THE GLOW

This is a work of fiction. Names, characters, places, events, locales, and incidents are either the products of the author's imagination or used in a fictitious manner. Any resemblance to actual persons, living or dead, or actual events is purely coincidental.

Copyright © 2020 by Sarah Aubrey Hadley
All rights reserved.
Cover and book design © 2020 Sarah Aubrey Hadley
Space photograph © Dave Morrow *(davemorrowphotography.com)*

For all the girls who have struggled to find their inner bravery.

CHAPTER 1

My hands are almost shaking too much to grasp the knob. Once I manage to get the front door open, I slam it behind me and collapse on the floor, gasping for breath.

I turn and reach to click the lock. A pink sticky note on the door catches my eye.

Harper, you'd better be locked in your room when I get home!

I toss Mom's note on the floor as I rush to turn on every light in the house. Then I check the locks on the doors and windows — not that I'm sure a door or window would stop that thing.

I sprint upstairs, shove my nightstand in front of my bedroom door, hide in my closet, and pick up my brother's baseball bat. My heart slowly returns to a normal pace. This is ridiculous, I'm seventeen and hiding in my closet like a little kid. Ugh. I wouldn't be in this situation if it wasn't for Mom.

Earlier today

My younger sister Olivia and older brother Brett were already seated on the couch when I walked through the front door. Across from them, Mom was leaning back into her shabby Victorian armchair, staring at me with that smug-ass expression of hers.

"It's 7:30 p.m., Harper. Where have you been?" she asked, tapping her foot impatiently.

"I thought it was another stupid scare," I said as I set down my backpack, trying to keep my cool. "Don't worry. I was just at soccer practice with a few friends."

Mom tilted her head and raised an eyebrow. "People are dead, Harper. That was very careless of you." Her voice sharpened.

"But it happened like thousands of miles from here," Olivia blurted.

Mom looked from Olivia to the window in thought. The evening sun highlighted her attractive, yet permanently scowling face, with faint wrinkles at the corners of her eyes. "It's always better to be safe than to take risks," she said quietly, practically to herself. "I shouldn't let you out of the house unless the authorities can prove the Syndrome is gone. Especially you, Harper."

"Especially me?" I forced myself to pause, trying to maintain composure. "What about Brett? He leaves all the time, and you don't care ... You've had me trapped in here for weeks. I needed some fresh air."

"Brett is responsible. When he left the house this morning, he was going to his job — not to play soccer with his *friends*."

"Yeah, but —"

She put up her hand. "And you're hanging out with those ... *girls* when you play soccer. Those reckless, irresponsible girls."

"So which part are you really upset about, then? The girls, or the soccer?"

"Both."

"Does this mean you're going to keep us locked up like last time?" Olivia asked, her big doe eyes full of concern. She swept her dark hair away from her face, exposing the slightly awkward thirteen-year-old features that she hadn't grown into yet.

"Oh, I'm such an awful mother, aren't I? Trying to keep my children alive," Mom added snidely for effect.

"More like dramatic," Olivia huffed, crossing her arms.

Preach, Olivia! I looked to Brett for support, but he said nothing and kept his head down. Typical.

"Do you know how they diagnose the RSE Sleeping Syndrome?" Mom asked. "They can't confirm it until you're dead, then they slice into your brain and find it full of tiny holes. There's no cure for it because the scientists don't know what it is. Does that sound like something you want to catch while playing soccer with your friends, Harper? Or hanging out at the mall, Olivia?"

My stomach lurched with annoyance. "You're blowing

the situation way, way out of proportion again. The breakout happened *on the other side of the freaking country.* There are *no* cases here. Do you realize how crazy controlling —" I snapped my mouth shut, but it had already slipped.

Olivia and Brett shrank into the couch.

Mom stood with enough force to make her chair slide back. To reinforce her point, she stalked closer to me, and stopped when we were nearly eye-to-eye. "Nobody leaves or comes into this house unless I say so! Especially you, Harper. Is that clear?!" Her breath beat hot on my face.

My fists tightened. The seconds of silence that followed lingered in the air like a pungent smell. I peered at the door and then back at Mom.

"Harper, don't you —"

She reached for me, but I was already out the door, pounding my anger into the ground with each step as I raced away. My feet carried me from the suburbs, through a creaky gate, and into the sagebrush-laden desert.

In the distance, the evening sun had sunk behind the great Sierra Nevada Mountains, the landscape darkening into a monochromatic gray stretch of bushes.

Antares, my favorite star, was one of the first to pierce the night sky. Away from the city lights, its ruby-red luminescence was brighter than even Mars tonight.

As my gaze lingered on it for a moment too long, my foot caught on a rock, and I crashed onto the gravel and skidded into a bush.

"Damn it!" I cursed. My leg was burning as I tried to wipe away the small rocks from my bleeding knee. But something on the ground caught my eye. Something fluttered. I turned. There was an odd glow in the not-too-far distance, and I froze.

Walking slowly towards me, almost floating, was a tall human-shaped silhouette — colors radiating off a black hole of a body at the center of what looked like a supernova.

I blinked over and over again, trying to correct my vision, holding the air in my lungs, so I didn't make a sound.

As it continued toward me, its flame-like energy cast distorted halos across the surrounding sagebrush and rocks. When it passed the other side of my bush, a gasp slipped out.

Through the branches sheltering me, I saw the thing pause. Then its featureless black head revolved like an owl spotting prey.

In a panic, my fingers scurried across the dark ground until they found a small, jagged rock.

The thing made a sudden sharp turn, heading for my hiding spot. I shot up, my heart about to rip from my chest.

"S ... S ... Stop!" I shouted like an idiot.

It did ... And for a moment, everything seemed to move in slow motion as colorful flames licked around its tall and slender body, but I couldn't make out anything else in its black silhouette.

It started hovering forward again, and I hurled my rock to slow it. The rock passed straight through the thing, as if it were made of smoke. My feet skidded on the gravel as I turned and raced home, too scared to look behind me.

Now I'm clutching this baseball bat in my closet, trying to make sense of what the hell I just witnessed. Was it all a hallucination?

I hear the front door open and tiptoe downstairs, still wary of my mother. Brett sets down a small pile of groceries and gives me an angry look. That's not fair. I should be mad at him for not backing me up with Mom.

He looks at my knee, which is still trickling with blood. Damn, I forgot about that. His expression softens. "What happened?"

"Harper!" Mom calls in her nails-on-a-chalkboard tone. I don't move, and I hear her walk inside.

"Why are you two just standing here?" she says in an accusatory tone, without so much as a glance at my knee.

"Because ... I think I saw a ... a ... ghost ..." Even with all that's happened, and everything racing through my head, I realize how dumb it sounds the moment it comes out. I don't even believe in ghosts. Well, didn't used to, anyway.

She slowly lifts an eyebrow. "Really? And is this conveniently timed *ghost* supposed to make me feel bad for you? Make me forgive what you've just done?"

Her eyes bore into me.

"I ... " I go silent, tightening my trembling hands.

"Are you doing drugs with those girls?" she says.

I have to clench my jaw to stop myself from screaming. "Why do you think I would do drugs?" I say through gritted teeth, shivering from both fear and rage. "My friends don't do them either. Forget it, alright? The desert was dark and hard to see."

"You went to the desert? After what we just talked about? Really?" she says like I'm stupid.

I don't say anything.

"Harper?" She snaps her fingers in my face.

"There was no one in the desert, Mom. It was fine," I say flatly, to hide the sting in my throat.

She claps her hand to her forehead. "I can't even, Harper. No more tonight, please. I'm done." She shoves a grocery bag into my hands and pushes past me. Brett follows behind her like the little lap dog he is.

After a silent meal full of glares and aggressive meatloaf cutting, I take the dishes to the sink and load them into the dishwasher. When I return to the dining area, Mom immediately points to my room. I get up and push in my chair.

"Not just her," Mom says, looking at Brett and Olivia "Everyone. Now." she roars.

"They didn't do anything," I say, watching Olivia hang her head.

"It's not great to have everyone pay for your actions, is it, Harper?" Mom taps her fingers against her arm, a threatening expression on her face.

Not fighting back would bring everyone the most peace so I hold my tongue and, like prisoners, we march upstairs to our bedrooms.

When I open my bedroom door, the papers on the wall give me pause: my printouts of dozens of nebula and space photographs are taped to the 70s orange oak paneling.

Fueled by my annoying, illogical paranoia, I rip them down and shove them into a box in my closet, promising them and myself that I'll put them all up again when I stop being such a baby.

The moment I hear Mom's TV turn on, I sneak across the hall into Olivia's room. When I open the door, I find Olivia reading a newspaper in bed.

"Harper! Jeez! Knock first! And don't be so *careless*!"

That hurts a little. "Careless" is Mom's favorite word for me. I know Olivia doesn't mean it. Mom was probably just going off about what a bad daughter I am when they all went shopping earlier.

"What are you reading?" I ask, answering my own question when I see, **The RSE Sleeping Syndrome Is Here!** in giant bold letters across the page.

Her voice quivers. "Mom said we should be ready, you know, if it comes here."

The inflicted fear in her big eyes presses against me like a hot iron. I want to stomp down the hall and yell at Mom for making this innocent thirteen year old girl feel this way. But I hold back my emotions and plop on Olivia's bed instead, wrapping my arm around her.

"What do I need to know?" I say cheerily.

"Well ... the first symptom is euphoria. It says to watch out for people who may appear intoxicated or on drugs. That's followed by the unavoidable urge to sleep. After someone falls asleep, death comes in about twenty-four hours."

"Strange," I say.

"Yeah. It's very strange. Like Mom said, they aren't even

sure what it is, but they suspect it's a super fast version of ... " She points to a spot on the paper and struggles to pronounce the words, "Bo-vine spong-i-form en-ceph-alop-athy."

I recognize the term from biology. "Mad cow disease?"

Olivia looks up from the paper, her big eyes get even larger. "So you know more?"

I recall that mad cow disease erodes holes in your brain so that it eventually looks like a sponge. But there's no way I'm telling Olivia that.

"You don't need to worry about it, Olivia. We have a better shot at winning the lottery."

"But if I *do* get it, they don't have a cure for it! Just like Mom said!"

Another wave of white-hot anger burst through me, but I say reassuringly, "Sure, everybody is panicking about it now, but it probably won't spread. The only case in the United States is that homeless shelter all the way in New York. And it didn't spread after it wiped out that small village the first time."

She frowns, seemingly unconvinced.

"Besides, why would anyone from New York ever want to come to crappy old Reno, Nevada? Everyone wants to get the hell out of this crap hole the first chance they get. They'd much rather go to California or somewhere way cooler ... Like us one day."

She smiles.

I grab the newspaper and toss it across the room, making it rain paper.

She laughs, which makes my anger subside.

"You want to have a slumber party like old times?" I ask her.

She grins, slides over in her bed, and pats my usual spot.

CHAPTER 2

When I finally manage to drift off, I'm standing in a hazy gray desert, where the glowing creature materializes. I throw rocks at it, tons of them, but they do no good. So I run. I run as fast and as far as I can, straight into an inky abyss. Then I hear funny noises, like a trombone trying to scream human words. Like the glowing creature is calling for me through the mist.

The strange sounds from my dream morph into human words.

"Olivia." Mom's voice drags me from sleep as she knocks on Olivia's door. "Your doctor's appointment is in ten minutes. Come on. I can't be too late for work."

"Oh sorry! I forgot," Olivia says.

The bed springs squeak as Olivia jumps up, and the bathroom faucet starts running shortly after. Mom and Olivia have left by the time my eyes are fully open.

I make my way to the kitchen downstairs.

"Hey Brett. About last night —"

"Harper. Dear God. Not right now. I have more important things to worry about than how you and Mom can't stand each other. I'm not going to be in the middle again!"

He's such a dick sometimes. Without uttering another word, Brett shoves granola bars into his backpack.

"I thought Mom told us not to leave," I say flatly, as I prepare a bowl of cereal.

He gives me a contemptuous glance. "I'm allowed to go to work, Harper."

"I hate being homeschooled," I huff. *"And Mom won't let me get a job,"* I say under my breath, bitterly shoving a spoon of cereal into my mouth.

"I called Mrs. Nunez next door." Brett says. He snaps his bike helmet on. "If you leave, she'll see you. And Mom is going to be calling the house every hour to make sure you're here. So don't go anywhere!"

"Got it," I say. Mrs. Nunez is a retired librarian who lives next door with her husband. She's usually knitting, watching TV, or snooping on the neighborhood by her front window. The most excitement she probably gets in life is from spying on us.

Brett takes his bike from the hallway and heads out.

The eerie quietness of the empty house slithers around me. I check the gold clock above the refrigerator. It's 11 a.m. *Crap.* Hilltop Park is about four miles from here, which means I can jog there in about twenty-five minutes if I hurry.

I quickly wash my dish, throw on my workout gear, and slather on sunscreen.

Before I leave, I pick up the home phone and call Katie.

"Sup, dude?" Katie says.

"Leaving now. Sending all my calls to you," I respond.

"Got it. See you soon."

I hang up on Katie and then input her number for call forwarding.

I sneak through the back gate and run around the block so I don't pass Mrs. Nunez' little spy zone.

About thirty minutes and one steep climb later, I reach the fence encircling the soccer field. The balding lawn smells musty from the morning sprinklers, which have caused the surrounding wooden benches to crack and silver over the years. An empty bag blows past my feet, skipping like tumbleweed.

You can see most of Reno from up here: a brown desert below, with patchwork of brown suburban neighborhoods, brown shopping centers, and brown casinos. Beyond all that, about fifty miles to the west, the massive Sierra Nevada Mountains are covered in *green* pine tree forests. If it wasn't for those mountains, I would've suffocated on all the *brown* a long time ago.

"Cute shirt," Katie says as I jog to my three friends standing in the middle of the field. She's the only one to notice my approach, as my other two friends, Maria and Jane, seem to be preoccupied arguing with each other.

"Another thrift store find?" Katie's lip curls on her long, yet symmetrical face.

I glance down. My t-shirt says "speed limit" with the letter "C" under it.

"Well you know, the thrift store is the only brand I can afford." I wink.

"What the hell is 'C'?" Katie asks.

I laugh. "The speed of light."

"You're hopeless, Harper." Katie shakes her head. "And why are you so sweaty?"

"Ran here."

"You're crazy, dude." She chuckles.

"Onto business then." I hold out my hand.

She gives me her phone. "It's yours for the next hour. Unless someone named 'California Boy 2000' sends me a DM on Insta."

"Got it," I say.

"I don't know how the hell you don't have a phone. Even homeless people have phones these days."

I shrug and put her phone into my shorts pocket. "Tell that to my mom."

"Don't lose it! Or sweat on it either!" She says shrilly.

"— That's not true!" Jane shouts at Maria beside us. Jane's frustrated hand gestures make her black studded bracelets glint in the sun.

Katie rolls her eyes at them. "They're arguing about the Sleeping Syndrome," she says with a sigh, bouncing her soccer ball from knee to knee.

I groan. "Not you guys too. Can we talk about anything else? My mom's being her usual self about it." I say it louder than is necessary, trying to distract them from their disagreement, but they continue.

Katie manages to impressively bounce her soccer ball from knee to foot. "Your mom would be. She flips over anything." Katie kicks the ball into the air and catches it.

"That's crazy!" Maria shouts. "Why would the government want to kill everyone who's got it?" Her eyes wander over to me from behind her thick horn-rimmed glasses. "Hey Harper," she says, finally acknowledging my existence. She motions me into the debate, which I don't want to be a part of.

"Think about where it first popped up," Jane says, also looking at me now. "They tested it in that small, isolated Maasai Mara game reserve in Kenya so they could perfect it there. Then it disappeared completely for six months. The only reason we knew about it was because some guy posted photos of the bodies on Reddit."

"Okay, so why would the government want it here all of a sudden?" Maria asks.

"Can't you see? The government used it to wipe out an entire homeless shelter in New York yesterday. Fewer mouths to feed. Duh."

"You honestly believe the government wants to kill homeless people?" Maria's mouth falls open.

"Ugh. You have to read We Know —"

"Come on. Not that site again —"

"Guys, seriously," I say, holding up my hands. "I have to tell you what happened last night." If you let her, Jane could argue her conspiracy theories for hours.

"Fine. But I have one more thing to add," Jane says, and a collective sigh comes from our group. Katie stops juggling her ball.

"Just do me a favor and get your survival supplies ready in case you have to make a quick escape. You can find a list of supplies on —"

"We Know!" I say.

Everyone but Jane laughs.

"We'll be fine," Katie says, waving her hand. "Look, I've got all the supplies I need." She pulls a vape from her bag and offers it to Jane, who makes a sour expression and bats it away. Katie giggles to herself and blows a small cloud from her vape at Maria.

"Katie, that nasty habit of yours is going to kill us before the government gets a chance." Maria says, shaking her head. "Now what did you want to tell us, Harper?" she asks, glancing at my t-shirt with an approving smile.

They all stare, and at that moment a funny suspicion comes prickling in. I sense more than just their eyes upon me: as if from beyond the fringes of the park, something else is watching us.

"Harper?" Maria asks.

Sweat trickles down my face. "Um ... I — my mom grounded me because she's worried about that Syndrome thing." I pull my gaze from the bush line of the surrounding desert.

"Jane, have you been talking to Harper's mom?" Katie jokes.

"Very funny," Jane says.

"Sometimes it does seem that your mom looks for any excuse to keep you locked in the house," Maria adds.

"Duh," Katie says. "Her mom's crazy. She probably doesn't even know you're here, does she?"

I shrug.

Katie laughs. "Here. I can help! I think I have a flask tucked away in here somewhere. We can make practice a little more interesting." She digs through her leopard print bag with one hand, holding her vape in the other, looking like a movie star in soccer gear.

"Katie ..." Maria warns.

"What?! Come on, Maria! Harper's got to have a little fun once in a while. When we're all old and wrinkled, she's not going to have any good stories to tell!"

"Maybe another time," I say. "I need to leave in about an hour so I can beat Brett home from work."

"Ooh. Sexy, tan, tall, muscular Brett," Katie says, fanning herself.

"So gross," I say. "Besides, he's an asshole."

"That's my favorite type! You know I've got a thing for the bad boys."

"He's too old for you, Katie," Maria says, pushing up her glasses.

"And ... and it would be gross," I remind her.

"Whatever," Katie says, continuing to fan her hand.

"Can we play soccer now?" I groan.

As the four of us dart back and forth across the grass, a group of older boys arrives with beers in hand, taking a seat at a picnic table.

An hour later, with the summer heat bearing down on us, we end practice.

"You guys enjoy your screwing?" I ask, using the bottom of my shirt to wipe the sweat from my eyes.

"You only made two more goals than me," Katie says.

"I'll buy you dinner later." I wink.

"Ha, like you know anything about screwing," Katie says. "You've never even kissed anyone."

Heat rises in my face. "Not true. There was Peter when I was twelve."

"That doesn't count. If you had a phone, we could remedy this situation right away." Katie makes a kissing sound.

"Leave her alone!" Maria says in a motherly tone.

"Fine." Katie takes out her vape and the guys at the picnic table whistle at her. She giggles and waves, smirking deviously at Maria, who's giving her a disapproving glare.

"It's your cancer!" Maria shouts.

"I wouldn't mind letting you be my cancer," one of the boys yells to Maria, who blushes.

When Jane walks over to throw away her water bottle they whistle at her too. She responds by flipping them off.

"I like your black nails!" a guy shouts. "I can get into the whole BDSM thing!" He and his buddies snicker, smacking each other on the shoulders like it's the best comment in the world. I roll my eyes.

To my surprise, Katie walks over to them.

"You should go get her, Harper," Maria says, covering her face with embarrassment.

"On it," I respond, jogging after her.

In the few seconds it takes me to reach Katie, she's already got the boys hanging on every word she says. As I approach their picnic table, all of their eyes move to me. When I stop beside Katie, there's almost a palpable shift in their enthusiasm.

"Hey are you one of those albinos?" The tallest guy asks,

breaking the awkward silence.

I hate that this is one of the first things people notice about me. "No, I'm not albino," I say coldly. Not that it's any of his business if I was. I'm what some people refer to as a "towhead." Pasty enough to blind you in broad daylight, with large green eyes and white-blonde hair in a pixie cut.

If he hadn't asked me if I was albino, I wouldn't be surprised if he'd asked if I was sick. That's the second most common question I get. No, I'm not sick either. The funny thing is, I have a fair amount of muscle definition on my arms and legs, which doesn't seem like something an unwell person would have ... but people just don't notice that part of me.

"She just needs more sunlight," Katie says.

The tall guy laughs over-enthusiastically.

I don't really know how to respond. Katie knows I sunburn instead of tan. I tug on Katie's arm a little harder than I should.

"Ouch!" she says. "*Fine*. Buh-bye now, boys." She grabs one of their beers with a flirty smile and we return to Maria and Jane.

Maria drops me off on the other side of my block. I cross the road and sneak back into the house. I've been gone a little too long — an hour and a half — but my brother hasn't returned yet, which means I've got away with it. I remove the call-forwarding from the home phone and hit the shower.

The cold water washes away the hot sun, and my eyes

flutter shut as it runs down my face, rinsing away a layer of sweat and grit. In the darkness behind my eyelids, there's a flicker, and the fiery silhouette materializes in a flash. My eyes spring open, and I whip back, pain blazing from my shoulder as I smack onto the shower floor.

I hear the front door open downstairs, followed by the sound of Mom setting her keys in the entry tray.

Olivia's voice echoes through the linoleum. "Can I watch Netflix?"

I stagger up and turn the shower off, still catching my breath from the fall.

"Sure," Mom says.

Footsteps stomp up the stairs and to the outside of the bathroom.

"Yeah?" I say through the door.

"You're still grounded, but Mrs. Davis really needs a babysitter until ten tonight," Mom responds.

For half a second, I'm excited at the prospect of getting out of the house. Then I remember Mrs. Davis lives on the cusp of our suburb, where the desert begins. It used to be my favorite thing about her house. The night sky is crystal clear there, with less light pollution. After her kids were asleep, I would crawl up on her roof, and even though my Mom would always tell me I was nothing special, I would think about how everything in the universe is made of the same elements, all created in the core of stars. That always made me feel better. That all of us come from the diamonds in the sky, like descendants of gods. That my life wasn't as meaningless as she made me feel.

"Why can't Brett do it?" I say, stepping into the hallway in my towel, reminding myself not to hold my throbbing shoulder, so she won't ask questions.

Mom crosses her arms. "He's busy. Mrs. Davis has an emergency at work, and I told her you'd do it. Besides, what have you been so busy with?" Her eyes hone in on the pile of clothes on the bathroom floor and I pray that she doesn't notice the fresh grass clumps sticking to my running shoes.

"The usual. Just trying to keep myself occupied while you've got me on lockdown. Did a workout in the backyard."

"I see." She pauses. "Well maybe you won't be so bored later this summer. We'll have an opening on the caretaker staff at the nursing home."

"Why can't I get a coffee shop job or something?" *You know, away from you*, I think.

She laughs. "You can't handle that much responsibility."

"I could always try."

"You can try whatever you want when you're eighteen. The nursing home is your only option until then." She checks her watch. "Well, anyway, go straight to Mrs. Davis' house and come straight back here. Nothing in between, Harper."

CHAPTER 3

Mrs. Davis' nursing uniform brings out the pink highlights in her hair. As she gathers her things to go, she reminds me of the emergency numbers on the fridge and how to turn on the Xbox to watch movies.

"The kids are asleep. There's some leftover pizza in the fridge if you want," she says before she darts out the door.

The moment she leaves, I shut all the drapes and windows, wishing that I had the guts to watch the stars from the roof tonight to clear my thoughts. Instead, I use a distraction tactic and pick up Mrs. Davis' phone.

"Hello?"

"Hey! It's Harper."

"Oh, hey. Whose number is this?" asks Maria.

"I'm babysitting for my mom's friend."

"Your mom let you out of the house?" she responds sarcastically.

"Shut it."

"What's up?"

"Just wanted to talk to someone," I say. "How was class this morning?"

"Oh, you know. The usual. Stuck in a freezing classroom while I watch everyone outside having a great time in the summer sunshine."

I laugh.

"Speaking of school," she says, "have you been giving college any more thought? I know you think you can't afford it, but I was thinking, have you thought about trying for a running scholarship?"

"Maria ... Not this again."

"Just hear me out. I did some research."

"And what do I need to go to college for?"

"You're always telling me cool stuff about space. Like that time you went on and on about that Rosetta spacecraft that had to do all those crazy maneuvers, using the gravitational pull of different planets, to reach a comet and put a probe on it."

"You mean Philae?" I correct her.

"Yeah! See. You know your stuff."

"Being a fan of the work is one thing, but being an actual astrophysicist is a very hard, different thing."

"Why not? You seem passionate about it. Everyone has to start somewhere."

"But *those* guys — "

"— And girls ..." she corrects me.

"Well, *they* need to be super smart to do that."

"And you're not?"

"I don't know if I'm *astrophysicist* smart ..." I pause, hearing a toilet flush upstairs followed by one of the boys' bedroom doors closing.

"And I don't know if I could leave Olivia alone with Mom either. Olivia would be completely brainwashed by Christmas." *Or much worse — But I dare not tell Maria about that part.*

"Well aren't you lucky, there are two schools, only four hours drive from us, so you could visit her on the weekend."

"Are those schools in California?" I ask.

"Yup."

There's no way I could go to California without Olivia. I've always promised her we'd go together. But I'm thankful for Maria's thoroughness and concern about me, so I pause, rolling the idea around in my head for a moment. "Maybe I could just go to the University of Reno ... even though it would mean four more years in this horrible brown expanse." I make a gagging sound over the phone.

"Reno doesn't have an astrophysics program."

"I'll think about it," I say, though I don't want to tempt myself. If it weren't for Olivia, I'd be out of this hellhole the second I hit eighteen.

"Okay ... well I'm here when you want to start prepping for the SATs and get some official racing times on record."

Maria and I keep the conversation going for another hour before she forces herself off to bed.

I hang up and wrap the blanket on the couch around me, covering my head like a nun. I turn on the TV. The blue light casts shadows from the furniture, which makes me constantly check the eerie movement it creates in my peripheral view. The sound of summer crickets creeps through an open window that I missed — I fix that really fast. I turn up the volume of the show I'm watching, a nature documentary, and try to repeat every word from the narrator in my head in order to keep my own thoughts from shooting off.

Another hour or so crawls by. At 11 p.m. I have to fight the gnawing in my gut. Mrs. Davis was supposed to be home an hour ago.

The phone rings.

"Hello, Davis residence," I say.

"Harper, dear, it's me," Mrs. Davis says. "I'm so sorry I didn't call earlier. There are some officials here saying ... never mind. Can I ask you a super huge favor? Can you stay the night to watch the boys? We're swamped at the hospital. If you need to go get your things, they'll be fine for a few minutes. I'll pay you double!"

"I'm ... not sure if —"

"Thank you so much, dear. I'm hoping to be home around nine o'clock tomorrow morning. You know where the blankets are. I'm being paged. Gotta go! Bye!"

Ugh. I just want to go home and curl up in my own bed. Still carrying the phone, I walk upstairs and check on the boys, who are sleeping soundly.

The phone rings again. I rush into another room so I don't wake them, hoping it's Mrs. Davis saying she's coming home ... "Davis residence," I answer hopefully.

"Hey, Harper." It's Olivia. "Mom said you were staying the night and needed me to bring stuff over?"

"You're still awake?"

"Yeah. Mom made me dust the entire house – if she finds one fleck of dust, I'm grounded."

My grip around the phone tightens. "How far are you from being done?"

"I think I'm almost there. But I'm not a hundred percent sure if it's dust I'm seeing. I'm exhausted and my eyes are blurry." She gives a timid laugh.

"Are you okay?" I whisper.

Her side of the line goes quiet. "Yes ..."

"Well, why don't you come and stay the night with me? There's also leftover pizza. I can help you double check the dust in the morning." *And get you away from Mom.*

"I don't know if that will make Mom mad."

"Why? You finished your job."

"Yeah."

"Sweet! If Mom doesn't agree, call and tell me. And make sure Brett walks you over, too. I don't want you walking alone!"

Olivia and I sink into the couch after demolishing the pizza.

She picks a kids' movie on Netflix and curls in close to me. She starts drifting off to sleep the moment her head rests on my shoulder.

"Hey Olivia?" I ask.

"Yeah," she says wearily.

"If I were to go away for a bit, how do you think you'd be with Mom?"

Olivia's head pops up, as if she's heard a startling noise. "How long is a bit?"

"Maybe —" My voice catches in my throat, "a year or so? But I'd visit you every weekend. I'd also call every night and check that things are okay."

"I thought we were supposed to go to California together?" She entangles her arm with mine.

"Yeah, but if I go to college, maybe I could eventually afford to put you through college too."

"I'm not the college type," Olivia says.

"Why do you think that?"

"Mom told me."

"That's not true," I say.

Olivia shrugs, laying back on my shoulder. "Don't go," she says softly as she starts dozing off. She shifts a little and her long, dark hair slides down the back of her neck, revealing dark purple finger marks blotted into her skin there.

I take a few steadying breaths, making sure I don't sound accusing in any way. "Are these from tonight?" I gently brush more hair away from the bruises.

I feel her go rigid, pulling the blanket up closer to cover the marks. There's a long pause before she responds, "Yeah. But she's been better. I shouldn't have snapped at her, I know that sets her off."

If only I could take Olivia away. "You have to stand up for yourself," I say. "Or you have to leave when she gets like that. She stopped hitting me when I stood up for myself."

Olivia sits up. "Okay, I'll try." She doesn't make eye contact as she uses her fingers to comb her hair back in front of her shoulders.

I sigh. "Olivia, I promise this won't happen again."

"Welcome back. Everything alright?" I ask as Mrs. Davis drops her enormous bag and kicks off her shoes when she gets home.

"Yeah." She sighs. "I'm going to go take a shower. Their father is going to pick them up in about an hour, so you can go now. Thanks again for staying."

"Sure! Anytime."

She frantically shuffles through her bag. She pulls out two twenties and holds them out for me, giving me a tense stare the whole time.

When I try to pull the money from her grasp, she doesn't let go.

"Everything alright?" I ask again.

She shakes her head and relinquishes her grip. "Sorry. Yes. Just fine. Have a good day, you two."

Olivia and I gather our things, say goodbye, and I walk Olivia to her friend's house.

"You stay here until I talk to Mom. I'll come get you after. We'll figure this out," I say, bending down to match Olivia's height, giving her a reassuring squeeze on the shoulder.

"Okay," she says timidly, her eyes on the ground. Her friend, Amy, is waiting for her on the front porch.

"None of this is your fault. I promise." I hug her goodbye, psyching myself up the whole way home. But when I get there, the house is empty. Mom must have work today.

Deflating a little, I make my way to the computer, feeling the exhaustion press upon me the moment I sit down. I'm supposed to be grounded from "for fun" computer use, but I surf using incognito mode, which blocks internet history. I check Reddit, pausing when I see photos of the Carina and Trifid nebulae slowly loading at the top of my personal feed, posted by the astronomy subreddit. "And goodbye to Reddit," I say as I close the window.

I'm a few days behind on homework, but I'm so tired. I lay my head on the desk to rest my eyes, just for a second. But in the dark of approaching sleep, glowing limbs start to appear, like nebulae in the black of space. I open my eyes before the body can finish taking shape. Stupid. It was just a rainbow in the desert ... Why can't I just let it go?

I move on to Instagram, massaging my temples as the slow hamsterwheel in this ancient computer strains to load the page. The first five posts are memes about the Sleeping Syndrome. Jane's posted a video with tons of conspiracy hashtags under it. After clicking on it, I have to wait for a second before it starts playing.

"He was being followed by the government, my boy was," says a rough man with stubble and a dirty baseball cap. "He was tryin' to get away. Came here to New York to find a job where they couldn't keep track of him. You know, work under the table and whatnot. Told me he found some job in construction."

"Why were they after him?" a voice off camera asks.

"Says he saw something. Wouldn't tell me what. Somethin'

in the woods when he was campin' with his friends. Came home all white-faced and said he had to leave. Said they'd find him."

"You think that was the government?"

"Oh yeah. Told me if anybody came lookin' for him, tell them I hadn't heard from him in months. Left his driver's license and everything. Then they must have found him and–" The man breaks down into sobs, wiping away the tears with the corners of his sleeves. "–killed him. The government somehow knew he was staying at that homeless shelter where all them people was killed in New York."

The video fades to black and a binoculars logo with the words we know underneath it fade in. I notice that Jane is also using the logo as her profile pic.

He saw something and wouldn't tell anyone what it was — just like me. Could it be the same thing?

I type 'we know' into Google and click on the link to the website. The page slowly loads with a stream of news content. I take a deep breath and type in 'glowing figure.' My heart races as the results come back with a mixture of links and images. I click around, scrolling through a few obviously photoshopped pictures. When I don't find anything of serious interest, I go back to the images in the search results. There are photos of little glowing orbs, soldiers under a night-vision green hue, and unidentified flying objects in the sky. There are even some personal sketches of fairies in there – the kind of crap that's been clogging up the internet as long as there's been an internet.

I can't bring myself to keep searching because it feels like something's trying to pull me in.

I jump when the house begins to creak. *What the hell is going on?*

The man's words from the video squirm in my thoughts: "*Says he saw something … Saw somethin' in the woods … Said they'd find him. Then they found him and killed him.*"

Could these things be connected?

I can't take being alone. I lock the front door, and begin to run.

CHAPTER 4

Maria lives in a one-story house six blocks from mine, it's easy to spot as it's the only house around here painted pink.

Maria's mom answers the door with a scowl, but once she recognizes me, she smiles and says, "Hello, Harper."

The house is heavily perfumed with cooking oil, and the walls are adorned with foil posters of saints and roses.

"Oh. Harper. I didn't expect you," Maria says from the couch. Her two younger brothers and sister are busy smashing together toy cars on the floor.

Her mom interrupts, and says something in Spanish. Maria rolls her eyes, and her mom picks up her purse and heads out.

"What was that about?" I ask.

"Dad's still out of town so she needs me to watch them tonight," she says, nodding to her siblings, "even though I have a debate club meeting in two hours." She sighs.

"This is so dumb. I can't miss another meeting. I'm going

to get kicked out, and I need the extracurricular if I'm going to get into a good school. My mom and dad don't care though. Sometimes I wonder if they're trying to sabotage me."

Tears swell in the corners of Maria's eyes. "They say it takes up too much time and we need extra money to pay for the house."

I plop next to her on the couch and sigh. "You'll figure something out, Maria. You're brilliant. Plus, I'm always here if you need anything."

She gives a soft nod and runs her fingers through her silky dark hair. "Hey, what are you doing here? I thought you were grounded?"

"I am." I smirk.

She chuckles softly and shakes her head. I grab a Kleenex and hand it to her. She blots her eyes.

"Did you see my message? I've been sending you DMs, but you haven't been responding."

"I didn't see any notifications."

"I sent you like three, I almost wrote a comment but I didn't want your mom to see."

"Are you sure? I was just on Insta and there wasn't anything."

"Look." Maria pulls out her phone and loads the app. "It's right ... hmm, that's weird. Did you delete your account?"

"No. I was just on there like ten minutes ago. Let me see that." I take her phone and search for my name. Nothing comes up. "This has to be a mistake. You mind if I log in?"

"Go ahead."

I put in my email and password. I get an error message that says my account has been deleted. I have to reread it a few times. The room seems to be shrinking around me.

"Harper, you okay?"

The video of the guy talking about his son comes back to mind. If they've deleted my Instagram account already, it probably won't be long until they figure out where I live.

I catch a glimpse of Maria's stunned face when I dash for the front door. Halfway across the street there's a tug at my elbow. Maria pulls me to a halt.

"I have to go home!" I try to tug loose, but her grip is unwavering.

"Harper! What's wrong?" She says, panting.

"Nuh—nothing," I say. I can't put her in danger too.

"I don't believe you! Tell me!"

"I can't!" My voice cracks.

"You're shaking! Please tell me! Everything will be fine, I promise." She rubs my hand. "I just told you everything that's been going on with me. You can tell me what's wrong with you. That's what friends are for!"

"I don't want them to come after you too ..."

"Who will come after me? Harper, is someone after you? Are you in trouble?"

Fine. I drag her behind a car and duck, pulling her down with me. I whisper into her ear, "You have to pretend you haven't seen me since last Saturday. You don't know me anymore, got it?"

"What? *Why?*"

"I saw something the night I got grounded. When I was running in the desert."

Her mouth drops. "What did you see?"

"I shouldn't tell you. They might come after you."

"Harper, tell me, or I won't act like I don't know you!"

Her eyes search my face. My focus bounces between her and the direction of my house. I'll be able to go home faster if I just tell her. "I saw something glowing. A black figure surrounded by rainbowish vapors, moving through the desert when I was running that night."

The seriousness in her expression fades a little. "Like a tie-dyed ghost or something?"

"Yes, actually. Except I don't think it was a ghost. I think Jane might be onto something with her government conspiracy theory. I know it sounds wild, but you see, my Instagram was deleted after I tried to investigate what it was online. Now they're trying to get rid of me."

"Okay. So what did this rainbowy thing do?"

"It just ... stopped and stared at me. I threw a rock and it went right through the thing! I think it — or whoever made it — is looking for me now!"

"Did it follow you home or something?"

"No. I only saw it in the desert."

"You've had a lot of stress and pressure from your family recently. I'm sure it was nothing. I've heard of tons of people seeing strange things in similar circumstances. Everyone was really scared when they announced the Sleeping Syndrome that day, too. Stress shows up in weird ways. Maybe you should talk to someone about this? My school has free counselors."

She doesn't believe me. Probably for the best. "You're right," I say. "Just remember, I never told you anything. I gotta go."

My chest seems to be getting tighter. I glance around at

the surrounding houses again, making sure that nobody is watching or listening to us. I start to rise and Maria grabs my arm.

"Please, Maria, I just want to go home and be in my own bed. I slept like an hour last night. I'm exhausted."

"Let me walk you —"

"Please, just let me go. I'll call you later. Promise," I snap.

"Harper —"

"I'm fine. Really. You should text Katie or Jane. Ask them to watch the kids so you can go to debate club."

"Are you sure?"

"Yes." I force myself to smile. "And if you don't get home soon, one of your snotty brothers could do something stupid and drop dead." *Like I might do soon.*

Maria hesitantly loosens her grip on my arm. I sprint home, which is still empty when I get there.

Up in my room, I slam my bedroom door, push my books onto the floor, and pull out my backpack, memorizing a list of things I'll need for Olivia and me to run away together. I'll pick her up from her friend's on the way to the bus stop. Maybe this time we can avoid being found out by Mom's friends.

When I'm in the bathroom, shoving Olivia's toothbrush into my backpack, the tightening in my chest explodes into a radiating pain, like needles bursting through my ribs and arm. With each excruciating breath, my vision gets more blurry, and I collapse.

CHAPTER 5

"Harper! Where are you?" Mom's voice shouts from downstairs.

The towels I grabbed as I fell are in a cold, sweaty tangle around my body, my insides vibrating with the remnants of the pain that has finally subsided. I tremble as I push myself up from the bathroom floor. I survived it. Perhaps it was a panic attack?

"Harper!" she shouts again.

I wipe away my tears and clop downstairs, freezing when I find Brett and Olivia standing beside Mom, Olivia's head hung in shame.

Why is Olivia here? She's supposed to be hiding out at her friend's house. How in the hell did Mom find her?

"Where were you earlier today?" Mom growls.

I pull my gaze from Olivia. "I was at Maria's because ..." I pause and debate whether I should tell her.

"Because she's trying to get you to play soccer with your

team on Wednesday? I saw her message on Instagram. You're not going!"

"W-what?" I stammer, my thoughts taking a moment to catch up. "*You've* been logging into my account?"

"I came home about an hour ago because Mrs. Nunez saw you leave."

Crap. I forgot to go around the back.

"And I know for a fact that Brett and Olivia have been on Instagram since you've been grounded, so your account shouldn't be logged in! I don't want any more of this, I've deleted your account. You'll get it back when you're not grounded. I don't know when that will be though, because you've just added another two weeks."

I can't hold it in any longer. I don't want to martyr myself for this insane secret. "I didn't leave to disobey you! I left because I was scared of being alone in the house! I saw something scary and —"

"Put a cap on it, Harper. Not this excuse again. You're seventeen years old. You need to stop being so self-centered. There are terrible things going on in the world and you need to listen to me! Why is it so hard to just stay in the house when I tell you to?" For a second, she looks like she's about to cry.

"Go to your room. I don't want to see you for the rest of the night." She points her finger upstairs as she hides her face with her other hand.

Olivia and Brett watch, Olivia combing her fingers through her hair nervously.

"Wait," I whisper.

Mom's hand drops, as if she's not sure if she's heard me

correctly. "What did you say?" She dares me to speak again.

"I'll go upstairs, after we have a family meeting about something."

Brett sighs.

Mom lifts an eyebrow. "Is this a joke? You're in no place for negotiations."

"I just want to make sure that you're not going to lay a hand on Olivia again, like you promised this whole family."

Mom's face drops and her hard expression softens. For an instant she looks like a little girl, puckering her lips at me and then Brett with big, shimmering eyes. "I, I didn't mean to," she sniffles. "I told Olivia I was sorry after." Her voice gets small and pathetic as tears start to roll down her cheeks.

I step closer to her. I'm nearly as tall as she is now. "If you touch her again —"

"Harper!" Brett says, putting himself between us.

"Why are you defending her? She choked our little sister! Don't you care?!"

"I won't do it again!" Mom says behind him, dropping to her knees, pleading to Olivia. "I'm sorry. You know I didn't mean it. I just get so angry sometimes, baby."

Olivia starts tearing up too. "It's okay, Mom."

"No! It's not okay!" I yell, Brett blocking me. "Don't apologize! Your apologies are pointless, Mom! Just stop doing it then you won't have anything to apologize for!"

Mom crawls over to Olivia and wraps her arms around her, sobbing into her t-shirt.

"Move, Brett!" I shove him out of the way and pull Olivia from Mom's grasp. "Come on. Let's go upstairs and talk. You don't need this fake bullshit."

As I shut Olivia's bedroom door, Mom is still blubbering downstairs, Brett repeating over and over again that it will be okay.

On Wednesday, game day, Mom and Brett are out again when a loud knocking erupts at my front door. I consider acting like nobody's home until I hear Katie's voice shout, "Harper! Open up!"

I rush downstairs. "Katie! You can't be here! I'm serving a life sentence now," I say, straightening up my pajamas, which I've been wearing since yesterday. I quickly run my fingers through my messy short hair, which is sticking up all over the place.

I open the door.

"Yeah, Maria told me, dude ... but you see ... that means you can't get into any more trouble ..." She twirls her car keys. "We've got no shot at beating Carson without you. Get dressed."

"Katie, I —"

"Dude! You're already grounded till like forever right? Or at least until you're eighteen. So who cares? Your mom is a jerk anyway."

"You should go," Olivia says. She pops up behind me, holding a bowl of oatmeal, giving me a smile.

"Thank you!" Katie gives her a high five.

I consider this. It's August and I wouldn't be eighteen until

February, but I've been grounded for much longer than that, and for much less. "Are you sure they'll even let me play? I've missed the last two practices. They've kicked people off the team for that."

"Don't worry, dude! Maria, Jane, and I have been telling them that you got a really nasty flu — which actually kind of freaked them out because they thought it might have been the Syndrome — but we told them it was more a vomiting thing. So yeah. Act like you're getting over a bug if they ask."

I turn to Olivia. "You want to come too?"

She shakes her head. "Maybe the next one. I was going to finish watching my show. Sorry, but I'm exhausted from last night."

I give her a hug. "I'll see you after the game."

"Kick ass," she says with a smirk.

Katie pulls her silver VW Bug up to Hilltop Park. Gravel crunches under our feet as we leave the parking lot. The old stadium lights glare on circling swarms of flying insects, and the sides of the field are scattered with people in lawn chairs and on picnic blankets. Small children are chasing each other around with miniature soccer balls on the field, and the evening air smells like sagebrush.

"You going to kill it today?" Katie asks enthusiastically.

"I guess," I respond, already starting to regret this decision, wishing I was safely at home.

"What's your deal, Harper? You've been distant lately."

I shrug. "Just got a lot going on."

She makes an odd face at me and lets it go. We reach the rest of our team in yellow uniforms.

"Hey! How you feeling?" asks Nick, a co-ed on our team. His messy red hair is already damp with sweat.

"Much better. That was a rough week. Dehydration can really get to ya after *that* many nights on the toilet."

"Um. Glad you're feeling better," he says awkwardly. "We've missed your speed! You're the only one who convinces us to run laps." He quickly looks for someone else to talk to. "Oh! Hey, John! You bring those extra shin guards?"

"Maybe that was a tad too much detail," Katie whispers.

"Alright, people!" Nick shouts, gathering everyone together. "The game starts in twenty minutes. Let's do two warm-up laps and then get into the stretching circle!"

Maria and Jane jog over. Maria studies me, undoubtedly searching for signs of instability.

We start to jog. My eyes keep drifting back into the darkness, over and over again, as if I'm looking for something.

The whistle finally blows and the game starts. Jane intercepts a pass and knocks the ball back to me. She sprints forward, pulling red uniforms with her. I pass a through-ball to the right wing of the field, where one of the red Carson midfielders left a hole to follow Jane. With a deft first touch, Katie advances the ball down the sideline. I cut inside, running toward the penalty area, where Jane is waiting for Katie's cross. She's got too many red shirts on her, though. Katie's seen it and she launches her cross slightly backward. I start sprinting faster, and for the first time in a week, I feel it again: a pure joy that only comes with the love of the game. With the joy, comes the hunger. I become angry at the thought of anyone reaching that ball before me.

I hear footsteps and heavy panting from behind me, but I'll get there first. The goalie gets into his stance as I pull back my right leg to shoot. His face drops when I let the ball pass between my feet. Jane, now free of defenders, sticks out her foot and sends the ball into the net.

"Fantastic fake out!" Katie yells as she runs toward us to celebrate. "Keep that up and we'll be eating pizza tonight!"

The remaining first half of the game is mostly a battle for possession. Carson makes a few good plays but our defense holds firm.

The equalizing play comes in the second half, when Nick screws up by attempting to slide tackle a red shirt that manages to get past his center-back position. Nick must be super tired to make a move that dumb. Our wing-back moves to cover, but thanks to Nick, he's momentarily outnumbered. The Carson strikers make it look painfully easy as they get around him with a skillful one-two pass. I groan as I watch the ball skim past our goalie's fingertips and into the net. Then they punch in a free kick with just two minutes to go.

"Come on guys!" Nick shouts. "We can do this!"

Our team drags their tired legs to the center of the field. We know we've probably got only one last shot before the ref whistles for the end of the game. Maria starts the action, exchanging a quick pass with Jane who knocks it back to me, reminiscent of our first play. Katie doesn't look at me, her head down, a sign that she's too tired to run for it. I switch up the play, kicking the ball into the air and over to our left midfield. Nick, with a perfectly controlled volley, one-times the ball to Maria. She exchanges a rapid succession of passes with Jane as they skillfully carve their way up the left wing of the field. The majority of the red team is rushing toward them along the sideline, trying to box them into the corner. Our entire team is now rushing the penalty box; even our goalie is making a mad run for it. Maria slips the ball between her defender's legs and fires a cross with her left foot. I can immediately tell the pass has too much weight on it; Katie is the closest but her nicotine-stained lungs are shot.

I'm barely past midfield, but I can't just stand here and watch Katie blow our chance. I dig my cleats into the ground and furiously drive every muscle in my body. Suddenly, there's a strong zapping sensation in my hands, like a bolt of electricity. Then, in what feels like only a second, I'm in the corner, just a few feet away from Katie as she stops the ball from going out of the sidelines. When she turns, she's startled by my sudden appearance, clumsily kicking the ball toward the goal. It flies wide and bounces off the low wall behind the goal. It lands back into the field and sputters into a slow, dramatic roll.

The referee sounds the whistle, and the game is over.

We lost.

Katie puts her hands on her head. "Harper, where did you come from? I was all alone out here! You scared the shit out of me and made me screw that up!"

"Harper, how did you do that?" I hear Nick, out of breath jogging up behind us. "It looked like you just ran fifty meters at a crazy speed!"

I bend over and take a breath. "I didn't want to lose!"

He laughs at my response, though I wasn't kidding.

Carson's team is mostly jumping in a circle, but a few of their players are looking at me. The small crowd behind them is also staring.

"I'll be right back. I'm going to get some water." I wipe away the sweat dripping down my face. It's been more than a week since my last workout and my stomach isn't pleased about it. Vomit begins to bubble up my throat.

I rush toward the bathroom drinking fountain and try not to pay attention to the gawking little kids. Why is everyone staring at me? Never seen a girl run that fast before?

I duck my head and hurry on. Not looking at where I'm going, I bump into someone hard.

"I'm so ... Brett?!" I nearly fall over.

"Harper," he says with a mirrored, awestruck expression.

I tense up and consider running for it, but he's just standing there. That's when I notice his brown hair is oily, and his t-shirt is covered in sweat stains. He's never come to one of my soccer games before. Does that mean Mom's here too? I whirl around but I don't see her.

My stomach gurgles loudly, I dive for the water fountain a few feet away. I take three large gulps and splash some of the water on my face.

"What are you doing here?" I ask, turning back to him. "Come here on a little mission from Mom?"

"No," he says defensively. "I, I didn't know you were playing here. Why *aren't* you at home? You're grounded." He says it with so much less conviction than I would have expected from him. He glances at all the people leaving, as if one of them might jump out and attack him.

"Mom said I could play tonight," I lie, guessing it might buy me another hour of freedom before she comes at me with a vengeance so severe that this might be what gets me locked in the closet until I'm eighteen. "What are *you* doing here?" I ask again.

"One of my friends was playing for Carson. Asked me to come along." Brett nods to indicate the tall, muscular figure looming a few yards behind him.

I hadn't even noticed his friend, standing there as stiff as a statue, quietly observing me.

"That's Max," Brett says. "We met at work a few weeks ago."

I reach out my hand. "Hi Max, I'm Harper, Brett's sister, unfortunately."

"Nice," Brett growls.

Max glances at my extended fingers. He looks at Brett, who nods, and then back at me. He gives a firm handshake. At least Brett's friend has some spine.

"Nice to meet you," he replies *very* formally.

We all stand there for an odd second, letting the noise of flushing toilets fill the silence. Then the sound of giggling girls wafts up from the field. Moments later, Katie butts up against me, joking with Maria and Jane beside her.

Katie is about to say something when her blue eyes zero in on Max. She bites her bottom lip. "Hey, haven't seen you around before," she says, twisting the end of her blonde ponytail around her finger. "You Brett's friend?"

Max turns his head quickly in her direction. "Yes," he says in the same serious tone as before.

Brett breaks in, "Well, we better get going. See you at home, Harper." He and Max walk off to the emptying parking lot. I'm surprised that he didn't call Mom to check on me.

"And I thought *Brett* was hot!" Katie says, fanning herself with her hand. "That Max is fire!"

"Gross. Remind me never to let you near my brother again," I say.

"You can't keep true love apart forever …" Katie claps her hands together.

"Anyway …" I respond. That's the last thing Brett —or I— deserve.

Jane holds her water bottle to her face. Her once tight ponytail now has stray hairs hanging from her temples. "I've never seen you run like that before, Harper. Damn. Maybe you should run track and field. If you can keep that pace up, there's no way you wouldn't get a scholarship."

"I told her that!" Maria shouts.

"Really?" I say, "It was that noticeable?"

"Dude. You were running so fast I thought my eyes were playing tricks on me," Jane says, sweeping up her ponytail.

"I hear Berkeley has a great track team," Maria says with a smirk.

"Well I'm starving," Katie says. "Who wants cheap Chinese food to forget about this stupid game?" She wraps her sweatshirt around her neck and searches in her soccer bag. "Where are those stupid keys?"

I decide to go. I'll take all the fresh air I can get before

I face Mom's wrath.

CHAPTER 6

We park our cars in front of a Chinese restaurant nestled into a row of other small shops. Inside, the walls are covered with Chinese food photos faded by the sun. At the center of each table are bottles of soy sauce and faux flowers in tiny vases.

We sit down. A waitress greets us with menus and chopsticks. Katie waves the menus away. "We'll take four number twelves, please."

The waitress nods and leaves us for the kitchen, hidden behind a metal swinging door.

In the corner of the restaurant a muted TV flashes in the large mirrors on the opposing wall.

Jane watches it for a bit and groans. "I almost didn't come to the game today because of the people who passed out in Florida. It's spreading. We Know can't stop talking about it."

"Jane! Can *we* please *not* talk about it. Especially what We Know posts. Maybe it freaks some of us out," Maria says.

Subtle, Maria. "People passed out in Florida? When?" I ask.

"How have you not heard about — Oh, that's right. Your crazy mom," Katie says.

"It happened this morning," Jane huffs. "They found seven people in a sleazy motel passed out but still alive. They've ruled out drugs and carbon monoxide, but can't find any other reason."

"Yeah, they're dying," Katie says.

"Well, their organs are failing," Maria corrects. "I saw on the news that they're trying all kinds of new treatments. Now can we change the subject?"

Jane takes a deep breath. "That's what they're telling you. We Know says the government is testing the disease in controlled areas of the population. They aren't going to save anybody. *They know* too much, whoever those people are, and they're going to die because of it. I think they're either old agents who went rogue or whistle blowers."

"That's ridiculous," Maria says.

"I can give you the link. It explains it all on the website. Another part of the population is going to get sick, then they are going to start putting new places under quarantine so they can experiment on those people too. Perfect the Sleeping Syndrome."

The waitress sets down our plates. The smell of the noodles is suddenly all that I can think about. The sight of the food seems to shut up Jane as well.

As I finish my last bite, Jane thoughtfully paints skulls on her empty white dish with a chopstick dipped in soy sauce. "Someone on We Know said her mom took her out of school when the Syndrome first started. They're packing up and heading for the hills next weekend. I'm trying to convince my dad to do the same. Maybe just for a few weeks. You guys should start packing up a bunch of supplies, just in case."

Katie smacks the table with one hand, holding her phone with the other. "*Dude*. Lay off of the internet. You're starting to sound like one of those crazy conspiracy nuts. Who cares what a bunch of wackos who live in their moms' basements think? I thought your whole conspiracy thing was just a phase ... but jeez, it's taking you forever to get over it." She glances at her phone.

We all stare at her. She notices the silence and pulls her eyes from her screen.

"What?" she asks defensively.

Maria throws a napkin at her. "Shhhh. That wasn't very nice."

"I'm not crazy," Jane snaps. "I'll send all of you a link. That will shut you all up."

"Yeah," I say, trying to disarm the situation. "Send over that info, Jane. We'll take a look." I give Katie a '*shut the eff up*' glare.

"Oh don't worry. I will! You'll see!"

"Can't wait," Maria says.

"Who are you talking to, Katie?" I ask, pointing at her phone.

"California Boy." Katie smiles deviously, choosing not to address Jane's death wishing stare.

"It better not be one of those college boys, Katie!" Maria shouts. The waitress clears her throat loudly from across the restaurant — a warning to keep our voices down.

"Who are you? My father?" Katie laughs. Her phone

starts ringing.

Her eyebrows lift. "Oh shit. It's your house, Harper. Should I ignore it?"

My stomach flies to the ceiling. Brett probably told Mom all about the soccer game by now. If it's Olivia, she'll leave a message."Ignore it," I say.

She nods and presses the dismiss button as though it might bite her. "Your mom is gonna be pissed at me. Not that she likes me anyway."

Maria shakes her head. "Anyway, Katie, you're never going to meet a nice guy—"

"Your house left a voicemail," Katie interrupts, pressing her phone.

Mom's voice shouts from Katie's speaker, "Harper! You need to come home right now—" Katie stops it. "Whew. You're in for a good one when you get home."

Her phone starts to ring again. She turns it to show me my name and picture lighting up her screen.

"Maybe we should go home. I'm over this whole restaurant anyway," Jane says, dropping her chopsticks so hard, they make her dish ding.

Then Maria's phone lights up with my number too.

"Ignore it. I'm going! I'm going!" I say. I dig through my bag for some money from babysitting.

"I've got this," Katie says, placing her sparkly gold credit card on the table.

"I'll give you a ride home," Maria volunteers when we start filtering toward the cars. "Your house is closest to mine anyway."

"Good luck on making it to eighteen, Harper," Katie says as I climb into Maria's mom's old black Jeep.

The inside of Maria's car smells like air freshener and the windshield's cracks run up the side like spider webs. I watch through the passenger window as we drive down the almost empty main road. We pass a park, a gas station, and construction workers putting up yellow tape to block streets on the way to my house.

I wait for Maria to say something but lean against the window, turned away from her to try to show that I'm not super open to questions right now. She keeps her eyes on the road ahead.

A few blocks away from mine, red and blue lights spin on top of two police cars in front of Mrs. Hernberg's driveway. Two officers are standing out front. Their heads follow our Jeep as we drive by.

"That's weird," Maria says, finally disrupting the quiet.

"It's probably just her drunk-ass husband causing trouble. I see cops there all the time," I say.

The Jeep's brakes squeal to a stop in front of my house. I take a deep breath. I'm almost home free, hand on the car handle, when she asks, "How are you doing? Any more signs of that thing?"

The words hang heavy in the air. She brought *it* up. Here in the dark. I wish I hadn't told her.

"No. I think you were right. It was just brought on by stress. I don't think I'll see it anymore. Let's just not talk about it, ever, okay?"

"You know I looked up what you described online. Trying to

see if I could find something to help. But all I found was rave gear and Burning Man pictures."

"What!" I shout.

She jumps.

"Why did you do that? I told you not to draw attention to yourself! Crap. Did you at least use incognito mode?"

"No. What's that?"

I smack my hand to my face.

"Harper, you might be overreacting. I think you're stressed."

Crap. Crap. Crap. Maybe she's right. Maybe I'm turning into Jane with the paranoia. "Just don't look up anything about it again, okay? Promise me!"

"Alright! Alright. I won't. But you know I'm here if you need to talk, like ever, right?"

"I know." I give a cheesy thumbs up.

"Well ... good luck with your mom tonight!" she says. I can tell she still has reservations, but decides to keep them to herself. *Good.*

"Thanks." I grab my bag, slam the door, and wave her off.

I walk slowly to the house and try to prepare myself to face Mom.

When I step on the porch, the front door makes a loud creak and opens on its own.

I push the door wider. "Hello? It's me. I'm back. Mom? Olivia? Brett?"

The sight in the entryway stops me cold. The floor is scattered with loose clothes, and the kitchen cabinets have all been rummaged through. I race upstairs. My sister and brother's rooms are torn apart, lamps knocked over and furniture overturned.

I run back downstairs, about to run out, when I see a bright pink sticky note slapped at eye level on the back of the door.

The note is hard to read with my mom's rushed handwriting.

HARPER - WE HAD TO LEAVE, STAY IN HOUSE OR COULD GET SICK! CALL YOU AT 8! STAY BY PHONE!

"Could get sick?" I repeat it out loud as goosebumps erupt all over my body. Is this a cruel joke? Is my Mom trying to teach me a lesson?

The gold clock above the refrigerator reads 7:55 p.m. I made it home just in time. Holy crap, why don't I have a cell phone? Why doesn't my mom? This would have all been solved with a text!

I go through the house, checking the locks and turning on all the lights. Then I wait impatiently by the phone. Every sound in the house sets me on edge. Finally, at 8:32 p.m., the phone rings. I almost drop it because my hands are shaking so much.

"Where are you?" I shout into the receiver.

"Harper, it's okay," Mom replies. For once I'm happy to hear her voice.

"What's going on? Was the house robbed? I could get sick? What are you talking about?!" I say quickly.

"They think Mrs. Hernberg has the Syndrome. Six square miles have been quarantined. You need to stay calm, Harper. You can't leave the area, and you definitely shouldn't leave the house. We had to collect our things in a hurry. That's why the house is a mess."

"But when I was coming home, there weren't any blockages!

Except maybe a construction crew setting up yellow tape. I can break out of some stupid yellow tape!"

"Not anymore. They're setting up fences and the perimeter is now heavily guarded. You must have gotten in right before they were set up. I was hoping you would head home long after that, so you would be turned away and not locked inside with everyone else ... " Disappointment echoes through her voice.

"So ... am I supposed to stay here *alone?*" I ask, not sure if I want the answer.

She pauses. "We made it out of the zone before it closed, so we can't get back in. They can't know we left either. So if they ask, you don't know where we are."

The phone slips from my clammy grasp. It bounces off my foot and under the pink recliner chair. After pawing around for it under the skirt, I finally press it back against my ear.

"—ello? Hello? Hel—"

"I'm back. So what am I supposed to do now?"

"Just wait calmly. Make yourself comfortable. You could be there for a few weeks. There's a good chance that everything will be okay and you'll be cleared ... once they see you're not sick ... Everything will turn out fine."

"So I need to sleep alone tonight?"

"I know you're scared, Harper, but you have nothing to worry about. The Sleeping Syndrome is not a monster that will creep into your bedroom while you sleep. The neighborhood should be pretty safe because the military is patrolling it."

"Why are you so calm all of a sudden? You get scared or mad when one of us coughs funny! Now you're perfectly okay with me being stuck in a quarantine zone with a killer syndrome?!"

She's stupidly quiet.

"Is there a chance that this makes you happy or something? That you finally showed your disobedient daughter that you're right?"

"No. I'm not *okay* with it, Harper," she says sharply. "I just don't want you to freak out. I promise there is no need for you to."

What the hell is happening? Maybe she's relieved that I'm the child who got stuck in here instead of Brett or Olivia. Or maybe the stress of this has sent her over the edge. Maybe this is her version of a breakdown: transforming into an irrationally calm person.

I take a deep breath. "Are Olivia and Brett okay?"

"Yes they're fine. We're all fine."

"Can I talk to Olivia?"

"Harper, is that really necessary —"

"Please," I plead.

She sighs and then there's rustling.

"Hello? Harper!?" Hearing Olivia's voice gives me a small sense of relief.

"Are you okay?" I ask her.

"Yes. I'm fine. Are *you* okay?" Her voice falters.

"Yes. Just a little nervous, but it's all going to be okay. It's probably just a stupid scare."

"But if it's the Syndrome, like the newspaper said —"

"Shhh. It's probably just a precaution. You know how overblown the media gets." I feel tears threatening to penetrate my voice, but if she knows how afraid I am, she'll worry too much about me. "Listen, I don't know how long I'll be gone, but I want you to promise me that you'll stand up for yourself and not take shit from Mom or Brett, okay? Don't let them manipulate you about bullshit. You're too strong and smart for that."

"I won't," she says quietly.

"Okay. Good. I'll be out of here soon and we can continue planning our move to California."

She laughs. "Sounds good."

She gives the phone back to Mom.

"I left a contact number for you on the fridge if you need to get a hold of us. Leave a message on the voicemail if I don't answer. Just don't tell anyone where we are."

"Okay," I say, worrying about the silence that will take over as soon as I hang up. "Mom, how did you know we were going to get quarantined?"

"I — I heard it through the grapevine at work, but I've got to go. Get some sleep. I'll give you a call tomorrow. Stay strong." Her voice sounds unusually empathetic.

"I'll try," I say, uncertain of how to interact with this version of Mom. "Take care of Olivia. She needs you."

"I always do, Harper," she says shortly. The phone line clicks. I place the phone back in the charging cradle. The inky dark outside lingers, waiting for me. I can't be alone with it.

I throw all of my essentials into a duffle bag, step outside and close the front door behind me.

The neighborhood is dead still, as if time itself has stopped. Light from a few windows sends a yellow glow onto the manicured lawns, and the moon's gleam runs down the sidewalks, leading my way to Maria's house.

When I step onto the sidewalk, two headlights flash on, glaring in my direction. Silence is replaced with the rapid pace of my heart. A loud click projects from that direction, followed by a booming voice through an intercom saying, "Please stay where you are!"

Frozen, I see the headlights bounce slightly as the weight inside the vehicle shifts. Two tall men wearing white get out of the car and walk to me with rigid, controlled steps. As they get closer, I see they're in hazmat suits.

"Ma'am, for your safety and for the safety of those in this neighborhood, we're going to have to ask you to stay inside."

I've heard that voice before ... "I know how this looks. It's not like that. Please, sir, my family is outside of the quarantine zone and I don't want to be stuck by myself tonight. I'm really scared!" My voice cracks. I'm sweating under the blinding headlights. "I just want to go stay with my friend tonight. Please."

"Please go back inside. We will come by tomorrow to see if you need any supplies," says the taller of the ghostly white suits.

"Max?" I ask, finally placing that formal voice.

CHAPTER 7

"You must be mistaken, miss," says the tall guy I think is Max. "Come on, let's get you inside." The guy grabs me by the arm and leads me back to my door. He taps his foot impatiently while I fumble with the lock, and then practically shoves me inside once I've managed to open it.

In the light I can see Max's brown eyes through the plastic face shield, and the breathing mask indenting into his strong cheekbones. "Do not tell anyone that you know me, got it? I'll be taken out of this unit if you open your mouth!" With each exhale, his mask fogs at the bottom.

"Just let me go. Come on. You know me, you're friends with Brett. Do him a favor. I won't tell anyone if you let me go!"

He huffs. "How about this. You keep my secret and I make sure you stay safe?"

"Can you get me out of here?" I try not to sound too desperate.

His eyes narrow. "No. There's no way anybody can leave right now. Not even me."

"What if you get kicked out because you know someone?" I threaten.

He groans, "Harper's your name, right?"

"Yes."

"This is serious shit, Harper. They've called in all kinds of things. Tanks, patrol, about four hundred men. You're gonna need all the favors you can get. I sure as hell can't get you out."

I examine his face suspiciously, looking for evidence of deception, but it's too hard to read with half of it obscured by the mask. "So you're in the army, Max? That's why you're here?"

The radio on his belt goes off. "Is she secure yet? We have to do rounds."

He picks it up. "Be right out." He looks at me. "I'm in the National Guard. They urgently needed a lot of people in the area, so I was recruited."

"We gotta go," the radio says.

"Coming," he replies. He extends his gloved hand to me. "We got a deal? We're keeping secrets, right?"

I contemplate for a moment. If I agree now, it doesn't mean I can't change my mind later. "Deal." I shake.

"Smart girl," he says.

"Don't patronize—"

"I'll see ya around. Got shit to do." He rushes to the door.

Through the cracks in the front curtains, I see the headlights dim away, and the house's emptiness rushes in around me again.

The phone rings. I rush to it, praying it's my mother calling to inform me that there's been an awful mistake and she's coming to get me.

"Hello?" I say.

"Oh my gosh! Are you okay? I was hoping you weren't home!" Katie shouts. "Your neighborhood's all over the internet and the news! Is your mom flipping out?"

"She's gone. My whole family left before I got home. It's just me in the house." I choke a bit.

"What! I can't believe you're there alone!" she says. A woman mutters something on Katie's end of the line.

"My mom says to turn on the news. Channel two!" Katie shouts.

I hold the phone between my shoulder and ear and flip on the little TV in the kitchen.

On the screen there's a newswoman among a slew of cameramen and photographers pushing against orange construction barricades. Behind it, I recognize the rooftops and trees reaching into view, and the old janky neighborhood sign that says "Sycamore Acres."

"That's my neighborhood ..." I say into the phone.

"I told you! It's all over Twitter too."

The newswoman turns back to the camera after a failed attempt to get a sound bite from one of the soldiers. I increase the volume.

"One of our own neighborhoods was put under quarantine tonight. A resident here reported to the nearby hospital, suffering euphoria and then extreme fatigue — symptoms associated with the RSE Sleeping Syndrome. Officials say that the resident and the neighborhood's inhabitants are all safe, and assure us that the situation is under control. We are lined up for an exclusive interview with one of the scientists working this case."

A balding man in glasses rushes onto the scene from the other side of some yellow tape. He glances around, confused, and then straightens up once he sees the camera. The newswoman stands closer to him, trying to fit him into the shot, the busy crowd bustling around them.

"We are joined here live with Dr. John McCrow, a scientist at the Centers for Disease Control and Prevention, also known as the CDC. Dr. McCrow, what can you tell us about the possibility of an outbreak here, and how likely it is to spread?"

"Well, fortunately, the only other confirmed outbreaks we've seen in the United States are in Florida and New York. Rapid-Onset Spongiform Encephalopathy — also known as the RSE Sleeping Syndrome — is interesting because it's not caused by a typical virus, fungi, parasite, or bacteria like other diseases with quick incubation. We've confirmed a unique prion protein causes it. Prion diseases typically infect their hosts for a number of years before symptoms surface, but the speed of this prion disease is unprecedented. The good news is that we've developed a test that detects the presence of the disease in the blood and certain tissues. Other recent scares have turned out to be false, so we are hoping this one is too."

"I see. Scary stuff. When is the CDC expecting to have the results for this area?"

"That will take a few days. We are setting up local labs so we can assist Reno as quickly as possible."

"Alright, Dr. McCrow, thanks for taking time out of your

hectic night to talk to us."

He nods and hurries off.

"Stay with us for up-to-the-moment news on what's developing with this possible outbreak. Coming up next: How the RSE Sleeping Syndrome has affected communities in New York and Florida and what Reno might have to prepare for."

"I bet this one will be a false alarm too," Katie says.

"I hope so," I say flatly. I can't believe this is happening.

"H ... have you spoken to Maria since she dropped you off earlier by chance?"

"No." I get a pang of guilt. I've been too consumed in my own crap.

"Oh," Katie says. "I called her before you. She didn't answer, but maybe her phone is on silent. I don't have her house number to check."

"I do." I say goodbye and dial Maria's house number. Then her cell. They both ring ... and ring ... and ring.

I call back Katie and relay the bad news. She tells me I should crack open a beer to relieve the stress. I say I'll think about it and we promise to call each other tomorrow.

As soon as I hang up with Katie, the phone rings again.

"Hello?" I say.

"Harper?" It's Jane.

"Yeah?"

"I saw the news. Katie texted me. Holy crap. You gotta get out of there. Maybe you can sneak out the side gate?"

"I tried. A *soldier* dude brought me back."

"You can't get stuck there! Remember what I told you would happen?!"

"That they'd lock—"

"Shhhhhhhh... yes *that*. We can't say any trigger words or they'll start listening! What do you see out of any windows facing the front?"

I stick my head under the curtains of the window that overlooks the front yard. Down the street, there's a black vehicle with its parking lights on. As I try to see whether there's a person inside, I hear the beating sound of a helicopter overhead. Its spotlight pivots up and down the rows of houses, turning night into day wherever it touches.

"Jane, there's a helicopter! What happens if they catch me? What will they do?"

"Do you have a tennis ball or something?" she asks.

"Yeah," I respond.

Following Jane's instructions, I sneak through the backyard to the side gate. I grab the metal latch and pull it open as carefully as I can. The rusty hinges protest with a series of squeaks. I freeze, waiting for movement or other noises. When nothing comes of it, I squat and roll the tennis ball down the sidewalk. It makes it halfway across the street, and bounces off a small rock.

Three sharp, red laser dots hit it. Then a spotlight follows the ball as it rolls into the gutter's edge. The light pivots to my next-door-neighbor's yard, searching the dense bushes nearby. The neighbor's dog starts barking like crazy and in a panic, I quickly slink back into the house.

The phone rings.

"Harper?!" Jane yells.

"They have the place under serious lockdown," I pant.

"Whoa," Jane says.

"Yeah. Any more suggestions?"

"I'll have to talk to my peeps." She hangs up in a hurry.

I stay awake until the morning birds began to chirp, and the sky changes from black to pink to blue. Finally, when the sun is full in the sky, I feel safe enough to sleep.

I'm coming home just in time for Brett, Olivia, and Mom to take me away with them. We escape to a house where we safely watch terrifying events unfold on the news. Familiar faces of our community collapse in the streets and the white suits madly collect and hide the bodies, like some sort of bizarre game. Police show up in riot gear and keep citizens from escaping. The power goes out, all goes dark, and my family and I start running for the car in a mad attempt to leave town. Olivia is going too slow and one of the white suits catches her ankle and starts dragging her away. I pull on her arms, but they're so strong, that I'm losing grip of her.

I wake up in a sweat, and take a long gulp of water from the glass on my nightstand, attempting to push the images away as I try to put out the fire in my throat.

The events of last night come rushing back, like a cruel headache.

The air is stale and thick by late afternoon, but when I move aside the sheets I've covered my window with and slide open the pane, the thousand-degree air from outside comes whooshing in. I slam it shut.

The street below is motionless, devoid of military activity apart from a few parked Humvees.

I scan the trees and rooftops, trying to figure out where those red laser lights came from last night. I take note of a house with a roof hidden by a large tree, and a pile of rocks in someone's side yard.

I fix myself some mac and cheese. Then I take stock of what's in the cupboards. It looks like there's enough food to last me for months. I guess Mom's weird, controlling paranoia has finally paid off. My house could feed the army outside. Jane would be impressed.

Every step I take echoes through the hall and up the stairs. Every clink of my spoon on the edge of a dish and every sneeze makes my location within the house painfully obvious. So I walk around on my tiptoes and watch for squeaky floorboards.

Holy hell, it's hot today. Lucky for me, our AC unit broke earlier this month and Mom couldn't afford to fix it. That means it's fridgcation time.

A cool relieving blast of air hits my face when I open the refrigerator door. I strip down to my underwear to avoid spontaneous combustion. My bare back leans against the cold glass shelves and I eat from a pint of ice cream.

Someone knocks at the door. In a panic, I dash into the living room, and turn the blanket on the couch into a makeshift wrap to cover my underwear.

When I answer, two officers in contamination suits stand like white statues under the blazing sun. I pull the blanket tighter around my ribs and wipe away the sweat dripping into my eyes. I try to make out the faces behind their masks, but the bright daylight gleam makes that impossible.

"Hello, miss. Are you the only one home?" the shorter one asks. The front of the house bends oddly in the reflection of her eye shield.

"Yes." I notice the big red badges with photos dangling from their belts.

"I see." She nods to her partner, who starts scribbling something onto a digital tablet.

"What's your name, young lady?"

"Harper Loomis."

"Harper, can you come out here and talk to us for a minute?"

I hesitate, embarrassed by my lack of clothing.

"That's okay, honey, we don't mind. We know you weren't expecting us."

I step out from the indoor shadows. She motions me to take a seat on the porch rocking chair.

There are more military trucks parked on the street now.

"Don't worry, you're not in trouble. How old are you?"

She leans closer. I can now see the badge from her belt reads cdc, atlanta in big black letters.

"I'm seventeen," I mutter.

"Ah, lucky you. Not quite old enough to be on your own."

I can't tell if she's being serious or sarcastic.

"Where is your family, Ms. Loomis?"

"Gone. They weren't here when you shut everything down."

"Oh." She turns to her colleague. "Do you know where they might be? We want to make sure they don't get anyone else sick." Under the shadow of the porch overhang, I can see her face and her bright green eyes.

"No." My hand grips tightly around the armrest.

"Hmm. Okay. I know you must be scared, being here on your own, but we're here to protect you." She pats my knee.

Her partner says something into the radio. Three other white suits pop out of a van, each of them carrying white coolers.

"We are going to have to search your house, Ms. Loomis."

"For what?" They walk past me, not giving a crap, and let themselves inside.

"They need to take samples and are going to spray something that could help fight any prions that could've gotten into your house."

This freaks me out. "Is the Syndrome airborne?"

The woman looks me over carefully. "I am not at liberty to release any info about the disease at this time."

She reaches into the square case at her side and pulls out a clear plastic bag. Inside is a giant Q-tip, some cotton balls, and a needle. I shudder.

"We're going to need some samples from you. We want to make sure you're nice and healthy. The sooner we know, the sooner we can get you and your neighbors out of here."

She plucks the Q-tip from the package and pulls apart its plastic wrapping. "Curious, do you have any eye issues?" She asks.

"No. I can see just fine."

"What about any bleeding problems, excessive bruising or random infections?"

"Nope."

"Do all of your siblings look like you? As in the same light hair, skin and eyes?"

"No. My brother is tan and my sister has dark hair. I'm the pastiest of them all." I throw in a little laugh, but she doesn't respond.

"I see. And you don't know where they've gone? It would be good to get samples from your entire family as well. Make sure everyone is healthy."

I shake my head.

"Well, I'm going to need a tissue and blood sample from you."

"Do I have to give you one?" I ask nervously.

Her partner taps his CDC badge. "Yes. All people in this area need to be monitored for infection. If you ever want to get out of here, you'll have to give us samples."

The lady with the green eyes breaks in, "Ms. Loomis, you look like you can hold your own pretty well, so can you trust me to do this?"

"I assume you know what you're doing since you have that fancy badge."

"Exactly. Open up." She rubs the Q-tip around the inside of my cheek and then drops it inside a plastic tube and gives it to her partner. He slips it into a manila envelope that has my street number printed on the side.

The smell of alcohol burns my nostrils as she blots my inner elbow with a wet cotton ball. She unwraps a needle and brings it to my vein. I look away.

"I think it helps when you look at the needle while I'm doing it. It hurts less when you know what's coming," she says softly.

"Sure." I smile politely and watch her. It pinches for a second, but she's right, watching does help. She fills up three vials of blood and hands them to her partner, who puts them into the same envelope. She then takes a cotton ball and holds it against the injection spot.

"See, that wasn't so bad." She holds my wrist up, making my arm into the shape of a V. "And now, to make you officially part of the club ..."

A light mechanical sound starts from her assistant's tablet. From a small opening on the side prints a thin, bright red strip. After the mechanical noise finishes, he pulls it out and hands it to the woman. She wraps the strip snugly around my wrist and snaps it shut with a tiny button. harper loomis: 17-z6 is printed on the wristband, alongside a barcode.

"That's just so we can keep track of your health," she says. "If you need medication or anything, we'll know who you are faster with that."

One of the men walks out of my house and loads his cooler into a parked military truck.

"I'll be right back. Wait right here." She goes and talks to him. He looks in my direction. He says something into his radio and follows her back to me.

"Because you're seventeen, we are going to have to watch your house. Your lookout should be here any minute. If you need anything, just ask him." He drones like he's tired of hearing his own voice. I bet this is the hundredth house they've been to today.

"Thanks for helping us out, young lady," the woman says. "You can go back inside now."

I grip my dress-blanket and stand up. The woman and her partner walk across my yard toward Mrs. Nunez's house. I bet Mrs. Nunez is having a great time watching all the action going on from her perch near the window.

CHAPTER 8

"Harper ..."

My hand hits the water glass on my nightstand, toppling it to the floor. A tall white suit stands over my bed, looming like a ghost in the early evening darkness.

I jolt up and fumble for the lamp, the light reveals Max's grinning face. He has the nerve to laugh at me. *Dick.*

"Ah, calm down. Guess who got assigned to be your night babysitter?" He shuffles a brown box under one arm and jug of water under the other.

"Really? Why did you sneak in here?! There's a doorbell, you know! Shouldn't you be sitting outside instead of watching me sleep like a freaking creeper?" I grab a dirty shirt from the floor and pull it over the sports bra and shorts that I've been sleeping in. Then I use another dirty shirt to mop up the water on my nightstand.

"Yeah, well, you like to sleep through doorbells. I even

knocked on your bedroom door." He glances at the nightstand that he's had to push out of the way to gain entry into my bedroom. "There wasn't an answer. I'm just checking to make sure you're still alive." He finally drops his smug-ass smirk.

"Fine. What's that?" I ask, motioning to the box and water.

"The water in the neighborhood's not working," he holds up the jug, then the box, shaking it. "And this is government-issued dinner. Hungry?"

"Thanks." I grab both and place them beside me. I've got enough food and water, but a little more won't hurt.

"Need some company while you chow down?" His tone has changed to a friendly one.

"Don't you have to get back outside? Wouldn't want to let on we know each other or anything."

"It's gonna be another twenty minutes before they drive by again. Unless one of your neighbors reports some suspicious activity." He pushes the bed sheets covering my window aside and peers at the street.

"What 'suspicious activity,' exactly?"

He sucks in air through his mask. "Violence. Signs of the Syndrome. Panic. Shit like that."

"What happens then?"

"They separate the infected from the rest of the family." He lets the sheet fall back into place.

"So how do they think my neighbor got it?"

His suit makes a crinkling noise as he leans against my door frame. "Sandy was a really cool lady. Let them examine her and her husband till the end. Wanted to make sure nobody else got infected. Even with all of that, they still aren't sure how she got it. Apparently she might have been hiking the day before or something? Anyway, that CDC lady said everywhere else has a trail, but your neighbor caught it out of the blue."

"Does that mean Sandy's dead?"

The muscles around his eyes twitch. He stays quiet.

"And her husband?"

He doesn't say a thing.

"That house is like five blocks from here! I'm just supposed to sit here and let it get me?"

"What can you do?" He turns and I see the gun attached to his hip. Was he one of the soldiers who pointed a laser at my tennis ball?

He starts stomping down the stairs.

"Hey! I want you out of my house!" I chase him to the kitchen.

"Do you really want to get rid of the only friend you have?" he says, placing the box and water on the counter.

I stop. He's got a point.

Max pulls a knife from his belt and breaks the tape sealing the box. I come closer but he puts his hand up. "Stay there."

Cracking open the tape, he pulls out what appears to be microwave-ready dinners, and stabs his knife into the plastic to open one. He slides it over to me and goes to the other end of the room, where our wall of photos hang.

I open the silverware drawer and grab a fork, poke it at my cold dish and take a bite or two. The dead phone sits on the counter beside me. I put it back in the charging cradle and wait for the flickering light that indicates a new voicemail. It's 8 p.m. and Jane was supposed to give me the latest info. The light stays dark.

I catch Max gazing at a photo where Brett is around thirteen, disheveled and buck-toothed. "Ha! Brett looks like a dork here!" he says, pointing at it.

"Yeah. That's before girls swooned over his every move."

"Yeah. I've witnessed it. He'd be a good wingman."

"So how did you guys meet again?" I ask.

"Like he said, we met at work."

"But you work for the military. You have two jobs?"

"The National Guard's a part-time gig."

"I see."

"You were a cute kid. Not bad looking now either," he says.

I'm not sure how to respond to that, so I say nothing.

He picks up another photo. "You and Brett get along okay?"

"Sure?"

"Uh huh. I don't make that face when I talk about my brother. He seems cool. You think he's a jerk? Give me the dirt."

I suppose it doesn't make a difference if he knows a little more about me now. It's nice not to have the house so silent. "Well, I just feel like he's always judging me. Ever since he moved here, he's gone out of his way to get me into trouble with my Mom."

"Where'd he move from?"

"Brett lived with my father. I didn't even know I had a brother before. Talking about my dad is off limits, so it's impossible to ask questions without being grounded for a week."

I recall, years past, when a strange man with a skeletal face and giant, bulbous blue eyes brought Brett to our door. Brett, who had to be about twelve then, was clutching a ragged suitcase with Transformer cartoons on it.

"These are your sisters," the skeletal-faced man said, nudging him forward.

Brett looked at Olivia and me with a pained, angry expression. Mom leaned down to his level. "I ... I haven't seen you in a long time, Brett," she said, and I was surprised by how unsure she sounded for him being her long-lost child. He barely spoke for months after that. Then we'd find random fist-shaped holes in the wall and the skeletal-faced man would come back and speak with him behind closed doors. Brett started being a suck-up to Mom after that, but was always bitter when he looked at me. Like I'd done something to him. Like it was my fault dad was dead.

"How old were you when your dad left?" Max says, breaking me out of the memory.

"I don't know. I can only remember my Mom crying and him hugging me goodbye."

"I can't believe she never told you that you had a brother. That's odd."

"Yeah, it's one of the many reasons we don't get along very well," I say.

"So why did Brett come back all of a sudden? Where did your dad go?"

I spin the fork around on the counter. "My dad died from a brain aneurysm, and Brett needed a place to live." My explanation is clinical, and I surprise myself, talking about my dad usually comes with a throbbing pain in my chest. Maybe the current situation is putting it into proper perspective.

"My dad left me too. It's got nothing to do with you. It's their own shit." He looks at my hand outstretched on the counter and I wonder if he's thinking about touching it. He pulls his glance to the clock above the refrigerator. "Well, I have to get going. We can hang out again tomorrow. I'll be in the military truck parked outside if you need anything."

I follow him to the doorway. Right before he's about to cross the threshold, he stops and looks me in the eyes. I look away, caught off guard. Is it possible he has a crush on me? At a time like this? I don't know. Nobody has ever had a crush on me before.

I head to the shower and turn the handle. Only a few drops of water come out. Oh, yeah. Max said the water isn't working. I go and get the jug of water and pour it over my head in the sink. The benefit to having short hair is that it doesn't require much to wash it. After that I give myself a quick sponge bath. Then I dry myself off and put on a comfy t-shirt and sweats.

Lying in bed, I pull out my homeschool study schedule, scatter my books across the blankets, and successfully finish three days' worth of assignments before the morning sun overtakes the light from my lamp.

My eyelids are heavy from the weight of the long night and even though I want to check the internet, the lure of sleep is stronger.

When I wake, well into the afternoon, a blip of light comes from the phone sitting on my nightstand. A new voicemail? I pick it up and am disappointed to find it caused by a blinking battery icon. Weird. I just charged it before I dozed off.

Climbing onto the frame of my window, I take a seat and push it open. The air from outside rushes in, damp and colder from the rain. The sky is a stormy gray and I can just make out the cackling of thunder in the distance. I glance at the phone. Maria's number sits at the top of the list on the screen, with the number twenty-six next to it ... the total amount of times I've called her without success over the recent days.

I sigh and press her number again. Why isn't she answering? The phone beeps with its last dying breath. I head downstairs to place it in the charging cradle but stop when something catches my eye: A folded sheet of newspaper has been slipped beneath the front door. I unfold it. A large, bright pink sticky note clings to the inside.

I can't call. The lines are blocked and the house is being monitored. We'll come for you tomorrow. If possible, do not let them test you. Destroy this note.

It's written in Mom's handwriting.

I yank open the door and search the street. I curse myself for not paying closer attention to see who delivered it. Are they watching me now?

Just down the driveway walks the same crew who examined me three days earlier. I close the door as quickly as possible and catch a glimpse of the CDC woman noticing me. *Crap.* I quickly stuff the newspaper under the couch cushions. Then comes the knock.

I open the door as casually as possible. "Hey."

"Ms. Loomis, what were you doing out here? Is something wrong?" the woman asks. She's gained dark circles under her eyes since I've seen her last. Her assistant stands beside her, holding his tablet.

"No, just trying to let in some of this nice cool air." I pull the door back and forth, like a giant fan.

She frowns. "We need an updated blood sample."

"What if I don't want to?" I say nervously.

"It's required," her partner says. "The situation's fluid, and we need the data to keep on top of things."

"Take a seat, my dear. This should only take a moment."

"Well, I don't have a choice, do I? I shut the door behind me and take my seat in the porch rocking chair. The woman draws two vials of blood and packs them into the same manila envelope with my address and barcode on it.

"That's good. My partner just needs to get a scan of your bracelet and then you're all done for today."

I hold out my arm and he runs the edge of his device over the barcode.

"You know, if you're having a stressful time, we have mental health staff on site, who can help with the stress of this situation. Are you interested in taking advantage of those services?"

"No thanks. Not right now," I say.

"Okay. We'll be back tomorrow. Let the guard know if you need anything. Just wave out the door. No more opening the front door to peek outside though, okay?"

"Okay!" I give her a slight smile and a thumbs up. I shut the door and turn the lock.

I pull out the newspaper and reread Mom's note. Then I turn my attention to the front page of this morning's *USA Today*. The main image is of a frail woman shouting as tears wet her cheeks. One of her hands is in a fist in the air and the other is holding a sign that reads DON'T LET MY LITTLE BOY DIE IN THERE.

Soldiers in breathing masks in the background are holding rifles, all lined up at a gate. Around them are different colored tents and exhausted looking campers. I turn my attention to the article.

SUSPECTED RSE SLEEPING SYNDROME QUARANTINE IN RENO, NEVADA

Hundreds of Nevada residents went into quarantine three days ago in an effort to curb the spread of a suspected RSE Sleeping Syndrome outbreak. The quarantine border encompasses about three square miles, which is believed to be the location where the first resident was taken ill. If confirmed, this would be the first reported case in Nevada.

Phone lines and internet connections appear to be down in the quarantine zone. Outside the quarantine zone, family members and friends have been gathering in protest while waiting for a formal announcement.

"I'm not able to reach my son or his kids," says Amie South, 56. "He usually calls me back within a few days. I know something is wrong in there. They keep telling us to leave, but I can't leave my son."

Officials say they will make an announcement as soon as possible, but are also looking at ways to clear the protest site. A spokesman for the CDC said, "We understand the concern, but we need to ask all family members outside the quarantine zone to keep a safe distance and allow our response team to evaluate the situation properly. The military is willing to use force, if necessary, to control the crowds, and has already doubled the personnel around the perimeter and blocked roads leading to the quarantine site. *The protesters need to remember they are putting themselves at increased risk by staying where they are."*

The same spokesman also cautioned, "If you or anyone you know is experiencing episodes of euphoria, slurred speech, difficulty speaking, fatigue, numbness or weakness, difficulty walking, or sleeping for unnaturally long periods of time, please contact us with the information listed on our website."

The president tweeted that he will make an official announcement about the quarantine zone tomorrow at 10 a.m. PST. Check out usatoday.com for live coverage.

If confirmed, Nevada will be the largest population affected by the RSE Sleeping Syndrome in the United States.

I read in slow motion as it sinks in that this incident is big enough to cover the front page of a national paper. What if Mom can't rescue me with all this security? How would she have the resources?

I drift into Olivia's room and wrap my arms around her pillow, which still emanates the scent of her lilac shampoo. My eyes burn. I could die in here. What will happen to Olivia if I do?

Still clutching her pillow, I fall into her bed. Through the tears, I weave in and out of sleep, until sometime in the wee hours of the morning, the slam of several car doors wakes me up.

CHAPTER 9

There's another slam and a metal clank. Someone's dropped something in the road. I creep to the window, keeping the light off to hide the shift in the curtains.

All the street lamps are off, which I've never seen before. As my eyes adjust to the darkness, I can make out faint outlines under the moon. There's more metal creaking.

A group of hazmat suits move slowly from Mrs. Nunez's front door. A white van silently backs up onto the sidewalk and the brake lights flood them all with red. Together, they heave two large objects into the van.

No. Mr. and Mrs. Nunez.

I shiver in the warm night. Hold it together, Harper. Mom's coming for you tomorrow — or today, now.

The van drives away, taking the white suits with it. I pull the blanket from Olivia's bed and crouch in a corner with it wrapped around me. I just have to hold out a little longer.

Olivia's lamp flickers.

I jump up and run into the hallway. All of the lights in the house start flashing on and off. *Hold it together. You have to hold it together! What's going on? Does the CDC know that I just saw them removing bodies?*

And then a terrible thought bubbles up from the depths of my mind.

Maria.

"Oh god!" I gasp. Maria googled the figure I described to her without using incognito mode! What if that led them right to her! What if *I* got her killed?

The house lights flicker again ... and then go out.

I kick open the front door and race onto the street. I pause. Max's vehicle is nowhere in sight. No lasers point at me. Strange. I look around for signs of anything, but the neighborhood is as lifeless and as dark as a graveyard. I glance at the Nunez' place and just make out a piece of red paper fluttering on their door. I look back at my house, which doesn't have one.

I race across the neighbor's backyard toward Maria's house. The silhouettes of bushes and trees are swaying to life, and my hair is whipping against my head. I climb onto their fence and realize I can balance along the central line of fences that goes down the entire block. Finally I make it to the end and onto the next road.

A small glimmer three houses down catches my attention. I rub my eyes, unsure what I'm looking at. It's a bunch of tiny lights, like glitter, circling in a small dust cloud. Are they fireflies? Surely not in Nevada? Or it could be ... *Nope* ... I sprint across the street. My feet make a clapping sound against the wet pavement. I jump on some trash cans and hop the next fence. I hear a loud diesel engine drive past in the distance, but I'm unsure of the exact direction it's coming from. The darkness is disorienting and so far there hasn't been a single light on in any of the windows to help me.

As I reach the next street, a helicopter flies overhead and I scramble to hide under a truck. When it's gone, I roll out and start sprinting.

Headlights slice through the night and I veer onto a nearby porch and duck behind some wicker furniture. *Crap. Did it see me?*

The Humvee slinks by, thank goodness. When I stand up, I knock over a metal watering pot and cringe at the clank it makes. Nothing in the house stirs. Nothing in the street stirs. The only sign of movement is something shaking in the wind. Taped to the door is another red leaflet, like the one I saw earlier. There's a large barcode on it similar to the one around my wrist.

Every house that I can make out has a red leaflet. It dawns on me what's nearby. Mr. and Mrs. Hernberg's house, the very first place infected with the Syndrome, is only a few houses from here, across the street. After triple checking for Humvees, I sneak over. There, flapping in the wind, like a morbid flag, is the same red leaflet that has been on every house I've passed so far ... except for mine.

I stare into the black windows. Wind chimes clank eerily in the distance and a ghostly howl whistles past my ears.

A Humvee roars down the block. I barely make it behind a garbage can by the time it speeds by. I lean against the crusty bin, trembling from the inside out, listening for the vehicle to fade away.

Then, to my horror, the brakes squeak to a stop. *Crap. Crap. Crap.*

It waits, idling, creating a racket that seems to ricochet off every house in the neighborhood. I lean closer to the gross, smelly can, angling my body to not be seen from the other side.

The Humvee clicks and revs in reverse, stopping just a few feet away from me. I hold my breath as a door opens and slams shut. Heavy, booted steps hit the pavement. Panic swells inside me as I consider running for it.

The boots step slowly, a flashlight beaming behind tree trunks and under parked cars. Then the light starts to round my trash can. I stumble to my feet, sprinting in the opposite direction.

Smack! The next thing I know, my nose is rubbing against the wet, rough street.

Someone pulls me up and warm liquid runs down my lips, the taste of blood fills my mouth. My hands are zip-tied behind my back, and a faceless white suit grabs me by the arm and throws me into the trunk of the Humvee.

The door slams shut. When I try to get up, my wet limbs slide around on plastic lining protecting the floor. The Humvee starts moving, and I slide into something else in the trunk. A cold, clammy object brushes against the back of my arm. I can barely scramble away on the slippery plastic. The Humvee goes over a speed bump and I'm lifted into the air. When I land, I look over my shoulder. There's a blanket covering whatever the object is. When I don't see movement, I reach to find what's touched me. My fingers close around someone's cold rigid hand, sticking out from beneath the blanket. I snap away, trying to get as far from it as possible.

"I got her." I hear the male driver mumble up front.

If I don't die in the back of this Humvee under that blanket, the driver may be taking me to die in a white tent; where my last breath will be studied with scientific indifference. A shudder rises in my chest and turns into a sob.

I thud into the body again when the engine abruptly comes to a halt. The trunk door opens. Under the light of the moon, a white figure stands in the road.

"Please!" I beg. "I don't want to die!"

He roughly lifts me out of the vehicle. I cooperate with him until he's got me on my feet. Then I kick at his nuts, but miss and catch his leg. He grabs my arm before I can sprint for it and I start kicking again like a wild animal.

"Calm the eff down! Damn it, Harper, I swear to God. You almost really screwed this up! You were lucky nobody was over there!" Max growls. "If you want to get out of this alive, we need to stay low and quiet until they get here."

"Until who gets here? Are you going to kill me too? Like whoever you've got stuffed in this trunk?!"

"I didn't kill her!" He tries to keep his voice low. "The Syndrome did."

"Well, don't I have it now? I've been touching her and shit cause you shoved me in there with her!"

"No. Apparently you're immune. You're the only person not showing symptoms yet, which is why I'm wrestling with letting you leave at all. Maybe your immunity can help people."

I pause. "Wait. You're considering letting me go?"

"Your mom and Brett talked me into it. If they weren't paying me serious money, there's no way I'd be doing this right now. They're the ones who gave me the body to replace you with."

"What?"

"Yeah. It's part of the plan you just messed up. That body was supposed to replace you in the house tomorrow. Then I was going to burn your house down during the president's speech." He reaches behind me and cuts the zip tie holding my hands. "Just follow me."

CHAPTER 10

Max leads me by my arm through a gate and into someone's backyard. We walk past a big swimming pool and huddle behind a shed, pressing against the fence.

"What's going on?" I whisper.

"We're improvising! I told you, you messed up the plan!"

I jump when a cat meows.

Then, to my surprise, Max meows back.

The cat meows twice in response.

"That's our cue," Max says, as he kicks in a soft fence plank, crouches down, and disappears through a narrow opening.

A helicopter drones by in the distance.

"You coming?" he asks from the other side. I crawl through the same hole. Black tarp, the kind I saw hanging from the quarantine fence on TV, drapes down from this side of the fence. Max holds it apart and offers me his hand. When I take it, he pulls me to the other side.

"Harper!" says a voice that I started to think I might never hear again.

"Brett!"

His arms engulf me and I evaporate into his hug, stress melting away into the night air.

"They're all dead, Brett. All of them." I cry into his shoulder. "I think Maria is too."

"Shhhh ... you're safe now."

Brett breaks the hug and looks at me. Even in the moonlight I can see his tired, puffy eyes. "Come on, let's get you a shower and some sleep. We have to hurry!"

He keeps me close with his arm around me as we walk. There's a bicycle leaning against a tree up ahead. This street seems to be almost exactly like ours except there are no cars in any of the driveways.

"Can't someone see us here?" I ask, alarmed by how easy we'd be to spot.

"No. It's cleared. The helicopter will probably be back around in about two minutes though," Max says, walking behind us.

Brett grabs the bicycle by the handles. "Harper, you stand on the pegs. I'll ride. We're going to meet Mom with the car — " His eyes stop on something.

Click.

I turn around. Behind us, Max stands rigid, his arm outstretched and his gun pointed at Brett. Even in the limited light, I can see the whites of his eyes behind his face shield. "I changed my mind. I can't let you do this, man."

Brett raises his hands. "Max. There's no need for guns.

Can we talk?" He takes a step back.

"No! Stay right there!" Max shouts. "It's not right that she gets to leave and everyone else is dead! You're both coming with me. Then you can tell me where your mom and sister are. You could all have some sort of immunity that could help other people, and it's my duty to save lives."

"I told you! Only Harper's immune. She can't help other people – it's a genetic abnormality that can't be replicated in other's genes!" Brett says.

What is he talking about? How does Brett know what's in my genes?

Max puts his other hand to his head, flustered. "Yeah. Yeah. So you've been telling me. If there's something special about her, the CDC can figure it out. You hired me right before the Syndrome broke out! That's fishy as hell!"

Something moves behind Max at the end of the block. Black shapes begin to enlarge and shift in odd ways. Silver outlines erupt from the edges and burn into feathery rainbows.

The figures morph into the humanoid silhouette that's been haunting me. It's the thing from the desert! No, it's three of them!

They glide closer, their waving flames shimmering around their black bodies like a sunset on angry waters.

"Brett!" I shout, pointing, because the rest of the words won't come.

"What is it?"

"Thoooose ... things!" I manage to choke out.

"What the hell is she talking about?" Max asks, glancing behind him, his gun still aimed at Brett.

Brett's face contorts with alarm. "What things, Harper? I don't see anything."

I look again, to make sure I'm not crazy. The horrible figures continue their approach. "You don't see those floating ... rainbow things ... over there?!"

"Run, Harper!" Brett shouts. "Run back home! Hide in your room!"

"No, you stay right there, Harper!" Max moves his gun to me.

Brett tackles him. "Run!" he shouts.

I dart to the fence and crawl back through the hole. I pause in the road, blood hammering in my ears. I didn't see how we got here in the trunk of the Humvee. I turn on another street, gain my bearings, and sprint through backyards to my house.

Back in my room, I hide in my closet behind a curtain of clothes.

"Be okay, Brett, you have to be okay," I whisper to myself over and over again, hyperventilating into the neck of my T-shirt.

A gun reverberates in the distance.

I get a sickly plummeting sensation in the pit of my stomach. *What do I do?*

Weird music creeps up from downstairs. How can that be? The power's out.

The neighbor's dog starts barking like crazy. I press myself against the back wall, hugging my knees to my chest. This has to be a nightmare.

The bedroom door bursts open and the sound gets louder, like an orchestra of flutes going off sporadically.

Through the gaps in the door frame of the closet, I see a glowing arm reach into my room from the hallway. A sizzling pop follows and the arm jumps back. The flute sounds get faster. Is that a language? Are they talking to each other? The glowing arm has disappeared. My room sits quietly in the moonlight.

A rod of lightning shoots from the doorway and strikes the opposing wall. I clench my mouth to keep from screaming. The smell of singed wood fills the room and the hole the lightning left behind reveals several rows of sizzling, black, sparking metal discs.

There's more lightning. The room starts bursting apart until nearly all of the wood paneling lies in ashes on the floor. Where the wood once was, are hundreds and hundreds of CD-sized silver discs, stacked on top of each other. Have those discs always been there? Hidden beneath the wood paneling?

The glowing figures start drifting around my room. They are tall — their heads nearly skim the ceiling fan. Their movements are quick and jittery, like a hummingbird.

"Harper!" Brett's voice booms from the doorway.

His appearance smacks me with a mix of relief and shock. What is he doing? Then I remember he can't see them. Do I stop him? Will they hurt him? He enters the room and the three figures freeze. Oranges, purples, and pinks radiate from them. Brett's worried eyes frantically scan the wrecked walls. Then he yanks open the closet door.

"They're behind you!" I shout.

That's the last thing I remember.

CHAPTER 11

My head is heavy with fog. *Brett.* But I'm too scared to open my eyes. I twitch my pinky. It's stuck, restrained by something. I take a slow, cautious breath. Weight pushes back all around me. It's made its way into the smallest crevices of my body: into my ears, under my fingernails, and between my toes.

I open my eyes. Mysterious dots of light, like fireflies, are drifting through the air weightlessly. I'm in a large room that gives the impression that I've been swallowed by a giant seashell, with a curving white floor, ceiling, and walls.

In the middle of the floor is a pedestal with strange gold and silver instruments on top. To its right is a translucent almond-shaped pod positioned vertically with — I squint— what appears to be a human figure inside. A face is breaching the surface — *it's Brett!*

I can't tell if he's breathing.

"Brett," I say. The jelly of the pod I'm stuck in squishes

against my cheek as I try to turn my head. Brett's face twitches and his eyes pop open. He gasps like someone waking up from a bad dream.

"Harper! Are you okay?!"

"Shhhhhhhhhhhh! Yes, I'm fine!" I keep my voice low.

"Where are we? What is this stuff?" He grunts as he struggles to move.

"I don't know!" I jerk and try to free my leg. As my foot's about to break the surface of the pod, the jelly hardens and turns solid, making a crystal cast around it, freezing my leg in place. The same thing happens when I try to free my arm. Whatever this stuff is, it isn't going to let us go.

There's another rush of wind. From behind a column, a rainbow figure materializes before me. I gasp.

The black center of the body fades away and the flames transform into a new shape: A solid, tall white being with an elongated head.

"She didn't do anything," Brett shouts. "It's not her fault! She doesn't know!"

He must be able to see this new form.

The being points one of its long three fingers into the air. It has the body of a slender humanoid in a black jumpsuit, with two legs, feet, arms, and hands.

The glowing dots that were aimlessly floating around bolt in front of the being and form into a hologram: a grid of lettering made from rectangular shapes and straight lines.

"How can you see me in my suit?" the being says to me in a female, auto-tuned sounding voice. It's coming from the tip of her finger, where a little light pulsates.

I open my mouth, but no words come out.

"I have other ways of getting the information I need if you won't give it to me voluntarily." She leans in closer, within inches of my face. Her two eyes are about three times the size of a human's with glowing opal-like irises and no pupils.

She maneuvers her finger over the right side of my face. A new hologram appears and the jelly I'm submerged in wraps around my eyes. I let out a guttural scream.

"Calm down. This won't hurt unless you struggle," she says.

"Stop it!" Brett shouts.

I think I'm screaming the same thing.

"She doesn't know what's going on! I'm the Sentinel!" Brett says. "I know where the others are hiding! If you leave her alone, I'll tell you! She doesn't know anything. Please! She doesn't know what she is!"

This is a sobering slap. "What are you talking about, Brett? What the hell am I?"

The jelly pulls away from my eyes. The tall white figure is staring at Brett. "Yes, human, what is she?"

"She's ... not a typical human," Brett says.

"Brett! Do you know what's going on here?!" I get a sinking feeling that I'm being betrayed.

The tall being puts her fingers to her temple. The slits that run down the center of her face open and close like gills, making those flute noises.

She paces to a wall and a bumpy glass post springs up from the floor, stopping at the height of her chest. From the post, she breaks off an icicle-shape and jabs it into my arm. I wince in anticipation, but all I feel is pressure. When she pulls the icicle away, there's a tube of my blood running down the center of it.

I look to Brett again while the creature busies herself. "Brett! Answer me!" I demand. "I know you can hear me!"

The being injects my blood into the post, where it swirls as it mixes with specks of light. A large DNA cylindrical strand appears as a hologram projected above us. She waves her hands through the air, zooming in on the details, as she makes more flute noises.

She returns to my side. "How can you see our suits?" Her glowing eyes send an icy-cold flutter through the pit of my stomach.

"Tell her," Brett says, finally acknowledging me, tears falling down his cheeks. "Tell her how you can see them."

"What the hell, Brett?!" I jerk violently in the pod. "I don't know!"

Brett closes his eyes.

"Very well," the being says, nodding at Brett. Her wordless lips move and I hear another gust of wind.

Two more creatures emerge, and pull me out from the jelly with ease. I feel cold ground on my bare feet. They've removed my shoes and covered my clothes with some sort of white unitard. They march me to a wall.

"Brett!" I thrash my arms. "Let me talk to him!"

A section of the wall parts and light pours in.

"Brett! Brett!"

I'm dragged through the opening.

CHAPTER 12

I blink away the blinding light. Every other thought I've ever had leaves my head as I try to comprehend where I am — hundreds of white skyscraper-sized structures rise into the air, holding up a massive latticed dome. The magnificent structures are like pine cones, draped with tendrils of vegetation, waterfalls, and connected via thousands of slender white bridges.

Platforms maneuver between it all like magic carpets. Sparkling fog hovers at different elevations throughout the dome, obscuring sections of the city and parting for the pastel-colored beings who walk through it on the ground.

My handlers tug me onward, snapping me out of my awestruck trance.

I pull back. "Please! Take me back to my brother! I need to know what's going on! Tell me what's going on!"

"You are not free to go, human," one of them says in an

auto-tuned voice. "Attempting freedom does not increase your chances of freedom. It restricts it further."

For a moment, I close my eyes, trying to calm the whirlwind in my head and chest. "Is there someone I can talk to? About what's going on?" I try to keep my voice assured, but it still trembles at the end.

They speak to each other in those flute sounds I heard in my house. We weave through the street level, passing more multicolored vegetation, pools of silver liquid, and large groups of pastel-colored beings running around. They have to be at least a few heads taller than most humans.

"It is not our place to tell you anything," one of them finally says as we approach a massive net made of millions of glowing threads. The threads untangle, revealing about fifty objects that look like black igloos lined up in rows. I'm immediately escorted toward them.

"Wait!" I yell as I'm shoved into one. The opening seals shut behind me.

I turn around. Sparks glide over the inner surfaces of a small domed room, like licks of flames roving through embers. On each side of the wall, two clamshell shapes protrude; large enough for a tall man to climb into. The clam shapes are filled with what appears to be a velvety pink fluff, almost like bubbles in a bathtub.

Something slowly rises out of one and I back to the other side of the room, flattening myself against the wall, shaking there.

The pink fluff falls from the shape, revealing another one of those beings. Her big, glowing gold eyes look me over for a second. "Why ah ye here?" she says with a thick accent. It's almost as if a flute is talking, as if she's singing her words. "Did ye kill someone?"

She makes a wobbly attempt to climb out of the shell. The tips of her copper fingers are noticeably black, and her face and arms are covered in giant welts. She's wearing a white hospital gown that stops just above her knees. *Where. The. Hell. Am. I?*

"No, I didn't kill anyone. My ... my ... brother ..." I choke, pulling at the unitard that's covering my clothes, which seems to be getting tighter with each passing second.

I turn and bang my fist against the wall. "Let me talk to my brother!" A heaving sob rises in my chest.

There's a zapping sound and I'm shot backward, landing hard on my butt.

"OOh!" The copper being hurries over, and bends over. "Ye can't be aggressive, they'll think ye're trying to escape so they'll shock ye," she says.

I wipe away tears and tug frantically at the unitard.

"Ye can't remove it. It appears they have concerns about what ye're wearing underneath."

"My clothes?"

"Oh. Yes."

The being stands up straight and makes a gesture like a reverse double-handed salute. Her elbows pinned to her ribs, she moves both hands from beside her head and down, pivoting her arms until they're pointing at me. "Hello. Me name is Rubaveer from Procell," she says, freezing there.

"Oh." I stand. "I'm Harper from Reno." I attempt the same movement.

She smiles. "Well at least I got roomed with a human. I love humans," her voice gets higher pitched.

"Who or what are you?" I stare at her, taking her in. Like the rest of her kind, her skin is iridescent, like a pearl. Other than the slits running down the center of her face that move when she talks, her tall forehead, high cheekbones, and lips are humanlike.

She gives me an odd glance, as if surprised. "I am an Enbrotici, but yer kind may know me by a different name. Ye must be a Sentinel because they keep Sentinels in the prisons. Sentinels call my kind thee Ancients."

That's what Brett said he was. "What's a Sentinel?" I ask.

Rubaveer's eyebrowless ridge lifts. "Oh, I didn't know they captured humans who are not Sentinels. Interesting ..." She ponders off for a moment. "There isn't much data on them in thee Procell database. What I do know is that thee Sentinels are a secret human group, who are opposed to my kind, thee Enbrotici." The glowing, curly pinstripes that run up the side of her elongated skull pulsate. The top of her species' heads reminds me of a squid or pharaoh crown."If ye are not ah Sentinel, did ye do something to upset them?"

"Not that I can think of. Maybe my brother did when he told them *he* was a Sentinel?"

"Hmmmm ... How did they find ye?"

"There was a sickness in my neighborhood. When we tried to escape, they captured us."

"Oooh." She bites her lip. Her teeth are a lighter version of her copper skin and made of a single smooth panel following the shape of her jaw. "Iiif ye're not a Sentinel, it's curious why they didn't just leave ye there. Thee Syndrome would have killed ye along with everybody else. There would have been no evidence."

My heart stops. "What do you know about the Syndrome?"

"Hmm ..." she hums again slowly, as if my words have carried her out of a daze. "Oooh, ye don't know?"

"No! Tell me!"

Her large gold irises roll to the side in more thought. "Well, human, isn't it all a bit obvious? We arrive on yer planet, which then suffers an outbreak of a syndrome that yer scientists don't understand?"

"*You* caused the RSE Sleeping Syndrome?"

She crosses her arms, offended. "Iii've done no such thing." Her voice is almost lyrical. "The Enbrotici here do not reflect our entire race. Iiin fact, our whole solar system knows nothing about this secret extinction plan."

"Extinction plan!" I choke out.

Her head pivots back, looking at me strangely. "Yes. When I found out by my secret research, I felt a calling to warn your kind. Iii snuck on a ship headed here, to help thee humans, but was found hiding before Iii could tell anyone —"

"— Does that mean you know how to stop it?"

"Well, it was genetically engineered on Procell, which is where I am from. It means that like any responsibly-made disease, it is controllable by responding to certain signals —"

A loud chime noise goes off, and I stumble backwards.

A hole opens beneath a hologram that appears on the wall and two globs of transparent orbs plop out and roll into a trough.

"Food!" Rubaveer shouts, reaching for them.

She shoves the squishy, warm orb into my hand and I hold up what looks like a giant water droplet.

"How do you stop the disease?" I ask urgently.

Rubaveer makes a loud slurping sound, sucking on the orb, that seems to shrink with every mouthful she takes. "There are a few ways," she finally says. "But there is no way to get out of thee prisons to do so. Not unless you have thee force of some sort of accelerator."

"And where is here exactly? A spaceship?" I place the orb back into the trough. Rubaveer's eyes follow it. Her red tongue runs around her lips.

"Iii believe we are on a base, not a spaceship. Iii do not know our location, which is another issue."

There's a clicking sound and the lights go out. A blast of frigid wind sweeps over my bare legs and arms, and I feel goosebumps rise all over.

A warm rubbery hand grasps mine. "Wwweee must hurry and get into thee sleeping pods. The light will be down for ah long time."

"How long?" I start to shiver, holding my arm to my chest.

"Iiit's uncertain. When ye entered, it was the first I'd seen thee light in many days. At least I think it's many days. It's easy to lose track in here." She places one of my hands on what I'm guessing is the clamshell shape and then guides the other to a soft, fluffy surface.

"Please hurry and get in. I'm very cold," she urges.

I pull myself over the rim and sink into the fluff. The softness inside envelops my whole body, surrounding me in what feels like down feathers and memory foam. I'm not sure how it's possible for me to breathe with my head beneath the thick density, but it is, and it's surprisingly warm and snug.

As I'm starting to warm back up, a hole opens in the fluff and exposes my shoulder to the biting cold. I adjust and roll on my back. The fluff shifts, exposing my face. I flip over and my neck is exposed.

I spend the next few minutes repositioning myself. Not too long after, it becomes clear that it's intentional. The black flesh I saw on Rubaveer's fingers and face come to mind. *Frostbite*. I feel sick.

How long until frostbite sets in? Twenty minutes?

First, the cold feels like the pain of hundreds of little knives stabbing, then, after a few minutes, it fades away and I go numb. The numbness takes a little longer on larger body parts, like my shoulders, hips and torso (which are also covered by the unitard).

As I lay there, battling with the cold, the worst pain comes from my chest, where it feels as though barbed wire is mangling my heart. The cure for the Sleeping Syndrome is a *few feet* away, and I'm helplessly trapped here as death barrels toward Olivia and everyone else I've ever cared about.

There's a zap, in my hands, like a bolt of electricity. Like the sensation I felt at the soccer game.

Brett's words solidify in my head.

"She's not a normal human."

"She has a genetic abnormality."

Could I? I raise my head out of the fluff and peer into the darkness. The air is like an icy flame against my skin and lungs.

I've got nothing else to lose. Without giving myself time to hesitate, I scream, leap over the edge of the pod and charge at the wall.

There's an immense blow of earth-shattering pain as I bounce from the wall to the hard floor.

"Hhuman! What are ye doing? Ye'll freeze in seconds! Get back in quick!" Rubaveer shouts from the other side of the dark dome.

Everything is spinning from the impact. I can barely control my trembling body as I crawl back to the pod, my head throbbing like a drum is beating on my skull. The light from Rubaveer's eyes is visible at the other end of the room, but the cold is overwhelming.

"Hhharper! Faster! The cold will take your limbs unless you move faster!" Rubaveer shouts. "Fffocus, human!"

My hand finds the slope of the sleeping pod at last. With what little strength I have left, I stand. The darkness spins more. I flop over the rim and fall in. The warm fluff consumes me and I sink to the center. I curl into a tight ball, my teeth chattering.

"Ddddid ye make it back, human? Are ye still awake?"

CHAPTER 13

A loud banging brings me back to consciousness. I open my eyes: light penetrates through the surface of the fluff. I'm not sure how long it's been, I only know that I can still feel the cold in my bones.

"Harper Loomis, please come with us," says an auto-tuned voice.

All the aching muscles in my body tighten.

I claw my way out of the sleeping pod and stand weakly in front of it. The intense light is relentless on my pounding head — my sore eyes drift to the spot I ran into last night. On the wall is a white starburst-shape contrasting all the black. Is that where my head hit? I did something! Something worked!

A door seam opens. Two ... *aliens* dressed in gold armor enter, far fancier than the previous ones who brought me here.

"You are to be moved to more appropriate accommodations," one says sternly.

"Are you taking me to my brother?" I say.

One of them gives me an intimidating glare. "Please come with us."

I back into the sleeping pod and wince from a sharp stab in my elbow. I look down at my arm to find that my elbow's turned a purplish blue, fringed on the edges with red, shiny skin. It must have happened when I passed out.

The Golden Guards approach and herd me to the door.

"What's going to happen to Rubaveer?" I ask.

"It is none of your concern," the guard says, grabbing my arm and pulling me out of the igloo.

"Stay strong, Rubaveer!" I say in a raspy voice as the door seals. *I'm going to try and come back for you.*

As the guards march me through the city, I look up at the massive silver dome that is so high; it could be a sky from another world. From the thick, geometric silver lattice design, light cascades out of its small openings, drenching the city in daylight: like a basket encasing a sun. Could this be the same sky I used to live under or is this Mars? The moon? Or did I travel light years through space to get here?

"Do you know what day it is?" I say to the guards.

They continue to look ahead as we march onwards.

"Or what Earthling day it is?" I add and still receive no answer.

They pull me down an unpopulated pathway. One of the gold-armored aliens flicks out his hand and presses it into a wall. Glitter rises from nowhere, like shards of metal drawn to a magnet. An expanding hole appears, and the beings tug me inside, through a long narrow tunnel.

When we reach the end, more towering pine cone-like structures are on the other side. The ground rises and falls in hills, covered by plantlike puffs in as many different colors as the aliens who live here. White cobblestone paths lead to each of the structures and floating balls of light line the road.

We stop at the base of a building, with no visible divide between the inside and outside, entering it by walking through an invisible force field. Past there is a massive lobby with towering white walls that elegantly slope down from the ceiling and rise up from the floor like white sand dunes. The guard parts a door at the end. I wait for him to step in, but he moves to the side and motions for me to go ahead.

"Only me?" I say.

He just gives me another severe look. His arm remains outstretched toward the door.

"Okay then." I hold my breath and step in.

I rise steadily on an invisible platform up the center of a shaft. Soon the speed slows, an opening appears, and the invisible floor pushes me out into a large room where a vast 180-degree window overlooks the city. At this height, I can see the point where the buildings join the top of the dome. I pivot my head and try to peer through the lattice holding everything up, to see if there are stars, red mountains, or a blue sky beyond it, but there is only pure white light.

I turn my attention back to the room. On the walls, foreign writing pulsates over an iridescent sheen. I run my hand over what I think is a couch that looks as though it's grown from the floor. Like most of the furniture in this room, it's a clean, simplified version of curving, organic shapes.

"Take a seat," says a cold, digital female voice, breaking the quiet. I spot her holding out her hand from the corner of the room: a willowy silhouette in shadow against the bright backdrop of the window. She must have been watching me the whole time.

Like magic, glass clumps grow from the floor and morph into a chair that looks to be made of icicles.

"Please, I insist. You are our guest."

Their guest? I place my hand on the chair to ground myself and am surprised to find that though it looks to be made of ice, it's slightly warm and squishy to the touch, like silicone.

"Let's talk about your brother," she says.

I get an uneasy lump in my throat. "Is he okay?"

A noise comes from her shaking shoulders. Something in that melodic native tone that breaks away from the accent of the digital voice: a laugh. At least, I think it's a laugh. It sounds like a group of flutes drastically changing pitch.

She steps out from the shadows — though she moves so effortlessly, it almost looks as though she's gliding. A gold suit glimmers into the light like fish scales, hanging from her tall, bony body. Her two purple eyes lock on mine, piercing against her pearlescent skin. Her bone structure is chiseled and jawline an elegant "v." She looks a little more human than the others, which is strangely comforting.

"Are you hungry? I can't imagine you've been enjoying our food. I know that you like macaroni and cheese."

"I'm ... okay." I say, with a growing sense of confusion and worry. How does she know I like mac and cheese?

She smiles elegantly and points her finger. A hologram

shoots out and she presses her finger into something on a floating interface. Another glass lump grows from the floor with ... a plate of macaroni and cheese on top.

I look at it with apprehension. I don't think Brett even knows it's my favorite.

"Harper," she says, "if I wanted to poison you, don't you think I would have done it when we were feeding you in the holding sector? This is a gift. The start of a friendship. That's why I've brought you here."

I slowly pick up the fork. If I eat some, this alien may trust me more. I take a bite.

"Wonderful!" She beams. "Is it to your satisfaction?"

I nod, though I can barely taste it over my thickening anxiety.

Her eyes trail off to the window. "Harper," her voice says slowly, "your brother has done terrible, terrible things to you."

The fork handle digs into my palm. "What do you mean?"

She draws a large circle in the air and a projection fills it. Two double-helixes spin side by side: DNA structures.

"This is your genetic code on the right and Brett's on the left." A few sections are highlighted as she zooms in. She looks at me, anticipating a reaction.

"I don't understand," I say.

"You and Brett are not siblings."

I recall the day Brett arrived at our house with the blue-eyed man. I remember how nervous he was, how sad he looked when he met his long-lost family. Is it possible some random kid has been living with us? His tan, attractive features ... the very opposite of me.

"Don't take it personally," The alien says. "He's a Sentinel and they are duplicitous. Brett's already confessed that he's been experimenting on you at night. Your mother hired him. She participated in it as well. In fact we aren't even sure if she's your mother."

What? I have to mentally replay what she's just said, to make sure I just heard what I think I did. "Of ... of course she's my mother. Maybe Brett doesn't look like me, but she does. She's always been there ... for as long as I can remember."

"Would a *mother* experiment on her own daughter? According to Brett, she wasn't very fond of you."

When I was younger, I remember sitting at the table each month as the blue-eyed man asked me questions. There were random math tests and occasionally physical benchmark tests, but I don't recall my mother ever doing any *experiments* on me.

"Why would she do that?" I say out loud.

"Because they were prepping you for the Sentinel army and didn't want your secret getting out."

"*No.* That's ... that's ... ridiculous. Mom works at a retirement home."

"That was probably a coverup." She sighs and gives me an empathetic frown. "Now *we* need to study you. Make sure that the Sentinels did no harm to you." She circles me for a moment, looking me over. "You see, you're a hybrid, and humans are not advanced enough to successfully create them. Most outcomes are ... immediately unfortunate. Other issues might not appear until you're older. Unless you're very lucky, cancer would be a certainty."

No. I want to tell her that she's lost her mind. "Why would I be a *hybrid*? I've never trained for this Sentinel army."

She lets out her flute laugh again. "They might not have trained you yet, but they had plans for you." She paces over to the window and looks out over the city. "Luckily for you, we have opted to welcome you into our hybrid rehabilitation. The reason you were born was terrible but you deserve a second chance. Here is a safe place where you can nurture your gifts and repair damage from the incompetent scientists that butchered your insides."

"Wait. Hold on a second. If I'm a *hybrid*, I'm a *hybrid* of what? A human and what else?"

She looks back over her shoulder. "Like the other hybrids here, you are partly Enbrotici."

I feel like I've been dunked in frigid water. I look at my hands. How? I don't look anything like these creatures?

"Don't worry. You will see. You are not alone. There are others like you. They understand your pain. After you and I are done here, you'll join your true kind."

"Do I—!" I check myself and soften my voice. "Do I have a choice?"

"A choice in what?"

"To go back to Earth."

She turns and faces me, crossing her arms, her gold suit sparkling where it hits the light at certain angles. "The Earth as you know it does not exist anymore."

I have to check myself again. "You killed everyone? Already?"

She shifts her weight, visibly uncomfortable with my question. "Harper, Earth is very sick... "

"With the RSE Sleeping Syndrome?"

Her large purple and blue eyes study me, narrowing a bit. "No, it was sick long before that. Humans are its disease. Earth is dying and we are here to help. Sometimes you have to make a choice for the better, even though in the short-term, and for some individuals, it is terrible. It is for the good of this planet and all other species here."

"So you're just going to kill all the humans?"

"Do you know why it's called the *Sleeping Syndrome*, Harper?"

"Because people fall asleep and die?"

"Precisely. And what do you humans do to sick animals when you care about them, but they are miserable and in pain?"

An icy chill brushes over me, like I'm back in the prisons. "Put them to sleep ..."

She walks to the window, her suit twinkles more in its light.

"But humans are changing!" I say. "We have electric cars, we recycle, we conserve endangered animals, we —"

"It's not enough, my dear. It's too late. The damage that has been done is just ..." She sighs, putting her face into her hand. "Without our help, *all* life on Earth will become extinct. You do realize that humans have poisoned the oceans and enslaved and destroyed *billions* of species?"

"Yeah, but —"

"It's a dire situation. Predeen, our artificial intelligence system, has calculated that by the year 2050, Earth's warming oceans will release their hydrogen sulfide, triggering a mass extinction that will wipe out humans, and 97% of the species you still have left. This would come after horrible waves of drought, famine, flooding, and nuclear wars over resources. We couldn't let that happen. There is no future for *any* life on Earth without our help."

"But you can help us," I say, stepping closer to her, so we're only a few feet apart. "Help us see the error of our ways. You have all this amazing technology. Surely you can help us fix Earth?"

"You mean 'them'? You are not human anymore."

"Yes ... them." I say coldly.

She intertwines her long fingers. "Humans' own scientists have been telling them this information, but humans still refuse to listen. They prize their routines and pleasures above all else, even their futures."

"But why do you even care what happens to Earth?"

"We've had a small part to play in what humans have done to the planet. It is our duty to correct it."

"What does that mean?" I ask.

"We'll explain everything during your training."

"What about Olivia?" I ask. "Is she?"

The alien maneuvers her hand through the floating interface, looking at what appears to be a list. "According to Brett, she is your mother's true biological child. No experimentation was done on her."

Does that mean that Olivia isn't my true sister? She does look more like my mom's real child, with her dark hair and eyes.

"Can I see Brett before I go to this training?" I say.

"Why would you want to do that?"

"I'd like to ask him all of this myself."

"Perhaps, I will think about it." She takes out a gray cube and passes it to me. "Your first belongings in your new home." She gives me a broad, uncomfortable looking smile, as if still learning how to do it.

"Oh!" She shakes her head. "How terribly rude of me. I was so eager to meet you that I almost forgot to introduce myself." She positions both hands at her temples and then drops them until they point at me — her arms held at a ninety degree angle, like Rubaveer did. "My name is Alexiuus. Welcome to the Base of Ki, Harper." She spreads her arms, indicating the entirety of the dome as she overlooks the city. "My Golden Guard will escort you to the medical center, then to your new living quarters."

A guard steps forward with a red flower-shaped tattoo on his shoulder armor, something that none of the others had. He doesn't seize me like the last two did, but halts there and nods.

"Wait!" I say as Alexiuus starts walking away. "You can save Earth without killing everyone. I know you can. Let me help you. I can be your ... your ... messenger to humans or something. You don't have to kill billions of people, who are just as real as you and me, *who have people they love*," I choke.

She gives that odd, large smile again.

"I'm glad to see you have such morals, Harper. But Predeen has put more calculations into this decision than you could make in a thousand of your lifetimes."

The Golden Guard moves closer, stepping between Alexiuus and me.

"Sontarx," Alexiuus says, looking at him, "is here to take you to decontamination."

CHAPTER 14

The jelly pulls away and I sit up in the crystal pod. I feel weird. A bit colder. A bit more exposed. A bit more naked.

It takes a moment to register that I'm staring at my own legs. I wiggle my toes, and the strange toes at the end of the strange legs wiggle instead. Something's not right. These limbs are too pale, even for me, pearl white and iridescent — like the belly of a fish or a lizard. Like an alien's legs!

"What did you do to me?!" I cry, seeing the white has spread to my hands and arms too. I frantically try to wipe it off. "Undo it! Undo it now!"

"This is your true appearance. You look better this way. No longer a filthy human. We've removed all the unnecessary artificial material," says Jenousis, the alien who performed this 'decontamination' on me.

"No," I cry, "give me back my skin!" I touch my face and then the top of my head, which is now smooth, "and my hair!"

"Your skin and hair were only camouflage, so you could blend into the human world." Jenousis's bulbous yellow eyes stare at me, hollow like a jack-o-lantern. Sontarx, Alexiuus' Golden Guard, stands back in the distance.

I jump out of the jelly pod, stumbling, and search for a reflective surface. I peer into a tiny slab of metal on the floor, the size of a butter knife. Before I get a chance to examine my missing hair, I'm caught by the strange eyes staring back at me. My pupils are gone. Now there are only irises. Solid discs of shimmering and glowing greens, like smaller versions of the alien's eyes!

"No! This isn't right!" I say, "This can't be! Change me back! Change me back now!" I fall to my knees.

"She needs to rest. They don't handle this part well," Jenousis says to Sontarx. "Bring her to her quarters."

"No! You have to fix me! Fix me now!" I spring on him and grab onto his black uniform. Sontarx easily rips me off, holding me back by the arms.

Jenousis injects me with an icicle and all my muscles go loose and warm. I collapse from a sudden lack of strength and will. Before I hit the ground, a soft web of radiating specks materializes and catches me.

I leave the room, towed on the floating web-stretcher by the guard. We journey over a thin bridge and come to another long corridor with gold lettering along the wall. We enter a place the size of a small hotel room, with a large window and balcony straight ahead of us. The floating web-like contraption lowers me to the hard floor and evaporates.

The place looks similar to the room I woke up in here, like the insides of a giant seashell, with curvy walls and a glowing interface.

"What quarter settings do you wish for?" Sontarx asks. He touches the surface of the interface and it ripples.

On the floor, I can feel my strength return, but it's no use to me now. I curl into a ball and turn away from him. *I hate them.*

"Since you have not specified, you shall have the default quarters," he says.

He taps the interface, and furniture grows from the ground. It's the same kind of simplified organic-looking furniture that was in Alexiuus' place: lumpy crystal chairs, a clam-shaped bed, and an orange light near the entrance.

I hear the whooshing sound of the door appearing again, and then the guard's footsteps are gone.

Fear of seeing my reflection keeps me glued to the floor. My unitard feels different. I look down and see that it's been cut open, exposing my clothes underneath. They are covered in white dust. I try to rip off the unitard material, but it's too strong. Defeated, I stuff my hands under my armpits and rock back and forth.

My body begins to ache from lying on the hard ground. I finally sit up and stare beyond my balcony. The dome's lattice has thickened up, shrinking the massive openings that once poured light into pinholes. The ceiling now looks like a night sky on Earth. I automatically start searching for my red star but stop myself.

I rise from the floor and wander over to the interface. As I approach, two illuminated circles bob up and down in the interface's dark reflection. I stop. The two circles stop with me. I spin around and check if there are two circles following me.

They are not.

What could those be? Some sort of weird dots in the interface? I wave my hand in front of my head to see if it will influence them. The circles blink when my hand goes in front of my face. I stop waving, my left hand frozen before me. The left circle is missing. I gasp. Those circles are my eyes. They're glowing like the aliens' eyes do ...

I'm standing about ten feet away from the interface. At this distance, it's too dim to see anything besides the illumination of my eyes. The only other light is coming from the window, a faint, silvery radiance produced by the fake stars and the shimmer of the night time city.

My heart thumps harder. What if I'm a monster? I stare at the two orbs before me, like two moons floating in the night. Holding my breath, I step toward the interface, moving quickly, before I can change my mind. As I approach, a couple of foreign words light up at the top of the mirrored surface. In the faint light, I see a hazy reflection. A strange, bald, pointy-headed silhouette with bony shoulders. The pale skin seems to cast its own light. I slowly comb my fingers over my rubbery scalp. I don't catch a single strand of hair or stubble. I step closer. My face is mostly the same, but my skin looks like it's been covered in a thick layer of white makeup. When I look down, I see that, other than my new tint, most of me still appears human. The hair of my eyebrows is gone and in its place is a slight purple undertone that matches my lips. My ears noticeably protrude from the sides of my pointy, bald head. In place of my hair are the pinstripe designs, starting at my temple and branching up and around the rest of my skull, all the way to the tip of it.

The patterns remind me of simplified graphic drawings of vines, with diamond shapes instead of flowers.

How can this reflection be mine? Vomit rises in the back of my throat.

I race to the balcony, lean over the side, and begin to hyperventilate.

How the hell is any of this even possible? This has to be a dream. My gaze wanders over the night-time city, where the architecture seems to have a slight luminescence and those little firefly lights move through it all like schools of fish. I search again and again for the glowing prison net, but can't find it.

In that moment, it occurs to me that I'm staring at an *alien* city. After all the astronomers that have looked to the sky in search of even the simplest of lifeforms; here I am, *imprisoned* by them. Supposedly one of them ... or half one anyway. All of it still seems fake. A 3D rendering or a dream ...

My eyes drift up. Above and below me are balconies every couple of feet. I reach forward and climb onto the railing, balancing there; trembling and calculating how far I'll have to jump to make it to the next one. I'm relieved that though I look different, my body seems to move and respond the same.

"You can't do it," whispers a human-sounding voice. I nearly lose my balance at the sound of her. Below me is a woman standing on the balcony next to mine. She's got random patches of human flesh next to purple alien skin.

"They don't understand human emotion all that well, but after the first of us jumped and killed themselves, they made sure it would never happen again. Besides, you have no reason to be upset. You'll be happy here."

"Who are you?" I ask, trying to steady myself.

"Tamera."

In addition to her strange skin, half of her face is more bloated than the other, one eyelid puffy and one eye glowing in the dark on the same side.

"Are you ... ?"

"A hybrid," she nods. "Why don't you get down? It's blocked." She throws something off her balcony. A previously invisible force field ignites as the object hits it.

I should have thought of that.

I step down carefully, trying not to gawk at the odd ... hybrid. Will I be as shocking to other people when they see me? "How long have you been here?" I ask eagerly.

"I'm not sure." She pauses, thinking. "A few months, maybe?"

"Are you in the training program? What have they done to you?" I wince. Perhaps I shouldn't have asked that last one.

"They spent weeks trying to fix what the *Sentinels* did to me, they've been nothing but kind to me here. There are other hybrids here too, you know. You're not alone. And soon we'll merge with the Ancients' society and become just like them." She sounds so happy when she talks about it, but I'm struggling to keep up.

"You don't have any reservations? After all that they're capable of." I ask with caution.

She sighs. "Trust me, you'll understand it after you've been here a while. There's a reason you felt like you didn't fit in with the humans."

"I admit I'm still figuring family stuff out, but I fit in just fine with my human friends."

"No, you're mistaken. You think you did, but the humans hated us." The harsh tone she suddenly takes surprises me. "The Ancients are willing to take us in and make us whole again. Soon we'll live down there, with them." Her eyes seem to twinkle and she gazes at the city below. "There's a plan for us to go to Cooms once they're done here."

"You know what they're doing to the human race, right?" I say in almost a whisper.

Tamera crosses her arms. "I was like you at first. I hated the Ancients too. But once you know what the human race has been up to, you begin to realize it's the kindest thing we can do. The Ancients are the good guys."

Why does she keep calling them Ancients instead of Enbrotici? I thought Rubaveer said only the Sentinels used that name. "But what I don't get is the reason for wiping the humans out? Look around. They have all this amazing technology. Their solution is awfully convenient."

She makes a very sour frown. "The Ancients didn't make the decision lightly!" she snaps. "You still have feelings about your loved ones, which is clouding your judgment." She jabs her finger at the ground. "Think about it. Humans don't bat an eye when they remove less intelligent, destructive species from an environment. Think of rat and cockroach infestations. Humans would be hypocrites to be against what the Ancients are doing. The Earth is *diseased* with *humans*."

"But you're part human ..." I say, taken aback.

"Humans never cared about me." She scoffs. Then her

expression softens and she glances away. "I only look like this because of what they did to me. You know, not many of us are lucky enough to be as cleanly spliced as you are." She motions to the patches of skin on her face. "The Sentinels wanted an advantage against the Ancients. That's why they created us. Not because they gave a shit about us as individuals."

"Why do the Sentinels and aliens hate each other so much?" I ask.

"Will you stop calling them *aliens*?" Her pitch sharpens again. "Call them Ancients, like they are, like they deserve to be called. They aren't some foreign *aliens* to you anymore. You're one of them — one of *us* — time to get used to it. Time to make it right. Time to see the light." She huffs. "Besides, I could not do the Ancient/Sentinel story justice if I told you. The *Ancients* will show you."

"Why do you keep calling them that?"

"What?"

"Ancients? I thought that's what the Sentinels call them?"

She shakes her head, clearly running thin on patience. "No. Not you. To you they are called Ancients. The Sentinels call them the Ancients out of fear. But in fear there is respect. And we greatly respect the Ancients. To us, to you and me, to all hybrids, they are sacred and should be respected, which a name like 'Ancient' implies. Old, sacred, and wise."

"I see. Who decided this?"

"The hybrids here," she says flatly.

"Okay. But I'm confused. Earlier you said that we were part of them, so if we are truly part of them, shouldn't we call them Enbrotici? Like what they call each other?"

"That's just how it is. Accept it. I'll see you at the Canopy with everyone else." She stomps back inside without another word.

CHAPTER 15

"Harper, is it?" Says a digital, British accent.

I sit up, straightening myself against the wall, having dozed off.

"Yeah," I say, as I peer up at the alien standing over me, troubled that I still haven't woken from this nightmare.

"Hello. My name is Innogen," she says. Her skin is pastel blue, complemented by a creamy beige suit. She pivots her hands away from her head in the greeting I'm slowly becoming accustomed to.

I stumble to my feet, feeling a sharp kink in my neck. "Hi. Yes. I'm Harper," I respond, and then realize she already knows that.

"Nice to meet you." Her accent rings like a pleasant bell. "Would you be more comfortable if I fixed your surroundings? This place can look however you want it to, you know."

"I did not," I say, rubbing my neck. "Are you here to start off my training?"

She glances around and and her eyes stop on the gray cube Alexiuus gave me. The guard must have left it there. She picks it up and twists it around to inspect it. "Not quite yet. There are some things we must do first."

She tucks the cube under her arm and goes to the interface hologram on the wall. "Let me see if I can recall your lovely home planet." She dips in her hands, and splashes what appears to be particles from the hologram on her face. It creates colorful steam-like swirls and specks of light around her head.

The room starts to shift. The roof over my head morphs into a blue sky. Fluffy clouds and snow capped mountain peaks materialize. A carpet of grass sprawls beneath our feet. She's transformed my room into a meadow. In the middle are blankets, pillows, and a picnic basket. Sunrays glisten overhead, and a breeze swishes through the foliage of distant trees.

"Isn't it beautiful?" She claps with an enthusiasm that reminds me of Rubaveer. "You can do it too, make it any place you want, all you have to do is remember it and the program will build it."

In utter disbelief, I bend down and comb my hand through the feathery-soft grass. *How is any of this possible?*

"Now. So sorry I have to do this, dear, but I need your Earth clothes."

"My clothes?" I pull my eyes from a bird that springs from the meadow and flies off into the sky. My fingers dart to my shirt, in protection of the grimy fabric beneath the slit in the unitard.

"Yes. Your clothes are not compatible with our technology here. I'm trying to do you a favor. You wouldn't want the guards to come here and force you out of them. The other hybrids weren't too fond of that."

The alien runs a little silver device along my spine. The white unitard falls off my shoulders, opening at the back. A thick puff of dust rises up, and I cough.

"Sorry about that. It's caused by the cells that came off when they removed your human skin. The machine can't get them all when you're wearing the protective suit."

My old skin. Turned to ash. Just like that. I run my finger down my exposed shoulder, making a streak in the dust. I pull off the stretchy unitard and hand it to Innogen.

"Here." Innogen gives me a squishy ball. "When you've taken off everything, including your Earth wear, remove all the dead cells with this." She passes me the gray cube. "And when you're clean, slap this cube against your chest."

I place the items on the floor and reach for the button on my shorts, pausing there. She's staring at me.

"Sorry," she says, "I always forget hybrids are self-conscious without clothes." She turns around.

My hands seem to go along on their own, pulling my clothes from my body as if I were simply getting ready for bed. Naked in the meadow, I run the squeegee ball up and down my bare skin.

Once I've removed the dust, I slap the cube Alexiuus gave me to my chest. At first, the cold, smooth liquid spreads over me, as though I've jumped into an icy bath. The gray liquid runs down my arms and legs until it forms into a bodysuit with shoes. When the bodysuit solidifies, the fabric is so light that I have to look down several times and check that I'm wearing something.

"Very good, Harper. Now, let's have a chat." A portal opens in the middle of the meadow, and I follow her through it to a large hallway flanked on both sides with a series of small gold plaques, like the room numbers in a hotel. As we pass them, I think of Tamera next door and question if every one of these rooms is housing a hybrid ... a hybrid who could help me get out of here ... if they aren't all brainwashed yet.

Innogen looks down at me pleasantly. "Before we found you, before you came here, did anything unique ever happen to you? Anything unusual?"

Panic builds inside me. Does she know? Did they see what I did? The sound of our footsteps seem to get louder in the lengthening silence. "Like what?" I say as casually as I can.

The hallway opens up to a long, slender bridge, majestically arching — practically floating — hundreds of feet in the air, spanning at least a good quarter-mile across; which makes me nervous when we begin to cross it. I try to keep my gaze on my feet.

Innogen shrugs. "Perhaps you can hear exquisitely well or breathe underwater? Or perhaps you can do something that is very unique for a human?"

"Can hybrids do those sorts of things?"

"Some can," she says.

Does that mean there are others like me here?

"So, do you have any special abilities, Harper?" Innogen says pleasantly.

"Oh. no." I give a laugh that I worry sounds too nervous. "Not unless you count clumsiness."

Her large blue eyes zero in on me. "I think you are doing human sarcasm." She looks forward again, nodding, as if assuring herself. "All right. Be aware that sometimes after we've removed human tissue interference from hybrids, special abilities have emerged. So you may see some strange symptoms in the coming weeks. You will let me know if that happens, correct? Anything out of the ordinary."

"I will," I say enthusiastically.

We complete a loop on the bridge, heading back to the hallway of rooms.

"Should special abilities emerge, I ask that you only tell me for the time being. There are a lot of new hybrids here. We don't want anyone getting hurt because they can't control their abilities properly."

"I see."

We come back to my room. "What about training?" I ask. "When will I meet the others?"

"Very soon," she says, patting me on the head like some sort of cute animal. "It was a lovely walk, but I must be on my way." She ushers me into my room. "The bathroom is where that little orange light is over there, when you need it. Cheerio now."

The door closes and it looks like there are mountains in the distance instead of an immediate wall. When I step closer, little beams of light appear and highlight where the real wall is. I press my head into it, holding back the urge to start kicking it open for freedom.

I sigh and turn around. The meadow looks so much like my Earth ... so annoyingly and dishonestly real, that I start ripping out fistfuls of grass and throwing them. But before they hit the ground, they decay into little ribbons of glitter that disappear into nothing.

I plop down on the picnic blanket and am hit with the fresh scent of laundry. Inside the picnic basket, I find a bottle of water, cucumber sandwiches, cherries and one of those weird squishy food balls Rubaveer likes. I'm not sure if I want to try any of it yet.

Folding the blanket like a pillow, I rest my head on it, staring up at the blue sky. I have to admit, there's some comfort in the familiar sights, smells, and the cushioning grass beneath me. Even if it is fake, it's like *home* — or the closest thing I have to it.

The longer I lay here, the more exhaustion sneaks in, and my thoughts carry me back to Reno.

I have to hope that wherever Olivia is, that she's safe. I can't bear to think about what happened to my friends; I'm just praying that I'll be able to figure something out before the Syndrome gets them all.

There's a TV flipping through channels at the center of a dark room. It switches between aerial views of a neighborhood, shots of military trucks, campers, and do not enter signs. Someone is adjusting the TV's volume until it's barely audible. The TV's voiceover says, "All of Reno, like Sacramento and

Tahoe, has been declared a 'no-go' zone by the CDC. The RSE Sleeping Syndrome infections have increased far beyond the available resources, causing the CDC to leave the infected dead where they fell in the quarantine zones. Because quarantine borders can no longer be secured, the CDC warns that anybody who enters a zone will face certain death from the Syndrome."

"It's getting stronger," a woman's voice says, leaning back on an old, ripped couch.

Her features take a moment for me to recognize. "Mom!" I shout. But she has no reaction to me.

"Yeah," says another, younger voice. "I just don't understand how it got this bad this fast. Harper was only quarantined like two weeks ago."

"Olivia?" I spin around, searching for the source of the voice and find a girl sitting crossed-legged on the floor. I drop to the ground. Her eyes remain fixed on the TV though we're nearly nose-to-nose.

I reach out to touch her, but my hand goes through her chest, as if I were made of mist. *What the hell is going on?* I quickly glance around. We're in a little room where most of the furniture is covered in sheets of plastic. Planks of particleboard are covering two small windows, where little slivers of daylight seep in.

There's a rustling and Olivia jumps up and switches off the TV, standing in front of it with her arms out. "Sorry, Harper," she says, her worried eyes fixed on something.

I follow her gaze to a mirror. My old human form stands there: ghostly pale, short blonde hair, jeans and a T-shirt. Why isn't my human self looking at me?

Before I can approach the mirror, my human-self steps away on her own, disappearing behind the frame.

Olivia chases after her, making it click that the mirror is actually a doorway.

I race after them, finding Olivia in a small dark room with peeling, frilly wallpaper. The human version of me is sitting on a cot, staring blankly into a corner. Light comes from a small, battery powered lamp that sits on a nightstand. The more I look at human *me*, the more I notice my nearly poreless skin, without so much as a single zit or freckle ... as if I've been eerily airbrushed.

Olivia takes a seat beside human Harper, lifting her arm to touch Harper's hand, hesitating before pulling away. "What happened to Brett is not your fault," Olivia says in a whisper.

The human Harper remains motionless and zoned out.

Olivia sniffs. "Please come back to me. I can't lose everything I know, Brett ... and now you. Please. I need you." A tear slides down Olivia's cheek.

"That's not me!" I scream.

They don't even glance up.

A vicious rage blazes through my body. I lunge forward, ready to jump the hell out of human Harper. A strong force yanks me back, as if an invisible rope has been tied around my waist, keeping me trapped in the doorway. "No!" I scream. "That's not me! I'm right here!"

Olivia startles, tripping backwards, eyes wide in my direction.

The scene is ripped from me as I wake up.

No! I'm back in the meadow.

"Come back!" I yell. My hands burn and I see that they're shimmering in waves of light.

"AAAhhhhhh!" I scream. The rage ... the lack of control ... is overwhelming ... *I'm going to* ... I run for the door ... I get a blast of wind ... and find that I've somehow transported to the other end of the room. I skid to a stop, barely avoiding the wall that lights up.

I pant, my heart thrashing against my ribs. *What am I going to do?* Break out of here? Go get Rubaveer? Then what? I don't even know where here or Brett is!

I let out another exasperated scream. My hands throb with a mixture of static and fire. I punch a nearby tree, sending bark shattering all over the place before it disintegrates into glitter. I drop to my knees, feeling extremely loopy all of a sudden.

My throat is sticking together from how dry it is. I crawl to the picnic basket, open it, and squeeze the water bottle into my mouth. I start swallowing, anticipating the cool relief, but nothing touches my tongue. When I pull the bottle away, glitter flies out from between my lips.

I spot the little glob of goo sitting beside the cherries and swallow a mouthful of it. Its room-temperature, gooey texture slithers down my throat. As I try to force a little more down, black spots erupt over my vision.

"Help!" I shout in a croak, hoping Tamera will hear me.

CHAPTER 16

Lights shine into my eyes. I open them. I'm in one of the medical places again. I squeeze my hands — no gel — thank God.

"Ah, there we have it," a blurry Innogen says in her pleasant British accent. She leans into my sight with a warm smile. "You feeling better? You gave us quite a scare. Your blood pressure was dropping quite drastically. It appears you were dehydrated. A nasty bout of body cleanse, it looks like. Don't worry, we've been able to knock it out with a good dose of fluids. Your blood drank it right up ... Though you wouldn't be in this mess if you'd eaten all of your food rations."

With my pounding head, her words seem to go by at a slower pace than they should. As my thoughts clear, I see a Golden Guard is looming in the background.

Innogen leans in so her head is right above mine. "Dear, is everything alright?"

I hold up my hand to block my eyes. "How did you know I passed out?" I ask groggily.

"Health monitor." She tugs at the collar of my suit. "We think it's just stress. Bodies have a funny way of showing it." She looks over at the Golden Guard. "But I've got some good news. I've discussed it with Alexiuus and I think it's time for you to meet the others."

At this, I sit up and jump off the pod. "I'm ready." I say, momentarily steadying myself against it.

Innogen holds out her hands as if she may need to catch me. "You can rest longer if you wish."

"I'm okay," I say, focusing on staying as still as possible. "I'm just very excited to meet my fellow hybrids."

Innogen brings up a hologram with alien writing on it. A light beam scans my body. "Your vitals are much better now." She says something to the Golden Guard in their flute language. I recognize that it's Sontarx by the red mark on his shoulder.

He comes over and leads me to the door.

"Good luck, Harper," Innogen says, waving, smiling again.

Sontarx takes me across a horrifyingly narrow bridge to an expansive white balcony with groupings of alien furniture arranged together like the seating areas of a big city's hotel lobby or airport.

At the center of the balcony is a large white table that could seat hundreds. Gold veins intertwine through the surface, and an abundance of legs merge into the floor like stalagmites.

To the left of me are about fifty transparent tubes the size of phone booths. Ahead of me is a large garden with paths winding through collections of plants. And on all sides of me, beyond the balcony, are the buildings of the city that fuse with the top of the dome, making this another place with an impressive view.

A glimmer in the distance catches my eye: A huge, chrome gold structure, like Sontarx's armor.

"What's that?" I ask.

He looks me over for a second, before he finally says, "Our headquarters," as he touches his chest.

"I see." It pains me to admit the beauty of the Base of Ki. Species exterminators should be evil-looking and ugly.

The sound of human laughter and conversation infiltrates the balcony. A group of strange beings flood in from another hallway — all a mixture of alien and human features.

My stomach does a quick twist. I'm not sure what my strategy is yet, other than trying to find the least brain-washed hybrids possible ... to help me ... somehow. Maybe someone in this group has useful powers or knows where this base is.

But as they continue in my direction, I worry. Will they like me? I've never been good at making friends, I just got lucky with Maria who introduced me to her friends.

"Harper," Tamera says, striding to the front of the approaching crowd. "Welcome to what we call the Canopy. Are you feeling better about all of this since they showed you?"

This is a promising start. "Showed me what?"

"Um." She doesn't answer.

"Hello," a shaky voice says. It belongs to a hunched hybrid with white whiskers growing from an oversized chin, nose and ears. "Name's Peet. That's an interestin' name you got."

"Thanks." I say. "My —" My tongue seems to catch as I

bring her up. "My *mom* named me after the author of *To Kill a Mockingbird*."

The rest of the crowd fills in around me, an excited chattering vibrating among them. As I look over the rainbow of faces, I wonder if they found out they were hybrids when they got here too.

"Never read that book," Peet says. "How'd you come to us, young lady?"

"Well you know … They sorta brought me here."

He grins. His human teeth look odd against his banana-yellow skin. "You see, I thought that too. Before I realized they saved me."

Tamera nods, holding her hands to her heart in thanks.

Peet lets out a cheerful, deep belly laugh that doesn't match his thin frame. "You know, the more hybrids I meet like us, the more I come to find that we have similar stories. Did you feel like you didn't belong, on Earth?"

I'm caught off guard by the assumption and everyone suddenly staring, anticipating my answer. My face gets warm. "Maybe," is the only thing I can think to respond with.

A few hybrids give a courteous laugh.

Peet beams. "Well, the presentation and David will help you finally see the light."

Tamera steps in front of him. "*Shhh*. Don't confuse her before her Leveling."

"The Ancients showed me the light too, honey," says a rod-thin woman whose face is severely sunken. "I was selling little pieces of myself to a different man every night, pieces of my soul to humans. They took everything I had for twenty dollar bills ... until there wasn't nothing left of me. I've been saved by the Ancients." She sniffs, then gives a heavy sob into her hand.

"It's okay, Camilla," says a short, female hybrid. She's uniquely pretty with smooth, round features and offers Camilla a ball to blow her nose into. Then the short woman's wide-set eyes move to me and her face is struck with a distant, sad look. "Not all of us have such tragic stories ..." she trails off.

"Yeah, Jacqueline's right. Not all of us are so frrrreeeeeaky," says a hybrid, who completes a full ballerina spin before he stops and grabs my hand. "Hi, I'm Adam," he says with a charming voice. "Don't worry. This is weird for everyone at first." He has to be in his mid-twenties.

Someone grabs my hand from Adam's. "I'm Tucker," he says. He has the odd roundness of a baby with the stature of a tall adult. "Nice to make your acquaintance, pretty lady, I can't wait to get to know you better."

"Thanks," I say, trying to free myself from his grasp.

"Tucker, aren't you late for a beer-chugging contest or something?" Adam asks.

"Adam ..." Jacqueline warns, her eyes still fixed on me.

"They don't have beer here, you dumbass," Tucker says, finally releasing my hand.

"I know. However do you survive?" Adam remarks.

"Whatever, dude," Tucker says, stepping back in a huff.

Adam leans in and whispers, "Iiiiiggggnore him. He doesn't think about how much he annoys others before he speaks." He pulls away, saying much louder, so that Tucker can clearly hear, "Soon he'll start blathering on about how he always knew he was special. That the Ancients —"

Tamera clears her throat. "Let her finish her training before you explain any more!"

"Fine," Adam says, deflating.

More hybrids chime in with their stories: A hunted illegal immigrant, an orphan, someone with Tourette's syndrome, and a couple of mental disorders. They come from all walks of life, from all over the globe, and it seems very few have lived a pleasant existence.

Through all the conversations, there's something moving just beyond everyone else, below the horizon of shoulders and heads. When someone finally shifts a bit to the left, I notice a slug-like thing, with what appears to be a melted human face on it, blinking and gurgling as it floats on what appears to be a sort of magic carpet. I almost trip over myself.

Tamera catches me. "That's Mandy. There's another one named Matthias," she whispers into my ear. "They're hybrids who got a bad mix of genetics from the Sentinels. She was a vegetable in a hospital bed for years. She stayed alive despite them disconnecting her life support." She shakes her head in disapproval, clicking her tongue.

"What you see is an improvement. The Ancients just got some of her facial muscles working. We've only found two like that so far, but expect to find more. The bastard Sentinels did that to them. Stuck like that with full brain functionality. Can you imagine?" She says dramatically. "Trapped in those mutilated bodies for years. They would've been better off dead. Just like the Sentinels should be." She runs her straight hand across her throat like a knife.

A light pulsates on her fingertip. "Yes, yes," she says, as

if she's listening to someone on the phone. She looks at me thoughtfully before holding her hands above her head and clapping. "Come on, Everyone! It's time for Harper's Leveling!" She grabs me by the wrist and takes me to the head of the massive table, where a middle-aged hybrid-man is waiting. He smiles at me with the poise of a handsome politician.

"This is David," Tamera says, bowing before him.

"Welcome, Harper. Please take a seat. We are here to help you see the light."

"Should I be worried?" I say cautiously.

He laughs airily. His fake-looking white human teeth gleam. "No. Everyone here has seen the light before."

That's worryingly obscure.

He points to the open spot at the front of the table, which I take hesitantly.

A hundred other hybrids are also sitting at the table now, gazes fixed upon me.

I spot Jacqueline a few hybrids down, our eyes meet again. I think she mouths, "It's going to be okay," but she quickly looks away before I can ask for clarity.

Should I just run for it now? But before I can come to a decision, David speaks up.

"I remember when they first showed me my light, my truth," he says, loud enough for everyone to hear. "The first thing I felt was disbelief. *Humans aren't that bad*, I thought. Then I started talking to all of you, and saw just how tragic the human existence truly is."

He waves his hands at the room, motioning dramatically in everyone's direction. "Your stories have shown me the true and unique depths of human evil. I think of stories like Sofia's here." He points to a meek woman leaning into another hybrid. "She was abducted for marriage, then beaten, lit on fire, and forced to drink her own urine for days by her in-laws." He begins to pace back and forth, his voice calm and powerful. "Or Camp Twenty-Two in North Korea, where people have been imprisoned for crimes their grandparents committed. Fifty. Thousand. People. And who can forget the humans' wanton, greedy destruction of our beloved planet Earth." His voice is surprisingly smooth and encompassing, as if I'm the only person here.

"We are here to change that. We are here to change what it *is* to be human." He slams his fist on the table. "The very definition of it. We are here to make it right —"

I jump when almost everyone shouts, "Because we have seen the light!" Except for a select few like Jacqueline, who keep quiet and look down.

"How many other creatures torture for pleasure? How many other creatures kill for no reason other than bloodlust?" He pauses. "Sure, we all know of 'good' people, like our mothers or a random stranger who holds the door open, but when weighing the good against the bad, we quickly recognize that the numbers are significantly skewed. Even the people we thought were good — even our own mothers —" He looks directly at me — "are just Sentinels using us for experimentation and personal gain."

A few hybrids wipe away tears. David looks at them, frowning, patting the back of a hybrid blowing his nose into a silver ball.

"It doesn't have to be like this anymore. The pain, the destruction. It will all end with or without us. We can all move on from it and be our own people without the scars. The future of mankind is up to us. It *is* us. Every single hybrid in this room who has felt hate or pain ... who has felt alone or abandoned ... even unloved ... that part of your life is now over. You hear me, everyone? The Ancients have made it *dead. Done. Over.*"

He goes quiet. The open space of the Canopy fills with the sound of sniffles and sad moans.

"The Sentinels may have wanted to exploit our minds for more evil, but we will use our minds for good. We are stronger than they could have ever imagined. We, as hybrids, will represent what a species should be. You will all know what happiness and purpose feels like." He reaches up his arms. "All of you have a purpose!"

"Because we've seen the light," yells someone in the back.

"Took the words right out of my mouth!" David responds.

"Now, Harper," he says in a quieter tone, as if telling me a dark secret. "Your brother admitted some disconcerting things."

It feels like David just drop-kicked me in the stomach. "Is he okay?!"

David laughs, as if my concern is silly. "Oh yes, he's fine. The Ancients are taking good care of him. He's being kept in a sleeping state where they keep all the Sentinels."

Rubaveer said they keep the Sentinels in the prisons.

David walks to the other side of the table, looking everyone over. "Don't worry about Harper's brother, everyone. That scumbag was a hired guard to keep Harper in line. Her mom didn't work at a retirement community like she claimed either, she worked with the Sentinels to monitor poor Harper daily."

"That's horrible!" someone says.

"Yes. They even had equipment in the wall to drain Harper of her energy so she was more controllable. They needed to use Harper like the Sentinels have been using hybrids for the last several thousand years."

How does this guy know all of this? And who the hell does he think he is? To stand here and tell everyone my personal business? I should stay friendly, to make a good impression on everyone, but when I catch a glint of his smug-ass smile at my obvious discomfort, it reminds me of my mother.

"Stop it!" I blurt out, fighting the urge to run from here, to clear my head in the desert in Reno, a Reno I may never see again. I get a sting in my throat. *No* — I can't think like that.

David gives a devilish smirk. "But you have not seen your light yet."

"I don't give a crap. This is not cool." My heart pounds.

David prowls over to me, stopping when I can feel his breath on my forehead. If he doesn't move out of my way really soon, I might punch him in his stupid fake-looking teeth.

Without breaking eye contact, he lifts his hand and snaps his fingers.

A large sheet springs over everyone at the table, engulfing us into a pitch-dark tent. Dots of light start to gather and the space around the table transforms into a desert. A desert with only shrubs and brown hills for as far as anyone can see. David draws my attention to an open space in front of the table, where a 3-D scene is forming. There's a bunch of tents pitched there, with large coolers and laundry swaying on wires. A group of digital people are gathered around the hood of a car, all looking at the screen of a tablet.

Like a ghost, a hologram girl walks past me, her dark hair blowing in the wind. She joins the people looking at the tablet around the car. Their features slowly come to my recognition. "O-Olivia ...? Mom!"

I run to Olivia, to touch her, but just like in my dream, my arm goes straight through her.

"They knew it was coming, Harper. That's how they got out of the quarantine zone in time."

Panic rises in me. "Why are you showing me this?"

"Keep watching."

From a tent comes a slender girl with white-blonde pixie-cut hair. She's exactly my height. Exactly my build. She's the airbrushed Harper from my dream!

"Who is she?" I say coldly, looking back at David.

"Oh, Harper, can't you see?" He shakes his head. "They've replaced you with another hybrid. As long as they've got a hybrid, any hybrid, they're happy. They already had all the configurations to make you. No need to reprogram or readjust. Copies are easier than originals. They don't need *you* anymore."

Olivia is now showing the airbrushed Harper something in a cooler. Is ... is ... it possible what I saw was more than a nightmare? That this clone is the same Harper I saw in my dream? Is Olivia in danger?

A blazing heat rises in my fingertips. I double over, trying to hide my hands in the fold of my body.

"You're all right. It's a panic attack. It happens to almost everyone. It will pass. Breathe," I hear Jacqueline's voice say, her hand suddenly on my back.

I take large breaths, attempting to slow the walloping in my chest, the heat in my hands starting to shoot down my wrists. I can't let them see what I can do. I'll lose my advantage.

More hybrids come over, stroking my arms and back, also murmuring that the panic attack will pass.

I close my eyes. *Not now. Not now. Not now*, I repeat to myself. Finally it recedes to my palms. I keep my fingers closed tightly to hide it.

"I think that's enough, David!" Jacqueline shouts timidly.

Suddenly the desert sky of home is gone.

Innogen arrives and a large group takes me back to my room, fluffing the pillows on the picnic blankets in the middle of the field. After I'm tucked in, assuring them I feel better, they leave me alone.

I pull the blanket over my head. The lifelines of my palms are still ignited.

Whatever's inside of me is getting stronger.

CHAPTER 17

A chime awakens me the next day. Innogen is standing there, seeming to have appeared out of thin air. "It's time for your presentation, my dear," she says. "You must hurry up and bathe so we can make it on time."

"This won't be like the last thing, with everyone watching, will it?" My hands tighten at the thought of Olivia with that awful clone.

"No," Innogen says. "You will see. Hurry. We don't want to be late." She waves her hand, to summon me out of my picnic blankets.

With my uniform still on, she shows me where a blinking orange light is and tells me to lift my arms and spread my legs like a starfish. Blue foam drops from the ceiling and twists around me like a tornado, making me feel like I'm in a carwash. I open my mouth, as Innogen instructs, and blue foam enters and runs across my teeth and tongue, with a bitter taste that makes me gag.

In only a minute, the foam rises back up to the ceiling like smoke, leaving me just as dry as before; but smelling of mint instead of sweat and unwashed pits.

"Very good. You shall clean yourself like that every morning." She glances at my pile of blankets in the middle of the virtual meadow. "Have you eaten your food rations in your picnic basket?"

"A bit." I say. But I've only managed to choke down a few swallows. That texture is too much to get used to.

"Well make sure you try to eat your portions. They'll keep you healthy, and last time you collapsed. Now come along." A hole opens up in the meadow, leading to the hallway of rooms.

As we pass the dozens of golden entrance symbols, I try to recall how many hybrids were at my assembly ... or *Leveling* ... It had to be at least two hundred. "How long have you been gathering hybrids?" I ask Innogen.

She peers down at me with her pleasant smile. "We first administered the Sleeping Syndrome in Kenya about seven months ago. Enbrotici DNA is not affected by the Sleeping Syndrome so imagine our surprise when we discovered surviving humans at the infection zones. Those humans turned out to be hybrids." She gives me an enthusiastic look.

She talks about exterminating humans so casually.

"How many hybrids do you think there are? All together?" I ask.

"We have an idea, based on how many we find in population densities ..." Her big blue eyes roll to the side in thought. "Hundreds more perhaps. I'm not privileged with that information, however. I'm just here to help the hybrids along their way." She looks ahead again, standing up straighter, seemingly content with the task she's been assigned.

I choose my next words and tone carefully, "Why not just let us disappear with the humans?"

"My, you are a curious little hybrid. That must be your Ancient DNA coming through." She pats me on the head. "We care because hybrids are half Ancient. We want to see what you're capable of when given a chance with our knowledge and technology."

"I see." We pass through another towering hallway.

"I can't believe how massive this base is. I've never seen anything like it. Where did you find a spot big enough to build it?" I say, then hold my breath.

She makes a fluty laugh and the slits down the center of her face contract. "We have many bases like this, all over the universe. You should see the cities of our solar system."

I want to pry further, but we turn into a doorway and my stomach rolls over: we're back at that awful place where my human skin was removed.

Jenousis, the genetic expert, creeps around the corner. His gaze sets upon me with a purpose. "Is your body functioning properly?" he asks, "Has anything been acting out of the ordinary?"

I'm worried he might be prodding. "Good so far. Though there was that one time I fainted," I say with sarcasm, attempting to shift attention away from it.

"Yes. We have that one time on record," Innogen gives a concerned frown. "Has it occurred again?"

"I'm fine. It was a joke," I say lightheartedly.

"Oh. I'm disappointed. I still do not understand human humor." Innogen shakes her head.

"It's time. Sit there." Jenousis points to a cloth that materializes out of the floor and levitates just low enough for me to sit on, similar to what the slug-hybrids were using.

I apprehensively take a seat. Innogen places a little vial, about two inches long, into my palm, with very fine, sparkling dust inside.

"There are answers about your origins in there," she says, pushing my hand holding the vial up to my nose. "You must inhale it."

What could be in here? Something about my parents?

Innogen and Jenousis go still, waiting for me to proceed.

I close my eyes and sniff. The depths of my sinuses burn, followed by the smell of blood. Then there's blackness.

I'm in the control room of an Ancient spaceship, looking over a desert of golden sand and sparse trees. There's a dim glimmer in the background that dances like fire. A small trickle of knowledge enters my mind. I'm not myself — Harper — I've taken the form of an Ancient. My name is Glock, and I'm on an expedition of some sort.

Another Ancient turns to speak to me. He sounds musical, and it takes me a moment to understand him. Then his words become clear. "Those are becoming the dominant species on this planet," the Ancient says, looking at the glimmer in the distance. "Do not fear them, they are friendly and do not interfere with our mining."

I want to ask him so many questions, but I have no control over Glock's body.

The spaceship lowers Glock and the other Ancient to the ground on an invisible platform. They hike to the rock formation as a fiery pink sun hangs low in the sky.

"Here!" the other Ancient says. They go to an open spot on the ground.

Glock pulls out two shiny eggs and pushes the pointy end into the earth. It grows legs that drill into the sand. The egg spins and liquefies, boiling and rumbling, sinking into the soil. Then a gold color starts to sprout from the spot, taking the shape of a balloon. It falls over, thumping heavily on the ground. Glock picks it up, his purple face reflecting on the solid, heavy gold orb.

"It seems there are many valuable metals here," he says. Glock pushes another egg shape into the soil. It spins, gets smaller and then a series of holographic numbers pop above it. "A 0.2% phosphorus crust," Glock says in awe. "The highest abundance we've seen in this galaxy."

The scene goes back to the rock formation. It's changed since I saw it last: I get the impression of time passing, like falling down a pit for five hundred years in an instant. There is now about a square acre of gold and silver balloons, lined up in symmetrical, evenly-spaced rows. Behind the acre of balloons are more acres of square black pools, with what looks to be a layer of fine white sand at the bottom.

Dozens of aliens are tending to it all, running little machines over the balloons that project holographic numbers into the air. Glock walks among them, looking over their shoulders as they work, occasionally stepping in to assist with moving larger balloons from the dirt to a small vehicle.

When darkness falls, Glock returns to the massive ship and enters into the main lobby where many cocoon-looking pods line one side. Choosing a pod, he makes the shell ripple and shimmer as he passes through the threshold. Snugly inside, Glock closes his eyes, concentrating, and sinks his head into the cocoon's soft wall. A few seconds pass, and he pulls it out. There's a chime, and a trough grows from the spot on the wall where he's just pulled his head from. A tiny vial rolls out and catches on the trough's lip.

In his private quarters, Glock sinks into his warm and welcoming sleeping pod, holding the glittering vial to the light beside him. Glock knows they aren't supposed to use the vials every night to get to sleep, but it's the only thing that calms his thoughts. He left Cooms two weeks ago and didn't know if the Council had approved his and Emmera's request to procreate. She's saving the news until she arrives tomorrow.

Having gone through all the protracted procedures the Council required, the couple were exhausted. In Enbrotici Law, only well-educated, well-intentioned, high-achieving, or genetically gifted Enbrotici have the chance to produce offspring and have a hand in raising them. All other offspring were sent off to training.

Glock felt fortunate for the fact that he had the chance to procreate with Emmera in particular, one of the youngest, most promising scientists in the past two generations. She might be two levels above him, but she'd still chosen him. Together they could pass their knowledge on to a brilliant child with limitless amounts of potential.

Tomorrow he would know. In the meantime, he couldn't wait to dream of her tonight, with the vial of good dreams and memories he held in his hand.

Emmera's spaceship arrives early that morning, just as Glock is finishing his inspections. Glock tries not to look too excited as she greets him with her all-encompassing smile.

"We've been approved! Our offspring will be ready in one year!" she says, her silver eyes and pointed features ablaze with excitement. "I even have reason to believe that the Council will approve us for another in the hatchery, should we make significant breakthroughs on this trip. I'm hopeful, I must show you what I've found, it will change so much." Emmera surprises him with a hug that nearly knocks him over with her enthusiasm. "There is much to update everyone on. I must meet with the Council. You will be on this project as well. I must go." She darts off.

Glock waits for her in his quarters that night, but doesn't see her until Morning Replenishment.

"I'm sorry. You know I wanted to see you. There was so much to talk about. There were not enough hours in the night to contain it all. Would you like to go for a walk?"

They leave the comfortable atmosphere of the ship for the hot, crunchy sand.

"Those are strange animals," she says, gazing at an orange glimmer in the distance. "I've been informed that they have been imitating our kind. It's very interesting."

"They aren't the first." Glock takes her hand.

Emmera nods. "This place is extraordinary though. The outlying asteroid belt, the magnetics, and most of all ... the abundance of phosphorus." She looks out over the black pools of water. "The rarest element in all the universe required for life and somehow *this* planet is full of it." She runs her fingers through the sand in wonder. "With my new Volucris design, Cooms will be saved." She takes a fist of sand and sifts it in the air, creating a dust cloud in the wind.

A screaming human man races out of the bushes, leading a stampede of dozens more.

"Is this some kind of greeting?" Emmera gives Glock a panicked glance.

The humans encircle everyone, including all the aliens working, pointing sharp shards of rocks on sticks with one hand and holding leather sacks with the other. They mutter a repeated rhythm together, bouncing their weapons. Two humans carrying smoking plants circle around the group, leading it in a chant. There's another yell and the chanting stops.

The circle breaks and a man with a skirt and a leather band around his bald head enters, carrying a staff.

He pushes out his chest. When he waves his arm, the circle

of humans bow. The man shouts in unfamiliar words. Emmera shakes her head to imply that she doesn't understand.

The man points to the gold balloons growing from the earth. One of his warriors tries to pick one up, but screams when his hands sizzle from touching the surface. The man in the skirt becomes furious and one of the warriors presses his spear against Emmera's stomach. She lets out a small gasp of pain.

"They must have seen that we can touch them. Give them some gold." Another Ancient says to Emmera.

"Where are the guards?" she asks.

"Give it to them!" The other Ancient urges. "The guards should come soon."

Emmera removes the gold balloon and holds it out for the humans to take. A man steps forward and hovers his hand over it, checking for heat. When he's satisfied, he takes it and nods to his leader. The leader points to Emmera and all at once, they stab the spears into several of the alien's chests. Emmera and a few others are swooped up by a net. The humans drag her away as she screams for Glock.

Glock, meanwhile, lies nearly motionless on the ground, a milky white liquid oozing from his stomach. "Emmera!" He calls after her in a weak voice.

A wild-eyed man with a piece of wood in his nose grunts as he forces a second spear through Glock's abdomen.

Glock wakes up to bright stars overhead, his body ablaze with pain. His colleagues lay in heaps of lifeless flesh around him.

"Emmera ..." he coughs out. A black shape moves, standing tall and bulky against the moon. Glock coughs uncontrollably, spitting up white blood. The shape squawks, rips something long and stringy apart, and flaps its wings. Glock cowers behind a row of gold balloons as the animal continues to busy itself. Glock begins to crawl away, back to the ship. There's another squawk and Glock pauses, certain he has been found by the creatures. He looks behind him, where more of the winged shapes have gathered, violently tugging on something between them: A severed arm with three fingers.

Glock feels sick as he watches the lifeless flesh being ripped apart and eaten.

A strong smell snaps him out of his stunned terror, and he sees the thick white plume of smoke rising from the ship's location.

After limping and crawling back as fast as he's able, he finds the ship's door jammed open with a giant log, more thick smoke billowing out, the smell so potent, it could only be burning phosphorus.

Holding his breath, he quickly locates one of the suits near the door and puts it on. He feels his way to the main hall, shouting for anyone who will answer. Deeper in the ship, the floor appears to be made of fire: Flaming phosphorus crunches beneath his feet like sand.

As he gets closer to the engine room, more and more bodies seem to line the way, including the bodies of the guards, whose job it was to protect them.

The engine room is a twist of melted metal. Glock attempts to get the system to suck out all the oxygen, to kill the fire, but creating a proper seal proves to be impossible.

His breath grows more labored with each passing second, so he changes course for the medical center. Thankfully, when he arrives, it has only been mildly affected by the fire and Glock is able to fully seal off the chamber.

A nearby pod senses his organ distress and drops down for him to climb into. The chimes on the wall beep, warning him of his plummeting blood pressure. He manages to get his suit off and then collapses into the pod, hoping that his injuries are not substantial enough to delay communication to Cooms.

The jelly in the pod thickens. Glock's body finally relaxes. His consciousness fades in and out amid the clicking sounds of the repairing machines. He should sleep. The procedure would require it soon anyway. He slowly submerges into a dream. A dream about him and Emmera bringing a brand-new offspring home. It's a beautiful little female with bright green eyes. Emmera watches the baby joyfully in her arms, its little hands pressing into her cheek.

Everything fades to blackness.

"That was the last time anyone heard from Glock," says a digital female voice in the dark. A light beams on, casting a hard spotlight on an Ancient who, even under the harsh shadows, has an innocent, childlike quality about her. "This incident happened 9,000 years ago, but we discovered this memory recording only a hundred years ago."

I look at my hands, which have returned to my own humanesque five fingers.

"Cooms sent twenty ships on the expedition for precious resources at the time Glock's fleet disappeared. When headquarters could not contact Glock's fleet, a rescue group of scientists and troops were sent to its aid. They found the shell of the ship, the insides melted, and all the mined resources taken. Because of the fire, very little data was salvageable.

"The humans only watched from afar as the investigations went on. The aides took note of this and examined the human communities in secret. It was found that though humans had indeed seen Glock's fleet, which was apparent from drawings and crop structures, the humans did not show any signs of aggression or hostility toward the investigators.

"It was hypothesized that Glock's fleet must have been attacked by another advanced species that had come and gone ... that humans, the original suspects, were too primitive to have been able to figure out how to use phosphorus to attack. We left concluding that Earth was a dangerous zone and should remain off limits because of unknown passerby species, whose technologies could potentially lead back to Cooms, endangering everyone there.

"That ban had been in place for nearly nine thousand years before one of our ships flew in close proximity to Earth a hundred years ago. They got a ping from our old technology, and found this memory attached to it ... "

Rough walls build in around us. A light source comes in

through a pile of rocks and boulders. The sounds of flute-like coughing and gagging reverberate around the space and continue down a long passage of the cave. Faint glowing eyes and head markings illuminate against the wall.

"Captain 4084 is begging for help. We've been captured by Earth's human species," his shaky voice says.

I turn and find the source of the voice on the floor, collapsed against a small boulder. He holds up his hand. The tips of his fingers have been hacked off, jagged pieces of flesh and milky white blood crusted among exposed bone.

"They've removed our communication abilities," he says. "They've been watching us for weeks to figure out how we function. They are much smarter than we thought — much more violent as well." He looks down at his legs — one of his feet has been sawed off.

More aliens materialize around me in the cave. A mess of missing limbs and battered faces, curled up weakly in the dirt.

The captain's body gives a convulsive shiver. "I found Glock, dead, just outside the ship." The alien sighs. "He had a memory capture in his hand. I was able to retrieve a small power source left in the fields that will last for a few thousand years."

There's a cracking sound in the background and his voice dies down to an urgent whisper.

"There's something else. Emmera was captured with us."

I spot Emmera, knees to her chest, rocking back and forth miserably. Milky tears streak down her filthy face.

I wish I could tell them all that I was sorry for my own kind ... or half of it.

"Emmera has an organic pregnancy," the Ancient says.

"She'll be showing in the next few weeks. I don't know why she would do something so foolish." He gives Emmera a disapproving glare. "Nobody has had an organic pregnancy for tens of thousands of years, but she wanted to experience it first-hand. If she lives, the humans will have her offspring."

There's another cracking and the simulation ends.

The space blacks out again and the childlike Ancient comes back under the spotlight.

"Details have since been lost to the centuries," she says, "but with the combined knowledge of hybrid genetic decoding and early human hieroglyphs, it seems the offspring somehow survived into adulthood. Evidence suggests that the offspring was manipulated into helping the Sentinels.

"But hybrids are not the only thing the offspring is responsible for. The offspring also used what was taken from the fleet's technology to help the Sentinels advance the human race at a dangerously accelerated rate, particularly after it got more knowledgeable in the last several thousand years.

"For comparison, dinosaurs were on this planet for 135 million years without any significant intellectual advancement."

A simulation of a planet forms behind her, displaying images that match what she's saying. "The first Homo sapiens, the modern-day human, only arrived about two hundred thousand years ago. And in that time, particularly in the last several thousand years, Homo sapiens have surpassed other species with strong intellectual promise, more so than dolphins or chimpanzees.

"The offspring, and its manipulators, the Sentinels, are

responsible for it. The Sentinels have been 'the man behind the curtain' as they say, pushing an agenda without anyone realizing. Analyzing Ancient tech and then selling what they learn about it as patents for billions of dollars."

The simulation shows a small alien spaceship hovering above Earth. We zoom inside and see a group of Enbrotici watching holograms of steam engines, a giant ship harpooning a whale, the Nazi regime marching, the atomic bomb, and smoke causing a whole crowd of people to clutch their throats and collapse.

"Enbrotici have been studying humans since we found Glock's message a hundred years ago."

More scenes flash before us. A smiling man ordering another to death and then watching him die by torture. Hundreds of sick-looking chickens stuffed on top of each other, struggling not to be crushed by the weight. Smokestacks that spew black pollutants. A seashore covered in litter and a cluster of seagulls tangled in fishing lines and spattered with oil. A child, inches from death with ribs poking through his skin, too weak to bat away the swarming flies. A fox being skinned alive, whose yelps twist my insides.

I seem to be frozen there as everything flashes by. "Stop ..." I say, almost out of breath, which won't be heard over the yelping.

"Stop!" I shout this time, as loud as I can, feeling hot tears run down my face.

There are more horrific sounds.

She goes on, "Genocide, wars, terrorism, mass extinction, rape, racism, multiple species enslavement, seven billion conscious beings slaughtered every year, the Earth's apocalypse from mass pollution and population ... Humans have quite a few marks against them. They are clearly not ready for the burden and power of the intelligence they possess—"

The sound of gunshots temporarily muffles her. Then all the noise dies.

"Do you understand, Harper? This is an Enbrotici burden. We have to stop it."

I cautiously remove my hand from my eyes. The Ancient is solemnly bowing her head. "And then there's you and your kind. Created because the Sentinels wanted to continue developing your skills, inherited from our offspring, to advance the human race. Preparing you to fight their war against us, should we ever return to Earth."

She comes closer and I see my white, still-foreign face reflected in her dark eyes. "But because you are not fully human ..." She puts her hand under my chin, making me glance up at her. "Your kind is capable of making a better race that we will help you build."

I look away from her and back to the spot where the horrible images happened only seconds earlier. "Will we replace the human population on Earth?"

"No. When we complete our task, Earth is not to have any interference for the next millennia to enable environmental repairs and allow other species the chance to evolve. All hybrids are to be transferred to Cooms soon."

CHAPTER 18

"Get up! It's time! It's time!" I hear Tamera repeatedly shout off somewhere in the distance. "To the Canopy, everyone!"

My eyes are shut, but I haven't been able to sleep, to dream of Olivia. My mind has been racing between the evil images I witnessed the day before, worrying that for a split second or two, I was convinced that humans were nothing but pure evil.

I sit up and see that the hole has opened up in my meadow. "It's time! It's time!" Tamera's voice continues to echo as she races down the large corridor outside.

If I can't make it out of here, which every day seems more impossible, are these the hybrids who I'll start a new race with? Would it be a better race than what I saw yesterday? I shake my head. I can't think like that. I know Olivia's not evil. I know Maria was — is not evil ... and I owe it to them to try and save them. I owe it to every good human like them.

Out on the Canopy, I find all the hybrids gathering around

the massive table.

"Hello," says a friendly-looking young man as he does a slight bow. "I'm Yori."

"Harper," I say, reaching out my hand, then switching to a slight bow.

He smiles. "I know who you are."

"Oh yeah … you were probably at … my thing," I say self-consciously.

He laughs in a friendly way. "Do not worry. Everyone here has had the Leveling done to them. Mine was hard as well. David showed everyone my father beating me as a child."

David's a freaking psycho. Then I feel oddly relieved that David didn't show any of those incidents with my mom. "I'm so sorry," I say quickly, trying to think of something better.

There's a shout of excitement and — speak of the devil — David suddenly leaps onto the table, above the murmuring crowd, as if he thinks he's some rockstar. Thunderous applause breaks out. David freezes there, giving everyone time to adore him.

"Yes! Yes! This is a great time!" he shouts, urging them on and flashing his blinding smile. The clapping gets even louder. "We've been approved to start training with the Ancients down in the city!" He dances and skips around. "The merger of our worlds has begun! You did it, everyone!"

Whoops and whistles erupt.

Two Golden Guards enter the Canopy.

"Follllooowwww them!" David bellows.

A line quickly forms, everyone's pressing shoulder to shoulder.

"Has anyone ever left the Canopy?" I ask Yori.

"No," he says. "We have been waiting a very long time."

The guards herd everyone through the living corridor, two sets of doors, and finally, an elevator platform. Each location that we pass has a set of guards, which seems like a lot of security for a group of hybrids who apparently idolize the Ancients.

When the last hybrid is lowered to the city street level by way of invisible elevators, we make our way down a long hallway alight with tiny blue hovering dots. We come around a bend, and bright light overflows from a doorway at the end of the hall.

It exits to an alleyway between two buildings so tall that they appear to be tilting and then straightening out again by the time they reach the top of the dome. The shadows from all the rows and rows of the building's mushroom-like overhangs are so large that only slivers of light filter through the blades. It's a different sensation from being in the Canopy, where we are up high, with open air, looking down on the world.

Everyone is directed out of the alleyway into an opening as wide as a prominent big city avenue. There, the light bounces and reflects on the shimmering buildings, creating a colorful kaleidoscope of patterns and colors.

Alexiuus is waiting for us at the center of the street. Her long slender neck curves into her sleek jawline and squared cheeks. Her skin is the color of fresh snow, and her gold scaly jumpsuit, with a sleeve on one arm, glitters in the daylight. She hovers on a milky glass platform that has enough room for many more Ancients to stand. A circle of guards surround her like a grand gold necklace.

"Hello everyone." Her lips seem to close around her words like silk, almost as if she were really saying them in English. She inspects the collecting pool of hybrids with her pale purple-and-blue eyes. She waves, and the enclosure of the guards breaks. Hybrids pour in around her, gaping up at her strange, yet ethereal beauty.

"We are very happy to introduce you to the citizens of the Base of Ki today. We've all been waiting for you to show us what you're made of. The Ancients here know of your quest to improve upon the human race, one that we'll all look to for inspiration. I am proud to be the one to introduce you to your new peers, friends, and family." She flattens out her fingers and pulls them up. Three milky glass platforms bloom from the floor.

Everyone applauds.

"But wait. There are many exciting things to touch on. First, Mandy and Matthias have been put into regenerative hibernation. The next time you see them, which should be a few months from now, they will no longer be missing arms and legs. They will be fully functioning hybrids with the ability to walk and communicate."

"Yeah!" Peet shouts. Then everyone else cheers and claps after him.

She raises her hands for silence. "Wait. Wait. That's not it. We have something else exciting coming up."

It goes dead quiet.

"There will be a celebratory, base-wide, Agility Game between the hybrid Daryl Pope and some of the finest Ancient competitors in our main stadium fourteen days from now."

Murmurs rise from the crowd, with "Daryl Pope" repeated many times.

"Who's Daryl Pope?" I whisper to Yori.

"Famous American basketball player."

"But," Alexiuus continues, "Forget not, this celebratory game is a community event. Therefore, you may all have the chance to participate in it too. Tryouts will be held in four days at the hybrid Agility Course."

There's more applause.

Alexiuus holds up her hand again. "And thirdly, right after the big Agility Game, you all will finally be leaving Earth and going back to your true home, Cooms."

It feels like I'm falling. *We're on Earth?* I look above the crowd, glancing around at the massive Base of Ki. Where can we possibly be? Underground? In the middle of the Antarctic?

"Now let us start this parade!" Alexiuus says. And the cheering that follows seems to come from some distant place.

A guard hoists Yori and me onto the platform. Alexiuus' eyes lower to me and she wraps an arm around my shoulder, squeezing me close. The guards transform into a brisk production line and assist each of the hybrids onto a platform, filling each with impressive speed.

When they are finished, the guards retreat back to a wide circle, making a stronger concentration around our platform. With a slight jolt, the floating platforms rise up about five feet and start to move forward, causing the riding hybrids to bounce against each other.

We commence slowly down the street, joining a steady flow

of low-flying platforms. The passengers of other crafts turn their heads to stare. The sides of the street are full of walking Ancients, all in the same black uniform. Signs blink above doorways in the foreign letters, the words appearing to hover in midair.

More and more Ancients start to notice us as we pass below bridges and beside them on the street. Only moments later, a thicker crowd gathers and I find myself being watched by a rainbow of eyes, glittering like a sea of jewels.

"Wave!" Alexiuus shouts. "Show them what kind of a new race you are. Smile, too."

A rumbling of cheering erupts, nearly shaking the city. Our floating platforms jolt again and rise above everything, just enough to clear the crowd of Ancients and traffic jam below. The guards on the ground beneath us weave through the thick crowd, struggling to keep pace. Sparks appear from nowhere and rain down on us like confetti. I feel like royalty and spot Peet blowing kisses.

As we continue, we pass more buildings, platforms, and bridges draped in vegetation. There's a massive stadium, which is almost a small city in and of itself. It has enormous, elaborate jungle gyms, multi-level climbing paths, zigzagging glass tunnels, and streamlined chrome apparatuses — I wonder if that's where the big Agility Game will be held.

Then there are expansive plazas with giant white statues of Ancients in heroic poses. The statues overlook gleaming pools fed by waterfalls that leap from the sides of buildings.

We pass massive outdoor dining halls with rows and rows of tables situated between fuzzy green, pink, and yellow trees that have to be at least twenty stories tall.

Among it all, I keep an eye out for the glowing prison net without success.

We rise up a hill, and the long road ends at a tower with branches connected on all sides, giving it the overall shape of a skyscraper-sized, sleek oak tree. At the base is a succession of brilliant, tall gold doors. Above the doors are massive windows laced together in a somewhat honeycomb pattern. A large projection floats one-third of the way up the building, scrolling their language like a stock ticker.

The guards assist everyone off their platforms. Together, the group ascends the mountainous stairs to the building. After huffing and puffing for a few minutes, we come to the grand golden doors and cross the threshold into an incredibly tall and airy chamber with shafts of light pouring in from the honeycomb-patterned windows, like stained glass in an awe-inspiring church. A wide podium rises over the swirled marble floor, at least three times my height. Behind it sit at least a dozen Ancients in silver uniforms, with Alexiuus in her gold suit dazzling at the center.

The shapes of all the Ancient's elongated heads remind me of an ominous jury of bishops wearing pointy hats. Their large eyes watch us fill the grand space, peering down at us with intrigued expressions. As we all filter in, the hybrids herd together like timid sheep, staying near the doors — a hiss of excited and nervous whispers echoing throughout the chamber.

Alexiuus stands. The shafts of light casting from the windows highlight her skin, giving it a pearl-like sheen. Her presence is so commanding that the hybrids go completely silent, without so much as a cough, sniffle, or sneeze.

"As I hope you have discovered from your studies," she says. "I have been elected the Abiding Matriarch and am first in command at the Base of Ki. The Council beside me are my advisers and I have asked them to assist in planning your fates in Cooms."

She leans forward over the edge of the tall podium, her large purple eyes so intense, that even from across the room, her gaze could pierce your soul. She waves her willowy hand and a series of glowing shapes appear in a shimmering hologram before her.

"Come forward, Dada," she says, her voice carrying across the large expanse of floor between us and the Council podium.

Murmuring erupts all around me, and then hybrids shuffle to the left and right, until they clear a path through the middle of our group.

A female hybrid steps forward, with lanky and sharp features, into the open space between the Ancients and us, her slender figure a mirror image on the shiny floor.

The Council members' large, pointed heads remain as still and as emotionless as statues, covered in shadow, with only quick flickers from their blinking, glowing eyes.

When Dada stops before them, Alexiuus makes her odd, fake looking smile. "Hello, Dada. Will you do a slow spin for us?" She stirs her long finger. "This is the Council's first time seeing the hybrids outside of a simulation."

Dada nods nervously and turns, not making eye contact with the hundreds of hybrids also watching her.

"Thank you," Alexiuus says.

There seems to be a collective nod from the council members above. A glowing holographic shape popsup in front of Alexiuus, lighting her face with blue.

"The Council has decided that you will go there," Alexiuus says as she points to a gold emblem near the back, mounted on the wall. Glancing around, I see that it's one of at least fifty, spanning every few feet, stuck to the walls of the massive chamber like the numbers of a clock face. Without hesitation, Dada goes where she's been instructed and waits there.

"Tucker," Alexiuus says, pulling my attention back to the podium.

Tucker rushes forward, stopping and spinning before the Council automatically.

A blue icon that looks like three stars flashes before Alexiuus in the air. "That is where we have chosen for you," she says, pointing at another gold emblem, across from Dada's.

Tucker does a slight bow and hurries to his spot.

"Harper," Alexiuus says.

It takes everyone turning to stare, for me to register that I've just been called. The crowd parts, clearing my way to the podium.

My footsteps seem to be louder than everyone else's as I approach the Council. What have they planned for me? My supposed *fate* in Cooms? I stop where Dada and Tucker did, nearly straining my neck to look up at the dozens of glowing Ancient eyes peering back at me.

Quiet flute noises begin to break from above, louder and louder until Alexiuus puts up her hand. Everything goes as silent as it was before.

"Can you turn for us, Harper?" Alexiuus says so softly that I wonder if I'm the only one who can hear it.

I do a slow spin and stop, waiting there. I can't be sure, as my heart is beating a million miles a minute, but it seems like the Council is taking longer on me, three of them scooting in for a closer look, my pale, bald head reflecting in a set of dark blue eyes.

A red icon flashes before Alexiuus: A large circle with three smaller circles inside. Then a blue icon with three stars, like the one Tucker got. The two shapes start flickering back and forth, flashing from one to another like fireworks.

Alexiuus fans her hand through the holographic shapes, and they shatter apart like sand. Her piercing gaze settles upon me for another long moment. "You'll go there," she finally says as she points to an emblem on my left.

As I turn to go, there's an outburst of flute sounds that halts nearly as fast as it started. I glance over my shoulder. Alexiuus is holding up her hand again.

"Harper," she says, her tone more impatient now, "I have it on record that you were interested in science, correct?"

"Yes," I say with confusion because she's not asked anyone else this. I get a pang of guilt. Did she learn that from Brett?

"Very good then. It's been decided. On you go." She motions to the same emblem as before.

The Council member's heads seem to track me as I walk to my spot. I glance anxiously at my emblem. As I get closer, I see it has an icon engraved into it: a large circle with three smaller circles inside — one of the two icons they were casting up. I glance at Tucker. He meets my gaze curiously from across the chamber, still waiting at his gold emblem — the one with the three stars. Where are they sending him?

"Camilla," Aleixuus says. A rod-thin woman with a sunken face comes forth, who I recall meeting at the Canopy.

Alexiuus glances down at David, who I hadn't noticed is standing beside the podium, nearly hidden by its lofty shadow.

Camilla perks up when she notices their interaction. "Please, great Ancients!" She shouts, lifting her arms as if to praise them, her raspy, rough voice thunderous against the hushed room. "Don't talk to *him* about what to do with me! I'm a good person, I promise. I'll do you proud in Cooms."

Alexiuus seems taken aback by this, glimpsing at David as if he'll give her an explanation. "Of course not, Camilla. Where you go is the Council's choice," she says reassuringly.

Camilla glances at David, who only looks at his feet. She makes a loud croak sound, which I think is a sob, and her shoulders slump in defeat.

An icon that looks like a bunch of squares and rectangles pops up before Alexiuus. "That way," she says, pointing Camilla to an emblem.

Tears fall down Camilla's face as she passes the crowd to her spot.

More hybrids come to Alexiuus' beckoning. For the next twenty minutes, a low murmur rises from the crowd as Peet, Yori, and several more are sorted and await their fates at their emblems.

Meanwhile, Camilla's reaction has my thoughts reeling. Is it possible the others know what's going on here? Should I be worried about my assignment? But when I search the room for some sort of indication, everyone's expressions are as clueless as mine.

"Jacqueline," Alexiuus says.

I spot her parting from the crowd immediately, giving Adam a nervous smile before she precedes to the podium. I get a little nervous for her, but when the same icon flashes before Alexiuus that I'm standing at, I think I feel relieved.

"Woodrow," Alexiuus calls next.

"Hi," Jacqueline mouths as she makes her way over to me.

I give her a little wave as Woodrow is given his emblem.

Jacqueline leans against the wall next to me. I follow her gaze to David, who's still standing in the same spot, now grinning at everyone like an idiot.

"Do you know what's going on between David and Camilla?" I ask.

Jacqueline shakes her head, her face blank.

"Do you think he works for them, then?" I whisper.

"Let's hope so," she says. "Otherwise he could end up with one of us, and then we'd have to see that fake smile every day. At least now, he's their problem."

Upon seeing her smirk, we both let out a small laugh that we have to stifle with our hands.

"Adam ..." Alexiuus says.

Jacqueline's attention snaps to him. He's now one of the last five who hasn't been assigned to an emblem yet.

"Going to give me a good one?" Adam says, jogging forward and doing a spin while pretending to tap dance for the Council. When he stops, he makes jazz hands.

Alexiuus' expression remains flat as an icon that looks like a spider web flashes up. She points to an emblem opposite of mine.

"Fingers crossed then," Adam says with over-the-top enthusiasm.

Alexiuus calls another name.

"Do you know what all these symbols mean?" I whisper.

"I'm not sure," Jacqueline says. She flicks her finger. A hologram shoots out and displays a ring shape with sections cut up by color.

"— Amadi," Alexiuus calls in the background.

"Is that alien tech in your body?" I say quietly, with a mixture of awe and worry.

"You haven't gotten yours yet?' She lifts a confused eyebrow ridge.

"No." My stomach does an anxious flip. *And I pray I don't get one. Keep that crap out of me.*

"Well, according to my Scanner, we're about to be in 'training' until Evening Replenishment."

"Oh. This is all for training?" I ask. "For what?"

"It doesn't say." She closes the hologram. "I guess we're all about to find out."

The last hybrid is sorted, and the low thrum of conversation drops off. Hundreds of hybrids are now standing at their emblems, in groups varying from one to ten, gazing up at the podium, waiting on what Alexiuus will say next.

Alexiuus' large eyes trace thoughtfully over all the hybrids one more time. Then, her arms lift as if conducting an orchestra, and the chamber echoes with yelps and gasps of surprise. There's a hiss behind me, and I turn to find a crack of light splitting the wall where my emblem is. In a whoosh, one after another, all fifty emblems open, turning into fifty doorways.

CHAPTER 19

Two guards are standing on the other side of the threshold. Without saying a word, they lead Jacqueline and me down a great hall of white arches. Then we're left in a bright room with a floor-to-ceiling window overlooking a rolling patch of grass and trees. The sight of it all gives me some reassurance: this place doesn't look so bad.

There's a quick jolt behind my ribs when in the distance, I spot the giant glowing net I couldn't find during the parade: the prisons, which have to be about a mile from here. I push away an image of Brett hugging himself and shivering in the sleeping pods.

My eyes lift to the dome's ceiling and try to follow it to the dome's end, but it's impossible with all the buildings obstructing it.

"Wow," Jacqueline says. "I wonder what kind of stuff we're going to do in here."

I turn my attention back to the room. In the center, there are a network of transparent tubes connecting containers that remind me of crazy straws. The walls on all sides are lined with shelves and drawers bedecked with neatly organized vials and funny little devices resembling metal Rubik's Cubes and 3-D, multi-faceted stars.

"Maybe we'll make some futuristic Frankenstein monsters in here," she says.

"Isn't that what we are already?" I respond.

She smirks. "Touché."

There's a swoosh of the door and two new Ancients enter.

The blue one is a bit shorter than the orange one. "My name is Vulgun," he says plainly in a masculine voice, without doing the Ancient greeting. All the features below his wide-set dark eyes seem to sag, leaving his mouth in a permanent frown. He glares at us.

"Be kind, Vulgun," says the orange one, ganglier with a long face and bright blue eyes, with a large noselike ridge down the center of his features. "How often do we get the opportunity to work with another species? They can help us with the workload. Oh! Or tell us about the hybrid who will compete against Enbrotici in the Agility Game."

"One opportunity is still too many," Vulgun says shortly.

The gangly Ancient sighs. "Do not take the anger you have for the Council out on the hybrids! It isn't their fault they're here." He turns back to us and I'm stunned by the contrast of his bright blue eyes against his orange skin. He waves both his hands away from his ears, bringing his arms to a ninety degree angle, in the typical Ancient way. "Hello, hybrids. My name is Arl." He leans in and whispers, "Vulgun's not upset at you. He's mad at the Council for giving him more to do. We are very busy and could use all the help we can get. Now, what do you call yourselves?"

Jacqueline and I tell them our names, returning the greeting gesture to each of them.

Vulgun conveniently glances out the window during the interaction.

Arl does a quick circle around us, leaning in to examine our features. He takes my hand and presses my five fingers to his three. His large eyes fill with intrigue. The glowing patterns on the side of his head pulsate.

Vulgun sighs impatiently. "Has their *one* dinky brain even been assessed, Arl? Can human hybrids even handle this level of work?"

Arl shoots him a look.

I turn and whisper to Jacqueline, "Do Ancients have more than —"

"Yes. Ancients — or Enbrotici — " She notices Arl and Vulgun staring at us and speaks up so they can hear, "Have six brains. The biggest one is in their head, the others are spread throughout their complex nervous system, helping with the control of motor function and biotech."

"You are correct, Jacqueline," Arl says. "And Vulgun! Humans have shown potential for large leaps in intelligence. And, might I remind you, these aren't just humans, they are hybrids. They have the combined intelligence of Enbrotici and humans! Perhaps some of them have more than one brain. Do either of you know if you have more than one brain?"

"I asked, but they're not telling us the details of our biology at this point," Jacqueline says, frowning.

"I see. Well, nonetheless think of everything we can learn from you two. We could do so many experiments!"

Jacqueline and I shift uncomfortably.

Arl puts his hand to his chest as though he's worried he's offended us. "No, not the way humans do experiments. We won't lock you into little cages and torture you. We aren't that primitive."

"If we must, where *must* we start them?" Vulgun says begrudgingly, as if he wants to get on with it.

Arl gives us a hopeful look. "What do you know?"

"In terms of what?" Jacqueline asks. "We don't know why we're here."

Vulgan laughs darkly, shaking his head.

Arl blinks a few times. "Oh. You two are training with us, here in the Science Sector," he says.

Jacqueline's face lights up and she replies immediately. "Molecular biology, protein purification, cell disruption, and cultures. I was also recruited to assist in research for injecting an engineered poliovirus into solid malignant tumors, which showed promising results. Some of the patients were already showing signs of remission."

It takes a second to process what Jacqueline's just said. *What the hell? She can't be older than twenty in human years.*

"Hmm," Vulgan says. "What you just described sounds like a basic level we teach to our young offspring."

"But your aptitude for science is better than nothing," Arl encourages.

Jacqueline's posture deflates.

"And you?" Arl asks.

I have to remind myself to close my gaping mouth. "Um ..." *Crap.* They're going to think I'm vegetative. My cheeks get hot. "I know ... I know ..." I search the room for an idea, and upon spotting what looks like a galaxy spinning in a jar, I say, "I know a little bit about space stuff ..." in a pathetically small voice. It probably means nothing to aliens who travel the universe with ease.

Vulgun stomps his foot. "Why are we training them? We have more pressing matters to attend to. The community needs us! There's a new infection in the food supply — probably contracted from this filthy planet. And you already spend half of your day contamination sampling in the Military Sector. We need to work on those things instead of this silly little social experiment they want us involved in," he huffs. "The Base of Ki depends on it."

Arl flips something on his Scanner, then starts yelling at Vulgun in their language, flipping back to English a minute later. "We can start with the basics. Come over here."

With a twitch of his hand, a glass table grows from the floor. He takes Jacqueline's finger and presses it against the table. The tip of her finger lights up and Jacqueline snaps back as if she's been bitten by something.

"I'm giving you data basics. Information for you to learn." Arl says.

Her eyes glaze over as if she's staring at something in the distance. "This ... I can't take all of this in. It's too much. It's like thousands of people talking over each other at the same time."

"I told you they have a singular dinky brain!" Vulgun taunts.

"Give them time. They aren't biologically integrated with the same technology as us ... And with that demeanor this will be a long process!"

Vulgun purses his lips, his eyes darting between Jacqueline and me. "An idea then. Let's chemically enhance that brain. Help ourselves, in turn helping the Base of Ki."

"But how will we learn about their natural learning process that way? This is such an interesting opportunity."

"Do you want to address our food contamination or spend days teaching slow learners? Let's make them useful. They should be smart enough to at least take over menial tasks, such as your Military Sector blood sampling," Vulgun says.

"Hmm. I suppose that is a good idea." Arl puts his hand to his chin. "Yes! All they'll have to do is complete a little bit of training!" The lines on his head pulsate again.

Vulgun shuffles through a shelf and pulls out a handful of little balls the size of marbles.

"This has a chemical that helps with brain absorption and long-term retention. Take one every day." He turns and starts searching around on another shelf, moving a bunch of silver cylinders aside.

"Don't let him get to you," Arl says. "Ask me if you have any questions. Harper, give me your Scanner."

"She doesn't have one yet," Jacqueline says.

"That is problematic. I will put in a request for one to be installed tomorrow," Arl says.

My stomach drops. "Wait! Um. I'm okay without one," I assure him.

"Nonsense. It is pointless in the Base of Ki without a Scanner." Arl waves his hand nonchalantly and holds out two pills. Jacqueline and I take one. He divides the remaining pills he's gathered into two small sacks that he gives to us.

"Now let's move to your first task."

We follow Arl to the top level of the Science Sector, an empty floor beside six rows of car-sized chrome bubbles that are smooth as river stones. Arl circles around one, and stops at its opening, which is large enough to climb into.

Arl places his hand on a bubble. "These are pretty easy to use. Simply go inside and everything will start. When you are finished with a session, just say it out loud," he says. "But be aware that hours can sneak by."

A loud pinging noise comes from Arl's finger.

He holds it up and his eyes glaze over. "I am needed," he says urgently. "You will figure it out." He speeds out the door, leaving us alone with the bubbles.

Peering into one is like looking into a dark, reflective cave that oddly distorts Jacqueline and my face.

"Ladies first?" Jacqueline says.

I tap the soft, silver floor. It ripples thickly, somewhat reminding me of the gel in the pods. "I guess we get in?" I say nervously.

"Looks that way." She hovers closer, nearly herding me toward the bubble.

"Are you in a hurry for something?" I say in a light-hearted tone, trying to hint that I need a little more space.

"No, why would I be in a hurry?" she snaps, looking almost offended.

We eye each other for a moment and I can't help but feel that she's sizing me up. Why, though? She doesn't seem like a confrontational person at all.

"Well I guess it's better to get this over with, then ..." I add a chuckle to lighten the mood, bending down to avoid hitting my head on the ceiling of the chrome bubble. My foot disappears into the pool of opaque silver, touching the bottom when it reaches my mid-thigh. The thick sensation reminds me a bit of the dreaded gel in the pods.

"I think you're supposed to sit down," Jacqueline says, watching me.

"Yeah," I say, with a flitter of nerves.

When I sit down, the silver goes up to my chest. It doesn't feel cold ... Or warm even. It's like a silky, light pressure. I take some in my hands. The silver slides around my palm, keeping its round shape.

"It looks like mercury," Jacqueline says, reaching in and taking a fistful. She lets it plop back into the pool.

When I lean backward, the bubble closes me into blackness. "Jacqueline? You still there?" I gasp, my voice echoing in the small enclosure.

She sounds far away when she responds, "Yeah! What's happening?"

Something moves in the darkness. "There are glowing shapes," I say.

At first, they remind me of the silhouette from the desert in Reno, but they remain small and simple, swimming around like odd sea creatures. "It looks like those things you see in your eyelids, right before you fall asleep at night."

"Cool. I'll give the other bubble a try," she says.

"Okay. I'll be in this black abyss if you need me ..." I call after her. There's a sloshing sound when I move. Luckily this silver stuff isn't as restrictive as the gel. I decided to relinquish control and embrace the experience, floating on my back.

The stillness soon gives way to the humming noise that only accompanies utter silence. A strange sensation happens in the weightlessness of it. My mind slips to the place between dreams and reality. Before long, I'm not sure if I'm asleep or awake.

The glowing shapes fizzle and morph into a grid of ovals with dots in the center. *Cells, those are cells, at different states in the cell cycle*, I think.

I'm not sure if that knowledge is from my own head or something that Arl made this pod do.

The cells start to shake and divide, then zoom into a group of x-shaped chromosomes being pulled apart by little things the shape of penne noodles ...

I jump, startled out of a trance.

"Please return to the Council Chambers," is written in blinding, glowing letters across the darkness, reminding me of where I am.

The shapes I was studying before fill the dark again, though the previous words are still burned into my retinas. Somehow I've managed to make it all the way from the cell cycle to molecular units, but I have no idea how much time has passed in between, just as Arl had warned.

"I'm done ... or finished ... " I croak, my voice rough from not speaking in a while.

The side of the pod opens, blinding me more in the full light. After catching my bearings, I stand, and the silver falls off of me in a sheet, making a slapping sound before returning to a perfectly flat surface. I leave a trail of silver footprints around the room, searching for the bubble that Jacqueline's in, but they're all empty when I look inside.

"Jacqueline?" I say.

The puddles I made on the floor levitate, break up into glitter and fly back to the silver bubble pod like a flock of birds.

I hear hurried footsteps and then, "Harper, you're done?"

I turn and find Jacqueline in the doorway, breathing hard.

"Where were you?" I ask.

"I had to use the bathroom but I came back to get you as soon as I received the notification," she says, panting.

That's weird. I don't remember feeling any bodily sensations in the bubbles. "Oh, I have to use it too," I say, but it's not true. "Where is it?"

"Um." She frowns. "Hold it. The other hybrids are waiting for us."

As we rush down the now dark and abandoned hallway, Jacqueline keeps her attention ahead of her.

"What did you think of the bubbles?" I say, breaking the rhythmic sound of our hurried feet.

Jacqueline continues to look ahead. "It was cool. What'd you think?"

"It was odd. Like someone else's dream was put into my head. What did you learn about first?"

"The same thing as you, I imagine."

She's deflecting. "Oh, so you got muscle fibers too?" That's a bluff. I didn't learn anything about muscle fibers today.

"Yeah," Jacqueline says, "I thought that was a random topic to start us on. Maybe they're preparing us for something medical, which will be such a pain in the vastus lateralis." She gives a half-hearted laugh. Then she nudges me. "You know, the muscle in the neck?"

I smile and nod. What the hell is up with her?

CHAPTER 20

A small digital screen lights up the darkness, revealing a group of people sitting together in a car. A man's hand presses something on the iPad, zooming into a map of where Nevada meets California.

"The Syndrome now has severe infections in every state," the man's voice says. "We'll need you to deliver Harper to California before you come back."

"The roads are dangerous now," *her* voice says. I feel a skip in my chest and find Olivia is next to me in the back seat, her face awash with the blue light of an iPad screen. *Thank goodness she's okay.*

"Harper is not in any condition to travel! Whatever happened to her in the quarantine zone has ruined her!" Olivia motions to the other side of me. To my right, is the perfect-skinned Harper, sitting on the other side of the back seat like an emotionless robot.

"Olivia, please!" Mom says, from the passenger side.

"No! We might as well kill ourselves now!" Olivia yells, with the loudest shout I've ever heard from her.

The man jerks violently in the driver seat, snapping around to give Olivia a threatening glare. His angular features and piercing blue eyes send a shock that feels like lightning through my body. It's the man who used to check on Brett!

"The whole human race will die if we don't do something! We need to assemble as many of *them* —" he gives the other Harper a contemptuous glance "— as possible. Somehow, these half breeds are our last chance."

"Don't call her that!" Olivia says.

The man glares at Olivia again, then back at my mother. "You'll leave in the morning, before the sun rises."

"Are you sure, Patrick?" my mom asks in a pleading way.

He nods, throws a paper map at her, grabs the door handle, and then slams it behind him.

It's nearly black without the glow of the iPad, the only light is coming from the digital clock on the dashboard.

"Mom," Olivia sobs. "We've already been attacked once. We stand no chance out there. Plus you and I could get the —"

"It's the only way he'll let us into the Nevada bunker, Olivia," she says coldly.

Mom gets out of the car, leaving Harper and Olivia alone, making my blood boil.

"I won't let these Sentinels take you. I'll protect you," she says, reaching through me to touch the other Harper. "This is not the way we are meant to go to California together."

No. I try to hug her, but she's no more than air.

"I'm trying, Olivia!" I shout. "I'm trying to help. To get to you. To go to California with you one day."

I turn to the clone. "Say something to her, you idiot!" I yell. "She needs you!" I smash my hands into her, but all I feel is wind.

A chime goes off somewhere in the distance.

I gasp, roll over, and try to breathe. I want to drive my burning fists through the wall and fight my way out of the Base of Ki. If only I knew where the hell I am.

Pulling the blankets over me, I press my forehead into my knees and rock back and forth.

Are these dreams even real? Or was it merely a crazy coincidence that I dreamed about the clone before my Leveling? Tears fall down my cheeks. My sister could be risking her life for a fake me, and here I am, no closer to getting out of here. There are thirteen days before they take us away from Earth for good; time is running out.

I hear someone talking.

Removing the blankets from my head, I find that my meadow is open to the large hallway again.

I wipe the tears from my eyes and follow a group of hybrids to the Canopy. Everyone is sitting around the massive table. A trench has formed down the center since I saw it last. Small holes line a ridge at the bottom with food orbs sprouting from them like bubbles. When a goo reaches the size of a baseball, it disconnects and rolls down the long trench, stopping in front of Adam and Jacqueline, who are sitting on their own at the end of the table.

She seems to know a lot about the Base of Ki …

"— I'm telling you. She must have been taken after we got back last night. She came to the Canopy with us," I overhear Jacqueline say as I approach them.

"Hi," I say.

They both startle. Their postures relax when they glance over their shoulders and realize it's me.

"Sorry," I add. "Is it cool if I sit here?"

"Uh, sure, have at it," Adam says. They both go quiet, staring off in worrying contemplation.

I scoot in close, so only they can hear. "Sorry again ... I didn't mean to eavesdrop," I whisper, "but who was taken?"

They both look me over. Jacqueline's gets the same sad expression that she had at my Leveling.

"Camilla," Adam finally responds after a long moment.

"The girl who was pleading to the Council about David yesterday?" I say in alarm, trying to keep my voice down.

"That's her," Adam says.

"Do you know why?" I ask with a sickening chill.

He sighs. "When you ask why, the Ancients usually call it 'gene treatment.'" There's a disturbingly dark tone to his voice.

"Does anyone ever come back?" I ask.

"No. Doubt we'll see her or the slugs again ..." Adam says.

My throat tightens. "How many have disappeared?"

"A few dozen, maybe. And who knows how many never showed up to the Canopy in the first place —"

Jacqueline elbows him. She quickly grabs a food ball and gives it to me. "Hungry?" she asks.

Despite the news, my stomach groans. I'm pretty shaky from how little food I've had. I've only managed to swallow a couple of bites since I got here. I take the ball from her and hold it before me, readying myself.

"You haven't eaten yet either, Adam," Jacqueline says, handing him one.

I put the ball to my lips and suck in a small mouthful, wincing as the sweet gelatin slithers across my tongue. I smack my lips, forcing some down.

"Jacq, you know how I feel about the snot," Adam says with a suddenly much more light-hearted tone.

"Stop being a baby. It's not that bad," Jacqueline responds. "Do *you* like it, Harper?" Her voice lifts.

They obviously don't want to talk about the disappearances right now. I'll have to dig more once I get them to trust me. "Um. Not particularly?" I say, "But you know, not many options otherwise."

"Tell me about it!" Adam says. "You know why it's so bland, don't you? The goo, which I affectionately refer to as Geeewwwwd ... because it's a mixture of goo and food."

"No. Why?" I respond.

"Ancients think you shouldn't consume food for pleasure. It enables addictions. They think the real pleasures in life should come from —" His voice rises an octave — "*Knowledge, self improvement, and a balanced community.* Annoying, right?" He wipes his nose while making a gross sucking sound. "Me, I see plenty of room for food in all of those other good things. For example, I can easily give Jacqueline a hug —" He wraps his arm around her — "And happily eat a nice juicy steak right after. There's no conflict for me."

Jacqueline drags his hand from her shoulder. "That's not

the only reason. According to them, their food was also their most significant contributor to damaging their planets and consuming their limited resources. They realized that a variety of complex foods and flavors were unnecessary for their species' survival. By moving to one highly nutritional and easily produced food source, they've become a self-sustaining species. The food is a mixture of electrolytes and algae, blended together to create the perfect balance of macronutrients, vitamins, and minerals. It also maximizes water retention in your cells, which is why there is enough water in two balls to keep us hydrated all day —"

Adam makes a loud snoring sound.

Jacqueline flashes with annoyance. She speaks louder, "And it tastes fine!"

Adam tosses his Gewd and catches it repeatedly. "That's just because you've been here too long." He points at her.

"Sup, Harper," Tucker says, taking a seat across the table from us. "I haven't gotten the chance to really talk to you yet." He reaches out his hand to shake mine, his eyes creepily run from my head to my chest – or lack thereof.

I let my hands fall under the table, safe from his sweaty grasp, trying to think of a way to get rid of him as quickly as possible, so I can keep my focus on befriending Adam and Jacqueline.

Adam stops tossing his Gewd and frowns. "You know Harper's like seventeen, right?"

Tucker drops his hand and looks me over again. "Age don't matter here. Peet's eighty going on twenty. We're going to live thousands of years, what does it matter if she and I are only separated by ten?"

"More like twenty years, Tucker. Twweeennnttty years," Adam says. "Don't you think that's a bit creeepppyy? Isn't there some girl here with self esteem issues your own age?"

Someone behind us loudly clears their throat. When I turn, Tamera is standing there with a courteous smile. "Harper? Jacqueline?" She says. "I need you two to come with me."

I hesitate after everything they've just told me about hybrids disappearing, but Jacqueline gets up without much concern, so I follow her lead.

Tamera takes us to a seating area on the other side of the Canopy. My stomach rolls over when I see David sitting there, sporting the most punchable face I've ever seen.

He leans back and pats the seat next to him but I sit as far away as possible, with Jacqueline on the other side of me.

"Thank you, Tamera." He waves her off. "I'm so happy you're out here with everyone, Harper. I'm sorry if you felt exposed the other night at your Leveling. Know that's not an unusual feeling. You're not alone."

"Why did you do it to me then?" I say sharply, not taking enough time to think it over. I don't know what happened between Camilla and him, but someone like David deserves to be stood up to.

"Leveling exposes our weaknesses and when you know everyone else's, they are no longer weaknesses. They are equalizers. Your hybrid community can help you heal."

"Everyone's life is their own business," I respond.

He maintains his calm composure. "No need to feel ashamed. It's part of your journey here, to get to know everyone.

When we find new hybrids, they'll go through the same thing."

"To be clear, I don't want to watch anyone else be humiliated. I don't get any joy *or weird satisfaction out of it.*" I make sure to look right at him when I say it, emphasizing the last part.

I see Jacqueline's mouth fall open in my peripheral view.

But David doesn't even squirm. "There's no way for you to avoid it, Harper, and the Ancients want you to see the Levelings. You don't want to offend them or give the impression that you think you're better than the other hybrids. That would be rude."

I try to come up with a good response, but all that comes to mind is a string of insults that would be wiser to keep to myself.

The thudding of footsteps approaches: Jenousis has arrived with a small silver rod.

"Ah the installer is here," David says as he pulls out a large, transparent marble that he gives to Jacqueline.

"Installer? For what?" I give Jacqueline an alarming look.

"Your Scanner, Harper," Jacqueline says, as if I should know this.

She's holding the marble in the center of her palm. It has two tiny gold cores with a tangle of gold threads surrounding them. "It will help you to navigate around here. It's a personal computer in your brain that connects what you think to the outside world and your finger. Receiving a Scanner is the next step to becoming a part of the Ancients' society."

Panic swells inside me. There's no way in hell I want that thing in me, but refusing could draw more attention or get me in trouble.

Jenousis aims the silver rod at the marble in Jacqueline's

hand. The hard transparent substance melts away, exposing the cores. The golden threads shift underneath, and lift the cores up, making it look like Jacqueline is now holding two golden spiders.

Jenousis waves the rod and one of the gold pearls breaks free from the threads, and clings to the rod like a magnet.

"Hold out your dominant finger," Jenousis says.

Jacqueline takes my right hand and molds it into a pointing gesture, positioning it upwards. My pulse is going so fast that I wonder if she can feel it.

I look to Jacqueline for some indication if I should be worried, but she's concentrating on my hand, her face is impossible to read.

Calm down, Harper, she's got one, I think to myself. *Every hybrid has one.*

Jenousis hovers the silver rod above my pointer finger. The gold pearl drops and lands among the swirls of my fingerprint. The pearl bubbles break apart into small shards, and are immediately sucked into my finger like water down a drain.

I gulp. *Ancient technology is now in my body.*

"The other one goes in your head," Jacqueline adds. "Don't worry, it doesn't hurt."

After the installation ordeal is finished, Jacqueline takes me to the other side of the Canopy, where the polished white floor gives way to a carpet of purple, plushy moss, connecting to a forest of dense alien vegetation.

"Come on, I'll show you how to use it in my favorite spot," she says.

As we walk, I run my finger over my head, where the

Scanner was implanted, trying to ignore the unwavering pangs of unease. "Does the thing in my brain know exactly what I'm thinking?"

Jacqueline gives me her studying look. "In Ancients it does, but not in hybrids with human-mixed brains. These Scanners can't yet understand our detailed thoughts. It guesses what you're going to do from your basic brain patterns, by learning the waves your brain makes when associated with a specific task —" She springs to the left, just avoiding a collection of opaque cactus-like plants.

"Careful don't let any of these poke you. You'll hallucinate for days."

Jacqueline takes the lead, showing me where to step through them. The air is suddenly perfumed with a cotton candy smell.

"The Ancients are genetically engineered to work with their technology," she says. "For instance, if one of us hybrids wants to make a selection, we need to flick out our Scanners to see and understand what we're doing. The Ancients are tapped into their Scanners and can process information, in their head, more like computers, if needed. Though as you have seen, they still use the visuals of their Scanners quite often."

"It's like magic," I say as my shin just misses a gnarly cactus spike.

The cacti diminish into a small grove of tree-sized puffs of smoke. Walking through it makes it seem like we're walking through clouds in the sky. Jacqueline stretches out to touch one, but the smoke-tree snaps out of her reach by creating a hand-shaped hole. Jacqueline laughs.

"What kind of things can we do with the Scanners?" I say, as more of the clouds sway out of our way, clearing a path for us.

"Loads of things. The most useful seems to be the automatic translation, which is helpful with how many different languages the hybrids here speak."

"What about what the Ancients say? In that flutey language of theirs."

"Their language is called Emi. And no, you won't be able to understand what they're saying. They don't translate for us unless it's by choice."

"That's a little weird. They want to invite us into their world, yet they keep us out of their language?"

"I thought so too at first, but as I understand it, the Base of Ki is top security. We aren't surrounded by Ancient civilians, we're surrounded by government personnel."

We come to an opening of thick green moss surrounding a reflection pool that contains water as silvery and still as a giant mirror.

"Do you trust the Ancients?" I ask, my eyes following little fluttering flowers meandering around the area like butterflies. One dips itself into the water, creating small, silvery ripples.

Jacqueline stops alongside the reflection pool. "Do we have a choice?" she says, almost impatiently.

"Maybe we do?" I say, standing before her.

She peers behind me, back to the smoke-forest we've just come from. As if not hearing me, she holds up her hand, and flicks out her finger. The colorful ring I saw on her hologram in the Council Chambers comes back again, forming from a swarm of tiny lights that appear.

"Flick your finger," she says flatly. "As you do it, concentrate on what you have to do today."

"Okay." I say agreeably, giving it a try. Like Jacqueline's hologram, specks of light come together and form a ring, cut up into different sections. Moving around the ring, like the hand of a clock, is what appears to be a stick figure without arms.

"That's you," Jacqueline says, pointing to the stick figure. "It represents where you are in your day. Imagine this whole thing is a really smart clock." She points to a section of the ring labeled "Evening Replenishment" at the six o'clock position. "See, your figure will be in that section next, because we will be eating after this."

"Cool," I say, enchanted by the truly magical effect of it. The projected clock follows my finger, leveling itself no matter which angle I turn my hand.

"Amazing, isn't it? All holograms are made with small flying bots called Volucris."

That's what the Ancients said they needed elements for in the Glock presentation. For a flash, I see the sea of Ancient bodies laying on the cave floor.

"Most Volucris, like the ones used for your Scanner, are nanobots, but some Volucris are as large as houseflies." She points to a school of the firefly things, twirling high above us. "They built this dome. Ancients sent them on a ship here before their arrival. Volucris are in the air all around us." She reaches for her hologram. Where she touches the clock, it breaks apart into glowing dust: a.k.a. Volucris.

"How do you think they built something this massive on Earth without being seen?" I ask.

"I'm assuming since Volucris are so small, they sent them here in phases, instead of all at once. Something as small as a balloon could potentially carry millions."

"Crazy." I pause, giving the moment time to settle, seeing the opportunity in it. "I keep wondering where *here* is. Do you think we're in the middle of the Antarctic? Underground? The moon?" I add as much wonder to my voice as possible.

"I have no idea where they've managed to build this base." Jacqueline narrows her eyes.

A flower lands on my arm and starts to twirl, and I peer upwards to the ceiling above us. "Have you ever been to the edge of the dome?"

"Harper, no!" she says sharply, looking as though I've just struck her. "You have to stop asking questions like this! Also, stop pushing David! You saw what happened with Camilla. He's dangerous."

I don't know what to say.

"Hey ladies." Adam emerges from the smoke-forest. "Just came to get Jacqueline for our meditation session ..." His eyes dart between Jacqueline and me.

Jacqueline frowns at him, turns, and says, "Watch out for the cacti on your way out," as she storms off.

"Alright ... " Adam responds awkwardly. "Catch you later then, Harper?" he says before he chases after her.

CHAPTER 21

The following morning, at the crack of dawn, I find Jacqueline on the Canopy as we board the platforms to go to training.

"I'm ... sorry about yesterday," I say, though I'm still not sure what exactly I did. There's something I trust about Jacqueline; and with all of her knowledge, I'd like to stay on her good side.

She glances at me blankly and I notice a clammy, pale sheen to her.

"You weren't at Morning Replenishment. Are you alright?" I whisper, so all the hybrids squishing in around us don't hear.

"I'm fine," she says with an odd slur.

Peet mounts our platform and flashes us a half-full mouth of teeth.

Jacqueline crosses her arms, where I catch her fingers twitchily drumming against the crook of her elbow.

"Everybody's on!" shouts one of the guards. Our platform lifts, along with the others, and we all travel out onto the nearly empty streets. There are a few Ancients strolling about. I spot two pulling a large cart which is spraying a stream of illuminated particles all over the road. I overhear some out-of-sight hybrids talking about the Agility Course tryouts tomorrow and then arguing about how Daryl Pope will stack up against the Ancients.

I glance over at Jacqueline again, who's staring off like a zombie, with that distant look in her eye she had when she downloaded data from the lab.

"Are you sure you're okay?" I whisper into her ear.

She jumps. "Yes, I'm f-fine." She sounds ... drunk. "Just make sure you stay out of my way for ... for ... the next bit."

"What next —"

"You 'right, miss? Should you see a doctor or somethin'?" Peet says, leaning forward as if he might need to catch Jacqueline.

She coughs, closes her eyes to focus, and says, "I'm fine." Her voice is suddenly normal sounding. "Just very tired. We will be with two trained medical Ancients soon. I'll check in with them."

I purse my lips. Peet looks to me for reassurance.

"I'll make sure she's okay, Peet. Don't worry. Thanks."

Jacqueline gives me a suspicious sideways glance, then stares ahead again.

Peet nods, though he never takes his eyes off us.

The platform comes to a halt at the bottom of the mountainous stairs. What's the next *bit*? Should I help Jacqueline? I decide to keep a safe distance as I follow her up the steps to the Council Chambers. She hurries past Arl, who is waiting for us at the Science Sector entrance. Arl gives me a confused frown before he chases after her.

She rushes into the lab, where Vulgun is in the middle of poking at something with a glass pick.

Jacqueline halts and takes a big gulp of air. "I'm ready for the next step of training," she demands. "I can do more than just learn in the learning pods. I'm smart. I can be helpful and I want to help with the real stuff!"

I find myself holding my breath.

Vulgun pauses and tries not to laugh. "There's no way you could have gotten to that point in training in one day's time. Enbrotici can barely do that."

"Try me," she says determinedly.

Arl looks at Vulgun with surprise.

Vulgun scans the room. Then he stops on something and says, "Create Volucris plasma. That's simple enough."

Jacqueline grabs three glass vials, presses something on her Scanner, and follows its map through the lab's cabinets. She takes out yellow containers and glass vials. Her Scanner draws lines on the glass vials, which Jacqueline pours the contents of the yellow containers into. When she's done adding everything, one of the vials is muddy with chunks floating around inside, a pillow of foam cushioning the top of the liquid.

Vulgun and Arl watch her with what appears to be confusion and worry.

Jacqueline holds up her dirty vial, and her Scanner shoots a laser through it.

I'm impressed by how well she can use her Scanner.

"That is not plasma," Vulgun says.

"Well, it's not yet." Jacqueline swirls the vial, with a faint tremble in her hand. She places the vial down on the table and glances around. She flips out her Scanner again and follows its directions to a lower cabinet. She pulls out what appears to be a big block of silver clay, places it on the counter, and tries to push the muddy vial into it. It won't go. The projection from her finger turns red. She looks to Arl. "I don't have clearance to run this."

Arl gives Vulgun a big, smug smile and runs his Scanner over the silver block.

"Thanks," Jacqueline says. She pushes the vial all the way in. Bubbles fizz from the top of the block, as though it's a pot of water boiling over. Then the bubbles spin and absorb back into the silver cube.

"After you," Arl says.

Jacqueline reaches into the cube and pulls out the vial. The liquid inside has gone completely clean and clear.

"There," she says.

Vulgun gives her a contemptuous frown as he examines her handiwork.

"I suppose it's decent, even though you only followed the directions from your Scanner. It's not sterile."

"I was only using my Scanner for measurements," she says. "The only way to make Volucris plasma completely sterile is to have it created in a factory. I assumed you just wanted to see if I understood the principles of how it's made. Its building blocks."

Vulgun's eyes narrow.

Arl claps his hands. "Most impressive! How were you able to improve your learning capabilities so quickly?"

Jacqueline shrugs. "I guess I just got the hang of things. As I said, I'm eager to get started! Maybe my one brain works better than you all thought," she says.

"She has tremors if you look closely," Vulgun says darkly.

Arl studies her. His mouth drops. "You do. How many pills have you been taking, Jacqueline? Not more than one a day I hope. It could kill you otherwise. Be honest with me. No punishment will come to you."

Jacqueline freezes. "I ... I ... " She bites her lip and looks at me.

Crap. I don't know what to do!

As she stands there, the tremors in her hands seem to get stronger. She hides them behind her back, her face getting pinker.

"Jacqueline?" Arl says. "You're worrying me."

"I ... may have taken a *few* extra pills here and there?" she says in a shrunken voice.

Arl and Vulgun have a quick discussion in Emi, making frantic gestures the whole time.

Arl flips his Scanner back to English. "Jacqueline! Though what you've done is most impressive in such a short amount of time, those pills were not supposed to be administered in the first place. We did you a favor and you took advantage of it." He sighs deeply. "We ... We ..." He clenches his fist. "Have to delay your cognitive learning or you risk an aneurysm. You could die in your sleep. Too much time could pass before anyone finds you and we wouldn't be able to bring you back from the dead.

It's very dangerous."

"So what am I supposed to do for training then? I just wanted to learn like *you* wanted. And Vulgun kept saying how dumb we were. I wanted to prove him wrong ..." Her bottom lip trembles, as if she's about to cry.

A pang of guilt descends upon Arl's face.

Arl and Vulgun get a little paler. They simultaneously switch their Scanners and begin talking. Vulgun shakes his head with a disgusted "no way" expression. Arl's shoulders slide down. They both switch back to English.

"We know you have intelligence, Jacqueline and Harper," Arl says. "To prove that I believe in you, you'll both work with me around the Science Sector and I will teach you things myself."

"The ships will be landing soon," Vulgan says in an impatient tone. "Maybe they'll be useful to you there."

My ears perk up. *Ships?*

"They're useful now!" Arl snaps. "Soon you'll see just how useful and smart they can be!" He shrugs himself into a calmer pose. "Now you are both banned from the learning pods for a bit. Give me your Scanner, Jacqueline." He grabs her arm and claps it against the glass pole that shoots up. It makes a beeping sound. "I need the remainder of the pills too."

"I'll bring them tomorrow," she says.

Arl gulps. "Harper? Yours?"

"I'll bring them tomorrow," I murmur.

"You better."

Arl reaches for the shelf and a slit widens. He pulls out a little glass vial and gives it to Jacqueline. "Take that, it will make the tremors stop and bind with the brain enhancer chemical to prevent further harm."

"Now, come this way, you two. The ships will be here soon."

Before we leave, he turns back to Vulgun. "I'll show you hybrids can be *very* helpful!"

We rush down the hall. Arl runs his Scanner over a gold emblem and we find ourselves in a room full of various-sized cubbies, stacked to the ceiling. Each cubby is fit to house its object, or many objects, perfectly. The largest cubby is twice as tall as me, piled high with gray blocks the size of apples. Arl takes three blocks from the top of the pile, handing one to Jacqueline and me.

He then slams a cube against his chest. There's a huge puff of air and an explosion of black fabric. For a second, Arl looks as though he's in a parachute. Then the black fabric condenses to the form of his body. As it tightens, the material on his shoulders swoops up into a hood-shape around his head, morphing into a helmet. Once everything has snapped into place, Arl stands before us in a fully-fitted bodysuit that makes him look like a super futuristic motorcycle rider.

He presses a spot on his right temple, and his face shield disintegrates. "This will keep you from contaminating the samples," he says.

Unsure what sampling has to do with spaceships, I slap the gray cube Arl gave me against my chest. There's a huge burst of air, and the fabric snaps tightly to my body. As it wraps around my head, the face shield shimmers into existence over my view. I hold out my arm. The fabric wraps around my fingers, turning into gloves. Up close, it looks and feels like scaly carbon fiber. *Neat.*

Jacqueline runs her hands over her suit, examining the intricacies of the material.

Arl pulls out a hovering cart from one of the lower cubbies. The cart has a flat tabletop and a closed storage compartment underneath. He leaves the cart in the middle of the room and goes to a spot where the wall is clear of cubbies. There, a crevice opens. He goes inside, where we hear him make lots of clinking noises. He emerges with three black sacks.

"We must go."

We race back down the hall and cross the Council Chambers into another entrance. This new sector looks like a stadium-sized bowl with a pool of water at the lowest point in the center. The floor is squishy like the rubber mats in children's playgrounds. Just like the layout of the Canopy, the bowl is divided into groupings of objects. Indentations run along the walls, large enough to lie down in, with fluff inside, stacked on top of one another like bunk beds.

"Hey ladies," says the annoying voice that can only belong to one hybrid. Tucker is waving, huddled over the other end of the pool, holding what looks to be a small electric device and rubbing it along the water line.

I glance back to where we came in. *I didn't see what was on the emblem of this sector.* Is this his sector? The other one I could've been put into? What has it got to do with spaceships?

I start searching for something that resembles a spaceship when I hear a loud thrumming noise, accompanying a bright line that appears in the roof of the dome. As the line grows wider, water falls from it, spilling all over the massive chamber.

"Ugh!" Tucker shouts, holding his arms above his head as he's drenched by the spray. The water on the floor runs down the slope of the bowl, draining into the pool at the center.

A cluster of about twenty semi-transparent ships, in the shape of sleek shark teeth, hover in. Wispy, glowing veins wind around a small yellow core, like some sort of angular-shaped jellyfish bodies. They're stunning in the way they silently move, levitating, as if gravity has no effect on them.

The ships touch down on elevated circular discs. I gaze back up at the tall ceiling, dripping with water where the opening was. How would I be able to get up there? My eyes follow the water to the pool below. I notice gritty crystal formations where Tucker was using his tool at the water's rim. Then it dawns on me. *Salt water.* I cover the mouth section of my face shield to block the view of my gasp. *The Base of Ki must be in the ocean.*

The ship closest to us ripples. A floating head pops out from where the ship's wall once was, followed by a neck, golden shoulder armor, and then golden legs and feet. The figure climbs from the ship, hops off the platform, and stands at a halt at the base of the docked fleet. Like a magic trick, almost a hundred soldiers in black uniforms appear from the nearly invisible ships and file into perfectly straight lines. Row upon row of statues, dressed in black from head to toe.

Arl waves his hand, and a lone, arched doorway and table grow from the middle of the floor beside him. "We need to sample their blood for any foreign bodies." He pushes the cart aside and pulls out his sack. He opens it, pulling out a device shaped like a gun and places it on the table. He pauses and looks to us. "Well," he says, "open yours too."

Still reeling from the ocean epiphany, I find myself opening my sack in a dream-like state. There's a gun thing, a small roll of string, and another sack. I place my gun on the table next to his. Two more arched doorways grow from the ground beside Jacqueline and me.

"You will each stand at your own arch," he says. He takes his roll of string and loads it into the handle of the gun. Then he looks to us to do the same. Arl waves to the troops. The first row breaks and they get in line at each of our arches, like they're in line for security at the airport.

"What are we supposed to do?" Jacqueline asks, holding up her gun.

Arl's arch makes a wall of smoke. A tall Ancient with square features is the first in Arl's line to walk through. Arl stands on his toes to reach the gun to the Ancient's neck and presses the trigger. There's a flashing light at the end of his gun. Then the Ancient leaves the area.

The Ancients waiting in mine and Jacqueline's lines march through our arches, and then stop and squat down to accommodate our height.

"The arch does a quick body scan and sterilizes against outside contaminants," Arl says. "After they've been scanned, you aim at the external jugular and extract a blood sample for testing. Human and Enbrotici jugulars are in identical locations."

My stomach knots up. I'm pretty sure they nick that artery to slaughter pigs.

Without any hesitation, Jacqueline pushes her soldier's head to the side and shoots the gun into his neck. A thread rolls out from the bottom of her gun with a tiny ball full of glowing white liquid. Another soldier comes through her line and when she puts her gun to him, another ball pops out, like a new bead on a necklace.

"Hey, Jacqueline!" I shout, frozen with indecision.

She turns around. "What?"

"How do I know if I'm poking the right spot?"

She puts down her gun and a collective sigh comes from her line. She slides next to me. "You push their head toward their shoulder. You'll see the vein pop out under their neck armor because it's so fitted there. The vein is obvious because the tendons in their neck are straighter and feel more like ropes if you touch them." She has me touch the Ancient's neck. "The external jugular almost always comes out at the center point of the clavicle. Make sure you stay in this small area so you don't hit an artery." She takes my hands, holding the gun, places it on his neck and presses the button. My gun makes a glowing white liquid ball of its own.

"Very good. Let's do it a few more times until you've got the hang of it."

She practices with me on three more Ancients without acknowledging my shaking hands. I pay attention as best as I can, so Arl gives me another chance to come back here.

"You're doing great. Let me know if you have any more questions," Jacqueline says. "I don't think these little machines will kill anyone. You have Arl here if you do anything seriously wrong."

Arl, hearing his name, holds up his finger and points towards the entrance. There, a Science Sector icon hovers above a gold emblem. "Harper, the Military Sector is equipped with an emergency supply of medical and contamination needs. Dying is an extremely rare occurrence for Enbrotici. Unless by choice."

"There you have it," says Jacqueline, shockingly cheery for how stressful this situation is. She returns to her sampling line and I notice her gaze fall upon the ships.

That's when it strikes me: *This* is the *bit* she told me to stay out of her way for. When we first met Arl, he said to us that we would help with *military* sampling after training. So she took too many pills to prove her intelligence sooner.

Holy crap. She's trying to get access to the ships. She's trying to escape the Base of Ki!

CHAPTER 22

"Jacqueline, I need to talk to you," I say.

Jacqueline looks up from her conversation with Adam at the long table.

"About what?" she asks, confused.

"Yesterday," I respond.

Adam stiffens beside her and some internal dialogue passes between the two of them. "Tryouts for the big Agility Game are in twenty minutes," Adam says.

"That's all I need from *Jacqueline*," I say, hinting that *he* should butt the hell out.

Adam holds his finger to his mouth to shush me, then changes his gesture to indicate that I should follow him.

"Adam! No!" Jacqueline stands, hitting her fist on the table.

A few hybrids look over at us.

"All okay," Adam reassures everyone with a charming smile. He holds a hand over the side of his mouth, so only Jacqueline and I can hear. "Not everyone is Rae," he whispers to Jacqueline. Her face drops.

"It will be alright. Trust me." He nods in my direction. "Come on."

We go to a steep slope near the edge of the Canopy. As we get closer, I notice it looks like a stadium sunk deeply into the floor. Within it — after what has to be a twenty-five-foot drop from the ledge on which we stand — is the near equivalent of a giant Mouse Trap board game. Weird stairs, paths, balls, and a giant cage.

"This must be an Agility Course," I say, watching a group of hybrids stretching by the big cage.

"Yup. Any bets on which hybrids will steal the show?" Adam responds.

"Probably Daryl Pope," I say shortly. Why has he brought me here?

"Ha, he doesn't count."

We slide down the slope until we're among a group of human-sized translucent spheres that look like hamster balls. Hybrids are running in two of them, making the balls spin.

"Since everyone will be warming up for tryouts soon, let's stretch here." Adam points us to a place between the Runners.

The three of us take a seat and Adam scoots in closer to me. "Lean in so you can listen. Make sure to look happy the entire time. Now let's stretch." Adam takes a seat, spreads his legs and reaches for one foot.

"What's going on?" I say.

"They can't listen to us here," Jacqueline responds.

"What?" I say, not sure if I heard her correctly.

Adam points to a huge jungle-gym-like cage at the back of the Agility Course. "Throughout the Base of Ki, if you look very closely, you'll see tiny bumps that look like pimples protruding from the ground ... about every fifty feet. But there aren't any here, between the Runners."

"What are they?" I ask, searching around, but don't see any.

"EMRS readers. At least that's what the guard that follows me for my job says they are. He told me that they scan the base for issues and send them to Predeen for analysis."

Jacqueline frowns. "They do more than that."

Adam nods. "There's a large control room, with every foot covered by 3-D projections of what the EMRS readers are monitoring. It seems you can inspect the whole Base of Ki from there. Ancients and hybrids included."

"How do you know that?" I say.

"I'm in that room everyday because of the training I got assigned. I don't know what you'd call my job ... Maintenance, maybe? It's exhausting." He smears his hands down his face. "An Ancient shows me two maps of the Base of Ki in that control room, which I have to memorize. One map is for collection and the other is for placement."

"What are you collecting and placing?" I say.

"Hundreds of these little contact-like lenses with gold wires inside. I don't know what they're for."

"And I'm guessing the Ancients can't see us now because there aren't any of those little pimples — or EMRS readers nearby?" I ask.

"Yup, because the Runners are intersecting them, causing this area to be too blurry for monitoring."

"Can they hear us?"

"I'm pretty sure they don't use audio. I think the EMRS readers read lips, or alien face slits, which is a problem if the images are fuzzy."

"Are EMRS readers in our quarters?" I say nervously. Is it possible they've seen what I can do?

"I haven't been able to see yet because of the holograms. I can't turn those off," Adam says.

"And how blurry are we talking?" I ask.

"Maybe as blurry as someone who really needs glasses? You can still see basic shapes."

"Hmm," I say. "I wonder if *EMRS readers* stand for..."

"Yes?" Adam says.

"Perhaps the E-M-R stands for electromagnetic radiation and the S at the end stands for sonar? *If* the English translation of the acronym is that exact. If the Ancients even have acronyms."

"Hmmm ..." Jacqueline pauses in thought. "It is possible with how their translation works."

"What does that mean?" Adam asks.

"Electromagnetic radiation?" I say.

Adam nods. "Yeah. I know what sonar is. It's used by bats and dolphins, but I don't know what —"

"Electromagnetic radiation is?" I smile, remembering my days of surfing YouTube, watching explanation videos about astronomy. "It's the wavelengths of energy all around us. In a nutshell, different types of energy produce different types of waves. Some that you can see, such as light, some that you can only feel, such as infrared, and some that are invisible to humans, such as radio and x-ray. So, based on the name of the device alone, it sounds like the Ancients are using multiple wavelengths to scan an area ... with sonar too ... which makes sense as to why some of those areas are blurry. Lots of those waves have problems getting through certain materials ... but ..." I take a deep breath ... "I wonder if it means they can see thermal waves. That would be helpful in monitoring technology, but they may also be able to see our body temperatures."

Jacqueline smirks at me. "Very good, Harper. How did you know that?"

"The electromagnetic spectrum is used by astronomers to see what a star is made of, how far it is, how old it is, and even the direction the universe is moving. As you can probably tell, I geek out on astronomy stuff sometimes. Or used to."

A series of chime noises erupt from all of our Scanners. Three small holographic Innogens float midair, one from each of our fingers.

"Everyone, please make your way to the Agility Course for tryouts," she says before the holograms end.

Someone gets out of a Runner and makes their way to the main course.

Jacqueline looks at me urgently. "Now, why did you want to talk to me, Harper?"

"Yeah. Does it have something to do with why you're all up in Jacqueline's business?" Adam says saucily.

The pace of my heart quadruples. "Because ..." it seems to get louder. "I want in."

"On what?" Jacqueline says, her and Adam's suspicious eyes boring through me.

My throat gets dry. "At first I wasn't sure when you seemed to be sneaking around the learning pods or whatever. Then you got access to the Military Sector ..."

They both continue to stare.

"You know ... where there are ships ..." I add.

They stay worryingly silent, examining every inch of my face. I try to hold a confident expression.

"Say we might be checking out some things," Adam finally says. "How do we know we can trust you?"

"Well, I haven't told on you or anything."

"Right. You haven't told on us for a thing you have no proof of," Adam chuckles to himself. "If there was an *in*, why do you *want in it?*"

"Because ..." The words seem to catch as I feel an unexpected sob coming on.

Jacqueline responds before I've even realized why. "It's that young girl, isn't it? Your sister in your Leveling?"

How does she — but when I look at her, she has that pained expression that she had when Adam mentioned that name at the table. "Who's Rae?" I ask.

"She's ..." Jacqueline trails off.

"Another hybrid who was in our group," Adam finishes for her. "You remind Jacqueline of her. You have a similar muscular build and head markings."

"She was rebellious like you, too," Jacqueline says quietly. "Spoke out against David."

"Was?" I say. "Nobody here has that name."

Both of their gazes fall to the ground.

"She disappeared two weeks before you came," Jacqueline

says sadly.

"Oh. Like Camilla ... "

Someone makes a whooping sound over at the main course. As we've been sitting here, the sound of an excited crowd has been growing louder by the second.

"Alright, so in theory, you'd want *in* to get back to your sister," Adam says.

"And her brother is locked-up here as well," Jacqueline adds.

"Oh yeah. That." Adam frowns.

"Well, there's more ..." I hesitate as it dawns on me how impossible this might sound. "I think we might be able to save the human race, too."

Adam goes still, sitting up straighter. "How in hell would we do that?"

"When I first got here, I think they thought I was on the Sentinels' side, so they put me in prison ... where I met an Ancient who says she came here to stop the Sleeping Syndrome. If we could get her on one of those ships with my brother, maybe he can take us to the Sentinels to fight the extinction."

They both ponder that.

"Report to the Agility Course immediately," Tamera's voice shouts from far behind us.

"Crap, we've got to scoot," Adam says, grabbing Jacqueline's hand and pulling her away before I can get another word in.

Confused by what that means for my proposal, I follow them out.

When we emerge from the cover of the Runners, a crowd of over a hundred hybrids is gathered along the Agility Course's edge, their legs dangling over the side, gazing down at us.

David, Tamera, and a very tall, athletically-built hybrid are standing in the middle of the Agility Course, turning to see the three of us approach.

"Oh, well, hello," David says to us in a way that makes my stomach turn. "Are you three volunteering to tryout first?"

"Um," Adam says in a gape, his eyes fixed upon the tall hybrid.

"Sup? I'm Daryl Pope," the hybrid says, reaching out to shake Adam's hand.

"I kn-know. Y-Your last season was incredible," Adam stammers.

"Thanks, bro. Excited to see whatcha all got today."

"Why don't you three come over here." Tamera points to a row of long, smooth silver runways which look like catwalks you'd see on TV.

"I've never done this before," I say to Tamera in a quiet, pleading tone, feeling the hundreds of eyes pressing upon me from above.

"Then we'll see if you've got any natural talent for it." She guides me to my starting platform.

"Alright, everyone!" David says with his arms above his head. "Let's see who will join Daryl Pope with the Ancients at the big Agility Game. Do you think it will be any of these three?" His eyes narrow in on me. "I've got some bets on Harper here." He gives me a wink, making my stomach turn over again.

There's applause.

I exchange nervous glances with Adam and Jacqueline, lined up on the runways beside me.

I need to stay average. Not draw attention to myself, I think.

My platform starts to move like a slow treadmill.

"Girls, prepare for your ass kicking," Adam says, leaning forward to quicken his stride.

"Shut it," Jacqueline says, swinging her arms broadly so her short body can keep up with her platform's pace.

There's a jerk and the platforms start to pick up speed. Sections of the silver runway sink, and the path turns into stepping-stones. The next minute, I sprint from one to the next, trying to maintain pace. After a few seconds, the surface goes flat again. Then, about half the runway in front of me, a silver mound rises up and forms into a humanoid shape. I glance over and see that Adam and Jacqueline both have the same humanoid shapes as well.

Ahead of me, the figure jumps and then slides forward. Two seconds later, the ground beneath me turns to thousands of tiny silver balls. And I start slipping all over the place. Then I understand: the figure is showing me what to do. I jump, giving me enough momentum to surf across the balls, so I can finish out in a spastic glide.

The balls fade away and more globs of silver rise up from the floor, forming into hurdles. The figure before me slides under two, does a front flip over the next, and then clears the last three in a single leap.

When the hurdles roar toward me, I duck under the first and crawl quickly under the second, stumbling up just in time to clumsily climb over the third. There's no way I can jump as far as the figure, so I do my best and leapfrog over the last three hurdles.

The figure collapses into the ground like a bucket of water

slapping into the pavement. The platform slows and pushes me to the end.

Jacqueline and Adam are already racing towards six massive walls of rings that look like very tall chain linked fences. I'm faster than them, so I reach a wall first.

When I start climbing, rings I touch change from white to either green, yellow or red. I make it a few feet up before a red ring explodes and knocks me to the ground. It causes a chain reaction all the way to the top of the wall, disintegrating an entire vertical line of rings, making it harder to climb.

As I rub my butt, I see that Jacqueline is almost halfway up her wall and Adam is about six feet below her on his. Before they move up, they tap rings with their hands and feet, exposing what color they are: yellow, green, or red. The red ones explode almost instantly. I must have gotten a red one right away. I notice the rings Jacqueline has her feet in are green.

I hurry back and start tapping around, exploding a few red rings instantly. Halfway up the wall, I notice that there's a pattern — sort of horizontal stripes — which helps me advance the wall faster. But by the time I reach the top platform, Jacqueline and Adam are already at the next challenge: Climbing through a large rectangular cage made of thousands of intersecting translucent ropes, like a 3-D grid, hundreds of feet in width and height.

"Come on! You got this!" I hear Tucker shout, then whistle.

The gaps in the grid are big enough for me to squat through. The ropes are rubbery, flexible, and bend beneath my weight. The deeper I get, the more I lose my orientation. The ropes are so thin and evenly distributed, making an infinite number of square shapes in all directions, that it's hard for my eyes to understand their perspective and distance.

I spot Jacqueline ahead of me, climbing across shaky ropes as she struggles for balance. I don't see Adam.

Then there's a loud hissing sound. The ropes at the other end of the grid are squirming: constricting on their own, like snakes, making the whole grid vibrate. The hissing sound gets louder as the ropes synchronize, weaving together in a twist, moving down the grid, shrinking gaps as the twist collects ropes to intertwine with.

If you got caught in it, you'd be killed in seconds, squeezed to death before you knew what hit you.

It hisses toward Jacqueline, who quickly scrambles up three levels in the grid, escaping to ropes that are not being pulled into the twist. Then, as if controlled by a giant weaver, the twist takes a turn in another direction: mine.

Like Jacqueline, I clamber up a few levels, safely away from the constricting ropes. The wave of tightening and hissing swooshes under me to the other end of the grid, leaving a long twisted braid behind it. Once the braid reaches the opposite end, it climbs a level and comes for me again, like that really old video game, Snake. I drop down and land on the older braid, holding firm so I don't bounce off.

As the second wave swooshes overhead, the braid I'm standing on unravels. I slip through the gaps, falling a few levels before I catch myself. I climb back up, then forward as fast as I can, blinking non-stop to try to help my eyes adjust and compute the infinity of ropes.

I hear Jacqueline groan as she pulls herself up another level, her arms trembling.

"You okay, Jacq?" I yell over the hissing.

"I'm getting tired," she says, grabbing the next row of ropes slowly.

The twisting ropes come for me again. I squat, stabilizing myself before I jump, skipping two rows of rope at once, hanging on for dear life. I keep moving forward like this, at first making progress against the twist, getting closer to a slowing Jacqueline, but the wave soon speeds up. I won't be able to outpace it for long.

"Come on, Jacq!" I hear Adam call ahead. He's standing on the finishing platform, only about a hundred meters in front of Jacqueline. Each rope she stands on trembles beneath her fatigued legs. I hold my breath when she nearly loses her balance.

The hissing sound speeds toward me.

I ascend as quickly as I can, which is easier than leaping ahead and balancing from rope to rope. I go up two levels, then leap forward two rows. I'm only about fifteen diagonal feet from the top before the hissing sound approaches again. *No. It's going too fast.* I climb up another level and the wave of twisting ropes sweep under me.

I take two heaving gasps of air before I see it aim for Jacqueline.

"Jacqueline go!" I yell. "You're almost there!"

She turns, and I can see her panic-stricken expression from fifty feet away. When she reaches for the next rope, she slips, catching herself by her knee, dangling upside down.

"I'm coming!" I yell and start jumping forward as fast

as I can, but the hissing to my right is faster, tightening up everything underfoot.

Jacqueline screams as she struggles to pull herself upright.

There's a blast of wind and then the world blurs. Jacqueline and I skid onto the platform and then fall off, hitting the ground. I feel a stabbing where my hip hits the floor.

Gasps and murmurs come from the crowd above. Jacqueline blinks at me, utterly confused.

No! I did it without thinking. In slow motion, the buzz from the crowd gets louder. When I turn, worried that they'll be in plain sight of what just happened, I feel a small wave of relief to see that the grid has broken up their view. Perhaps they saw *something*, but they couldn't be sure what it was, right?

Adam rushes over to us. "Are you guys okay?"

I stand, rubbing my hip. "Yeah. Fine."

Tamera appears. "What happened in there? Our view of the grid was corrupted when Harper went for Jacqueline," she says.

I feel another wave of relief.

Jacqueline gives me a warm smile. "She was great, she grabbed me and pulled me out of the way."

"At that speed?" David says, climbing up onto the platform, Daryl Pope in tow.

"Yeah," adds Daryl Pope, "Looked like you just went half a basketball court in less than a second."

"Must have been the perspective you saw it from," Jacqueline says.

Tamera's mouth twists. "Well, you have the rest of the course to finish." She gestures to what appears to be a white, rocky mountain ahead.

"Yes, Harper," David adds. "You were so quick, you could finish first."

"I can try, but that last part took a lot out of me," I say, pretending to hold a stitch in my side, enjoying the fact that it makes David's face drop in disappointment.

"Shouldn't we go?" Adam says. "Everyone is waiting."

"Yes," David responds, flashing his dazzling white teeth. "Finish strong you three." He turns to the now dead-silent crowd and shouts. "Everything is alright. They will continue now!"

Jacqueline, Adam, and I line up.

"Go!" David yells.

We slide down the platform slope and then race up the white mountain, made of fairly steep, various-sized stairs. I let Adam reach the top first, to keep the focus away from me.

"Very good," Tamera says when Jacqueline reaches Adam and me. "Now please move aside so the next group can try out. We will let you know if anyone made it tomorrow."

We're given Gewd to rehydrate, which I notice Jacqueline and Adam don't even touch. I want to ask them more about the escape, but we're told to sit beside Peet and watch another group of hybrids try out.

When the other hybrids run the rope grid, there's a giant hologram screen above the Agility Course so everyone can see. That must be the view my ability corrupted. If it did that, I wonder what other things it might be useful for against Ancient technology ...

CHAPTER 23

I search for Olivia in my dreams, but keep waking from nightmares of Glock's crew, stuck in that cave, lying in bloody messes in the dirt, crying, "Humans are violence. Humans are violence," over and over again.

"They're not all like this," I keep saying, but they hold up their severed limbs and point to missing eyes, repeating the same thing.

With only *nine* days left to figure out how to get back home, I search for Jacqueline and Adam the next day at Morning Replenishment, but don't see them anywhere. When the hybrids arrive in the Council Chambers, I find Adam and Jacqueline busy in conversation with Yori, so I still don't get a chance to talk to them.

"Why are your eyes glazed over like that?" Arl asks when we arrive back at the Science Sector. "You didn't take more of the learning pills, right? You have them for me today?"

"Just couldn't sleep last night," I mumble, pulling the sack of learning pills from my pocket and giving it to him. He opens the sack and looks inside, appearing to count them. Jacqueline gives him her pills too.

"It seems there is the right amount in here," he says, satisfied. He flicks out his Scanner and glances at Ancient writing, or as Jacqueline told me their language is called: Emi.

"The military won't be arriving until this evening," he says. "In the meantime, you two can help me with another task. Come this way."

We go back to that supply room with all the cubbies and containment suits in it. When we get there, Arl throws our sacks of learning pills into an incinerator.

"Now. There are a lot of chemicals that are carried and used throughout the Science Sector. Cleaning bots and Volucris take care of most of what spills or splatters, but sometimes those methods are not strong enough to remove it all. I volunteered you two to take over. I think it's a good way to introduce you to our equipment." He goes to a cubby and grabs a containment suit cube for each of us. "You'll need to wear these."

I take my cube and slam it to my chest. There's a cold rush of air, and fabric explodes out around me. With a swish, it snaps to the contours of my body like thick, carbon-fiber-made spandex. A portion of the material rises and encases my head, making a helmet with a face shield. Once the outfit's finished forming, I have to admit; I feel a little superhero-esque.

Glancing at Jacqueline's delighted smile, I get the impression that she feels the same way in hers.

Arl goes back to the section of the room where the cubbies

are parted by a blank wall. It slits open. He disappears into the doorway and returns with a device that looks like a silver tube with a ball on one end. This is the sprayer," Arl says, and hands it to Jacqueline. He disappears back into the depths of the doorway and reemerges with a second device. It kind of looks like a clothing iron with a really big sole plate. He gives that to me. "While Jacqueline is spraying, you will follow her with this skimmer."

We go to the main hall of the Science Sector. There are other Ancients moving about, looking at diagrams on their Scanners or talking in groups. We reach the end of the hallway, where it ends at another gold emblem indicating a door.

"You can start by cleaning the main areas first. They haven't been cleaned in a while."

We reach the corner of a hallway, open our Scanners and press an icon that Arl points us to. A force field forms around Jacqueline and me. The projection on my Scanner widens and highlights a stain on the floor, in our force field zone.

"Oh good. It's working," Arl says. "Now Jacqueline, spray at an angle so the spray goes toward Harper. Harper you get down and hold the skimmer and try to catch as much of the spray bounce-off as you can."

Jacqueline aims her sprayer at the stain and presses a blinking button. Spray and mist flies everywhere in our force field.

"Stop!" Arl shouts.

Jacqueline turns it off. Mist swirls around us.

Arl sighs. "Harper, you must turn on the skimmer!"

I hold out the skimmer, twisting it around, spotting a little light pulsating on what looks like a button. I press it. There's no noise, but the mist floating in the force field sucks into it and I feel a breeze of clean air hit my contamination suit on the other side.

"Good. Jacqueline, your goal is to aim your spray that bounces off the wall into Harper's skimmer as much as possible. Try now."

I squat down and hold out the skimmer like I'm a catcher waiting for a baseball. Jacqueline turns on the sprayer again. It jolts back causing spray to go everywhere, including all over my face shield. She apologizes and wrangles control of it. With some practice, the spray finally makes it into the skimmer successfully. However, as much as we try, we can't get everything in. Something always splashes out.

"That's okay," Arl says. "It's impossible to make it perfect. It's just best to get as much of the bounce-off into the skimmer as you can."

Arl watches patiently as we finish. Jacqueline and I continue working until the highlighted stain fades from our Scanners. After the rest of the mist has filtered through the skimmer, my Scanner goes off again, an arrow pointing to another spot where a stain highlights.

"The Volucris have found your next spot. Just keep following the notifications until I contact you to meet me in the Military Sector. When I do, you will need to replace these suits. Just go back to the place where you got them."

"You can count on us!" Jacqueline says.

"Good. Contact me if you have any questions."

We move over to the new stain and begin working at it.

I've been nearly bursting to discuss the escape plan with Jacqueline since yesterday, but there are EMRS readers everywhere. Perhaps I'll try to whisper in her ear on the platforms, where there are more hybrids around, so it looks less suspicious than it would now.

After we wait a few seconds for the skimmer to finish clearing the air, we go to the next spot. After completing that spot, our Scanners lead us to a dirty corner that highlights stains all over the place.

Jacqueline aims her sprayer at a huge stain on the floor, creating a large puddle of liquid gas around our feet, filling the entire bottom of the forcefield.

"That thing you did yesterday ..." Jacqueline says, surprising me. "Has it gotten any weaker since you got here?"

I glance nervously at the EMRS readers on the ground. The puddle she's created is momentarily covering them.

Maybe I should make my ability sound weaker than it is to give me an advantage? But I need to seem like a valuable teammate, worthy of bringing on. "It's gotten stronger," I finally say.

"Really ... " She thinks for a moment, moving the sprayer in small circles, causing more steam to rise up around us. "How long have you been here?"

"I don't know. A week and a half?" I respond.

"Have you been eating all your food portions?"

"Not really. I don't like it very much."

"That explains it then." She looks me over.

"Explains what?" I hold up the skimmer, trying to keep too much steam from gathering around our faces.

"Their food weakens *things* ... and if you want *in*, we need your *thing* for something."

There's an excited flutter in the pit of my stomach. "I want in," I blurt.

"Good. I'll tell you more tomorrow." She moves the sprayer from the floor to wall. The puddle starts to dissipate, along with our cover from the EMRS readers.

I wave around the skimmer, trying to catch more of the steam. What did I just volunteer for? What if my ability can't do what they ask? What if they dump me?

The group of stains keeps us busy for an hour. As we go on cleaning, I keep battling with my thoughts, noticing just how many EMRS readers there are. Even though we don't make it very far down the hall with all the stains — maybe a hundred feet at most—there seem to be hundreds of them.

Arl sends us a notification to meet him for the military sampling a few hours later. Oddly, Jacqueline leads us back a different way than we came.

As Jacqueline powers ahead of me in a brisk walk, I notice her head pivoting around as she passes all the open doorways, peering inside each of the rooms. Trying to figure out what she's doing, I follow her lead. I also glance inside the rooms as I tread through the corridor: rooms full of metal boxes, rainbow-ceilinged rooms, rooms with tubes everywhere, and rooms with floor-to-ceiling beehive textures.

Then Jacqueline comes to another doorway. She suddenly slows as she passes it, glancing inside. When I pass the doorway, I see it holds a stockpile of Gewd: A giant mound of it is sitting on a lumpy glass pedestal. Why would she be interested in that? I thought she just told me their food weakens *things*?

"Come on, Harper," Jacqueline says as she disappears behind a corner ahead.

She's already stripping off her containment suit by the time I reach the storage room. After she shoves her suit into the incinerator, Jacqueline seizes my skimmer and takes it into the blank wall that Arl retrieved it from. "There are a lot of weird-looking devices in here," she says, her voice echoing out of the closet-like crevice. There's a muffled noise and Jacqueline comes back out, holding something up. "Look! The Ancients have buckets!" she says, showing me what does look like a large white bucket with a handle. "There's a lot of them in here."

"Yeah, sure looks like a bucket," I say, not sure what she's getting at.

"It's just good to familiarize ourselves with the kind of tools they have. In case we need to help in an emergency or something. Just like what we were doing when we were walking around earlier. Familiarizing ourselves with everything. We need to be helpful."

Is she saying that for me or the EMRS readers?

Arl's voice rings from Jacqueline's Scanner, "Please hurry!"

In the Military Sector, I stand frozen, unsure of what to do. My Arch is blinking red, making an obnoxious loud pinging sound. The three lines of soldiers all back away and a force field forms around the soldier at my arch.

"Uh oh. Looks like you broke something!" Tucker huffs as he jogs by slowly, trying to complete his second lap around the place.

Arl rushes over and brings up his Scanner so he and the soldier can both see it. Between them it displays a diagram, with a red spot highlighting her right boot. The soldier lifts her foot. Wedged between the crevices of her boot is a bright green wad of chewing gum.

Jacqueline and I exchange looks: there's only one planet she could have stepped on that.

Arl dashes into the emergency supply storage, indicated by a gold emblem.

He emerges juggling several items in his arms and places them on the table beside my arch. There's a sprayer, a skimmer, a metal wand with a sharp tip, a transparent cube, and two glass balls with pink and yellow bubbles fizzing inside.

"Watch this you two," he says. He grips his right wrist and squeezes five times. A white layer sweeps over the gloves of his containment suit. "This works with the protective barrier around the contaminated subject."

He takes the glass cube and wand and reaches into the force field with them. The soldier lifts her foot. Arl begins scraping at the stubborn gum and pauses, as if waiting for it to come alive and defend itself. He finally manages to remove a piece, making a huge green strand from the gum to the box. "What a strange substance," Arl says. He works at the gum on the shoe for the next few minutes, eventually removing most of it into the glass box.

"Now it is up to you to finish the task." He passes Jacqueline and me the sprayer and skimmer.

In cleaning mode, our force field combines with the

contaminated soldier.

Jacqueline turns on her sprayer and aims at the highlighted foot. I turn on the skimmer, aiming to catch the spray. The remaining gum comes off in a matter of seconds. When we try to turn off cleaning mode, we get another warning sound.

Arl holds up the glass balls he got from the emergency supply storage. Pink and yellow bubbles rise like carbonation inside them. "Not yet, hybrids. You'll need to use this X-231 for complete sterilization whenever we encounter outside sources. The special Volucris within it will dismantle any microscopic weaponry." Arl pushes a ball through the force field. It shatters when it hits the ground, and thick purple smoke rapidly encases Jacqueline, the soldier and me, with the overwhelming stench of burning plastic — making us cough despite the protection of our suits.

Seconds later, the force field clears, and the purple smoke disperses throughout the entire Military Sector. The contaminated soldier leaves my arch casually, joining the other soldiers, who have started doing various exercises in the Agility Course.

"That was dope," Tucker says, his hands on his knees, puffing for breath. "You ladies are so impressive. It's hot."

Ew.

"You are being disobedient, hybrid!" a Golden Guard shouts at him. "Continue your training!"

Tucker's eyes widen before he continues another lap.

"I'll have to look into this odd substance," Arl says to himself, looking at the gum in the box, possibly forgetting his translator is on. He turns to us. "Please return the objects to their proper spaces." He motions to the items he retrieved from the emergency supply storage.

The emergency supply storage room is a smaller version of the other one, with different-sized cubbies stacked like Tetris blocks. These cubbies are different, however, because they are filled with bottles of liquids and powders instead of devices — an Ancient pharmacy. Jacqueline flicks out her Scanner. As she moves around the room, the names of the substances in the bottles pop up on her hologram. I recognize some names, like epinephrine, somatic stem cells, and anesthesia. But other names, like desryaneaxly, c615, and nuritaissmisis, are a complete mystery.

"Ah, here we go," Jacqueline says, finding the other X-231 glass balls. She places the unused ball into the empty slot at the front. I put the wand back in a container of others. We hang the sprayer and skimmer on pegs on the wall.

I'm tempted to talk about the chewing gum, but spot EMRS readers on the floor.

"Hurry up!" Arl shouts in the distance.

We return to our arches and continue sampling, but end up returning to the emergency supply storage three more times because of contamination alarms for a leaf, stick, and small pebble.

When sampling is over, Arl decides to throw a few of the X-231s into the open Military Sector for good measure, which creates a thick, purple haze over everything.

The burning plastic smell starts to give me a headache, and it's difficult to see more than a few feet in any direction. As we're packing up, I hear a lot of water splashing into the pool.

With the sound of a light breeze, the purple fog momentarily parts for a new ship slowly hovering down from the ceiling.

"There are no more ships scheduled today," Arl says, flipping out his Scanner in confusion. "Oh ..." He glances at us with a hint of worry. "Quickly now, you two. You're going to be late for your ride back to the Canopy." He practically pushes us, through the fog, to the exit with the cart. "Go dispose of your containment suits before you meet the others. I will see you tomorrow," he utters before he disappears into the sea of purple.

The door opens and Jacqueline takes the cart to exit, but I grab her arm to stop her.

"What?" she says, surprised.

I hold my finger over my mouth and nod toward the ship. "The EMRS readers probably have a hard time seeing through all this haze," I whisper.

She frowns and her eyes dart around. After thinking it over for a second, she whispers back, "Fine. Two minutes tops."

Since we know most of the soldiers are at the Agility Course, we slink around the other side, staying hidden along silver storage boxes.

We find the ship perched on a landing pad. The breeze it generates makes a small clearing in the fog, so Jacqueline and I can make out most of it from afar, safely hidden behind our boxes.

The sides of the ship ripple and a gold soldier pops out of the side, with an unconscious human man levitating before him.

I gulp, a chill running over me. Could that be a Sentinel or a hybrid?

Arl approaches the unconscious man and stabs the icicle-looking syringe into his arm, drawing a blood sample. A DNA hologram appears above him. Since Arl's back is turned to us, I can't see his expression.

The unconscious man is whisked away, disappearing into the purple haze.

Shocked, I look at Jacqueline, but her attention is still fixed upon the ship, her hand over her mouth in a gasp.

When I look back, three more humans have appeared. Arl is now drawing their blood too.

Like a jolt of electricity, my finger vibrates and the ring-clock shoots from my Scanner.

I quickly dodge behind a larger box, trying to keep anyone by the ship from seeing it. Jacqueline rushes over, reminding me of the reverse flick gesture to close it, which I barely manage to do.

"We're late," Jacqueline whispers. "We have to go!" As she crawls to the next set of boxes, I notice her adjust a bulge in her pocket.

I take one last look as Arl continues drawing blood from the *humans*.

We'll see if any of them show up at the Canopy.

CHAPTER 24

Another frustrating, Olivia-less night scrapes by, passing like I'm lost in a dark, blank dream. Is she dead now? The question feels like a chasm in my chest, sucking away what grains of hope I've been clinging to. Maybe none of it was ever true. Perhaps it was all just my brain's desperate attempt to cope. But Olivia wouldn't want me to give up. Neither would Maria.

I pull the blankets from my head and roll over in my meadow. *Eight days left.* According to my Scanner, we will be training at the Canopy today. There's a new green section highlighted at the end of my clock labeled: Levelings. I feel cold, wondering if it will be anyone from the ship yesterday.

"Hey, guys," I greet Jacqueline and Adam at Morning Replenishment. Upon seeing the pile of Gewd in the table's center trough, hunger pangs set in from having skipped Evening Replenishment entirely the night before. The small mouthfuls of Gewd were better than nothing.

"Hey," Adam responds lightheartedly. "Sleep well?"

"Yeah," I lie, fighting the urge to beg them to tell me what they need my ability for. *Eight days left*, I think again.

"Sit down," Jacqueline says, to my dismay because it means I'm going to have to practice extreme patience today, which is in short supply at the moment.

"You see we have Leveling this evening?" she says as I take a seat across from them. I notice they're both holding Gewds, though I suspect they don't really eat them. What abilities are they trying to protect, I wonder? I grab a Gewd, watching them. How long have they gone without eating?

Following suit, I press the Gewd to my lips, pretending to take a sip. "What are we supposed to do for a Canopy training day?" I ask.

Jacqueline flicks out her Scanner and a list appears with what looks like four bar graphs. "Unfortunately, it's going to be a boring day for me. I'm all caught up."

"Caught up on what?" I ask, flicking out my Scanner, whipping my wrist around, wondering how she got that view, because all I get is the stupid ring clock.

"Alignment." Adam rolls his eyes. "You're supposed to complete all four subjects as soon as possible." He shows me how to do this funny swipe gesture to get to it. Four percentage bars display on my Scanner: Health, Culture, Knowledge and Mental. Mine are all at only two percent.

"It's like a video game leveling or something?" I say.

"Exactly." Adam gives a cheesy wink.

"Hmmm. You're very behind on your training," Jacqueline says, leaning over the table to look closely at my list.

"Though I guess you got here when we were approved for city training. The rest of us were stuck in the Canopy for months with nothing to do but achieve Alignment. Perhaps we should take you to the Archives after this, add to your Culture and Knowledge achievements. They could be useful with *things*."

"Yes. It's very important to be Aligned. It will help us all when we arrive in Cooms," says a very smooth sounding accent, coming from across the table. Two young adult hybrids take a seat, their features and jawlines as sharp and sleek as cheetahs. I recognize one immediately. She was the first hybrid assigned to her training sector in the Council Chamber.

"Hello, I am Dada, and this is Amadi," she says, assuming the Ancient greeting. "We have not introduced ourselves yet."

"Harper," I say, returning the gesture. Adam and Jacqueline nod as if they know them already.

"We were just discussing why you have a meadow for your living quarters? We thought you were from the desert like us?" she says with a big smile.

They must have helped me to my quarters after my Leveling. "Where are you from?" I ask.

"Kenya," Dada says. "And you?"

"I'm from Nevada in the United States, which is the desert you saw."

"Is that not your happy place? Your home? Kenya is mine. It's what my quarters are."

"Well," I pause, "Innogen, the British alien —"

"You mean Ancient," Dada corrects. Even her pleasant accent doesn't mask her judgmental tone.

"Yeah, well, she set my quarters to a memory she had of

Earth, so I've sort of just left it that way ever since."

They both give a shy laugh.

Yori scoots over to join the conversation. "Mine's of my old bedroom in my parents' apartment in Japan." His voice now has a slight digital accent, which means my Scanner must be translating him. "It has my gaming system with all three of my glorious screens in it — not that the computer in the simulation really works. I usually sleep in my old giant beanbag in the corner."

"Mine's my old hunting shack in the woods," Peet says from down the table. "They even got my fur blanket right. Smells like campfire."

Taking my chance to find out more, I ask, "And what's yours, Jacqueline?"

"My office at my university with all my books, paintings, and plants. Boring old people stuff," she says.

"Why do you have an office at a university?" I ask.

"I'm a college professor," she says sheepishly.

"How old are you?" I respond with astonishment.

"Twenty-two."

"How are you already a college professor at twenty-two?" My mouth hangs wide open.

She waves her hand dismissively. "I just graduated high school a little early at fourteen."

"Pssshh. A little early," Adam mocks.

"Enough about me." Jacqueline laughs, turning dark pink. "Adam's quarters are much more interesting than mine."

"You're just jealous you didn't think of it first," Adam says, patting his chest. "A garage is a perfectly normal happy place."

"Keep going ..." Jacqueline says.

"Okay, it's my garage with my Audi A7 parked in the middle."

"He sleeps in it too. I've found him asleep behind the driver's seat a few times," laughs Jacqueline.

"Whatever. It's the sexiest car you've ever seen. The jealousy in this place is unparalleled. You people."

"If I may chime in," says a wide-jawed guy with a slightly built frame. Small lines are just starting to show between his thick eyebrow ridges. "We are encouraged to move beyond our worldly possessions and onto our new existence. David encourages us to make this place our own and change our living quarters to that of the Ancients, so that we may absorb their great wisdom."

Adam nudges me with a smirk. "Your favorite dude."

The wide-jawed guy frowns with disapproval. "David has been chosen as our leader for his gifts of humility and intelligence. His leadership is exactly what Glock would have wanted. We are all fortunate to be in his presence." His eyes narrow in on me and his voice loses some of its accusatory tone. "Young lady, please feel free to talk to me any time you wish. I am happy to help. I can answer any questions." He doesn't give Adam another glance before as he scoots back down the bench to his huddled-up friends.

With that, Jacqueline stands and I notice her Gewd is gone. "Come on Harper, let's get you to the Archives to improve your Culture and Knowledge achievements."

"Sure," I say, hoping this is code for her finally telling me what the hell they need me for. I try to casually slip my Gewd back into the center trough.

Adam follows us, laughing to himself as we walk away. "God. How up David's butt was Taylor back there?" He shakes his head. "Yeah, David's the leader because of his humility and intelligence ... *that's* it ... not because he just happens to be from the first group abducted from Kenya." He stirs his finger around his head, mouthing "Cuckoo."

"He's from Kenya?" I ask.

"He was there on one of those religious missions. Converting the locals or something," Jacqueline says.

"And Taylor's one of his minions in what Jacqueline and I like to call 'The Cult.' They think the Ancients are gods sent here to save us from ourselves. That we're the chosen ones and should accept our fate here as *divine intervention*. They're why all the hybrids started to call the aliens 'Ancients' instead of 'Enbrotici,' because calling them 'Enbrotici would imply that we think of them as our equals. *God* forbid — or *Ancients* forbid.'"

"Yeah, Tamera told me a little bit about that when I first got here. If you're not in the Cult, why do you and Jacqueline call them 'Ancients' too?" I ask.

"Because that's what all the hybrids call them," Jacqueline says. "I didn't find out about the reasoning until after the name stuck." Jacqueline covers her mouth, pretending to sneeze. "And now I don't want to seem like I'm disrespecting anyone ... or stick out."

"But not everyone is in the Cult, right?" I say.

Adam shakes his head. "No. We also have the athletic bunch, obsessed with the Agility Course. There's Sue, that really fit girl who could bench press me. Gene, another buff guy — Oh! And

Daryl Pope, of course."

We approach what looks like dozens of tall glass tubes, a little larger than phone booths, lined up near the edge of the Canopy.

Adam continues, "There's also the hybrids who keep to themselves most of the time, they're the ones who always look like they're thinking of weird stuff ... like Woodrow and Vihaan over there." He points to two hybrids, leaning against a column near the edge of the Canopy. Upon noticing Adam's pointing, they glance at us sharply, with warning looks.

"See? They're being weird AF right?" Adam whispers. "Anyway. Then there's also the hippies. One of them is actually named Flower. They usually hang out in the garden. Then there's the different cultural groups and the floaters, who don't really have strong thoughts either way."

When we stop outside the tubes, Jacqueline says, "Adam, you should get in some Archive training with Harper." Her hand passes through the glass of a tube like it's breaking the surface of water.

Adam makes a grossed-out, wincing expression. "Ugh. So boring. I'd almost rather let the Cult have me. Pretend I can see apparitions from Glock or something. Maybe then Tamera will like me."

"Doubt it," Jacqueline responds, her whole arm now inside of the tube. "Come in, Harper. I'll show you how to use the Archives, since I've finished everything anyway."

Walking through the threshold feels like walking into a warm, steamy room. The walls of the tube change from clear to frosted once we've fully entered. The air around us starts to fill with wisps of colors and specks of light that float and swirl in every direction.

My heart races, anticipating what she's going to tell me, but my hopes falter when her voice stays in that matter-of-fact tone she uses when she's teaching me something. "The Ancients have given us access to a huge archive of knowledge," she says. "You can either follow a syllabus or go exploring on your own. If you have any questions, it kind of works like your Scanner, using brain waves to understand you."

She pauses to catch some of the floating, smoke-like particles in her palms. "When you ask, try to visualize your question. The blood vessels in your nose give the particles the fastest access to your brain."

She sucks the particles through her nostrils and then exhales. The particles bound from her nose like she's breathing out steam. They start to spiral, faster and faster, until enough gather to make 3-D orbs. Soon they become recognizable as planets.

"The first thing they like to teach in the Archives is about Cooms," she says aloud, her stare concentrated. "This is the Cooms solar system. It's five hundred light years from here, where the main planets are Giro, Aetas, Procell, Foglo, and Techeous." Each planet lights up as she says its name. "There are also surrounding dwarf planets and many moons."

She takes another deep breath. "The Ancients started off on one planet, Giro, like us with Earth, and then eventually figured out how to travel and adapt to the neighboring planets.

"Giro, the original planet, is in ruins now — every living thing almost became extinct because of pollution, which is why they moved the majority of the population to Aetas and Techeous."

A bright stream of light jumps from one planet to another, highlighting each one as Jacqueline talks about it.

"Aetas is somewhat like our Mars. In the beginning, it didn't have a dense enough atmosphere to support life. When the Ancients first settled there, it was covered in environmental domes, but eventually the Ancients figured out how to make a substantial atmosphere and the domes were no longer needed."

Something resembling a ball of hair highlights next. The negative space between the hairlike strands starts to fill in, making the object appear fuller. The whole thing then swells into a solid planet.

"This one is Techeous. It started as a large space station for the overflow of Ancients that wouldn't fit on Aetas. It eventually grew into a planet made of harvested asteroids and Ancient technology.

"Foglo is a water planet, with a core made of level-seven ice. There are a few settlements there now too."

She takes another deep breath, inhaling more particles. "And finally, Procell."

A planet with a surface that looks like sandstone grows larger.

"Procell is a gas planet that has an environment hidden within. It's where scientific and military communities of Ancients live. And it's where most of the Ancients' top technology comes from."

That's the planet Rubaveer is from.

"And another interesting fact," Jacqueline adds, "to match the orbit and rotation of Giro, their day cycle is three hours longer, and the Ancient year is 473 days —"

"Jacq, I need you for something," Adam asks, sticking his head into our tube.

The planets dissolve with Jacqueline's concentration.

"Right," she says, looking at me. "I'll be back for you later. Why don't you start with government structure." She shows me how to use my Scanner for selections in the Archives and picks my first lesson on government.

"Wait!" I say. "I want to ask about where Cooms is. If it's only five hundred light years away, that means it's in the Milky Way Galaxy. Also, have they figured out dark matter?"

"I wish we could ask it questions like that," Jacqueline sighs. "But you can only access approved lessons for now. I must go. Have fun with your training." She disappears through the wall.

The little lights gather and make three icons. A voice that sounds like Innogen's says, "The Council is a government system that has been perfected over hundreds of thousands of years. There are three parts to the government. The Public Council is in charge of surveying and understanding the public's needs. The Future Council is responsible for addressing the species' long-term goals, and the Abiding Council is composed of representatives who have served on both the Future and Public Council."

"There is a leading representative from the Abiding Council in every district. Alexiuus is the Abiding Matriarch here in the Base of Ki."

"However, it's not only the councils that decide the fate of our species. Cooms' core artificial intelligence, the Predeen system, was developed thousands of years ago. Its founders spent hundreds of years studying population patterns and behaviors to create it. It predicts the effects of laws, wars, population changes, space travel, natural disasters, and much more with 99.99% accuracy."

About an hour later, Jacqueline sticks her head in the Archive. "Time to add to your Health Achievement?"

We head toward the Agility Course, and Jacqueline weaves me through a crowd of hybrids watching some kind of futuristic version of exploding Jenga.

When a loud bang goes off, I nearly jump as Jacqueline whispers into my ear, "At the top of the Science Sector, you'll follow the hallway all the way up to a doorway at the end. Do you remember what the Scanners look like before they're implanted into your finger?"

It takes me a second to understand why she's telling me this. Then it strikes me: *This is it*. There's cheering and cackling coming from the game, drowning us out. Panicked for a second, I take stock of who's around us, noticing the feet of the crowd blocking the readers.

"Yeah," I say quickly, recalling the little glass marble with the gold core that David was holding.

Jacqueline pulls me to a stop in the thick of the crowd, and we both face the game, as if we're watching it. Another series of pops go off like fireworks.

Jacqueline leans in close again, smiling like she's telling me something funny. "Adam has seen a room full of unformatted

Scanners at the top of the Science Sector. My theory is, since you possibly move as fast as light, and distort alien technology, they won't be able to see you take a couple."

I pretend to laugh, though my stomach feels like it's in a free-fall. "Are they guarded or anything?"

"No, because they're unformatted, so they don't work yet. They're pretty much a bunch of useless blank keys."

"Are you going to format them?" I scratch my nose to add extra blockage for this question.

She pulls me onward, leaving the cover of the crowd. "Bring at least two back and hide them in the closet. The EMRS Scanners are blocked in there. We'll tell you more after." She smirks as two hybrids call someone a bad loser.

"What closet? When?"

"When I ask you to get the buckets," she says as we breach the crowd and set foot on the open Canopy.

Fear wracks me. I've never gone more than a few feet with my abilities before. Would I be able to hold my glow all the way to the top of the Science Sector?

"Hey-o, guys," Adam says, jogging over. "Ready to get our sweat on?"

"Sure, we were just on our way to the Runners," Jacqueline responds.

"Cool." Adam looks at me. "You alright? You seem a little ... paler than usual."

"I'm okay," I say, with probably an unconvincing grin.

We come to the Runners, half of them in use by other hybrids. I glance nervously at the Agility Course, reminded of what I did there only two days prior.

Adam sits on the ground and starts stretching his back.

"Hello," says Tamera, approaching us, "I wanted to introduce you to our newest residents."

Two worried hybrids, that I've never seen before, are standing behind her. One's ribs jut out like a giant comb beneath his uniform, and his features are so gaunt I can see his skull. Beside him is a young purple teenage girl with large doe eyes. I don't remember either of them being carried from the ships, and why are there only two? There should be four.

"This is Dae-Jung and Aleena —"

The purple teenage girl interrupts Tamera, "I'm not sure if my real name is Aleena, so it might change when my memory comes back. Aleena is the best I can remember for now," she says in a quick and nervous way.

Tamera nods. "They found *Aleena* with a serious head injury, so she doesn't remember a lot." She turns to her. "But even if you do remember, I wouldn't mind if you kept Aleena. It's a pretty name."

Aleena smiles shyly. "Thanks."

"It could be a good thing," Adam says, "You could wake up one day and realize your real name is Bertha." Adam lowers his voice, "This way nobody has to know."

She giggles.

Tamera clears her throat. "Yes, well, you can learn more about them later. You'll hear their stories tonight." She pauses, shaking her head. "Humanity is just so — never mind. Come on, you two." She leads them off toward the gardens.

"So it's them tonight ... " I say, feeling anger rise as I watch Aleena glance around the Canopy in innocent, wide-eyed wonder.

Jacqueline nods. "Looks that way."

A giant tent envelops everyone at the table, making it pitch black. David flicks his finger, and a small cluster of floating lights emit from his hand, shining up his face menacingly as if he's about to tell hundreds of hybrids ghost stories. He carries the ball of light with him as he stalks around the massive table, his eyes fixed upon Dae-Jung and Aleena, who are sitting at the head.

"Dae-Jung is from a concentration camp in North Korea," David finally says, motioning to him. "When he saw one of the glowing Ancients in his camp, he thought that starvation had finally killed him."

In the darkness, sparks fire, large hills form on every side, the land barren and brown, with dead grasses, shrubbery, and trees. Twenty-foot-high fences with loops of razor-sharp barbed wire spring up around us. Long, gray buildings made of raw cinderblock and mud materialize from the dirt.

Starting as shadows, people emerge, solidifying into figures even more emaciated than Dae-Jung. All traces of fat or muscle are gone: nothing more than skeletons within sacks of skin.

David's voice punctures the horrified silence of the crowd. "Dae-Jung informs me he was sent to this camp because his brother was standing near a crumpled-up flyer on the street that contested the rulings of North Korea's 'Supreme Leader'. His brother was just waiting for the trolleybus." He shakes his head, clicking his tongue, extinguishing the light in his hand.

"Dae-Jung lived three hours from that brother, by the way. The North Korean government will arrest the entire family of a person who breaks the law. And not just his immediate family either. Three generations, because that stops anyone from speaking out against the regime."

"Dae-Jung's wife was also sent to the prison camp with his family — then later executed because in North Korea's concentration camps, pregnancy is not allowed. Even if someone is raped."

David turns to Dae-Jung. "Why don't you tell them what they did to your wife?"

Dae-Jung pulls his eyes from the gray sky. His face goes cold and distant, his voice dry as he speaks. "She was tied naked to a tree for days. They knew because her belly was large. She had been trying to hide it, but it's difficult when everyone is so malnourished. Anyone with a swollen belly sticks out," he says with a scratchy digital accent.

"Then from that same tree, they finally hanged her. She was so weak, she didn't even fight them. And there was nothing I could do as I watched my wife and unborn child die. If I cried, they'd torture me too."

He closes his eyes tightly, making his face wrinkle up like an old man.

"What a horrible experience, Dae-Jung. I can't even imagine." David says with the sincerity of a used car salesman. He lays his hand on Dae-Jung's shoulder, which makes him flinch.

"The Ancients found over 150,000 people in those labor camps, tortured all day long," David says. "The Sleeping

Syndrome ended all the suffering, all the cruelties humans had inflicted upon one another." He strolls around, making eye contact with as many hybrids as possible. "And not only did the Ancients end their suffering, they gave them a sense of euphoria before they passed. The Sleeping Syndrome is a tough thing for them to administer, but they do it with kindness. Honor. That's more than Dae-Jung's wife got. That's more than so many poor souls at Camp Twenty-Two got!" He raises his voice.

David lets that thought linger in the air. It makes me recall when my human skin was stripped away. That doesn't even compare to what's been done to people like Dae-Jung.

The scene zooms into one of the buildings and goes inside a small room. There's crying, screaming, painful moaning, and the sound of water hitting the concrete floor. Thirty or so men and women are mid-squat, their arms tied and lifted behind their back, their wrists hitched to a bar on the wall. The bar is too high for them to sit down but too low for them to stand up. They appear as though they've been at it for hours, maybe days. They're shaking all over, and their clothes are covered in blood, urine, vomit, and feces. The smell is unbearable.

A hybrid in the Canopy begins to cry, "Humans are so awful. So awful." She repeats over and over, the mutual feeling of disgust creeps through the tent like a heavy fog.

My eyes close, but I see flashes of Glock's crew in the cave there, so I open them again and try to look away.

The scene fades, the sound of the yelling guards is the last thing to go. I look to Dae-Jung, who seems unaffected. Perhaps seeing so much death does that to a person.

"It's one thing to hear of human cruelty, isn't it?" David asks. "It's quite another to watch it; as we have done at this table over and over again." He holds his hands to the sky, as if asking it for mercy. "This is the exact thing the Ancients are trying to save us from. Our own barbaric nature."

At that, David shifts his attention to Aleena, sitting beside Dae-Jung, with a suddenly charming grin. "And you, young lady, tell us about yourself." He slinks over to her, effortlessly shifting moods.

Aleena goes completely still, taking a moment to realize that it's her who's being addressed. "They found me in the forest?" Her voice trembles. "I don't remember much."

David puts his hand to his chest. "My dear, they didn't just find you in the forest." He gasps. "It was much worse than that."

With the flick his hand, a new scene surrounds the table. We're in a birch tree forest. The foliage is surprisingly green and the ground is carpeted in purple flowers. A human girl is darting through the trees, hiding behind boulders and crawling among shrubs. Her face is covered in mud and smears of soot. Her brown hair and clothes are singed, as if she's just escaped a fire.

"Run!" a man shouts from a distance.

The scene pauses.

"Do you remember any of this, Aleena?"

She shakes her head.

"You escaped from a Sentinel camp. They were trying to get you back."

A gun fires in the background and the shouting man in the distance screams some more. Aleena runs until she reaches a steep hill. She slips and starts rolling down the slope until she comes to a stop, knocked unconscious. Blood dribbles from her head, and deep scrapes cover her legs. Purple flowers are tangled in her short, dark hair.

The real Aleena quivers, shrinking into her seat.

"My oh my. That's not all we found," David says, "Your bones had numerous old fractures, which is evidence that you were frequently beaten." David brings up a 3-D version of the hybrid Aleena.

The real Aleena's large eyes shimmer and she draws her knees up to her chest.

"Stop!" I shout, shooting up. "She's seen enough!"

The Canopy goes so quiet that all I can hear is Aleena's ragged breath and feel the gaze of hundreds of eyes upon me.

"She needs to know how terrible the Sentinels and humans are," David says. "She had three old skull fractures, consistent with being beaten like this …" The model of Aleena on the table is knocked to the side by an invisible force, her hands reaching up to stop the blows.

Adam stands too. "Stop, David. She gets it. We get it. The Sentinels and humans suck. Can we finish this little meeting now?"

David looks to Tamera, who's biting her bottom lip so hard, she might not have one soon.

David snaps his fingers and the tent fades away, revealing the Canopy again.

"Fine, I guess that's a good place to stop for now," he says, coming over, putting his hand on my shoulder and whispering into my ear, "I do hope you two aren't punished for this."

CHAPTER 25

When Adam and I make it through pretending to eat at Morning Replenishment with only a slight scolding from Jacqueline about Aleena, and then to the city without a visit from David, I feel a bit more at ease for now.

Arl is busy, so Jacqueline and I are given free rein to continue spraying and skimming the Science Sector on our own.

"Let's start on a different end of the Science Sector today," Jacqueline suggests.

We walk the path we've gone before, passing the room of Gewd, making my stomach protest loudly. *Would it really be so bad if I just stole one Gewd? I could ration it out over a few days,* I fantasize. *Get this metal flavor out of my mouth, especially after the workout I had yesterday at the Agility Course: I'm dying.* Then I remind myself of how much Dae-Jung truly starved, and decide I should stop being so selfish. I look ahead at Jacqueline's quick pace. How long has it been since her last meal? Come to think of it, she does look a little skinnier since I first met her.

We continue on, around the corner and down the hall, where Jacqueline pauses, turning on cleaning mode, which highlights multiple stains in the area.

"Look how dirty it is," she says.

I nod and turn on my cleaning mode, joining our force fields and crouching next to her as she sprays, feeling a little faint from low blood sugar.

An hour later, after multiple stains, we end up by the Gewd room again. As Jacqueline sprays and I hold the skimmer, I try to keep my eyes from lingering on the mound of Gewd, gloriously glistening in the light. I *never* thought I'd be craving the stuff.

Plenty of Ancients come by and take a Gewd and leave, not knowing how lucky they are to just eat it that freely.

The stain in the doorway eventually disappears and Jacqueline turns off cleaning mode.

"I wonder how long until we'll be called to sampling?" She flicks out her clock. The section labeled "Military Blood Sampling," takes up the rest of the day. But it is faded out with a "pending" status under it. So it's not officially on the schedule yet. It means the military could show up any time.

"Hmm. I'm worried that if we get started on a new stain, we could get stuck here for too long."

An Ancient approaches from the hallway and squeezes behind Jacqueline to get into the room. Jacqueline, not paying attention, starts to say, "Maybe we should —" and smacks into him. They both go tumbling to the ground. Her sprayer goes off, hits the pile of Gewd and sends it flying everywhere. In a panic, Jacqueline slips all over the wet floor as she scrambles to stop the sprayer, which is spinning, wildly spraying the entire room.

After a few slippery attempts, I manage to catch the sprayer and turn it off.

"I'm so sorry!" Jacqueline says to the Ancient she's run into, who's fallen to the floor, soaking wet, clumps of squashed, mushy Gewd all around him.

The Ancient looks utterly surprised at the sight of us and the disaster we've created. He starts speaking, first in Emi, then opens his Scanner and switches to computerized English. "I am sorry as well. I did not see you there. We need someone to clean this up."

"No. No," Jacqueline says, "Don't worry. It's all my fault. We are perfectly capable of doing it. We've been properly trained." She motions to her containment suit. "I just didn't see you there."

The Ancient looks at something that lights up on his Scanner view. His tall forehead and thin mouth purse. "Very well. I would help you, but I have somewhere I need to be. Should I call anyone?"

"No. No. We're fine."

"Thank you." He stands, liquid dripping from him, and steps carefully over the lumps of Gewd covering the floor. From the pedestal, he takes one of the few Gewds unaffected by the spray. He apologizes one more time before he hurries away with it in hand, leaving wet footprints behind him in the hall.

The sweet smell of all the broken Gewd wafts through the suits, making my stomach rumble. I should be worried about this mess, but I'm so damn hungry I could lick it all off the floor.

"This much material won't go through the skimmer if I spray it." She pauses in thought.

I look at her. Is she up to something?

"Harper, can you go get two buckets from the containment suit room? You'll find them in the closet. If I were you, I'd start bringing them back from there. I'll start scraping it into a pile with my hands in the meantime."

Her words send a flare of shock through me. I'm an idiot. *Oh my god. She just gave me the signal.*

"Harper?"

"Right. Get the buckets. I'm going."

I swiftly walk down the hall, back to the closet, thinking of Jacqueline's words, *I'd start bringing them back from there.* My heart is beating so fast that I worry I could set off my ability this instance. Yesterday, she also said that the EMRS readers are blocked in the closet, which is where I'll have to 'disappear' and come back without being seen. Otherwise it will look like I disappear from nowhere, which would be suspicious as hell.

I pass two Ancients, trying to maintain a calm expression before I turn the corner and enter the large storage room. My whole body is clammy as my eyes dart around — I find the blank spot on the wall and go into the closet. If the storage room were organization heaven, the closet is organization hell: empty vials on the floor, a pile of silver blankets, a tangle of gold pipes, several large containers of an oily substance, what look like corroded crystals, and then the pile of the white buckets Jacqueline pulled out two days prior.

It's the first non-perfect thing I've seen in the Ancient world, a surprising reminder that they do have flaws. A reminder that we may be able to use those flaws against them.

I turn and face the door, finding that my hands are already tingling from the nerves. I swallow dryly, cold sweat dripping down my forehead. I feel sick with the anticipation of it, like I'm about to do something as foolish as leaping off a cliff. I close my eyes tightly, trying to picture all the people I'm trying to save.

Olivia's face flashes up; I can see her in that car with that blue-eyed man. Suddenly a strong pulse in my fingertips shoots up my hands and arms like fire. *It's now or never.*

I race out the closet door, and it's as though I'm running through a strange dream-version of the Science Sector. There's a funny blur to it as if Vaseline has been spread over my eyes. Odd, colorful light is shimmering on *everything*, like the reflection of rippling water is shining onto the floor, walls, and ceiling.

I go to the left, then to the right and pass a series of Ancients, all frozen mid-step, like statues. I follow the hallway to the top as Jacqueline instructed. As I see the last doorway at the end of the hall, a trembling sensation tears through my body, like I'm holding onto a jackhammer.

Through the last doorway is a room with transparent pipes lining the wall, straight and spiraling into various see-through tanks. Then I see what looks like a chandelier made of glass balls with gold specks in them: Scanners.

I rush over. The Scanners come off easily, like removing magnets from the fridge. I take two, as Jacqueline instructed, and hold them tightly as I make my way back. The jackhammer sensation keeps building — going all the way to my teeth, making them throb.

My legs and arms feel like I've been trekking through chest-high mud for hours and I'm still two floors from the closet. The blurriness of the world begins to sharpen and the shimmer fades.

Crap. Oh crap! I'm not going to make it back in time! Dread washes over me until I see them: my glinting saving graces ... the learning pods.

I veer to the right, and it's like I smack into a wall just outside an open pod. I quickly crawl into it, getting hit with a flash of light and lose grip of a Scanner. As I splash into the silver liquid, I hear the Scanner make a shattering sound as it hits the floor outside the pod. I gasp for breath, my lungs burn, and my head spins like I've just run a very, very hard race.

"What was that?" a human voice echoes with approaching footsteps.

Shit. Shit. Shit. Shit. Work again! I push my hands together but all I can manage to stir up are tingling fingertips.

"Hello ..." I hear *him* say.

My stomach plummets. David and Tamera peer into my pod. "What a pleasure," David remarks with an oddly satisfied grin on his face. He covers his mouth, which makes me wonder if he knows about the EMRS readers. "What are you doing in here?" he says.

"Learning," I say hoarsely, knowing I'm not convincing at

all. Why would I be in a learning pod with my containment suit on? I just pray he doesn't notice my clenched hand or the crushed Scanner somewhere on the ground.

He studies me for a moment, his expression unreadable. Tamera continues to look back and forth between us, as if waiting for an indication of what to do next.

"Tamera, why don' t you go finish what we were doing before." He nods at her. She obeys, hurrying off in submissive silence.

"Funny," he finally says to me, keeping his voice down, his hand to his face as though he's making a thinking expression with it. "I thought you're supposed to be cleaning the Science Sector two floors down."

"Well, I came up here because I'm behind on —"

In a swift movement, David grabs the sides of the pod and sticks his head in, so his nose is only a few inches from mine, almost touching my face shield. "I know you're not supposed to be up here. Don't *lie* to me," he says in a menacing way that echoes through the small compartment of the silver bubble.

"I–I'm not," I stammer, "I'm just catching up on —"

He puts his hand on my face shield, where my mouth is, to tell me to shush. "I'll tell you what," he says as if it were a negotiation, "I've given it some thought. I didn't complain to the Ancients about your little backlash last night and I won't tell them about this little exploration. But that will be on one condition ... you must agree to compete in the big Agility Course."

He removes his hand from my helmet.

"I'm not an idiot, Harper. I know that you played soccer

and excelled at running. I need as many viable competitors as possible. To show the Ancients our eagerness to merge with their world ... and to give the Base of Ki a good show."

His eyes glare into mine dangerously, rendering me silent.

"Great. I'll see you at practice tomorrow then." He slowly pulls himself from the pod, stands up straight, adjusts his gray uniform, and hurries off.

I lay against the back wall, still panting, my whole body trembling, swaying between relief and dread. Have I just endangered the plan?

Two hallways. That's all I have to do to make it, I repeat to myself. Judging by the silence outside the pod, it sounds like David has gone.

I close my eyes and picture Olivia trudging through a desert on her way to California, to deliver the clone, to deliver what she thinks is me. In the silence, I try to reach her, to see if I can find her like I can in my dreams. Then in an odd way, that I can't be sure is completely sane or not, I sense that wherever she is, that she's hiding from something. Alone and afraid.

I'm coming for you, just hold on a little longer, I try to tell her. Just seven days.

With no more time to waste, I leap over the pod's side, and find the busted Scanner marble on the floor, wedged underneath the now blurry pod, which would explain why David didn't see it.

I scoop it up, the other Scanner still safe in my hand, and head for the door, feeling like I'm running upstream, against a rapid river. Black spots start to swell over my vision, but I am relieved to see my surroundings shimmer and blur again.

A second later, I turn the corner and collapse into the pile of blankets in the closet, the world spinning a million miles an hour. With the last atom of strength I have left, I shove the two Scanners a few layers underneath the blankets and everything fades away.

"Harper! Harper! Are you alright?" Someone shakes me.

"Jacqueline?"

"You didn't come back, so I came to check on you."

"Oh crap," I sit up, and instantly regret the swift movement because it makes my skull pound.

"Did you get them?" she asks, with a worried look on her face.

I reach under the blankets and pull out the Scanners, holding them out for her in my palm. Her eyes immediately go to the one that I dropped: with a huge crack and a big glass chunk missing out of the side.

She takes the cracked one and examines it. "This might be problematic."

"I'm sorry. I —"

"The military ships will be landing in ten minutes. We have to hurry and clean up the mess. If anyone asks, you fell asleep in here." She shoves the two Scanners back in the folds of the blankets and then grabs my hand and pulls me up.

"How long has it been since I left?"

"About fifteen minutes." She frowns, handing me one of the white buckets in the closet. "I know you must be dead, but you've got to come back and help me."

Back with the Gewd mess, I begin shakily helping Jacqueline scoop it off the floor and plop it into the two buckets.

We hastily pick up as much Gewd as we can by hand. Then Jacqueline puts the buckets into the hall and we spray and skim what's left in the room, noticing new orbs of Gewd already replenishing on the pedestal.

The way back is a shaky balancing act of full buckets, sprayers and skimmers. Jacqueline carries three buckets, while my lack of strength only allows for one full bucket and a skimmer.

In the storage room she sets her buckets on the floor.

"Give those to me," she says, taking mine, before dumping the Gewd in the incinerator. "Come on, Harper, we have to hurry!" She rips off her contamination suit and throws it into the incinerator. She moves quickly and puts the sprayer, skimmer and buckets back into the closet. We both put on new suits and rush to the Military Sector.

CHAPTER 26

At the bottom of the mountainous stairs, without sight of Adam, Jacqueline and I mount the platforms after the military sampling session. Jacqueline is about to set foot on the platform with Amadi and Dada, but I pull her back onto a less crowded platform with hybrids we don't know as well.

Once we're in the air, with no EMRS readers in sight, the sound of the wind muffling our voices, I lean in, and before Jacqueline gets the chance to ask the questions I know are plaguing her, I say, "So what's the escape plan?"

She doesn't appear surprised. Good. She knows she owes it to me after I got her the Scanners.

She subtly glances at the hybrids at the front of our platform then at all the platforms around us, to double check nobody's within hearing distance.

"Before you came along, the plan was to sneak off and hide in storage containers during the Agility Game, when the whole Base of Ki — including the military personnel — will be watching it. According to Adam, the ships are scheduled to take off immediately afterwards, when everyone else will be celebrating, so they won't know we're missing until the ships have already landed on Earth."

Something loosens inside my abdomen, like a giant knot that I didn't even realize I've been carrying around. *There is a plan*, I tell myself. "What about Rubaveer and Brett in the prisons?" I say.

She nods. "Yes. That's complicated things quite a bit. We're still trying to figure all that out, which is why we needed you to get the Scanners." She glances around again. "What happened with that, by the way? Why were you passed out and why is one of them broken?"

"I ... I got up there okay ... but my glow couldn't hold."

Her eyes enlarge and her voice goes up an octave. "Oh no. Is there any chance the EMRS Scanners or someone saw you?"

I explain to her what happened with David and how he wants me to compete in the big Agility Game in exchange for his silence about the incident.

She's quiet for a minute, wind whistles past our ears as the Canopy comes into sight. I worry she's going to ask me to step away from the plan, since it seems I might have to compete. Will I be forced to go with the hybrids to Cooms, light years away?

"Rae had the same problem," she finally says. "She couldn't hold hers for that long either, but she was working on it. I just assumed, since you seemed to carry me the length of the grid when you saved me, that you could do it longer."

My heart gives a hard thud against my ribs. "Rae could glow?"

"Yes. We were going to use her ability to help us escape too."

There's a bump and the platforms start losing altitude, rapidly approaching the landing dock on the Canopy.

"Tomorrow is a Canopy training day," she says. "Let's meet in the gardens after Morning Replenishment then."

I wake up to aching hunger and a pinging sound on my Scanner. My clock's holograph is floating next to my bed with the words 'Change in schedule' blinking. I rub my eyes and see that in about a half hour, there is a new section cut out that says, 'Agility Game training with Daryl Pope.'

I groan. Stupid David. "I got it," I say groggily, swatting at the hologram, making it fade away.

How is it morning already? I don't remember falling asleep, thinking about Rae and then trying, infuriatingly, and fruitlessly, to contact Olivia. The suspicion of her death starts to creep in — No. We've got six days to figure out how to get back to Earth. Six days to figure out how to penetrate those damn prisons, too. I'll see her then.

I hurry out to the table for Morning Replenishment, to find Adam and Jacqueline already there amongst everyone, balls of Gewd filling the center trough of the table.

"Good morning, Sunshine," Adam says in a cheery tone.

"Good morning," I reply in a hangry croak. My stomach makes a loud growl as my eyes drift to the food, and I feel simultaneously faint.

"Sit here," Jacqueline says, patting the open spot on the

other side of her.

And torture ourselves by staring at it? I think. "Didn't you want to go meditate in the garden or something?" I say, trying to get them to move along. We've got to figure out how to get into the prisons, I've got more questions, and stupid David needs me soon.

"Breakfast is the most important meal of the day." Jacqueline smiles.

"Yeah I know." I sigh, they aren't getting my hint, so I plop down onto the bench, enviously watching everyone at the table reach for the Gewd. Am I truly supposed to starve for the next six days?

Just as I'm starting to salivate, I feel something soft and wet press against my hand beneath the table. I freeze. Beside me, I see Jacqueline's arm slightly outstretched in my direction. I take what she's giving me, my fingers prodding it for answers. Its squishiness tells me ... it's a little ball of Gewd?

I send her a confused look.

She lifts a small Gewd to her mouth and says quietly, "Go ahead. It's not from the Canopy. It's safe." She takes a slurp.

I thought all Gewd hurt our abilities? I glance at Adam, who takes a huge slurp of his food too. It actually appears to be shrinking, which means he truly has to be eating it.

If it's not from the Canopy then, where? — Oh. Jacqueline must have snuck some of the Gewd away from the mess yesterday.

Well, if she says it's okay... I suck in a big mouthful. The flavor alone feels like it's given me more energy, and instantly alleviates the repetitive metal flavor that has been lingering in my mouth for days. I take a slower second bite so it doesn't go as fast. I wish I could ask Jacqueline how much she has stored up so I can ration myself. But I look over and watch her portion vanish so I decide to eat all of mine too.

"Well that was refreshing," Adam says. "How about that little garden meditation you wanted, Harper?"

I check my clock. "Okay. But I haven't got long before I have practice with David."

We find a spot in the thick of some bushes. After *looking at some plants*, a.k.a *checking on EMRS readers*, the three of us sit in a close circle and get into a proper meditative pose that Jacqueline shows us: crossed legs with our hands on our knees.

I hear snoring coming from Calvin, an arrogant guy who hangs out with Tucker. He's taking a nap on a bed of spongy-looking plants, some thirty feet away.

Jacqueline notes him and shakes her head, covering her mouth. "He's not close enough to hear us." She scans the rest of the garden. "Nobody is close enough to hear us if we keep our voices down."

Adam changes from the meditative pose and lays on his stomach, resting his chin in his palms, so his fingers cover his nose and lips. "Alright, Harper, we're ready to answer your burning questions."

I look at him, unsure how he knows that. Then I shift and imitate his pose on the ground. "Well, as you probably know, Jacqueline told me the basics of the plan."

He nods.

At that, I continue, "So then, how are we going to get Brett and Rubaveer?"

"Riiiggghtttt." He gives me a playful, yet serious look. "So for that, we're going to need your ... services again."

In an almost apologetic way, Jacqueline quickly adds, "We need you to take the two unformatted Scanners and replace them with formatted ones." She fans a round blue leaf in front of her face, to hide her mouth.

It's like I've been punched in the gut. I don't know if I can do it *again*. "Where?" The word cracks when I say it.

Adam winces. "Have you ever seen that huge gold building from here?"

I hesitate. "Yes. I saw it on my first day in the Canopy. Sontarx, the Golden Guard I see hanging around us sometimes, said it was their headquarters."

"Good. Well. You're going to go there and swap the unformatted Scanners with formatted ones ... because Golden Guard Scanners can get into anything."

"Isn't that really hard to get into?!" My voice rises to a shout. I find myself on my feet.

Jacqueline quickly stands and grabs my arm, fanning herself frantically. "Harper ..." she pleads me to sit back down.

"It's not guarded or anything. All you have to do is walk in. Sontarx takes me through that area sometimes. It's about a mile and a half from the Canopy. At the center of town. Remember, everyone at the base of Ki is government personnel, so things aren't heavily protected," Adam says, as if it's no big freaking deal!

"Sure, apparently it's just the prisons they care about!" I say, the anger boiling up.

Jacqueline keeps motioning with her eyes to the ground as she fans herself even more frantically with the blue leaf. I seize it from her, so I can block my mouth before words erupt, "How in the hell do you think I'm going to be able to do that, when I couldn't even make it up two stories?" I say through gritted teeth. "You're asking for me to get caught! There's no way in hell."

"That's what practice is for," Adam says, still keeping his cool. "There are rooms that we've been looking for, ever since we were trying to find places for Rae to practice. Rooms that don't appear to have any monitoring or EMRS readers. Jacqueline can help you."

"And what's your ability?" I ask her, wondering why she hasn't been able to take some of this on.

She picks up another blue leaf from a pile of fallen ones on the dirt. Then she acts like she's scratching her nose with one in hand. "I've got special eyes. I can see at night, zoom into details and see really far away. We've been using it to help us locate EMRS readers."

"That's cool," I huff. "And you think you can help me control mine in only a few days? That I'll be able to travel a mile and half, up a few stories, swap something out and then come back ... which, by the way, sounds like it's more than twenty times the distance of last time? Which I failed at," I say sardonically.

"It's worth a shot." She does a hard nod towards the ground again.

Fine. I plop down, back to my stomach, putting my chin

back into my hands, like Adam is still doing.

"I know it sounds scary," Adam says. "But don't worry. Sontarx and I were there just the other day when he was acting all funky around me. I checked, and there are plenty of spots you can stop at along the way. It's not guarded —"

"Wait. Back up." Jacqueline interrupts. "What does *funky* mean? Should we be worried?"

"What?" He says.

"You said the guard was acting *funky*."

"Oh. Yes. It's a good thing. At first, he was an emotionless, soulless void, because those are the only species that don't find me hilarious, but I've finally gotten him to open up a bit, since he's been acting *funky*."

"Adam ..." Jacqueline gives him a withering glare, running her hand down her face with annoyance. "You're not telling him too much or anything? You don't feel he's onto you or anything, do you?"

"No. No. No. I've just been feeling his sadness. When I asked him if he was alright, he asked me about you. Said he's seen me hang around you a lot, that I shouldn't get too attached."

Jacqueline makes a choking sound. "Well that might have been worth mentioning sooner, Adam!"

"No. It's not like that. He was warning me because his brother had developed romantic feelings, which isn't common for Enbrotici. He said that pairings in the Enbrotici world don't always match with emotions. That you and I could be separated onto different planets. It was more of a manly bonding to get him —"

My Scanner goes off.

"Crap. I've got Agility Game training. Maybe I should just skip it?" *I have so many unanswered questions.*

"No. That would look suspicious. You should go now." Jacqueline sighs. "But you'll need to figure out a way to get out of the big Agility Game."

Leaving them, I race to where the Agility Course once was and find myself at the edge of a dark, giant swimming pool, the size of a small lake.

"They're over there, Harper!" Peet points to my left. He's sitting with Yori and Dada on a bench, with tens of other hybrids, looking out over the dark water.

My gaze follows Peet's finger to a group of hybrids standing on a white, glossy platform, spanning out into the lake, Daryl Pope's blue head and shoulders towering above the others.

"Thanks!" I say.

"Good luck today!" Peet shouts as I run off.

David is in the middle of addressing the group when I approach the end of the platform. "It is so important that you do your best —" He pauses, making my entrance painfully obvious.

"My, don't you have a talent for showing up at the last minute?" He shakes his head as though I'm some sort of silly, small child. "Welcome to the official Agility Seven." He waves his hand to each of them. "Amadi, Sue, Gene, Vihaan, Jun, and your little friend, Aleena."

"Hi Harper!" she says enthusiastically waving. She looks even more scrawny than ever, next to this tall and muscular bunch, smiling at me with her big eyes.

"Isn't she too young for this?" I shoot back at David.

"She could get hurt."

David shrugs. "She made good time in the tryouts. She's as qualified as everyone else here."

Daryl Pope cuts in, lifting an eyebrow ridge at me, "No offense, but why is *Harper* here? She didn't have a good time at the tryouts."

David's hand goes to his heart, as if he's just heard something offensive. "I don't think that was her best day. Did you know she used to be a very good runner on Earth?"

"No way. What college you run for?" Daryl says.

"I —"

"She was still in high school, so she didn't get the chance to compete yet." David doesn't let me finish. "But I think with some training from someone like you, dear Daryl, she could really do well next week."

In the corner of my eye, I notice Sue and Gene, two hybrids that I suddenly recall Adam saying were in the athletic group, assessing me. Sue puts an arm on her hip and gives her chiseled bicep a flex.

"Fine," Daryl says. "Now, let's get this show on the road." He clears his throat. "You're probably all wondering how this huge-ass swimming pool got here. The answer is, I have no idea as this Ancient shit is crazy, but I do know that the Agility Course can change every challenge." He taps his head "It's to keep you on your toes. To test all levels of athleticism and intellectual adaptation. I also figured, none of you has practiced in water yet."

Daryl presses something on his Scanner and the whole lake boils around us for a moment. A second platform rises from the water, next to the one we're standing on, with a pile of what appears to be swimming gear on it.

Daryl lifts what looks like one of many oval glass bowls from the pile. He holds it over Aleena's face, which makes the gray fabric from her hybrid suit reach up, as though it's made from thousands of thread-sized tentacles, and fasten around the bowl, creating a helmet suitable for scuba diving.

Second from the pile, Daryl retrieves geometric-laced fins and attaches them to her feet. Finally, he ties a mesh fanny pack around her waist.

"You'll all need this for collecting stars," he says.

There's a gasp from Jun and Vihaan as they stumble away from the edge of the platform. I turn just in time to see the bend of a giant creature sinking beneath the water with a splash.

"We're going in with that?" Vihaan says, his eyes wide.

Daryl gives a sly smile. "If Agility were easy, everyone would be doing it. Now everyone, get your gear on."

Once we're dressed, Daryl lines us up at the water's edge. Another platform rises from the water, at the other end of the small lake. "You'll all be racing to that. But as you can probably tell by your gear, this isn't no freestyle swimming. You'll have to collect the stars along the bottom of the lake to move forward. Sound good?" But he doesn't wait for a response before he shouts, "Go!"

I plunge into the water, and with little protection from my hybrid suit, the cold temperature makes my limbs go rigid. When the chaos of splashes, bubbles, and my competitor's hands and fins disperse, I find myself hovering above a clearing of stoney hills, curling into abstract shapes, splotched with growths of colorful algae. Past the clearing, in the direction of the finishing platform, is a dense, dark forest of kelp-like plants. A school of transparent little creatures zooms past me, the shape of raindrops, with a singular pivoting eye in the center of their transparent heads.

Sue is already swimming down to the rocks, propelling quickly because of the fins, toward something that's twinkling. She puts a star into her fanny pack, where it still twinkles through the mesh fabric. Then she continues along the bottom, collecting more.

The other hybrids are not far behind her, ascending into the depths, in a race to collect as many stars as possible.

I hover as my skin numbs to the cold, watching the frenzy – which reminds me of an Easter egg hunt. My original intention was to be last today and get kicked off the "Agility Seven." *But, thinking of being unprepared against whatever that giant monster thing was worries me* — and I don't want to be forced to glow in case the others might see it.

I spot Aleena, gliding through the water effortlessly with her fins, as if it's her natural state of being. I swim to her, delighted by the force of the water pushing against me, making me feel powerful and fast; a confident sensation I haven't felt since running in Nevada. Definitely not something I've ever felt during my glow.

"Aleena!" I say as I approach. She continues on and I have to tap her on the shoulder to get her attention.

"Do you want to be on a team?" I ask.

"No. I've got this." She gives me a thumbs up, does a backflip and swims off into the forest on her own.

Maybe I'm too worried about her and that competing in Agility is exactly where she belongs.

I find myself alone in the rock clearing, other than the revolving school of funny transparent fish with one eye. The kelp forest Aleena disappeared into looms ahead, its foreboding shadows promising danger. Supposing that I'll be in need of protection, I spend the next few minutes collecting four stars, hoping that everyone ahead of me has cleared a path.

Only a few feet into the forest and the once shimmering water seems to grow murkier, the tall weeds only let in blinks of light in the ebb of the current. The deeper I get, trying to remember the direction of the finishing platform, the more I have to weave through the thickening growth and untangle myself from the snaring branches.

A *click, click, click* sound starts to echo all around me, as if someone is tapping rocks together. *Click, click, click.* My hand hovers over my fanny pack, questioning if the stars can be used as a weapon, like ninja stars.

Three small glowing red eyes emerge ahead of me. I pause, starting to reach for a star in my pouch.

Neither the creature nor I move for what has to be a minute, before a shifting beam of light finally reveals a little crab-like animal, with twice the amount of legs of Earth crabs, and three eyes which follow me like satellites. Its legs move together in a sway making the *click, click, click* sound I heard earlier.

I swim around the crab, faster, pushing through more slimy weeds, when I feel little pointy legs prickling down my hip.

With a scream, I slap it off. But in an instance, there are

dozens more of them on me, prickling down my torso.

In a panic, I scrape my hip across some kelp and manage to remove most of them, praying I reach another clearing soon. I feel one pulling at my pack, trying to tear the mesh holding the stars. Then it hits me: that's what they want. I flick him off and swim faster, my breath heavy in my helmet.

There's a shrill scream overhead — Aleena?

Somehow, I move even faster, my calves cramping from the unusual movement of kicking with the fins, finally seeing the light ahead, the end of the forest near.

Click, click, click, comes from every perceivable direction, as if the entire forest were made of the sound. A mass shadow absorbs me into it and I find myself in a thick layer of crabs, their combined weight pulling me to the bottom, their thousands of little legs like static all over my body. Flinging them off my arm, I manage to get my hand into the pack and around a star. I take out two and throw them a few feet away.

What feels like thousands of them jump off and pursue the stars, giving me enough time to make for the exit.

I burst clear of the forest and into another rocky clearing. Swatting more crabs off me, who scurry back into the protection of the kelp.

The clearing is eerily still. At the other end is a giant white monolith rising all the way to the water's surface: The finishing platform.

But where's everyone gone? Where did that scream come from? Suddenly, I'm dragged down behind a rock, flailing hard until I'm staring into Amadi's face. He holds his hand over his face shield, where his mouth is, with large eyes that beg me to be quiet.

There's a loud sucking sound. Amadi peers around the large rock he's pulled me behind, waving for me to look.

What appears to be a giant sea slug turbos out of the forest, with a massive round mouth of spinning teeth that reminds me of a jet engine. It swims low, over the rocks, creating a whirlpool of sand that sucks up though its great mouth and spits out an orifice at the back of its body.

As it turns to circle back, I see one large pivoting eye in the middle of its transparent head.

It turns again, this time moving even faster and knocking itself against a cluster of rocks, making the ground shake.

"Sue, Gene, Vihaan, and Jun have already finished," Amadi whispers.

"What about Aleena?!" I say in a panic.

"Trapped by the creature." He nods to the cluster of rocks the slug is smashing itself against.

I panic. How long could the rocks hold? "How did the others make it past the slug?" I say quickly.

"I didn't see how Sue and Gene did it, but Jun and Vihaan snuck by when the slug was chasing Aleena."

Think. Think. Think. I touch my fanny pack. "Have you tried throwing a star at it?"

He nods. "It's not attracted to the stars like the sea spiders are."

I glance back at the forest, where thousands of little red eyes peer out from the darkness. "It might be attracted to crabs ..."

"Excuse me?" Amadi says.

"If it's sifting through the sand like that, it's probably

looking for small animals to eat."

He lifts an eyebrow ridge, still not understanding.

"Give me your pack," I say, reaching for it.

He pulls away. "I need to finish with stars or I will lose. David will not be happy if I lose."

"Fine, keep the stars, put them in your pockets. Give me your fanny pack. Hurry!"

He moves his stars to his pocket, giving me his pack.

The slug releases a furious, gurgly roar and starts swimming around the finishing platform in swift, small circles.

In a rush, I remove my fanny pack, where the two stars are still glowing strongly through the mesh. I tie mine to Amadi's, making a long rope from the straps. I take the biggest rock I'm able to carry and tie the end of the fanny pack rope to it.

Amadi watches me shaking his head.

"In sixty seconds, I need you to start banging rocks together as loudly as you can, to draw the creature away from Aleena."

"Then it will eat me!"

There's another loud thud as the creature smashes itself against the pile of rocks again.

"No. I'm going to distract it, I promise."

He studies me for a moment. "Very well," he finally says with a nod.

Making sure the giant slug is facing the other way, I swim to the edge of the forest. Taking a deep breath, I hold on to the rock end of my rope and toss in the stars in my fanny pack, like a fishing line, into the mass of red eyes.

The giant shadow of crabs descend upon it within seconds, hundreds and hundreds of them, nearly reaching the end of the rope.

I hear the banging sound from Amadi and a gurgly roar from the monster.

With all my strength, I kick my legs against the rocks at the bottom – the crabs emerge in a clump so big, they're nearly a quarter the size of the giant slug.

My legs are on fire as I move into the clearing. I find a spot to place my rock, smash it into the ground and make a loud enough sound to draw the slug away from Amadi.

It works. The slug comes turboing through the water, barreling through the thick cloud of crabs, who retreat back into the forest.

Amadi swims for the monolith and I dart for Aleena, finding her huddled in a small cave, shocked when I grab her by the arm.

"Come on!" I shout, pulling her out. Her leg has a big gash so I practically drag her toward the finishing platform.

Then there's a big roar and I get the sinking feeling that the slug has finished with the crabs.

"Swim, Aleena!" I scream, the finishing platform is only a few feet away.

My hands heat up. *No, I can't do it here.* Finally, my fingertips graze the top of the monolith, breaking the surface of the water.

The world around us dissolves into glitter, the whole water environment evaporates away, turning what was once a teeming habitat into a giant sterile pool.

I help Aleena climb onto the finishing platform. Daryl, David, and everyone else wait for us on top.

David's smile fades. "My, that took you a long time."

He looks at my hips where my fanny pack should be.

"Do you have any stars?"

"No."

"And she's technically last," Daryl says.

"But she saved me!" Aleena protests.

"It's okay, Aleena," I say. "I don't think I'm cut out for this. Pretty much had a side ache the whole time. It was super hard for me." I bend over and put my hands on my knees, pretending like I'm holding back vomit.

Aleena gives me a confused look.

"Besides," Daryl says, "Agility isn't about saving anyone. Nobody was in any real danger."

Aleena holds out her bloody leg.

"Small battle wounds — I'm sure the Ancients will heal these up. But maybe Harper's right, David. She might be too out of shape for the big game."

In the corner of my eye, I think I see a vein pop in David's neck, as his face turns a shade darker with anger. Tamera, right beside him, is mirroring his expression.

"Give her another practice," David says. "I think she will do better then."

CHAPTER 27

"Come with me," Arl says, grabbing the handle of the cart in the supply room the next day. "Change out of your suits. I have something new for you."

Both Jacqueline and I were surprised when he notified us to meet him in here today, instead of the Military Sector after spraying and skimming.

He takes our sprayer and skimmer, then disappears with them into the storage closet. I hold my breath, thinking of the Scanners and Gewd hidden there, until he emerges unfazed.

After we remove our suits, we follow Arl through the Science Sector and down the hall. We enter a room, through an open doorway, where the walls are made of waves and large honeycomb-textured arches, where thousands of tiny lights blink everywhere. It's as if we've walked into the depths of a glittering, white beehive. Jacqueline seems to be in awe of it all, her mouth gaping.

Arl leads us around a large bend of the honeycomb material to a heaping pile of blood samples on the floor, behind a cluster of tiny, straw-sized pipes. There, the blood samples are tangled together like Christmas lights that have been through too many moves. There has to be at least a month's worth of collections in the pile.

Arl picks up a thread connecting a string of blood balls, unwrapping it from another strand it's tangled to. Once freed, he feeds the end into a blood-ball-sized-hole in the wall. The balls make a *glut, glut* sound as they're sucked in. "Put the samples here," he says, tapping the hole. "The machine will alert you if anything is off."

"What about the Military Sector sampling? Who will help you with that today?" It could take him hours on his own.

Arl glances at the exit, bouncing on his toes impatiently. "I will be taking that over until further notice. I am very behind here, which is where I need the most assistance from you two."

"I thought we got instant results if anyone is sick?" Jacqueline asks, picking up a string of balls. "Why are we testing these samples now?"

Arl inches closer to the door. "The arches only do basic diagnostics. Blood samples are detailed work. I try to test once a week, but with our new food crisis, we've been very busy, so now this can be your work."

"When do you need this done by?" I say.

"It will take you a few days," he says, rounding the bend of honeycomb, halfway out of sight. But he pauses. "Oh!" He sighs, and turns around. "I almost forgot. You can't use your Scanners in here. You'll have to go outside the room to contact me."

"Why can't we use our Scanners in here?" Jacqueline says eagerly.

Arl perks up, appearing pleasantly surprised by her interest, "Because the vast amount of oscillating magnetic fields are not compatible with the Volucris used for Scanners. It's the same reason the sprayer and skimmer won't work in here either. Also, it's better to not have other technologies interfere with the purposes of this room."

"What are the purposes of this room?" Jacqueline says even more eagerly than before.

"It's for processing vast, vast amounts of data," he says, his eyes bouncing around the twinkling lights thoughtfully.

"Well, we're happy to help wherever you need us," Jacqueline says. "You've been such a wonderful teacher." She holds her hands to her heart.

Arl's orange cheeks get two shades darker. "Right. Thanks, Jacqueline." He returns a coy smile. "I must be on my way. The lab waits for no Enbrotici." He finally disappears around the bend.

The moment his footsteps fade off, Jacqueline's face lights up. "This is one of the rooms, Harper!"

I'm surprised she's not covering her mouth. "What?"

"One of the rooms Adam and I have been watching for monitoring. You don't remember us passing it a few days ago? When I was looking around, when I found the room of Gewd?"

"Kind of ..."

She starts jumping up and down like a giddy child. "This room doesn't have EMRS readers ... and you heard Arl ...

It sounds like a lot of their technology doesn't work in here because of the magnetics in whatever all of this is," She motions to the walls.

I'm surprised her defenses have fallen so easily. "Do you think they're monitoring us in other ways, though?" I cover my mouth with my hand because I can't help it.

"We have no evidence of that. There are other rooms in the Science Sector that don't appear to have EMRS readers either. There's also a pure white room that doesn't have them, a room of vapors ... anyway." She goes to the pile of blood samples and lifts off a strand, which is stuck to a knot of others. "I've been asking Adam to keep an eye out for them when he's in the control room. He's never, ever seen a room that looks like this." She starts picking at the giant knot. "So, how about you practice and I'll sort?"

I glance around anxiously, still a bit uneasy about this place, but with only five days left, and probably even less time until they want me to sneak into Golden Guard territory — I gulp — it seems we haven't got many options.

"What about the open doorway around this wall?" I point past the bend Arl just disappeared behind.

"Nobody can see us from the hallway in this little hollow. I didn't see the blood samples over here when I examined this room all those times we walked by it. I've never seen an Ancient in here before either. I think it will be alright. I'll watch for you."

"Okay," My stomach does a sudden drop. "So how do I *practice?*"

Jacqueline puts her knot down and reaches into her pocket.

She pulls out a handful of vials filled with glitter. "We can trigger you with these."

"Where did you get those?!"

"Adam," she says.

Of course. "But those didn't trigger my ability when I sniffed a vial for the presentation before ..."

"You probably had some Canopy Gewd before. It's been two days since you've eaten any. With a less emergent dose of the vials, I think you'll feel more like yourself too, which can help you control your ability."

"What's on them?"

Jacqueline frowns. "Adam suspects that they're recordings of crimes committed by the human race." There's a tinge of guilt in her voice.

I get a flashback to my presentation, when the alien was showing me the evils of humanity in that dark room. What horrible pain and suffering could *these* vials have in store? I take a yellow one from Jacqueline's hand and turn it over.

This is bigger than me, I remind myself.

The vial twinkles from all the lights blinking on the wall, which gives me a thought. "Are you sure these aren't made of magnetic material?" I say. "What if I suck it up my nose and then the glitter's pulled through my brain and kills me?"

"A valid point," Jacqueline says as she pours half of a red vial into her hand and flings it into the air. The glitter flutters straight to the ground. "It doesn't appear to be magnetic." She flicks her finger to bring up her Scanner. A hologram starts to form but malfunctions and scatters apart like sand in the wind. "Looks like the magnets are on now, too."

She takes back the yellow vial I'm holding, gives me the half-full red glitter vial, and then pulls out a small piece of black fabric from her pocket. "If you start showing signs of your ability while under, I'll have you smell this rag. Then we'll try to trigger you from the smell. They don't have much here in the perfume department, but I rubbed it on some of the flowers in the Canopy garden. It smells special, I think." She gives the rag a sniff.

Wordlessly, I sit down, crossing my legs on the floor. I'm so nervous I might throw up. I put the red vial up to my nose, readying myself.

"Bon appétit," Jacqueline says with an encouraging smile.

"Bon appétit." I sniff. There's a sting, followed by the scent of blood.

I'm staring at filthy water: cloudy and brown with pieces of trash floating in it like disgusting soup. The air is thick with the smell of garbage and sewer. I gag. *The dream-like scene glitches.*

I sit up. I'm surrounded by muddy roads, garbage, and shacks constructed out of planks of wood, roof panels, blankets and brush. A child is crying. I turn to find a hut beside me and in its doorway stands a rail-thin woman in colorful garments, rocking an even thinner toddler. The baby's slender arm drapes over his mother's shoulder as she bats away a swarm of flies.

There's gunshots down the way — *and more glitching.* The woman jumps, glancing frantically in the direction the shots came from. She presses her son to her chest as she disappears into her hut and covers the doorway with a plank of wood, followed by the sound of hammering.

Three young soldiers march through the street, strapped with guns, who can't be any older than seventeen.

As they approach the woman's hut, one of the soldier boys yells something in another language. When there's no answer, two of them start smashing their boots into the plank until it cracks in half. They pull the woman out, with her arms still wrapped tightly around her small son, both of them shrieking.

They shove her against a tree, and the woman protects her son even more frantically, kicking at them, tears streaking down her face.

The soldier boy points his gun at her, reaching for the child. The woman steps back, shaking her head. The two other young soldiers grab her.

"No!" I shout, but they can't hear me.

Her son is ripped from her arms. She's bashed over the head as they take her child with them. *More glitching.*

"No!" I shout. A funny smell fills the air, like roses.

The woman sobs as she lay in a heap on the ground, reaching for her child as he vanishes down the street. Her shrill screams transform into,"Harper! Harper, wake up! Harper!"

Jacqueline is standing above me, slightly blurred, waving

slowly, her words almost inaudible. I gasp, rolling over, the piece of black fabric lies beside me, my body buzzing with electricity.

"It's leaving! Try to hold it!" She urges.

But I can barely sit up for a moment, my body trembling from fatigue. I put my head between my knees, "I can't —" I struggle for breath as my hands cool.

"You glowed," she says, as if surprised.

After a few more breaths, I look up at her and see that she's biting her lip, narrowing her eyes at me.

"What's wrong?" I ask.

"You look like *them* when you do it ..." she trails off, as if haunted by some dark memory.

"Like who?"

"Like the glowing figures that capture hybrids."

I'm one of *them*? The image from my nightmares? "What do you think it means?" I finally say.

"I don't know, but if the Ancients can do it, it must be powerful." She continues to peer at me.

I look at my hands and then my arms. *How is it possible? Why me? Why ...* "Did Rae look like that too?"

"I never saw her in action. She just said she could move really fast, like you can." Her eyes glaze over as she talks about her. "But you've got to learn to control it." A determined look replaces her sad one. "We need it if we're going to save humans." She clears her throat. "They'll need us back at the platforms soon and who knows how many days Arl will let us in here."

I try a few more attempts to glow, sniffing halves of other

vials with terrible things on them. Each time my glow seems to be weaker than the last.

Finally Jacqueline says we've practiced enough. On the platform on the way back, she leans in closely and says, "I'll give you all the food rations tonight. Maybe your body hasn't had enough food to properly recover from the last time. I'll try to give you most of the food from here on out."

I glance at her shrinking frame. "But you and Adam —"

"Your ability is the most important right now. We need it for the Scanners and ..." she trails off.

"And what?"

"It's the next phase in the plan. There's not time to talk about it now," she motions to the approaching Canopy.

Convenient, I think.

At Evening Replenishment Jacqueline gives me all three small Gewds under the table. I eat them guiltily, watching Adam and Jacqueline act like they don't care ... but they have to be starving.

"Thanks," I say before I push off to stupid Agility practice.

Trying to save precious calories, I take my sweet time at it, despite Daryl Pope's threatening shouts. As I run through an evolving maze, marked by changing colors, I come in last place by more than five minutes.

At the end, I overhear Daryl complaining about me to David, saying that he still doesn't think I'm right for Agility. I smirk at how much it's probably pissing David off.

The next day, with four days until the big game, Jacqueline and I spend a few hours practicing my skill in the sorting room.

Jacqueline has me sniff a vial, experience the simulation, then awakens me with the scented cloth when I'm glowing. I manage to maintain the glow for a few seconds and move a few feet across the room in a second. But the following day, three days from the big Agility Game, I'm worse than on my first day of practice. At best, I manage to glow for about a half second, in my time, and then have to fight to keep down the extra food rations.

The vials give me such vivid nightmares that it's impossible for me to slip to that black in-between space where I can see Olivia. The images from the vials creep into the daylight hours too. When we're around Arl and Vulgun, Jacqueline has to step in to fix my mistakes and calm my shaking hands before they notice.

On the fourth day of practice, merely two days before the escape, I sit on the sorting room floor, surrounded by the blinking lights, the pressure to succeed crushing down on me. I pull the little black piece of cloth from my pocket that smells like Canopy flowers. I haven't managed to glow at all today.

Jacqueline holds out two glitter vials.

"Pick another one," she says.

"I'm sorry. I can't," I say. "Those things are getting to me." I shiver.

"I'm not saying it's pleasant. But we need to get you to glow again," Jacqueline pushes, marching around. "You haven't gotten it down yet. We're running out of time. We've got *two days*. You've got to replace the Scanners soon or we're going to have to leave without your brother and friend ..."

"Yeah. I've definitely noticed that!" I shout, fighting back tears. I flip the piece of cloth in my hand as I take a second to gather myself. "I haven't smelled it yet today." I hold up the black cloth. "Maybe we could try without the simulations? Maybe it's all just been too much?" I can't bear to look at her; I'm so ashamed.

"Okay," Jacqueline says, "I can understand that. Give it a try."

I slowly take a seat on the floor and straighten my back, crossing my legs.

"Just try to think of something that gets you going," Jacqueline says.

No shit, I think, trying to forget that she's there. I close my eyes and recall a vial from yesterday — I can see the dank, large warehouse, the smell of urine makes the air acidic. Rows and rows of bears in lifted tiny cages, their bodies covered in large calluses, trembling as they make low noises that sound like throaty barks.

A man pulls out a syringe, and the bear's barks get louder. The closer the man gets, the more the bear shakes.

A sizzling goes off in my fingertips. I sniff the piece of fabric, and the smell of roses intensifies. Heat grows around me. I take deep breaths, smelling the cloth, honing in on the dark thoughts.

"It's working," Jacqueline says. "In your hands. Keep going."

Stop talking, Jacqueline...

The man easily reaches around the outside of the cage and injects the bear. Then goes to the next one and does the same. By the time he is on to the fourth bear, the first one is loopy and drops, passed out. That's when the rest of the group of humans descend. They open the first bear's cage and adjust it until its belly is pressed against the bottom wires. Then a woman goes under the lifted cage with a tube and cup. It's then I see the permanent catheter, coming out of the little bear's abdomen. The woman attaches the tube to it, and yellow bile drips into her cup.

Even though I want to rip the lady and the man into unrecognizable pieces, the warmth in my hands doesn't intensify: It starts to fade.

Then, a sharp pain digs into my throat. I open my eyes and see that Jacqueline is dragging me by something around my neck. As I claw at it, black spots appear in front of my vision. I can't get a good enough grip to tear the thing off. I can't breathe! I thrash back and forth to try and force her to let go. She doesn't let up.

I give the biggest lurch I can and Jacqueline crashes into the wall behind her. I can finally breathe again, taking in as much air as my lungs will allow.

I jump up, preparing to fight her, but she just lies there, stunned, rubbing the back of her head. She pulls her hand out and it's covered in blood. There's some on the honeycomb wall too.

I stand, readying myself. "What the hell, Jacqueline? Are you trying to kill me?!"

"Wait!" she gets up, holding up her hands in surrender. "I needed to see if you're still capable. It seems like these vials are not strong enough to fully trigger you anymore. You need to trigger a bigger fear response ... a.k.a. more adrenaline."

"Great. So does that mean you're going to choke me every

time you want me to glow!" I shout, angrily rubbing my neck.

"Well, if even that works ..." Her voice trembles and her eyes get a little more shiny. "Harper ... we didn't want to put more pressure on you, but the last part of the plan, to save Brett and Rubaveer, needs you to glow too..."

I stand there, wanting to run somewhere, away from the shame of letting so many down. Especially after they've given me the food out of their mouths. I turn my head and blink away the brimming tears.

"During the Agility Game, you're going to use the Golden Guard Scanners to get past the prison guards, into the gate. Then you'll glow to bring Brett and Rubaveer back to the storage containers, where we'll hide until the ships take off for Earth."

Despite the light clicking sounds coming from the walls, I can still hear my heart thrumming in my ears. Well, that plan might be screwed. The only other option is to escape with them, without Brett or Rubaveer ... or maybe I should just compete in the games, as a punishment to myself for not being able to pull this stupid thing off ... go back to Cooms with everyone afterwards. I fully deserve it.

"I've got another idea," Jacqueline says quietly. "There was adrenaline in the emergency storage closet in the Military Sector ..."

"The epinephrine?" I get a cold chill. "They use that stuff to save dying humans in shock ... Can't that kill me?"

"It could kill a *human*, push them into cardiac arrest. You're not a normal human though."

"What do we do if I go into cardiac arrest?"

"We could start out with only a little bit. Go from there, but

I haven't got much. I only managed to sneak one small tube. Probably only enough for one event..."

"So I'll have to choose between using it for stealing the Scanners or saving Brett and Rubaveer?" I say.

"Yes. That's if it will even work for you at all."

By the time I make it to Agility practice that evening, Daryl already has the "Agility Seven" divided into different drills to perfect techniques that may be useful for the big game, only another day away. There's the silver runway where the floor morphs into different obstacles, the ring wall, a small swimming pool to perfect your stroke, a miniature rope grid (similar to the one I saved Jacqueline from), and a large hologram with different mental puzzles.

All the drills are so spread apart, it's hard to see everyone at once. But I don't really care how my competition is doing, as I need to get out of this for good.

When Daryl finally approaches me on the silver runway, where I go at a slow jog, jumping over small hurdles clumsily, he gives me a few pointers about leaning forward and leading with my dominant leg to get a smoother clearance.

It does improve my form, but at the next silver hurdle, I see my opportunity. Making sure my back leg doesn't quite clear it, my foot catches the rim of the hurdle, sending me rolling off to the side of the silver platform.

"Ouch!" I shout, holding my wrist, rocking back and forth on the ground.

"Oh shit! Are you alright," Daryl says, rushing over.

"Yeah." I slowly stand and hold it out. Then with perceived caution, I move my wrist and pretend to shout out in pain. "I think I tweaked it," I cry and snap my arm against my body protectively.

"The Ancients should be able to heal that in time for the big event," I hear Tamera say, as she and David hurry to the scene — The Agility Seven not far behind them.

David takes one look at me, clicks his tongue and shakes his head in a weird, insincere way. *Why isn't he more upset about this?*

He glances at each hybrid gathered there. "How nice of you *all* to come and check that your dear teammate is okay: Jun, Amadi, Sue, Gene, and Vihaan, you're all so kind."

I almost fall for real when I don't see her there, after checking twice. It's when I look back at David, his expression a kind of excited anticipation, that I feel icy-cold all over. "Where's Aleena?"

Everyone gives me a grim look, including Daryl.

David puts his hand on my shoulder. "Unfortunately, the Ancients said she won't be able to compete. She had some genes that needed to be repaired." He pushes me off to the side, away from everyone, his fingers dig into my shoulder blade painfully. He speaks lower so only I can hear. "But I have a feeling that, if you do really well on the big day, *like I know you can*, she may come back."

"If you hurt her —"

"Now, now, Harper. I wouldn't have to do that unless you give me a reason to. Since you're ... *injured*" He licks his lips as if the word tastes bad in his mouth "why don't you take the next day off and *heal* ... get yourself together ... and I'll see you the day of the big game, ready to beat all the other hybrids, except maybe Daryl Pope, of course."

Waves of disbelief and shock batter through me. As I look into his evil square face, white-hot anger builds with the force of a thousand suns. Heat ignites in my palms and moves up the tendons of my hands and forearms.

"Harper ..." I hear Jacqueline's voice behind me, in that pleading tone she always assumes when Adam acts out. They must have been watching me practice.

David still stands there, unfazed, daring me to knock out his fake, white teeth. I want to hurt him so badly, to beat him into the ground so he can feel an ounce of the emotional pain he's caused everyone here. To break him until he tells me what he's done with Aleena, Rae, Camilla, and every other hybrid who has gone missing ... but as hard as it is, I must aim this feeling at a higher purpose.

Without giving David the satisfaction of another second, I turn and storm off in Jacqueline and Adam's direction.

"I just heard about Aleena ... I'm sorry ..." Jacqueline says as I pass her. And by the thinness of her voice, I can tell that she means it. This must remind her of losing Rae all over again.

"Don't be, Jacq," Adam says, giving me a nod before they both follow me in a jog, out of the Agility Course, past the table and through the garden into a thicket of fluffy bushes.

"Is this a good place to talk?" I say in a hurry.

Jacqueline quickly scans the area. "Yes?" She narrows her eyes suspiciously.

"Good. Give the unformatted Scanners to me." I hold out my

hand, where the lifelines in my palms glimmer.

Her eyes widen and she pulls them from her pocket.

Adam grins and nods in approval. "I'll tell you how to get there."

CHAPTER 28

With the world shimmering and blurry like it was when I walked the Science Sector, I find my way to the vine in the garden that Adam told me about. The vine — pink and wiry, with little pine needle-like leaves — cascades over the ledge and onto many floors below. There's a lurch in my stomach when I grab what appears to be a flimsy limb, and try not to look at the several-hundred-foot drop that could end me, should it snap.

I spot the hollow I'm looking for in the tangle of spindly branches. As instructed, I shimmy through the narrow opening to avoid the forcefield that protects hybrids from jumping. To my relief, the deceivingly strong plant doesn't budge as I descend two stories. Luckily, the little needles are like feathers against my skin.

I pull myself onto the lower level and follow a ramp, weaving through a crowd of frozen, shimmering Ancients, crossing a vast lattice of dozens of bridges, feeling like I'm walking around in a hazy dream. *Third bridge to the left,* I think, recalling Adam's directions. Then I see it: the building with the giant gold blades and the bridge that will take me to it. It's about another half a mile from there, where I have to continually zigzag through the motionless commuting Ancients. The closer I get to the golden blade building, the more frozen Golden Guards I start to pass, making the knot in my chest tighten.

Up close, the golden building is engraved with pinstripe patterns that remind me of the ones that decorate the heads of the Ancients and hybrids. The patterns continue inside, engraved on the vaulted ceiling and walls, the chrome-gold floor reflecting the massive corridors like water.

Repeating Adam's directions in my head, I pass more guards and find my way down a long hallway, and turn right at a second corner that leads me to a spiral ramp and up to the third floor. My legs start to shake, but I'm almost there. I picture Aleena's face to keep me going.

When I turn the bend, the third floor emits an orange glow. Turning the corner, I don't expect to see the orange net encasing the back of the room because Adam didn't say anything about one being here.

The net is protecting a display of containers full of various colorful substances, glitter, and needles. Beside them is a stacked pile of gold cubes, which I assume is Golden Guard armor. Behind that, mounted on a free-standing wall like a show of jewels, are rows and rows of what I'm looking for: Scanners. I reach in my pocket and feel the unformatted ones I'm supposed to replace them with.

But how am I going to get in? I spot a Golden Guard, halfway through the net, making a small gap in the net's forcefield. I try to squeeze in there, but it's too tight. Pushing the guard out of the way doesn't work either. It's like he's stuck to it, somehow. Unmovable.

A vibration sensation starts in my hands and the world pulses between blurry and sharp. *No.* I'm running out of time. I circle the net frantically again, seeing that the only way in is by the guard. Since he's unmovable, I try to pull open the net to squeeze inside. But when I touch it, it's like my hand snaps to a magnet. There's a sucking sensation and it looks like light is pulled from my hands and into the net. I try to pull away, but it's strong. I yank harder, finally freeing myself, flying backwards. As soon as I break the connection, the dreadful jackhammer sensation arises, starting from my gut and swelling through the rest of my body like needles.

No! I have to get the Scanners! In a panic, I try to shove the guard out of the way harder. When my shoulder is pressing against the guard's ribs, my eyes stop on something I didn't see before, in the crack of a closing door, that could only be seen from this angle. Pale aliens float in large tubes, their faces lax and their eyes closed. There's a small Ancient at the end — and then I see that its hand has five fingers instead of three. It's a hybrid. Why would they have a hybrid here? The trembling builds as I continue to push against the unbudging guard, but I can't look away. She's familiar. She's the same pearl color as me, with my muscular build, but a slightly different face — Rae? Why is she — It's like I'm hit by a giant hammer, as the second wave of violent vibrations pummels into me. The shimmer covering my surroundings glitch.

I have no option but to go back. With one last fleeting look at Rae, I go as fast as I can, back down the corridor, back over the bridges and back up the vine, returning to where I left a frozen Jacqueline and Adam in the thicket of bushes.

I collapse on the ground, heaving for breath as the world around me comes into sharp focus again and the wavering light dwindles away.

They both blink at where they last saw me standing, glancing around frantically until they spot me on the ground.

Adam shakes his head in disbelief. "Harper, did you already do it?"

"Yes," is all I can manage to say through my labored breaths, trying to get to my hands and knees.

"You made it back!" Jacqueline snaps her hand to her mouth because she said it too loud. Then she rushes over and attempts to help me stand. Small vibrations still send painful shocks through my arms and legs.

"Harper ..." Jacqueline's tone turns fearful as she and Adam finally get me on my feet. "What happened?"

"I ... I ..." I gasp. "I made it ... but I couldn't get in."

They look at each other and their troubled silence almost kills me. I hesitate, for another moment, before I tell them. "I ..." my voice catches. "I think I saw Rae."

Jacqueline's mouth opens as if she wants to speak, but no sound comes out.

Adam turns his ear toward me. "Come again?"

I try to explain to them everything that happened.

Adam shakes his head in disbelief. "I don't know what to

say. The net wasn't there when I saw that place with my guard. I've also never seen aliens floating in tanks. That must be a secret room or something."

Jacqueline puts her hand to her forehead, her eyes watering. "What could they be doing with Rae?" Her voice tightens with a sob.

Adam wraps his arm around Jacqueline. "It doesn't matter. We can't help her. We can barely help ourselves at this point."

Another terrible silence falls upon us, as does the realization that this is all my fault. Because of *me* Aleena was taken. Because *I* couldn't pull my shit together and stay longer to figure something out, we can't save Brett or Rubaveer ... Or Olivia.

I wake up screaming Aleena's name, my blankets in the meadow soaking wet with sweat, my heart about to rip from my chest. I wipe my face with my sleeve. Gray clouds have overtaken the sky of my meadow, covering everything in gloom. I flick out my Scanner and see that there are still a few hours before we leave for sector training. I try to roll over and fall back asleep, but the dilemma of staying or going tomorrow keeps slashing its claws through my consciousness like a rabid animal.

I stare into the swirling, dark clouds, and try to think of Olivia, attempting to reach her, as if she'll somehow send me a sign about what to do. A sign if she's died. A sign if it's worth leaving Brett, Aleena, and Rubaveer behind to come and find her ...

Hours later, groggy and puffy eyed, I make my way to the

Canopy for Morning Replenishment. Each step feels like I've been through a shredder, lifting arms and legs made of cement.

At the table, Jacqueline tries to push her and Adam's food rations on me, but I only agree to take anything if they eat their own rations. The strategy seems pointless now anyway.

When we reach the Council Chamber, I'm relieved when Arl tells us we'll be helping with military sampling instead of sorting, as I can't take another vial.

In the Military Sector, we go through the usual motions of drawing blood, all of it happening routinely until my arch starts blinking red. I look around for the containment breach, but only notice the floating line graphs that have appeared over my soldier's head.

Arl rushes over. "Something is making your soldier's armor malfunction," he says, whipping out his Scanner.

One-by-one, the same line graphic starts appearing above every soldier's head, and four of them are blinking a warning red.

"Their bio info shows they're overheating," Arl yells at us, then yells in Emi at the affected soldiers, who collapse where they stand.

"Should I get the Nii Ten gel?" Jacqueline says as she hurries over to help.

Arl glances up, both surprised and happy. "Very good, Jacqueline. Each of you get as many as you can carry, in case we see more overheating."

As more soldiers collapse, I run with Jacqueline back to the emergency supply room. She flicks out her Scanner and follows it to a cubby piled high with packs of blue gel. She grabs a big pile and shoves them into my arms, giving me so many that I start dropping them. Then she takes her own huge amount, balancing her pile carefully.

Arl has four unconscious soldiers out of their armor, which is in heaps on the floor beside them. When we run up, Arl takes the gel packs and begins squeezing out globs on the soldiers' bodies, like rows of toothpaste. He puts extra on oozing wounds that remind me of severe burns.

"What did this to them?" Jacqueline asks in shock.

"Sentinels, most likely," he responds in a solemn tone. "Each of you needs to put the gel where all the largest hearts are and on the burns. It's the quickest way to cool the blood. Hurry!"

Jacqueline gets straight to it, but I find myself clenching my pile of blue gel packs, unable to move. The chaos of the situation is closing in around me, spiraling down further and further. I start to get woozy.

Jacqueline grasps on my arm. "You got this, girl. Be present," she whispers into my ear. In the patient, teacher-like manner she has, she reminds me where the Ancients' hearts are, despite the chaos of more falling soldiers.

We manage to get the situation back under control, with Arl repeating how proud he is of us for handling the situation so well.

"Harper!" Tucker shouts, smacking me out of my haze. He and Marshall approach me, both looking me up and down. *Gross.*

"Where are your buddies at?"

I spin around, searching the crowd of waiting hybrids at the loading platform. Jacqueline must have just slipped off to find Adam.

"They're over there," I lie and start to creep toward my made-up direction.

"Wait up. You're going too fast. I'm sore from working out so much," he says, catching my arm.

I pull free of his hold, giving him a glare.

"Sorry, sorry," he laughs. "I was just wondering what you're doing after the big game tomorrow? After you've finished crushing all the other hybrids in the game, I thought we could hang somewhere, away from your little friends and everyone else at the Canopy." He winks.

His friend Marshall nods in approval.

"Shhheeeeee's seventeen, dude! Seeeeevvveeennnteeennnn!" Adam yells as he and Jacqueline approach, causing everyone to stare.

Jacqueline jabs Adam with her elbow.

A vein throbs on Tucker's forehead. He glances around before he zeros in on me. "Let me know when you want to stop hanging out with these losers, and have some actual fun," he says. "You're too serious all the time. You need to lighten up. Let a real man show you the ropes. Not some pansy."

He turns and finds Adam standing right behind him. "'*Pansy*' is an offensive word, Tucker. It's almost as if I called you lard-ass."

Their eyes lock for a tense moment. Adam breaks it by slowly reaching out and caressing Tucker's cheek. "You've really got to work on those toxic masculinity issues of yours,

Tucker. It's not very becoming," Adam says mockingly.

"Screw off!" Tucker shouts, as he jumps back, his hands curl into fist. "Marshall, let's get away from this creep." They barge off, and disappear into the crowd.

Jacqueline crosses her arms. "You really couldn't keep your mouth shut, could you?"

"Ooohhh come on. He was assskkking for it. Someone his age only hits on seventeen-year-old girls to take advantage of their ignorance about the world. No offense, Harper."

"None taken," I respond.

"Good, just watching out." He has a smile that seems out of place, that remains plastered across his expression.

Jacqueline continues eyeing him, shaking her head and lifting an eyebrow ridge.

Adam turns to her. "I know. I know. I don't want to draw attention to myself."

"Please do more than just work on it. Just do it! We need to blend in!"

Yeah they do, especially if they leave without me. If I compete tomorrow, I could at least get Aleena back. I'm only an extra liability for their plan anyway. They deserve their shot at freedom.

The platforms land and the crowd starts pushing forward. Adam holds us back, until the last hybrids are lining up, leading us to a platform with only a few others on it.

We go to the other side, away from two hybrids who are arguing about how good the Ancients will be in the game tomorrow.

As soon as we lift off, Adam says, "Why are you two so

glum today?"

Jacqueline shakes her head and sighs, not even attempting to address him, watching the buildings whizz by listlessly.

"I think I'm going to stay," I blurt out, wind whipping softly over my face. "I've been thinking. The Ancients must have figured out how to travel by defying spacetime, because the Ancients said that Cooms is fifty light years away. But the Ancients were able to come here rather quickly after only watching us for one hundred years ... according to the presentation. That means they must be able to travel faster than light."

They both give me blank looks.

"It means I might be able to transport back to Earth after I've found some other way to cure the Syndrome. With some time on Cooms, maybe I'll figure out how to bring Aleena, Rae, Brett, and Rubaveer back to Earth." But as I say it, it dawns on me how unlikely that would be. I have no idea what awaits the hybrids in Cooms.

Adam frowns. "I'm not really sure what you mean by *spacetime*, you little nerd, but I don't think all that will be necessary."

"Why?" Jacqueline says, looking over from the view.

"Because our plan *was* like Swiss cheese, but now it's a block of parmesan. Solid as eff." His odd smile returns. "There have been some very significant developments." He pauses again, relishing the drama. "I have a way to get into the prisons."

"What?" Jacqueline and I say at once.

"You know my buddy guard, Sontarx? The one you were so upset I was talking to?"

"Yeah ..." Jacqueline says cautiously.

"Well it turns out, that little red tattoo on his shoulder is a memorial mark for his brother, who always told him that the Enbrotici didn't love enough. With that little thought-cloud hanging over his head, Sontarx has been very moved by his visits to Earth and his interactions with the hybrids. He said that human relationships remind him of his brother. That when I talk about my relationship with you Jacqueline, it makes him think." He grabs her hand. "The Ancients wiping out the human race has really gotten to him ... and I might have helped by reminding him of all the good humans the Ancients are killing."

"So he's going to help us?" I say.

"Yup." Adam pulls out two little transparent marbles from his pocket, keeping them low in front of his chest. "You're looking at two Golden Guard Scanners." He quickly stuffs them back in his pocket.

"A-And you don't sense any deception from him?!" Jacqueline asks. "Are you sure your ability doesn't work differently on Ancients?"

"Your ability?" I say, peering at Adam.

"Yes," Jacqueline responds quickly. "Adam can sense emotions, like a *human* lie detector."

Adam winks at me, before addressing Jacqueline. "I've felt every Ancient walking around this place and I've sensed everyone on the Canopy just fine, so I don't think there's any issue that it works on Ancients. Sontarx is putty in my hands."

"Isn't Sontarx concerned that they'll connect the hybrid

he's guarding with our escape?" Jacqueline says.

"No. He thinks they'll blame our escape on the Sentinel spying or something. Apparently they're worried they've been infiltrated."

"Do you think Sontarx is involved with that?" Jacqueline asks.

"It's possible. It was hard to get a clear reading when I asked him," he responds.

"So I'll still need to get past the guards?" I say.

"No, because he also gave us these —" Adam opens his other pocket to reveal an array of black cylinders. "Hallucination powder. It will put the guards into a dream-like state where their surroundings stay the same, as if nothing has changed. So we'll be able to sneak past them."

"What about the EMRS Readers and all the surrounding buildings that will be looking down on us?" I ask.

"X-231," Jacqueline says. "I took some more today. Just in case."

Adam nods, as if he knows what she's talking about.

"More?" I reply.

"I took two during the first infection scare and two today. Thought they might come in handy. We can drop them around the prisons. The smoke will give us some cover to remove Rubaveer and Brett. It's not as subtle as you glowing — in which case they'd be completely invisible during transport — but it's a good backup plan. It just draws more attention than I would like."

"Yeah." I get a knot in my stomach, but then a small flicker of hope ignites. "I'll still try to glow. If I can't, I'll try the epinephrine."

"If you're sure, Harper," Jacqueline says.

"I'm sure," I say, though of course I'm not.

Adam does a triumphant fist pump. "So it's on then."

The wind blows past our ears for another minute, filling the otherwise wordless silence.

"I still feel guilty about leaving Aleena and Rae," I finally say, tears threatening my eyes as the Canopy comes into sight.

"You don't really know if you're the real reason Aleena disappeared," Jacqueline says sympathetically.

"Yeah," Adam agrees, adding, "And even if you are, think about it, they have no reason to keep Aleena in captivity if you leave. They may have never given her back to you in the first place either. It's David we're talking about."

"True," I say, as our platform hovers lower, readying to dock. "But I want you two to promise me, if the epinephrine makes me sick or kills me, you must try to stop the Syndrome without me."

Jacqueline and Adam nod slowly, and their eyes glance at the approaching loading platform.

CHAPTER 29

The day of the big Agility Game between Daryl Pope, the Agility Six, and the Ancient contenders has arrived. Jacqueline and Adam pull me into the garden before Replenishment, and fill me in on the details of the plan.

Later that morning, Jacqueline and I undertake the military sampling so the military Ancients can make the game too — everyone has a half-day of work assigned so the whole base can attend the game in the afternoon.

We finish sampling and Arl asks us to drop off blood at the lab before we go, so Vulgun can do some testing.

As soon as Jacqueline and I drop off the blood samples, the plan will start. We're going to meet up with Adam in the Council Chambers while everyone goes to the game. From there, he'll show us the way to the prisons. We'll still be dressed in our containment suits because anybody cleaning throughout the Base of Ki wears a containment suit, so we won't look suspicious.

With us, we'll have two additional suits for Rubaveer and Brett to change into. Then we'll wait for the game to begin.

We bring the cart to the golden emblem that marks the lab entrance. When the door opens, it reveals a lab in disarray, with many open cabinets and lots of empty containers everywhere.

I push the cart to Vulgun and open the storage compartment for him. On the inside sits a coil of fresh blood samples. But I worry about what's shoved in the back of the cart, hidden behind everything.

Vulgun grumbles as he tears his eyes away from the Emi on his Scanner. He bends down and reaches into the cart, his hands searching the coil. His hands stop, as does my breath. Then he plucks off three blood balls and drops them into a jar with a clink.

"That's good," he says, "You may go now."

Arl glances up from another task, sorting hollow blue crystals that need to be stacked like Russian dolls.

"Good luck!" He waves with the content grin of a proud parent. "We will truly miss you two when you leave for Cooms tomorrow." Then he lifts a satisfied eyebrow ridge at Vulgun.

I think I might miss both of them too.

A loud bang erupts from the wall next to the entrance. Arl pauses and sets down his tools. "What was that?"

The door slits open and four Golden Guards rush in shouting. They go straight to Arl, who points at Jacqueline.

In an amazingly fast swoop, they grab her and pull her out of the room.

"No! Wait!" I shout, chasing after them. Arl stops me by

tugging at my arm. He stabs me with something and a warm calm washes over me. Before I know it, I'm staring up at Arl from the floor, his outline is fuzzy.

"It's not the right time yet," he says. "Be patient."

"They're bringing them to the holding cells," Vulgun says, looking down and out the window. "There's another male hybrid with her."

I scramble to my feet and join Vulgun at the window. Below, Adam is being thrown into one of the igloo cells, in the prison net, flailing his arms and legs in protest. Jacqueline is just up the street behind him, hanging her head.

My hands are getting warm. Whatever calming stuff Arl injected is leaving my system. I feel it coming on, and start shaking all over. *What the hell am I going to do now?*

Arl comes up beside me and leans on the window. The force field pulses against the pressure. "Funny thing," he says, "The room where we test the blood samples from the military expeditions records everything that happens ... you know, for documentation."

"How? There are no EMRS readers in there!" bursts out of me before I can stop it.

He nods. "For that very delicate room, we use technology for oscillating magnetic manipulation to control and observe things as tiny as atom anisotropy. Vulgun and I got a warning about very unusual magnetic fluxes. Imagine our confusion when we couldn't find the source in the equipment. So we adjusted the monitoring to see a broader view of the whole room."

"That's when we saw you," Vulgun says. "Your power

source — I've never seen anything like it."

"Vulgun and I debated turning you in, but for a while at least, decided to let you continue out of scientific curiosity."

"We were amazed that Predeen didn't detect your upcoming escape," Vulgun says. "It typically has an accuracy of 99.9888%."

"Which is astounding," Arl adds. "That led us into a whirlwind of our own. After a long debate, we've theorized that Predeen was unable to predict your escape because it doesn't yet know enough about hybrid or human behavior. It took the first Predeen thousands of years to get enough data about Enbrotici to accurately predict our behaviors."

"In short," Vulgan says, "The whole thing is interesting enough to send the scientific community into a research frenzy ... and reporting you would put us at the head of it."

My mouth goes dry. The burn intensifies in the tip of my fingers and I clench my hands shut.

"But for some reason, our recording system has been acting up," Arl says. "So that data is corrupted. I think that one of the generators set off a damaging pulse again. It wiped out everything from the last month. Such a pity."

Vulgun replies, "Yeah. Useless thing. I've been telling them we need new recording devices for ages. I think it also took down all the EMRS readers on this side of the Base of Ki."

"Ugh. How can they expect us to do our job with malfunctions like this? I guess there will be no more blood testing for a while ..." Arl's eyes meet mine and drop to my hands. I follow his gaze. My hands are glowing.

"You must be stressed," he says, his voice calm and steady. "Did you know we have things that can alleviate that?"

He goes to one of the cabinets and pulls out a vial full of little gel balls. He places it on the counter nearest to me.

"These work quite fast. About thirty seconds after they hit your tongue, you will be sound asleep."

Vulgun says, "Injecting it makes it work faster, though."

"Oh that's right, instantly," Arl says. "The injectors, you know, the same ones we use that pierce the soldier's armor —"

"Even gold armor," Vulgun adds.

"Yes, well, you can inject yourself to go to sleep. That calming serum I gave you earlier might give you a little pep in your step later too."

"The Agility Course, Arl!" Vulgun shouts.

"Ah yes. We must go or we'll be late. Have a good nap, Harper. I hope your dreams are pleasant. I will tell them you had to be sedated over being so upset about your friends. Very good luck to you."

With that, they both leave with only a quick peek back.

It takes me a moment to put together everything that's just transpired. *Holy crap ... I'll have to do this whole thing on my own.*

But how? Everything is so different. Is it even possible? I try to think. What else do I have at my disposal?

Arl told me the guns go through the guards' armor. Of course! I wish I'd thought of it myself. The plan might still work, it just needs some major alterations. I open the cart, throw out the blood samples, and grab the black sack hidden in the back, to make sure I have everything: sampling guns, reloading twine, two balls of X-231, four containment suit cubes and ... no epinephrine. No! That can't be right!

I turn the sack upside down to make sure I've emptied all of its contents. How am I supposed to do anything if I don't have that? Or Adam's Golden Guard Scanners or Sentinel weapons?

Then, with shocking clarity, another plan comes to me.

After waiting for the sounds of the Science Sector to subside, I push the cart into the main corridor.

My footsteps echo throughout the long passage and bounce off the disproportionally tall ceilings. The Council Chambers are nearly empty, except for a few Ancients filing out of their sectors and another containment suit swooshing over the marble floors with shiny cleaning dust.

I keep my head turned away from them, so that the hood of my containment suit hides my face.

I cautiously approach the Military Sector as its door opens and a group of soldiers comes out. I look away again, but look back just in time to catch a glimpse of the Military Sector behind them, before the door closes. There are still a few stragglers who haven't left yet.

I pivot for the grand engraved doors that lead outside, but a human cough stops me in my tracks. I peek back over my shoulder and see the face of the other containment suit cleaning the floors: Tucker.

Turning around fast, I feel a wave of relief when I hear him start to work on the floors again.

There are only a handful of Ancients rushing about the city now, all hurrying to the arena. Signs and walkways blink for nearly no one. The Volucris who usually dance in the air above the crowds are now dancing around the street like fireflies alone in the forest.

I push my cart full of supplies past closed shops and empty transportation platforms. I'm not a hundred percent sure where I'm going, I just know the general direction of the prisons from the view from the lab's window. Adam was supposed to show us where to go.

I know I've chosen the right way when I see a glow from the prison nets reflecting on the buildings at the end of a small alleyway. The closer I get, the more I start to shake. I can't believe that I'm about to do this. But I keep reminding myself that Jacqueline, Adam, Brett, and Rubaveer are screwed unless I try. Then there's Olivia and possibly the entire human race.

A booming sound vibrates the city, followed by a loud cheer and a song of sorts, that sounds like it's sung by a thousand Ancients in their native tongue. The Agility Game must have started. David must be livid I'm not there to compete.

I peek around the corner of the alley, hiding behind some silver storage boxes. Two Golden Guards are standing at the archway at the entrance. I think about all of the surrounding buildings with a view of the prisons. Their floors and floors of stacked windows, all with a perfect view of what I'm about to do. This could be a suicide mission.

I don't want to chance using the X-231 because I think a random cloud appearing will give the Golden Guards a reason to call for backup. I also don't know how much they know about Adam's plan, so I need to be in and out as quickly as possible.

I pull out the gun injector, the vial of sleeping medicine, and the reloading twine and lay all three of them on the cart.

My adrenaline is rushing so intensely that it's nearly impossible to keep a proper grip on everything. I turn the vial over, and two bright green gel balls fall into my hand. *Crap*. Arl didn't tell me how to get these things into the injector. I turn it over and don't find any other openings, so I squish four of the balls into the pin-sized hole at the tip of the injector, smashing in as much as I can. The green gel goes everywhere. I really wish I could test this theory first.

Since I don't have an accessible pocket, I open my face shield and tuck the container of gel balls under the tight fabric of my containment suit. I wiggle it over to the side of my shoulder, so it's easy to reach, keeping the face shield open.

I take a deep breath and charge out of the alley in the direction of the two Golden Guards watching the arch.

There's a blast of wind, and I'm astoundingly happy when the world around me blurs and shimmers as I start to glow. *Thanks for the pep in my step, Arl.*

Before I know it, my arm is around one of the guard's necks. The tip of the injector digs into his artery and I click the trigger. I release him and jump for the other guard.

I'm moving so fast, the other guard is in the same position when I inject him.

The green vial of sleeping pills drifts past my nose, mid air, as if I'm floating in zero-gravity. It must have escaped from my suit. As it does a slow spin, I grab it, stuff it back into my containment suit, and run back to the alley, in case this whole crazy plan doesn't work.

I take slow breaths until the world sharpens slightly and wait for what seems like a minute before a guard's arm lifts and then goes limp with sleep. Both of their heads slump over and their postures start falling forward. Crap! I forgot to use the reloading twine! I grab it from the cart and dart back over, shoving a guard against the arch (holy hell, he's heavy) and fastening him to it, so he appears to be standing. From close up the twine is visible, but from further than a few feet, it won't be.

Still glowing, I go back and grab the cart just in time to catch the second falling guard. He almost knocks me down with his weight. I exhaust myself getting him into the cart's storage compartment. He barely fits inside.

Swiping his hand for entry at the arch, I take another long breath and wait for the security light to blink green for entry. In about thirty seconds my time, which I can only guess is less than half a second in real time, the net within the arch disappears.

Black igloos protrude out of the ground like rocks in a dried riverbed. As I make my way down the center aisle, the weight of my legs set in and I feel as though I've just completed a marathon. The once-frozen lights of the prison net start to slightly move again. There's a massive tremble through my body and things become sharp. I push the cart, which feels the heaviest it's ever been, to the igloo where I last saw Rubaveer ...

CHAPTER 30

I pass the igloo I saw Jacqueline and Adam thrown into. Where could Brett be in here?, I wonder. I bring the cart to a stop at the end of the igloos, in front of Rubaveer's door, peering over my shoulder to check for danger.

I bend down as if I'm digging through the storage under the cart, getting ready to swipe the guard's hand over the entry Scanner. What if I remove his armor? I reach inside the cart and try to pull off his helmet. It doesn't move and I don't see any release clasps anywhere. I try the same thing with his boots and gloves, and get the same results each time. I sigh. Not happening. I swipe his finger on the entry Scanner and the door opens. Even from outside the igloo, the cold air blowing out turns my breath into bursts of steam. The room appears empty, other than the shell beds — Icicles hang from the ceiling and the walls are wallpapered with frost crystals.

"Rubaveer?" I whisper loudly. The extreme coldness numbs

my face. "It's Harper. I need your help. We're getting you out of here."

When there's no response, I start again, "Rubave—"

"DDDooon't think a human voice will rattle me! I won't tell ye anything, ye human torturers!" a flutey voice says. She then says a few words in Emi.

Rubaveer's head lifts from the foam. Her right eye is swollen and purple. The gaze from her good eye settles on me.

"Juuussst as I thought. There's no Harper here. Ye think her voice will rattle mee?"

Her accent has improved a lot since I saw her last. Though her "e's" and "a's" are still drawn out and her "c's" and "s's" still sound like low notes. It's weird to hear an Ancient not talk with a computer twang.

"No, it's Harper, I promise." I step closer, praying I look enough like my old self for her to recognize me.

She squints and places a hand missing a fingertip to her chin.

"Ye look like Harper for the most part. But ye do not look like aaa normal human. Where is thee fur on thee top of yer head? Why is yer skin that color? Why are yer eyes like mine?"

"Because it turns out I'm a human and Ancient hybrid."

She frowns and carefully studies me. She opens her mouth to say something and then closes it.

"I'm here to break you out, Rubaveer."

She laughs, an almost insane flute laugh that hits all kinds of pitches, that seems to go on for at least thirty seconds. "III told ye, I'm not telling ye anything. I'm better off dead. Let me die. I'll be just as useful to ye, then." She bows back into the foam and disappears.

I tap the cart's storage and open it, revealing what's inside.

"Look Rubaveer!" The unconscious guard's gold uniform sparkles and reflects the blue light from the interface on the wall. "We don't have much time to get everyone to the ships. Please just trust me. If I were lying, how much worse could it get than what they've done to you already?"

Her head rises into sight again, only this time her lower lip is trembling. "IIf ye're lying to me, hybrid Harper ... "

I push the cart hard and it slams into her bed. "Please, we have to hurry! You can use the weapon on his right hand and shoot me if you think any of this is untrue."

She hops out of her bed, landing stiff and wobbly, as though she's grown elderly. It takes her a few tugs to get the guard out of the cart and I worry that I've made the wrong decision. Perhaps she's gone crazy in here. Is she actually going to try to shoot me? Should I run?

She pushes the cart away, reaches past the guard's hand and places a finger on the guard's chest plate. There, she makes a loop-de-loop as though she's signing her signature. The guard's helmet lifts off. Underneath, his face is slack and both eyes are closed. All the breathing slits down his nose ridge expand and contract calmly. He's snoring.

"Hhhe *is* unconscious," she says.

"How did you pull that off?" I ask, feeling a mixture of relief and amazement.

"I remember my commander's code from Procell."

"Can you wear it?"

Her tone goes sour. "Thee armor?"

"Yes. We'll look less suspicious if we've got guards with us."

She nods and removes the chest plate, placing it on the floor. "What is yer plan?"

"I'm going to free a few more prisoners and bring them to the military ships. Then everyone is going to hide in transportation boxes and leave with the military, right after the game."

"How are you going to get us there?"

"Well, I only have two extra containment suits with me, which doesn't quite cover everyone we need, so I don't know ... maybe ... *glow* ... and carry —"

"Glllow?" She stops.

"Yes. I *glow*. I know it sounds funny. I get hot in my hands and it spreads all over my body. Then the world goes all blurry and shimmery. When it happens, I go invisible and move really fast."

"Are ye capable of that without aaa suit?"

"Apparently for bursts of adrenaline I am."

"IlI've never heard of that before."

She goes back to messing with the armor. After she takes off the guard's last boot and places it at the bottom of the gold jigsaw puzzle she's created, she removes his stretchy black bodysuit underneath, quickly gets naked, and dresses him in her white robe. She wiggles into the black suit. It's a bit too big for her and bunches up around her knees and elbows.

"How do ye plan to get into thee Military Sector?" she asks, placing the chest plate on herself and redrawing the loop-de-loop she did earlier. The whole pile of gold pops up off the floor and snaps into place, turning Rubaveer into a Golden Guard. I catch her wincing before the helmet flies on.

"HHHarper, what is yer plan?"

"Right, sorry. I have access to the Military Sector. Another hybrid and I were training with the Science Sector. We took blood samples from the soldiers that returned from the field."

Rubaveer runs her hands over the armor, making adjustments on her shoulders.

"I don't know if wee will have a good chance of escaping by simply hiding in storage containers," Rubaveer says, "Especially since yee have made this guard unconscious."

"I was sort of hoping we'd make it out of the Base of Ki before anyone noticed ..." I feel a stab of panic. I'm such an idiot for not thinking this through more. "Well ... then ... maybe we can... *you can* fly a ship out of here."

"III am not formally trained in ship operation, Harper. Thee most I've done is type in coordinates."

"That's more than I know. Isn't that all you need to fly those?"

"Hmm ..." She zones out. "It's possible."

A loud ping noise booms from outside followed by thundering applause.

"OOOh. A Big Agility Game?" she says. "I haven't seen one in ages. Is that how ye plan to get by unnoticed?"

"Partly."

"I suppose if we go fast enough, it may take some time before thee EMRS readers notify the control room. If ye are moving us by glowing, they might not notice us at all."

"The EMRS readers have been disabled."

"HHHow did ye manage to do that?"

"It wasn't me. It was two Ancient scientists that I trained with."

"Who?"

"Vulgun and Arl."

She smiles and the lines on her head pulsate. "Vulgun and Arl are great scientists."

"Are they trustworthy?" I ask.

"If they have been enlightened, they are trustworthy."

"I don't know what that means."

"I don't know if they have seen thee truth or not. So I'm unsure."

"Okay. Moving on. Have you heard of anyone named Brett here?"

Rubaveer sighs. "He is aaa very high security inmate."

"Where is he then?" My heart thunders in anticipation for the answer.

Rubaveer goes back to her bed, sifts around and lifts out a limp human missing an arm. His entire forehead is black. She lays him on the ground.

I let out a yelp as I race over to him. "Why didn't you tell me right away? Brett! Brett! Wake up." I shake his only remaining arm, but he doesn't stir. "Why is he in your bed?"

"Hhhe's been unconscious for days. When he started getting worse, I kept hearing him shout yer name and thee name of someone called Oliviaa. After that he started talking less and less. Then he began to go in and out of consciousness. I pulled him into my bed when he stopped responding all together."

"Is he going to die?" I choke.

"Not if he gets treatment, and soon. Sometimes they

prolong suffering to scare ye. So when ye give up, ye beg for death ... but they take that away from ye too. They rarely kill anyone."

"Let's put him in the cart. Hopefully the other two are in walking condition."

"Ye'll have to leave him here for now, if you want to open more doors," Rubaveer says, motioning to the unconscious guard on the floor.

The thought of leaving Brett here longer in the depth of the cold makes me ill, but she's right.

Rubaveer and I gently lift Brett back into the shell bed, drag the mostly-naked guard back in the cart, and shut the igloo door.

"IIIs thee other guard restrained?" Rubaveer says.

"Yes. He's unconscious and tied up out front. Don't worry — he looks like he's still standing."

"Very good," she says.

"The other hybrids are in this cell," I say, waving toward the igloo I saw Jacqueline and Adam taken to from the window in the lab.

"OOOh. I wonder how much they'll look like ye." She claps her hands together.

To anyone who might be watching, Rubaveer and I look pretty convincing: just a typical contaminant suit and Golden Guard checking on prisoners. Her limp is the only slight giveaway.

Rubaveer stops. "Wait. But other hybrids, Harper? Is that really necessary?"

"What?"

"BBBringing them too. Thee other hybrids."

"I can't leave them. This whole plan was theirs. They're being held for trying to escape. They're done for without me."

"I would love to meet them, but ye know, Harper, the ships we are going to escape with don't typically hold a lot of Enbrotici. They are made that way to keep them light and agile. I'm not sure how it will perform with five of us onboard. I'm unaware if it's possible. It would be preferred if we had someone with more flying experience."

"Well, we don't have another choice."

She points a finger into the air. "Actually we do." She seizes the cart and turns around, rushing back towards her cell, pausing at the one next to hers. She bends over, behind the cart, and swipes the guard's hand over the entrance.

"MMMedical check!" she shouts in a deep pitch. She then says something in her native language and it echoes throughout the igloo.

A very tall Ancient arises from his bed, hovering a good foot over Rubaveer in height. He has a long and lean build, with athletic shoulders. At first I think he must be riddled with frostbite, but as I get closer, I see the frostbite only accounts for some of his more significant markings. He's silvery gray with natural black and white freckles all over his entire body.

Rubaveer says something to him I can't understand. He shakes his head.

"Hhhe's alone," she says to me.

"Okay," I nod.

He springs out of bed, landing light on his feet, like a panther. Rubaveer holds up her arm to stop him.

"We need to get the other guard, Harper. Topazious is going to take that guard's armor. The chances of all five of us making it to the Military Sector without looking suspicious are better with two Golden Guards. Golden Guards are rarely questioned."

"Okay ... I'm assuming he's a pilot?"

"Yes. Of course. Hhhe is one of the best!"

"And how do you know he can be trusted?"

"HHHarper. Remember how I told ye that I came here by sneaking on a ship? It was his ship. Hhhe discovered me hiding and didn't say anything. He's just been incarcerated for taking the humans' side!"

"How'd *you* end up incarcerated then?"

"It has nothing to do with him. There is no time right now. We need to get him into the other armor."

"How are we going to do that without anyone seeing?"

"Ye! Ye're going to glow and swap me for the guard standing at the entrance."

"No ... I can't glow on command! I have to be really, really stressed out for it to work!"

Another ping sound goes off from the Agility Course.

Rubaveer looks around as if she's embarrassed for me. Then she leans in and whispers, "Are ye not stressed out now?"

"Not enough to glow! If I can't, how am I going to swap you two? You'll need to hide inside the cart, and the cart only holds one. And we need the guard that's already inside to open all the doors ... " I look at Topazious' smoking breath, his bright yellow eyes blinking in puzzlement. I'm not sure if he understands what I'm saying. I continue, "I have X-231. If I can't glow, we can use that. Smoke up the whole place. Give us some cover."

Rubaveer looks at Topazious and puts her hand on her chin. "X-231? That could be useful. How much?"

"Four balls."

"I believe that will provide good cover within thee prison compound, but not outside the gate, where ye'll need to replace the guard. Ye need enough X-231 for both outside and inside thee prison compound, which ye do not have."

"Right." I gulp. I cross my arms and stare at the bright light coming through the open igloo entrance. "Okay then. Say I can glow. I'm thinking you'll ride on top of the cart, the guard will stay underneath in the cart's storage compartment, so we can use his Scanner. Then, after I drop you off out front, I'll carry the unconscious guard back to Topazious. Does he know how to open the armor? Like you did? Can you give him your code, or whatever it was?"

"NNNo. It takes weeks of muscle memory training to learn."

"Should we —"

Rubaveer interrupts, "HHHarper. IIIt's simple. Topazious will change into my armor now. He will be the one to switch with the guard outside. Ye will bring that guard to me. I'll open his armor and change into it."

"Then you, me, Jacqueline and Adam will walk out of here? You in the golden armor and Jacqueline and Adam in the contamination suits I brought."

"I assume those are thee hybrids ye were referring to?"

"Yes."

"There's also Brett," Rubaveer says. "What do ye plan on doing with him? When we all leave together?"

"Dang it. I can't hide him in the cart because we need to

keep the guard in there to open the doors. There was an alley out there! When I bring Topazious to the gate, can Topazious hold Brett on the cart with him? I can hide Brett in the alley and we'll pick him up on the way out."

"III think so," Rubaveer says. She turns to Topazious and has a brief conversation in Emi. Topazious rips off his white robe and stands before us in nothing but his freckles. Rubaveer, to my shock, does the exact same thing, tapping her chest and causing all the gold pieces to levitate to the floor, whipping off the black bodysuit just as fast.

Two stark naked Ancients stand there, both lanky with bones sharp under their flesh and shiny black wounds from frostbite.

They trade spaces and Rubaveer slips on the white robe with a quick tug over her head. Topazious struggles with the black stretchy suit. Once it's on, he positions the chest plate and Rubaveer draws her loop-de-loop on it. All the pieces on the ground rise and snap into place.

"Wwwe are ready," Rubaveer sings. "I'll be waiting here."

Topazious marches beside me as we return to the igloo containing Brett. Topazious helps me lift Brett out of the clam bed and onto the cart. Topazious jumps on, wrapping his arm around Brett, and then hangs onto the front of the cart as though he's about to ride a bull at the rodeo.

Everything suddenly feels stiff. Topazious stares at me in anticipation. His stare alone might be enough to make me glow, I'm so damn nervous. I close my eyes and listen to the sound of my heartbeat, feeling it quicken, focusing on the tornado of nerves rolling through my chest and gut. I repeat to

THE GLOW

myself: *Brett, Jacqueline, Adam, Rubaveer, and Topazious will die without me ... Brett, Jacqueline, Adam, Rubaveer, and Topazious will die without me ...* A drop of sweat creeps down my forehead and the shaking starts from the pit of my stomach and swells outward. I open my eyes and the steam from Brett's breath is stock-still and blurry. I don't know how long it will last.

As swiftly as I can, I snatch the cart and push it to the entrance. That's when the weakness sets in. I don't think I'll be able to hold my glow for much longer. I wait about thirty seconds (for me, in my glow's super sped-up time) for the gate to open after swiping the guard's hand.

After making it outside, I rush to the alley across from the arch and hide Brett between some of the metal storage boxes. I return to the arch and pull Topazious off the cart (who must weigh like three hundred pounds) and prop him up against it.

Then I dash to the other side and break the strings that are holding the other unconscious guard upright. I'm on the verge of collapse as I use my last bit of energy to push him on top of the cart.

I've done everything so fast that the gate is still open, which means it must have taken me less than a second. Just as I make it back inside the entrance, I feel as though I've smacked into a wall. I know my glow is fizzing out. As fast as I can, I dodge behind an area hidden by the arch and fling the cart forward, aiming its trajectory to hide behind the first igloo.

The world slows to its normal speed again and the cart makes a crashing sound out of sight. I vomit, collapsing there into a fetal position, the rainbow lights of the net above spinning. The head and shoulders of a Golden Guard pop into view. How did Topazious get back in here?

"HHHarper. Sit up. Put yer head between yer knees." Rubaveer's voice emanates from the armor. She pulls me up by the armpits and I gag on an empty stomach. She hands me a Gewd. "Drink some when ye can. IIIt has electrolytes."

"I can't."

"Just aaa little sip. It's good for ye. I don't mean to rush ye, but we have to get yer friends."

"You changed fast," I say.

"I heard the crash and saw you. It was smart to get him out of sight."

I take a sip of the Gewd and try to focus on keeping it down.

Rubaveer helps me forward and places my hand on the cart.

"HHHang on to this for support. Ye need to look like ye're walking on yer own. Come on."

Slowly we walk back to the igloos. We reach the one I saw Jacqueline and Adam thrown into. When we run the guard's hand over the door, it opens with a blast of cold air.

"Adam, Jacqueline, it's Harper. I've come to rescue you."

"Haaaarrrrppppeerrr!" Jacqueline shivers. She lifts from the foam, wearing a white robe, hugging herself for warmth, a tear frozen to her cheek. Her eyes widen when she sees the Golden Guard beside me.

"Don't worry," I assure her, "this is Rubaveer. We've managed to get her into the armor."

"How?!"

"We can go over it all later."

"We need help!" Adam shouts from the opposite bed. He jumps out, runs to a third bed beside his, and tugs out a shriveled gray Ancient.

Though I had guessed that seeing the conditions of the long-term prisoners wouldn't be pleasant, nothing prepares me for this: Out of the bed falls what I can only describe as a rotting zombie. A hole in her cheek reveals transparent bone; strings of muscle and tendon stretch across the top and bottom of her jaw.

"She's been moaning in horrible pain. We have to save her!" Adam says in a panicked plead.

"Wwwe can't bring her," Rubaveer says.

Adam makes a funny expression, which I think is both from Rubaveer's non-digital accent and what she's said.

"She'll slow us down. Topazious has informed me that thee ship will already have difficulty maneuvering quickly with this many of us."

"Who's Topazious?" Adam asks.

"We found a pilot," I say. "He's outside."

Adam looks more surprised. "If we found a pilot then we'll just fly slower."

"I'm unaware if we'll have thee resources to save her. We risk our escape and she has only aaa low chance of survival."

"So what are we supposed to do with her, then? We can't let her die. Are you sure?"

Rubaveer kneels over, examining the Ancient's jaw. "I have not seen these kinds of cruelties from our race before. I've never seen someone this unhealthy." Rubaveer lifts the white robe and assesses the damage underneath. "She is severely injured. Wee can't help her with our resources."

"So what are our other options?" Adam asks.

"Wwwe can leave her here or —" Rubaveer holds up her arm, pointing the weapon at the sickly Ancient, waiting for Adam's word.

"Are you kidding me?"

"I am not kidding ye, though I am unsure what thee word '*kidding*' means."

Adam sighs and turns away. "Fine. Do it."

"Ttthey may not be trying to kill her, but she will be tortured for who knows how long." Rubaveer twitches her arm and the sound of crackling follows. Sparks sizzle on the Ancient's head. Rubaveer shoots three other spots on the Ancient's chest.

"That's where the largest Ancient brains are," Jacqueline says to Adam and me.

Rubaveer checks the Ancient's pulse. "Worry not, hybrids. She's not suffering anymore."

A red light bleeps on the wall.

"Put her back in. We've got to go now," Rubaveer says.

"What's that light mean?"

"It's a loss of life. I was unaware they were monitoring vital signs. They didn't want her to die, just suffer. We must hurry."

"Won't that light send someone rushing here?!" Jacqueline says. "A death?"

"Not with the EMRS readers disabled. It's the same system."

"The EMRS readers are disabled?!" Jacqueline says.

"Yes. Arl and Vulgun disabled them," I respond.

Jacqueline's mouth drops, but she doesn't say anything.

"I'll tell you later, Jacq." I reach into the cart, grabbing two of the four containment suit cubes. "Take off your robes and put these on as fast as you can! Jacqueline, you come with me.

Adam, you go with Rubaveer and Topazious, and show them the way to get back to the Military Sector."

"Why can't we all go together?" Adam asks.

"A group this large is bound to draw attention. Two Golden Guards, three containment suits and a cart. I've never seen anything like it."

"True."

When we all leave the igloo, a subtle red light is also blinking on top of it.

"That's bound to draw attention," Jacqueline says.

She's right. It looks like an emergency signal — unless! I stop. Adam and Rubaveer continue walking to the gate. Jacqueline stops with me, puzzled. I bend down and reach into the cart and around the guard folded up inside. My hands land on the two orbs. I pull them out and throw them at the igloo. Smoke fills the entire prison compound.

Adam and Rubaveer look like ghostly silhouettes when they rush back to us through the smoke. Adam smiles, "X-231? Niiiiiice. Let's get out of here."

Jacqueline, Adam, Rubaveer, the cart, and I hurry onward, huddled closely together so we don't lose one another.

We reach the exit and I swipe the guard's hand. It opens and Topazious is waiting on the other side of the arch.

"Hhhe says some Ancients have walked by," Rubaveer says.

"Okay, you two follow Adam back to the Military Sector," I say. "Jacqueline and I will go swap the guard in the cart for Brett. We'll meet up again in five minutes tops."

"HHHarper. Be as fast as you can. It won't be long before someone notices the missing guards and thee warning sign when thee contamination smoke clears," Rubaveer says.

"Don't worry, we'll be right behind you," I say.

Jacqueline and I push the cart to the alley where I stashed Brett. When I see Brett, crammed between the two boxes, I find myself frozen to the spot. He looks so lifeless. I have to really focus to see his chest rise and fall with each breath. God, I hope he makes it back to the ship.

"Is this your brother?" Jacqueline asks.

"Yes."

Her eyes trace over the black stump where Brett's arm once was. "Was that from being imprisoned?"

"Yeah."

She sighs. "I'm sorry, Harper. I don't know what else to say."

"Don't worry about it. We just have to hurry."

I reach around Brett's chest to tug him to the cart, but he's heavy. I glance over at Jacqueline, who has already managed to get the guard halfway out of the cart's storage.

I prop up Brett before I go and help her.

That's when I hear a shrill scream and a crack. I spin around and see Jacqueline on the ground. The previously unconscious guard, who I've stupidly dismissed as harmless, is halfway out of the storage compartment. His gaze travels from Jacqueline to me, with a look that sends terror rolling through my core. I reach for the tranquilizer gun beside the cart. He rolls out effortlessly and lunges at me. I want to be brave, but my eyes close on their own, in preparation for the blow … the blow that doesn't come. I open my eyes, and he's frozen there, his arm outstretched, just inches from my neck. It's a hell of a miracle I have any juice left. My fingers close around the gun, just a foot away, and I inject him with it. The world's speed returns to normal, and he smashes into me, crushing my body to the ground, his hands like steel ropes tightening around my neck. Black spots and fireworks burst over my vision. Everything starts fading into darkness ... and then it all comes back.

There's a soft thud beside me. My neck is suddenly free, and my lungs heave desperately. With the strength of a kitten, I push myself up and make my way over to Jacqueline, crawling over the unconscious guard.

Jacqueline is whimpering as she stares up at me, clutching her ribs. Tears have left shining streaks down her face. She lifts her hands to show me. The right side of her chest has an unnatural indentation to it. Her teeth are chattering from the pain.

"I must not have normal human anatomy anymore," she shivers. "Otherwise this would have caused a collapsed lung. I still have ribs though, in fact I can feel where they're broken."

"We're going to get you out of here, Jacqueline," I say. "Just wait here one second. I'm going to go put Brett in the cart —"

"Cccaaannn you use that on me?" Jacqueline says, pointing to the gun I'm holding. "Knock me out."

I bite my lip. "You have to try to walk there with me —"

"Harper, I can't —"

I take her arm, giving it a light squeeze. "I need you to try. We all need to be brave. I'll inject you as soon as we get to the ships, I promise. They probably have something in the ship we can fix you with ... or maybe in the medical supply closet."

I turn so she can't see me wipe away a tear.

"Let's hurry then. The pain is making me woozy. I might

pass out."

    I heave Brett into the cart. I shove the guard between the boxes and pop one of the leftover green gel sedative balls into his mouth for good measure. Jacqueline cries out when I help her up.

    "Do you want to hold onto the cart?" I ask.

    "No, that will make it worse, I'm just going to follow you. Don't walk quickly."

    "I won't," I say.

    She tries to stand up, placing both arms straight at her side. "Ready," she says.

CHAPTER 31

We reach the Council Chamber lobby, after a slow climb up the mountainous stairs. The windows project light patterns onto the floor and the gold emblems sparkle, marking the entrances they keep safe.

Jacqueline bends over, opens her face shield and yells a string of cuss words into her shoulder.

"You did great, Jacqueline," I say in a pant.

She releases another painful moan. "Where are they, Harper?" Her face is beaded with sweat.

"I'm not sure."

"That doesn't make sense. They left before us."

"Maybe they had to go a different way or got held up?" I say.

"And if it's the worst-case scenario? Should we try to leave without them?"

I sigh. "We can't. We can't fly a ship." I'm surprised the thought even crossed her mind.

The door of the military entrance opens.

"Jacqueline!" Tucker says, still in his containment suit. He turns to me. "Harper?!"

"Hey ..." I say and exhale with some relief. At least he's not a guard.

"Weren't you supposed to be competing?" he says.

I try to keep the nervousness from my face. "I couldn't because I tweaked my shoulder." I run my hand over it. "Thought I'd stay and help Jacqueline here instead. Make myself more useful."

"Help Jacqueline with what?" Tucker asks, his eyes darting between us.

"We've been asked to clean up some biowaste while everyone is off at the big game," Jacqueline says. "That way, there are fewer people around to get contaminated."

Tucker purses his lips. "The general thinks I didn't do a good enough job, huh? Jerk. I'll tell you. Nothing is good enough for that bastard. Just because I'm not a freaking Ancient." He kicks the air.

"Where are you going?" I ask.

"The general said that if I finished, I could catch the last part of the game. So that's where I'm going." He looks me over with that dumb expression I hope never to see again. "But I can stay and help you, pretty ladies, if you want. That's much more interestin'."

"That is very nice of you, Tucker. However, you don't have any training for this kind of stuff. It wouldn't be safe," Jacqueline says.

"I've practically been cleaning shit for the last hour. What's so different about what *you're* going to do?"

"Do you really want me to explain why exposing you to toxic waste is bad? You don't have the proper training," I say.

His expression goes blank. "You two are so fancy. Fine ... but only if you promise to sit by me at Evening Replenishment tonight." He nudges me with his elbow and winks. "I could help you out with that shoulder of yours."

I hold back a grossed-out shudder and reach out my hand to shake his. "Sure," I say. "It's a date. When the game is over, wait for me at my quarters. I'll meet you there as soon as I finish here."

A thousand-watt smile lights his face. "Of course, Miss Harper." He steps aside and bows, then walks off. We hear a happy whistling until the front doors close behind him.

"Tucker actually thinks he has a date with you." Jacqueline laughs softly.

"Had to think of something." I shrug and shake my head, too exhausted to deal with Tucker on top of everything else.

I go to the front of the Military Sector entrance and put my finger over the emblem. The slit opens and I look inside. It's empty. Thank goodness. I go back to Jacqueline. We wait for the others in the silence of the Council Chambers. I'm too worried to speak, lost in unthinkable outcomes. I open the storage compartment of the cart and make sure Brett's still breathing, staring at all the purple on his face. Just as I'm about to propose hiding in the lab, Rubaveer, Topazious, and Adam burst into the lobby.

"What happened?" I shout.

"III apologize. Adam had to lead us thee long way,"

Rubaveer says. "A group of Golden Guards were on the main street and we had to avoid them."

"Let's go," Jacqueline says as she waves her finger over the golden label and opens the entrance to the Military Sector.

Inside, reflections from the large pool of water ripple on the ceiling. The ships huddle quietly together like a flock of birds perched on sticks, with more than one hundred yellow cores pulsating at different rates as they charge and repair.

Topazious and Rubaveer rush forward while Adam and Jacqueline disappear into the emergency supply storage, reappearing moments later.

"Wwwell take this ship," Rubaveer says, pointing to one. "It looks like it has thee most charge and thee least damage." On the stem holding up the ship, she signs the signature.

Topazious runs to the cart, pulls out Brett and hoists him over his shoulder. The ship lowers to ground level and Rubaveer disappears inside.

"What the hell are you doing?!"

Both Jacqueline and I spin around. Tucker is standing at the entrance.

Topazious points his arm at Tucker.

"What did you do to that guy?!" Tucker asks, looking at Brett. "Where is his arm? Is he human?"

Jacqueline waves at Topazious to lower his arm.

"No," she says. "He's a hybrid who hasn't been stripped yet. Before he's stripped, Arl asked us to disinfect him."

"But you told me I had to leave because what you guys were doing was toxic," Tucker says.

"Yes. It's toxic to ... breathe in ... Top secret. Anyway, you should go, Tucker. We've got it all under control. We have two guards here to assist us," Jacqueline says.

"The one that just went into the ship is not a guard."

"What?" I say, stepping up to him. "Of course she is."

"She's got an accent. None of the Ancients who fly these planes got an accent like that. They use them computer voices and shit to speak English. Besides, why the hell would you need a ship now? I know for a fact that nobody is leaving till after the game."

Topazious lifts his arm again.

"Don't freaking shoot me!" Tucker holds up his hands and looks around. "Are you trying to escape? It looks that way. If you are, I want to come with you. Take me away from this place. I hate it here. Please."

"Wwwe should not take him," Rubaveer says, who's just reemerged from the ship. "Why should he go when we've left so many behind in thee prisons?"

"If you don't take me, I won't let you leave."

"How is that, you pathetic lard?" Adam asks. "You going to tell on us? How can you if we shoot you first?"

"The roof won't open unless you enter a code. It's your lucky day, as I know the code."

"How? You're nothing more than the janitor here," Adam says with a hiss.

"There's a new code every day. It's passed around on a little piece of metal so only a few military members know what it is. They've been freaked out about Sentinels for a bit. Well today, everyone left in such a hurry for the game, that my dick-hole general left it in his military suit pocket when he changed into civilian clothes. Guess who puts the huge pile of used military suits into the sterilizer? *Me*."

Jacqueline turns to Rubaveer. "Is it true? Does the roof really need a password to open?"

Rubaveer talks to Topazious and then replies, "IIIt's possible."

"So just shoot him and take it!" Adam says. "Problem solved."

"Maybe I ate it. Maybe I only have it memorized, or maybe it's hidden somewhere ... you want to take that chance?"

Rubaveer shouts, "We must take thee inconsiderate hybrid! We have to leave now."

"What about the weight?" I say.

"Our chances fall faster the longer we stay. Let's go!" she says and shouts something else to Topazious, who takes Brett and darts for the ship.

Adam and Jacqueline start running.

"Come on then, Tucker!" I yell.

Passing through the transparent shell of the ship is like breaking through a squishy membrane. The innards are nearly empty, other than the yellow blinking core that sits below the floor line, and four lumpy glass chairs — mounted in the middle, facing the outside.

Topazious and Rubaveer are strapped into two of the seats. Adam and Jacqueline are strapping Brett into another. Tucker runs for the fourth. I cram in around everyone's legs on the floor. Then Adam and Jacqueline also join me on the ground. Jacqueline is looking a little pale and damp. Adam grabs her hand and kisses it. I pat her foot reassuringly, praying she doesn't have any internal damage.

"JJJust hang on to something! Ye can strap up later!" Rubaveer says.

Topazious taps around on the dashboard. The ship rises up to the ceiling and the whole interior turns red.

"PPPassword!" Rubaveer says.

Tucker reaches into his pocket and pulls out a sliver of metal. Topazious takes it, reads it and types it in.

"Oh for god's sake," Adam says. "If only we'd searched your pockets and left you!"

We burst through a ceiling after a little resistance. The Military Sector is instantly replaced with sheer blackness.

Rubaveer rushes out of her chair, stepping carefully to avoid our limbs on the floor and starts sliding her hand over the wall.

The landscape around our ship changes from darkness to swirling colors and then blinks back to darkness. It's like a strobe light between the two states: color, black, color, black, color, black. It's making me nauseous, so I close my eyes until Rubaveer says, "Wwwe must wake him."

A slit that wasn't there before opens above Rubaveer's head, with little glass bottles clinking inside. She's holding what looks like an icicle, with a tube of red liquid running through the core. "Wwwe must find out where the coordinates of the Sentinel base are."

"Is that epinephrine?" Jacqueline says, holding onto her rib and the base of the chair Brett is strapped into.

"Similar."

"We have nothing to keep him stable once he's awake!" Jacqueline warns.

Rubaveer swipes the wall with her hand and a long silver ribbon appears. "IIIʼm going to freeze him after we get thee information we need. It will sustain him until we can provide proper medical treatment."

Before anyone else can say anything, she jams the icicle into Brettʼs chest.

In an instance, Brettʼs eyes and mouth are wide open like a fish gasping for water. "Brett! Itʼs me, Harper!" I say, trying to calm him down, my grip firm on his only arm.

His gaze falls from the ceiling to me. "Youʼve been turned." His voice is a hoarse combination of disgust and sadness.

"Iʼm still me, Brett. I just look different!"

His eyes lock onto mine. The light continues to change: color, dark, color, dark.

"Listen to me, I know thereʼs a lot to try and understand right now, but we donʼt have time to fill you in. We need to know where the Sentinels are. Do you know the coordinates?"

"Hell if Iʼm gggoing to tell you, Ancient," he slurs and tries to push me away.

Rubaveer appears beside me, grabs his face, stares him straight in the eye and says, "It is me, Rubaveer. Yer friend from the prisons. Those who watch and do nothing, watch evil prevail."

Brett blinks a few times, as if something profound has registered in his head. "39.592654 and -119.947472," comes out of his mouth robotically.

"What the hell does that mean?" Tucker says, clinging to a chair.

"It is where we are going," Rubaveer says.

Brett's eyes roll back into his head. He passes out again and starts shaking violently.

"Brett!" I shout.

"He's having a seizure!" Jacqueline screams. She and Adam rush to his side, and hold him.

"Bring him here!" Rubaveer demands, clasping the end of the silver ribbon.

Adam and Jacqueline drag him over and Rubaveer winds the silver ribbon around his waist. Suddenly Brett is in the air and the coils of the silver ribbon start winding around him like a spider wrapping its prey. Before long, he's snug in a silver cocoon with only his head sticking out. His seizures cease.

"Hhhe is safe now," Rubaveer says.

"Are you sure he won't die?!" I pant.

"Yes. He is frozen in his current state. He will neither advance nor decline until we release him," Rubaveer says.

The blinking of the light slows around us and there's a thud. We've stopped. Snow pelts down from all directions, making no sound as it hits the ship.

"Where are we now?" Adam says.

"Thee humans call it Nevada."

CHAPTER 32

"Already? How long was that? A minute?" Adam says.

Rubaveer's mouth forms into a line of disapproval. "III know, hybrid. It should have taken half a second. We had to slow down to avoid ripping aaa hole in thee planet's atmosphere. Every time thee light changed, wee were hitting different parts of thee Earth. Thee change in light depended on where Earth was in its rotation facing thee star."

Adam returns a childlike grin. "Dope."

"So they can't track this ship?" Jacqueline asks.

"Not easily. We are using a Repeater. Iiit mimics and reflects the nearby environment so wee are not detectable. They cannot detect us unless they know our sync settings, knock into us directly, or our power source runs out."

"That's neat," Adam says. "Sure happy you came along."

"Thank ye, hybrid. However, there are still ways of finding the ship. For instance, they can look for the magnetic disturbance it leaves behind, but it fades quickly. Wee confused them by overlapping trails, which was risky considering all thee Enbrotici ships currently surveying Earth's surface."

Silence follows, and we all gaze out at the snow. It's mostly dark, but I can tell it's not very deep. The bottom of the ship is pressing into the mud and the thin blanket of fresh snow extends out into the darkness. Is Brett taking us to the Nevada bunker my Mom talked about in the car with Olivia? Is it possible they made it back from California?

"This doesn't look like Nevada," Adam says. "I thought Nevada was a desert?"

"It's not all a cactus desert," I say with a little laugh, thinking back to the brown expanse I used to know. "It's a high-elevation desert that gets all the seasons." I feel a pang of longing for those times, like a firm tug on my gut.

"Where are the Sentinels?" Jacqueline asks.

"These are not thee exact coordinates," Rubaveer says. "We are eleven miles away from thee numbers Brett gave us."

"What? Why?" Tucker whines. "Pick up this thing and park it where it should be. I'm not going to walk eleven miles in this storm. Looks cold as shit outside. Plus someone has to carry the armless man!"

"It would be unwise to leave the exact coordinates in thee ship," Rubaveer responds. "And if thee other Enbrotici are able to eventually track it, Iiii don't want to lead them straight to the Sentinels."

"It's a good idea," Adam says, glaring at Tucker, daring him to utter another word.

Rubaveer pulls a silver glitter vial from a slit that forms in the control panel. She holds it out for Jacqueline. My stomach turns to knots at the sight of it.

"Are you giving me a vision?" Jacqueline asks.

"No. Volucris to inspect yer injuries. I want to make sure it's safe for ye to walk."

Jacqueline opens her face shield and sniffs the vial. I half expect her to daze off, like I probably do when I sniff the glitter, but within seconds, little specks start highlighting on her suit, as if she's being hit by thousands of tiny laser pointers. They collect on the spot where Jacqueline was kicked by the Golden Guard in the alley. The ship beeps and a holographic paragraph of Emi floats in the air.

"Two broken ribs and internal bleeding," Rubaveer says. "Thee Volucris can repair the bleeding tissue. Healing bones takes aaa few hours."

"Wow. Thanks," Jacqueline says.

Rubaveer beams.

"How come we can't heal Brett like that?" I ask.

"Jacqueline's repairs are small and she will not die during the healing process. Brett is in a much more urgent situation. He needs to be fully submerged on life support."

"Can't you heal him while he's frozen? Repair him slowly that way?"

"No. Volucris cannot move through frozen tissues. They use the blood's circulation to travel. His human heart is not beating."

"I see." I look at Brett, strapped in the chair in his silver cocoon. So pale and lifeless. "How did you know that saying, Rubaveer? The saying that made Brett tell us the coordinates?"

"III heard him crying it in his sleep when he was imprisoned with me."

"Oh," I say, surprised.

"So, as Tucker somewhat brought up, is what we're wearing going to be enough to avoid freezing to death out there?" Jacqueline says.

"Yeah!" Tucker says, pouting. "Right?!"

"Ooof course not, Jacqueline," Rubaveer responds. "Containment suits are not equipped with Repeaters or thee equipment needed to enact Stealth mode. You need interplanetary armor."

"Well, that's an issue," Adam says. "Seeing that we don't have any."

Rubaveer blinks, confused. "Wee do, hybrid." She maneuvers between us, weaving through the crowded cockpit. On the other side she runs her hand over the translucent wall, and a slit opens. She turns around and glances at me, Adam, and Jacqueline. She shuffles through various items and takes out four black cubes covered in shiny scales. With them in hand, she returns to the main dashboard and places the cubes on it. She taps around on the hieroglyphic-like interface. The cubes each spark blue. She removes them from the dashboard and hands one to Adam, Jacqueline, Tucker, and me.

"Ooour Golden armor can calibrate for this environment, so Topazious and I do not need to change. I've just synced everyone's armor so thee Repeaters will work properly together, as long as ye stay in a range of 400 feet. When thee time comes, all of ye will need my code to remove yer armor. Now remove yer containment suits," she says.

Adam clears his throat. "We took off those white robes they had us in, in prison. So ... um ... Jacqueline and I are naked under here."

"Thee armor is only a little less comfortable against bare skin," Rubaveer says.

"Okay then," Adam nods slowly. "Why don't the dressed people change first?"

"What about our gray uniforms, Rubaveer?" I ask.

"Yes. Those work with the armor," she says.

I set my cube on the ground and remove my containment suit. Adam, Jacqueline, and Tucker are all watching me in my gray bodysuit.

I pick up the cube. "Slam it against my chest?"

"PPPrecisely," Rubaveer says.

The cube makes the sound of shattering glass as it hits my body. Wet, cold, silvery liquid spreads over me like a thick layer of oil. It disperses outward, enveloping my arms and legs, spreading to the tips of my fingers and toes. A helmet materializes, then I feel a sharp prick on my neck. I smack my hand against it. "Ouch!"

"Iiintravenous connection," Rubaveer says. "For replenishment, monitoring, health and pain management."

Tucker's eyes widen. "How bad did that hurt?"

"Just a little sting. Your turn."

"Alright." Tucker removes his containment suit and slams the cube against his chest. When the black has spread over him, he looks like a shorter version of the iridescent black soldiers in the Military Sector. *Much* more badass than the containment suits.

"Oh come on. It didn't sting that bad, Harper." He winks at me.

Adam clears his throat. "Now you all turn around. The Adam and Jacqueline show isn't free. Tucker, you cover your eyes! Harper, you keep your eyes on him!"

"I'm not gonna peek!" Tucker says defensively.

They both change while all of us face the snow.

"Sweet! I'm a badass ninja," Adam says, crouching down and swishing his arms through the air. He hits Tucker, pretending it's an accident. "Oopsie!"

"Hey! Watch it, buddy!" Tucker says, taking an aggressive step toward him. Jacqueline gets between them and warns Adam with a glare.

Tucker scoots closer to me. "You look nice in this stuff, Harper."

"Creep," Adam says.

A series of beeps comes from Topazious' direction. On the walls of the ship, thin beams of light begin drawing an expansive landscape of hills around us, as if we've been smacked into the middle of a 3-D blueprint. Topazious swipes at the air. The simulated 3-D landscape moves forward as if we're moving hundreds of feet at a time.

"What's that?" I ask.

Rubaveer answers, "It's aaa land survey —"

"No, that over there." I point to a hill ahead on the simulation, where angular shapes are just peeking over the horizon. "What's there?"

Topazious grabs the air and pulls it forward. The blueprints slide over the hill and reveal a strange sight: Empty steel building frames, dented street lamps, and cars sitting on axles, their structures riddled with holes.

"That's not good," Adam remarks.

Topazious rolls the survey further, down one of the bigger streets. The simulation comes to an arch, and the blueprints begin to trace out shapes. In half shattered neon letters, atop of a heap of rubble, lays the giant word, 'Reno'.

Outside the ship, clouds in the night sky look like marble, plump with snow and highlighted by the pale moon.

When we get far enough away, the ship disappears into the environment as if it had been a mirage, leaving the six of us amongst little snow-covered shrubs that remind me of cotton balls.

We move so silently that I have to turn around and check that the others haven't disappeared, as if we're ghosts. As we approach the city, the snow behind us remains perfectly smooth and untouched.

"Where are our footprints, Rubaveer?" I shout ahead at her, hoping she can hear me through the armor.

"That was painful! Speak quuieter!" Her voice says as though she's beside me, from some sort of speaking system in the helmets.

"Thee armor stops traceable markings from happening. Just like thee Repeater for thee ship and yer suits, it is aaa function of Stealth mode."

We come to the top of the hill.

An eerie aurora borealis of blues, pinks, and greens is

winding and twisting through a skeleton of a city. Below the haunting colors, at ground level, fallen clumps of cement lie on the street, bars of steel clawing out of them like bony fingers. Icicles drape from neon signs, power lines string across rusted cars, and all the colors of the sky above tint everything in a ghostly glow.

"Jeez, you'd think a nuke went off or somethin'," Tucker says, cutting through the thick atmosphere like a blunt knife.

"Yeah," I choke out.

"Thee Volucris work quickly. My guess is that they were released here sixty Vala ago. After they finish euthanizing the humans of an area, they eliminate all signs of the species."

"What's a Vala?" Tucker asks.

"A Vala is 100,000 gi, or what the Ancients call a full day," Jacqueline says. "So sixty Vala is roughly two months."

Topazious adjusts Brett on his shoulder and then opens his palm. A little wisp of glowing blue smoke rises and breaks apart, creating a dotted line that leads down to the main street. The group follows it.

The wind howls through the city as if it were the voices of the dead themselves. Windows from the dark and empty buildings stare, hollow as skulls.

A loud clang comes from somewhere to our right. Topazious and Rubaveer immediately lift their arms, and aim their weapons.

As we all turn around, a black crow pauses atop of the hood of a rusted van, and seems to look straight at us, a nut of some sort in its beak. After it appears to have examined us, it goes back to banging its nut against the van.

"I think it can see us. I hope this Stealth mode is working, Rubaveer," Adam says.

"Do not worry. Iiit is still enabled," she responds.

The group continues through downtown like a funeral march. Without much to identify, I try to remember what it was like before it all fell to pieces. I hadn't been downtown many times, but it's so strange that this is the same city where I grew up. I struggle to compute that nearly everyone I've ever known was here and may be dead. My friends. My soccer team. All those lives turned to dust.

Olivia and Mom made it past this part, I think. I hope.

About three hours outside of town, halfway through a mass of steep rocky hills, the snow picks up and the world around us becomes blindingly white. Anything further than a three-foot radius is hard to see, including the dots that Topazious has been using to navigate.

As we go onward, Topazious develops a limp that seems to get worse with every mile.

"Shouldn't we wait for the storm to pass?" I finally say to Rubaveer, who I can barely see at the rear of the line. "We should rest. We can't lose each other."

"There are only six miles to complete now," she responds.

Tucker huffs, "I'm. Real. Tired. And hungry."

"There was that little dug out we passed a minute ago. The ground was relatively flat there," Adam says.

"Yes. Stop there. Please," Tucker begs.

"Is it safe to sit still until the storm has passed, Rubaveer?" Jacqueline asks.

"Yes. Iiif it isn't for too long."

"Let's give it an hour and go from there, then," I propose. "The weather here doesn't usually last long."

We backtrack and find the dugout.

Tucker plops down first. He lies on his back and spreads his limbs like a starfish, groaning with contentment. Then he looks at me and pats the spot beside him. I pretend I didn't see it.

The rest of us huddle and lean against each other's backs in a circle. Topazious places Brett, still wrapped snugly in the silver cocoon, at the tip of his legs, safely in sight. The snowfall gets so heavy, it's like being stuck in static. I have to tap my fingers on Jacqueline to remind myself that I'm not alone. She gives me little squeezes on the arm for reassurance.

"Hey, Adam," I say, "how did you guys get caught? Did Sontarx betray you?"

"I don't think he betrayed us intentionally," he says darkly. "I think he was up to something else and got caught. We were out collecting discs when they arrested us. They said they would question me after the Agility Game and dropped me off at the prisons. Thank God you saved us. Who knows what we were in for."

"Are you sure he wasn't betraying us the whole time, Adam? Perhaps it was his plan all along," Jacqueline says.

"Unless he's got some sort of psychotic disorder that can change his mind without a trace of his old emotions, I'm positive I didn't sense any dishonesty."

"But why only you and Jacqueline? Why not me too?" I ask.

"Because I hadn't told Sontarx about you, Harper, he only knew I wanted to start a life with Jacq, so I'm assuming that's why they took her too."

"I see. Where did you put the epinephrine, Jacqueline?" I ask. "It wasn't in the cart."

"It was in the pocket of my uniform, under the containment suit. I forgot to take it out."

"Oh." We all go quiet.

"Poor Sontarx," Jacqueline says, "If he truly didn't tell on us, I hope he hears of our escape and knows that we're grateful. May his suffering be minimal."

Adam takes a deep breath. "Well, thank goodness our hero Harper came along. That was some impressive bravery. How the hell did you manage to pull all that off?"

I relay everything that happened after Jacqueline got captured: how Arl and Vulgun helped disable the EMRS readers, and all the other things that popped up along the way.

"Very well done, Harper," Jacqueline says. "Thank you so much for what you did."

"I know you guys would have done it for me," I say.

"We sure would have," Adam says. "Take that, ya asshole Ancients!"

Rubaveer huffs and crosses her arms. "Iii am not sure what that means, but thee way ye are saying it, I assume it means wee are bad. In addition to Topazious and me, ye also had thee Golden Guard and two other Enbrotici scientists who assisted ye. That means there is a chance that more could be persuaded, if presented with thee proper evidence."

"I only meant the ones who tried to keep us down," Adam says. "But you're right, some Ancients are pretty awesome. Especially you and your bad-ass pilot friend here."

Rubaveer's expression lightens. "Bbbad ass sounds like aaa good word."

"It's the best word," Adam says.

We all chuckle, for the first time in a while.

"What do you guys think the Sentinels are really like?" Adam says. "Do you think we're walking into a death trap?"

For a split second, I wrestle with telling them about my dreams, but decide to keep them to myself for now ... not without a tinge of guilt.

"I think there's more to the Sentinels than we're being told," Jacqueline says. "It's fishy that the Golden Guard helped Adam, and that they suspect the Base of Ki has been infiltrated. Maybe Arl and Vulgun are involved with the Sentinels, and that's why they helped us?"

"I've been thinking about that too," Adam says.

"What if the Sentinels kill us when we meet them? We don't look human anymore," Tucker says.

"I don't think they'll *kill* us." I look at Brett's form in the silver cocoon. "I mean, my family were Sentinels and they didn't kill me. They probably want more hybrids on their side for the army the Ancients have been telling us about. The Sentinels might not be good, but they might help us get the Ancients off of Earth."

Rubaveer breaks in, "III do really hope to meet thee Sentinels! I'd love to meet more humans! But I do find thee fact that thee Sentinels still exist here to be unlikely. If they survived the Sleeping Syndrome thus far, they would then have to avoid being found by thee vast amount of Volucris in thee area. The chances of that seem very low. I did not expect the process to be this far along." She ponders for a moment. "Iiiin order for thee Sentinels to sustain themselves, they would need an airtight environment and find a way to block our heat-sensing technology, among many other issues. They would also need a way to deal with Volucris contamination. I don't know if they had time to prepare for an undertaking that large."

It's another blow to my hope of finding Olivia alive.

"Wait," Tucker says, "So you're saying we could have escaped for no freaking reason? The Ancients might be jerks, but I left two square meals a day and a roof over my head to live like a freaking nomad."

Adam scoffs. "If you recall, nobody wanted you to come."

"Iii'm unsure what our survival chances are if we don't find thee Sentinels," Rubaveer says. "And thee Volucris can be programmed to hunt specific beings. If we ever leave Stealth mode, thee Base of Ki could find us."

CHAPTER 33

Early morning sun glitters on fresh, thick snow. Topazious leads the way up a rocky hill, his limp better after the enforced rest during the blizzard. Even with Brett slung over his shoulder, he effortlessly seems to glide through the terrain full of millions of ankle-twisting rocks and bushes. Rubaveer is not far behind, leaping from stone to stone as if it were a simple hopscotch game.

For hours, we forge through lofty hills and zigzagging paths of endless snowy bushes. No matter how far we walk, the large mountains always seem to remain the same, taunting distance away.

Then, out of nowhere, a giant oak tree rises over the desert, towering over a valley of monotonous little shrubs.

"Thee coordinates," Rubaveer says, pointing at it.

When we reach the base of the tree, Topazious removes Brett from his back and leans him against the trunk, which has the girth of a minivan. The rafter-sized branches break up the sky like stained glass, and sunbeams make bright fractals on the gravel where the tree has protected it from snowfall.

Topazious runs his hands along the trunk's bark, leaning in close to examine it.

"Now what?" Adam asks.

Rubaveer replies, "III don't know."

Topazious continues his examination of the tree, doing laps around it and climbing around the limbs.

"I guess we wait?" Adam says.

Tucker picks up a stick and hurls it. "Anyone want to go on a hunting trip with me? I think I saw a rabbit back there. I need some real food."

"Ye should not be hungry. Ye are receiving replenishment and hydration intravenously."

Tucker smacks his lips loudly. "Well it's not doing anything about the taste in my mouth. Nothing that a little rabbit wouldn't solve." He wipes snow off a branch and holds it out in front of him. "Or a bite of snow. This desert's got more moisture than my mouth." He knocks on his face shield, which sparks at the pressure of his knuckles. "Let me get this off and get a taste. Whet the palate a little."

As he says it, I feel my throat stick together when I swallow, my tongue dry against the roof of my mouth. It's gotten really stuffy in these suits because we've been breathing recycled air for hours. It's a bit claustrophobic, too.

Fluffy snowflakes begin to drift lightly from the sky. I imagine letting them land on my tongue and the fresh, cold air on my face.

"Is it safe, Rubaveer? To open our face shields and get some fresh air?" I ask.

"If you had no problems breathing your native atmosphere before, I think you will be fine."

"And the Volucris won't attack us?" Jacqueline asks pleadingly.

"Stealth mode will protect ye from thee Volucris that are not synced with us. And as ye should recall, Volucris will not attack any Enbrotici or any Enbrotici-made material. Harper was not affected by thee Sleeping Syndrome. Since she is a hybrid, my guess is that her Enbrotici DNA protected her from harm. So I would guess that it protects thee rest of ye hybrids as well."

"That's how they said they found the first hybrids," Jacqueline says. "They found the Kenyans in the Canopy because they weren't killed by the Sleeping Syndrome."

"When was thee last hybrid brought in?" Rubaveer asks.

"They were brought in randomly all the time," Jacqueline says. "Maybe even last week."

"So it would appear hybrids are still not harmed by Volucris or the Sleeping Syndrome."

"So, we cool to open these things then?" Tucker says.

"Be our guest," Adam responds.

Tucker flicks out his Scanner and opens his face shield, his finger hovering over the button to close it again. The silence stretches out for a good few seconds before he intervenes with his big, relieved laugh. "Dang! It's cold out here, but it feels nice!" He takes a big breath and then slowly exhales, creating a puff of steam. "Nothing like the smell of fresh, crisp, cold air!"

He breaks an icicle off a branch and starts sucking it. "Oh that's the best icicle I've ever tasted."

He quickly breaks off two more and crunches them down.

"Well, it seems safe," Jacqueline says, lifting her hand to activate her Scanner, freezing with apprehension.

But I can't wait any longer, so I open mine. Cold, refreshing air rushes over my face and scalp. With a few deep breaths, I feel a pleasant little sting in my lungs. Then I spin and stick out my tongue, catching as many snowflakes as I'm able.

"See. Good stuff, huh?" Tucker shouts.

I stop spinning. Specks of cold hit my cheeks and forehead. "Good stuff," I agree.

Tucker gives me an icicle and then breaks two more off for Jacqueline and Adam. They remove their face shields and we all toast one another cheerfully.

It's weird to taste something that isn't Gewd. The dusty-icy flavor brings to mind eating snow on Christmas. Then the memory of my sister and brother sledding down a hill.

I get another tickle in the back of my throat, then I'm wheezing. My fingers close around my neck. When I try to speak, nothing comes out.

Someone is giving me the Heimlich maneuver.

"I think she's got some ice stuck!" Jacqueline shouts from behind me.

No I don't! But I can't speak to tell her that. My lungs heave. The world begins to spin. Adam tries to hold me up.

Rubaveer shoves Jacqueline aside and grabs my wrist. "Your Scanner, Harper!"

Through the fog, I barely manage to make the gesture.

Sparks light up in front of my face and I hear the whooshing of air.

"Wait, hybrids!" I hear Rubaveer say.

My lightheadedness fades and I begin to feel stable again. My breathing slows.

Rubaveer's helmet drops into view, and I see myself laying in snow in its reflection. "That's it, Harper." Rubaveer pats my shoulder. "Ye will be okay."

"What the hell just happened?!" Adam shouts.

"Harper can no longer breathe Earth's air."

"What?" I cough.

"Cooms has much higher levels of carbon dioxide than oxygen. When ye removed yer face shield, Harper, ye weren't getting enough carbon dioxide, and lost the ability to breathe."

I try to sit up and Jacqueline rushes over to help me.

"How did I breathe when I lived on Earth then?" I say in a raspy voice.

"Ye must have had an implant converter of some sort. Ooor something's been altered since they've changed ye at the Base of Ki."

I motion to the others. "How are they breathing then? Without implants or whatever?"

"My guess is that since thee DNA is mixed, some of thee hybrids will be more adapted than others."

"So are you saying some of us could be adapted to breathe in both atmospheres?" Jacqueline asks, her hand steadies my shoulder.

Rubaveer shrugs. "It's possible. It's also possible that some of ye may have implants to breathe at the Base of Ki. Maybe

Harper's Earth one was damaged."

Everyone turns their face shields back on.

I'm shaky and weak after the ordeal, so Jacqueline helps me over to the giant tree so I'm able to rest. As my eyes trace the branches, running over them like a mouse through a maze, something catches the light, glinting from one of the tallest limbs. I squint, but can't make much out.

"Jacqueline!" I say. She glances up from drawing in the gravel with Adam. I point at it. "What's that?"

She hurries over and holds her hand over her eyes to block the sun. "I don't know, looks like a silver ribbon? Maybe a piece of garbage?"

There's a loud squawk and four crows descend upon the branches, cawing at each other, loud and thunderous against the otherwise motionless snowy desert. One of them hops down closer to Jacqueline and me, his black, beady eyes staring in our direction. The bird utters two more loud squawks, returns to the others, and they all fly away together.

"I swear they can see us," I say.

Jacqueline frowns.

I look around the tree. The silver glinting object is gone.

Dusk sets upon the desert and Topazious leaves us to go scouting for anything unusual. Jacqueline makes a mancala game by digging two rows of small holes in the mud. With the help of the moonlight, we're able to find enough similar-sized pebbles to play the game and before long all the hybrids alternate playing one another. An owl perches in our tree, but flies away when Adam throws a stone and does a victory dance after beating all four of us. That's until Rubaveer comes, learns the rules, and then beats him in two moves. She makes sure to fill in the Mancala holes and scatter the rocks as soon as we're done.

Tucker argues for a campfire, even though everyone is plenty warm. Rubaveer points out that contained fire is unnatural and could draw attention, which seems obvious to everyone else.

After that, Rubaveer agrees to keep watch while everyone else sleeps.

In the middle of the night, the sound of someone calling my name wakes me. "Olivia!" I say, but there's no answer. After failing to fall back asleep, I open my eyes and find Rubaveer sitting on a large branch overhead, her leg dangling over the side, swinging back and forth.

"Did you call my name?" I say to her in a whisper, so I don't wake the others.

She startles, and peers down at me. "Ye are awake now? No, Harper it wasn't me. I've adjusted the sound so only ye and I will hear each other."

I nod. "Any sign of Topazious?" I ask, climbing in the tree to join her.

"Not yet."

Between Tucker's snores, the night is so silent that my ears hum.

"Ye were talking in your sleep. Like yer brother,"

Rubaveer says.

"He's not my real brother."

"He may not be genetically related to ye, but he cared for ye thee same."

"It's hard to know what's true."

She leans back, gazing at the night sky. That's when I see my star, Antares, glinting brilliantly red amongst the cloudy appearance of the Milky Way, because there's no longer any light pollution to obscure it. How is *this* the same star I saw so many months ago? The same star I gazed upon the moment all of this started.

Rubaveer sighs.

"What are you thinking about?" I ask.

"Hmm? I'm wondering if I'll ever see Cooms again. I wonder if the main population will ever find out what's happening here. I suspect Earth isn't thee only place Alexiuus is doing a mass extinction."

"How many other species are out there?" My eyes follow a shooting star.

"Countless," she says, "Which is why I'm so happy that out of so many, I got paired with ye humans." She grins. "Our species seem to have some relatable similarities."

"I agree, Rubaveer. If only we could have met under different circumstances."

A wolf howls in the distance.

There's a crunch from our right. Then another from the left.

Rubaveer and I freeze. She lifts her arm, pivoting her weapon in all directions.

Then dozens of yellow eyes lift from the bush line.

"Can they see us, Rubaveer?" I ask urgently.

"I ... I ... don't know how it is possible," she says slowly.

My heart hammers. "Adam! Jacqueline!" I scream, worried they might not hear me.

Jacqueline jolts up. "What?" She says in surprise.

"Grab Adam and Tucker and get in the tree!"

She looks up at me and Rubaveer. I slowly motion to the eyes surrounding us.

Jacqueline reaches for Adam and starts pulling him into the tree. With her other hand, she grabs Tucker's arm. He wakes with a yelp.

"Get in the tree! Get in the tree!" she urges.

I glance at Brett, who's too far away for anyone to reach. I pray because he's frozen, that they presume him dead.

Two wolves leave the protection of the sagebrush and sniff around the trunk, so close to Brett I can hardly contain myself.

Adam pelts the wolf with a snowball. It jumps and then sticks its nose in the air, moving in our direction.

"I'm not sure how well these suits are working here, Rubaveer," Adam says.

A third wolf exits the sagebrush, smells the air, and sits directly below us. In his mouth hangs a long, silver ribbon.

"Jacqueline, is that what was in the tree?" I say.

"I have no idea," she says, making a snowball and hitting two wolves with them.

"Is Brett going to be okay down there, Rubaveer?" I ask.

"The substance Brett is wrapped in is strong. He is safe for now, but it can be worn down enough to break through," Rubaveer says.

"How long does it take to wear down?"

"They are kind of cute, aren't they?" she says.

"Rubaveer ..." I urge.

"Oh yes. I am unaware of the strength of their bite. How strong would you say it is compared to a human's?"

"I don't know. Three or four times as strong?" Adam says.

"Hmm ... maybe it would take them about 1,200 gi to break through, at full bite strength."

"Jacqueline?" Adam says with exasperation.

"About twenty-ish minutes?" Jacqueline responds.

"Well, that's not great news," Adam says.

"Can you shoot them or something?" I say.

Rubaveer holds up her arm. "Yes, but shooting could give away our location, other Enbrotici might be able to trace it."

"Maybe they should just use wolves and crows to find us!" Adam says.

"Would you like me to shoot, Harper?"

I hesitate. "Just wait. Let's see what happens, maybe they'll leave him alone?"

As if they heard me, a wolf wraps his teeth around Brett's feet and begins to tug at him. The other two help.

"Holy shit!" Tucker shouts. "They're gonna eat him!"

"Should I shoot now, Harper?"

"Wait. Just wait a little longer!" Panic swirls through me.

More wolves leave the sagebrush and help pull Brett into the dark desert.

"Harper?" Rubaveer says.

"Yes. Do it!"

I close my eyes and look away, waiting for the sound of

shooting that doesn't come. Opening my eyes again, I yell, "Shoot!"

Rubaveer is still, her arm outstretched.

I can just see the wolves' heads in the bush line now. "Rubaveer! They're taking him away! Shoot!"

She leaps from the branches, and dashes in the direction of the last wolf. Just as she's about to disappear into the dark, she turns and yells, "We must go!"

CHAPTER 34

My legs don't seem to carry me fast enough, still aching from the escape and hike. With only the starlight, I swerve between and leap over hundreds of bushes in the direction I saw Rubaveer and the wolves go.

"Wait, guys!" Tucker shouts somewhere behind me.

Finally, I almost smack into two golden figures standing in a clearing. My foot nearly trips over a rock they're looking at.

"Hello, Harper." Rubaveer waves.

It takes me a couple of seconds to register the scene before me. Topazious is now kneeling over the black stone that almost killed me. Brett is lying unharmed right next to him, encased in his cocoon, and Rubaveer has the command of the three wolves, who are sitting at her feet like enthusiastic dogs.

Adam and Jacqueline run up, gasping for breath.

"What the hell is going on?" Adam huffs.

"Topazious has been watching thee tree from afar," Rubaveer

says, "scouting for visitors. He noticed thee same birds and wolves coming and going from this spot. He suspects there is an opening because thee animals disappear here."

A wolf starts to bark and whine.

Rubaveer looks down at it. "I'm sorry. Iii do not speak yer language, but I hope ye will teach me while I'm here."

Topazious dusts snow off the black stone to reveal a carved symbol on the surface — the figure eight on its side: an infinity sign.

A wolf howls, and the icy hum of his voice shivers through the quiet. The rest of the pack joins him and the dead of night becomes a haunting choir, so strong that it echoes off the hills and my insides.

A jagged crack splits in the ground beneath Brett. Topazious grabs him, and yanks him to the side. Mud and snow separate, accompanying the sound of an electric whir. The crack pulls apart. At first there's just a giant muddy hole. Then rocks begin to stack like stairs, leading down into a tunnel.

"Guys, guys," Tucker pants as he finally reaches us. "Is everything okay?" He puts his hands on his knees. "You went a little — what the?" He pauses when he spots the tunnel and then the wolves. "Topazious?" he says.

The howling halts. The wolves lower their heads and hurry past us to the tunnel.

"Ooooohh. I think they want us to follow," Rubaveer says, as she jumps and claps her hands.

"Should we?" Jacqueline asks with apprehension.

"It could be a trap," Adam says.

"Or exactly what we've been waiting for," I say keenly. "Why would the Ancients go through all this trouble when they could just scoop us up back at the tree? This has to be Sentinels!" I turn and chase the wolves.

The stairs drop down a hundred feet. A glowing ball, I'm assuming sent from Topazious, leaps before me, lighting my way.

The walls of the tunnel are made of loose clay mixed with roots and rocks as if it were freshly dug. The only tracks on the floor are paw prints.

I find the pack of wolves ahead at a dead end, their tails thump against the ground with excitement.

Rubaveer arrives at my side. "Harper, are ye alright?"

"I'm fine. The tunnel just stops."

"Do you think it's broken?" Adam asks, leading Jacqueline by the hand. Topazious, Brett, and Tucker arrive behind them.

The wolves pant and scratch the dirt — an adrenaline-filled minute passes uneventfully.

"I'm getting a bad feeling 'bout this place," Tucker says, backing up slowly.

That's when the electric whir sound resumes, and the ground beneath our feet collapses.

We move fast, sliding down a dark slope to an illuminated doorway ahead.

We land in a room with glass walls. Looking in on us are more than fifty humans pointing Ancient-looking weaponry. Other than Brett, this is the first time I've seen real humans in I don't know how long.

Humans beating each other with bats.

Humans strangling each other.

Humans killing themselves with guns.

I shake my head to rid myself of all the awful images I saw at the Base of Ki. The lights flicker and I search the crowd for Olivia, my mom, or my clone. But I don't recognize anyone. Maybe they're just not here right now. Or somewhere in the back.

Glancing around, I see we're not in any normal cave. This is a command center.

A beeping sound begins and the wolves squeeze through a small opening that leads out of our glass enclosure. Then they go into another area, beside ours — they can move freely but we're in a sectioned-off glass hallway.

The wolves push through each section, first sprayed with steam, then showered with sparks, and finally flashed with fog. When they've made it through the entire hallway, they join the people in the cave.

A man steps forward, the crowd parts for him, and it takes a second to realize that I'm not in one of my dreams. *It's him.* The man who brought us Brett. The man who sent away Olivia with the clone.

He's dressed in a gray turtleneck and pants. He has a serious face with wide, pointy cheekbones, deep eye sockets, and bulging blue eyes. He throws something to the wolves and they gobble it with excitement. A wolf pounces forward and starts pawing at the other side of the glass from where we're standing.

"I can't see you, but I know you're there," he says. His voice is coming from speakers in our glass enclosure. "Funny thing ... some animals can sense Ancients, despite all the fancy technology. Show yourself or we'll set fire to that entire chamber. Then we'll have to see what you look like as ashes."

"Hhhumans!" Rubaveer says excitedly to our group. "Though they do not seem like friendly humans." She frowns.

"I ... I ... know him," I say. "He knows where my sister is." I reach for the glass but Rubaveer holds me back.

"Can we trust him?" Jacqueline asks.

I search the room again for my sister and mom, hoping that they must be somewhere right behind him. "I don't know," I say breathlessly.

"I suppose it makes sense that not all humans are nice. Not all Enbrotici are nice." Rubaveer taps her face shield thoughtfully. "In that case, I will keep ye in Stealth mode until we figure this out." She touches something on her wrist and her figure flashes yellow.

A gasp escapes the crowd of humans.

The man flinches, steps back, his head lifting to meet Rubaveer's tall stature. His bulging blue eyes drop from her helmet, and trace her impressive golden armor.

Lights continue to flicker, contouring everyone in shadow. Rubaveer opens her face shield and her copper skin shimmers when the lights are brightest. "Hhhello, great human. We come in peace. We seek asylum from thee Ancients. We escaped a few days before and wish to see thee Sentinels."

"The wolves have indicated that you have a human or humans with you. Is that true?" the man says flatly.

"We have one pure human, four half-human hybrids, and two Ancients. We believe thee human is aaa Sentinel."

The man glances at those around him. "Make the pure

human visible first."

Rubaveer taps her wrist and blinks yellow again, taking Brett from Topazious.

When Rubaveer reappears with Brett lifelessly hanging over her shoulder, the crowd lets out another gasp. Even though Brett is wrapped in silver, his puffy face is still visible through the helmet.

"We did not do this to him. His injuries are from his time in prison. We saved him. He needs immediate medical attention once he's been unfrozen."

"Do you know his name?" the man asks.

"Oooh, yes. He told me his name is Brett Loomis."

The crowd hisses. A woman comes forward and stands beside the man, eyes wide, mouth hanging open. At first she's just another middle-aged, prettyish, tired woman. But on second glance, shock grasps me. *Mom!* She looks ten years older. Her cheeks have hollowed from weight loss, and the shape of her clavicles are like hangers under her dark green shirt.

I want to scream through the glass and beg her to tell me where Olivia's gone, but I'm not sure what the right next move is.

"Please place *Brett* in the next chamber," the man says. "We need to get him medical treatment immediately."

The door next to our chamber opens. Rubaveer doesn't move. "I would love to hand him over, human, but we need thee guarantee of safe passage. We need to stay with him."

The man folds his arm, his face stagnant. "How do we know you won't cause us harm? How can you guarantee that you are not colluding with the other Ancients? You are wearing the armor of a very well-trained fighter, after all."

"Ye can see we are in Stealth mode. Thee seven of us have been for nearly two days. There was no one else in range when we disappeared into yer hiding place. Yer underground fortress will block any outside communication, which is why I guess ye have built it down here. That and to avoid Volucris. Ye know we are no longer traceable." She pauses, awaiting a response. The man taps his foot, seemingly unimpressed.

Rubaveer continues, "Ooone of the hybrids we have is also a sibling of Brett."

The man and my mom both perk up. "Which one?"

Is this a game? Are they asking about the clone?

"We will reveal the sibling when you let us enter," Rubaveer says.

"Give us proof. Tell us something that only they would know."

Rubaveer taps her wrist which then flashes, returning her to Stealth mode. She looks to me with anticipation in her bright copper eyes, resting a hand on me.

I'm the one who's not a clone, I think.

"Harper?" Ruabaveer says. "Think of a fact about yer mother without being too specific, in case another sibling is more valuable than ye."

"My Mom ... she ... has a scar under her left foot from stepping on Lego."

Rubaveer nods and flashes back. "Thee mother has a scar from a lay-ae-go on her left foot."

The man lifts his hand in the air like a composer and

swooshes his finger downward, causing a bunch of collars to rain on us. "Each one of you must place a collar around your neck for safety reasons. If you are deceiving me, those collars will cut off circulation to your brain and you'll pass out ... or worse, if you really piss me off. Once you've put them on, step into the next chamber and wait for further instructions."

Rubaveer doesn't put her collar on, but asks us to, then has us enter the next chamber. She stays behind, adjusting Brett so her arm is around his neck.

"Iii'm going to make ye all visible now," Rubaveer says. Then she says something to Topazious. Topazious nods and taps Adam's wrist. Adam flashes, and the people in the crowd suddenly go very still, staring with wide-open eyes and mouths.

"What ... is that? What have you done to that Ancient ... human ... whatever it is?" the man says with revulsion.

"He's a hybrid," Rubaveer says, as if it's the simplest thing in the world to understand.

"That does not look like any hybrid I've ever seen. He looks like something concocted in some Ancient lab."

"Hey buddy, watch yourself!" Adam points his finger at the glass. "They said you guys made me this way."

Mom comes forward. "Humans do not make hybrids. Only Ancients make hybrids."

"That's not entirely true," says a slender boy, about my age, standing near the front. A wild mop of black, curly hair falls just below his ears. Tattoos peek out from under the sleeves of his black shirt. Like almost everyone here, he looks like he hasn't seen sunlight in a while. "There are plenty of humans who have worked with Ancients to build hybrids. We have proof."

"Well they don't look like that," someone says in the back.

Adam responds, "That's not what I was told when they pulled me apart."

Rubaveer claps. "Hhhumans. When ye are finished reprimanding someone for an appearance that they have no control over, ye'll be shown the other hybrids."

"Go on then," the man says.

Topazious presses Jacqueline's wrist, Tucker's, and lastly mine. Topazious disappears once I leave Stealth mode.

My mom approaches. The room goes so quiet that I can hear the thundering of my hybrid heart.

"Harper, is that you?" She places a hand on the glass.

I get a sting in my throat. How can I hate her and miss her so much at the same time?

Her eyes shimmer. "What have they done to you?"

"They said you did this to me," I whisper. I almost can't bear to look at her. She's so close it's unreal, like I'll wake up any second back in the Base of Ki and she'll wisp away.

"Where's Olivia?" My voice shakes. I feel Jacqueline take my hand.

Mom looks down with a sad expression that terrifies me.

"There will be time for catching up later," the man says forcefully. "Where is the other Ancient?!"

At that, Topazious appears, towering over everyone. Mom stumbles backwards. The lights finally stop flickering.

"He's friendly," I say to her. "They're all friendly. Both of these Ancients were imprisoned for trying to help humans.

We're here to help the human race now."

Mom studies us for a moment. "We should let them pass."

"Your daughter could have been brainwashed," the man says. "We've heard what they're trying to do with the hybrids."

"If they're any trouble, kill them," she says, with a sudden harsh tone. "Put them under watch for a few weeks. We've got nothing to lose. More Ancient knowledge can only help us."

"Molly, you're —"

"Rubaveer can help stop the RSE Sleeping Syndrome!" I shout, pointing to her.

Rubaveer looks at me, tilting her head. I should have told her sooner, but with everything going on, it didn't occur to me.

"Impossible. How?" The man responds.

Rubaveer smiles. "Iii know how it was engineered on Procell." She claps her hands. "Though I have yet to see what human technology can do."

There's a burst of murmuring.

"Let them in, Patrick," Mom says. "We need every shot we can get. We're losing out there!"

"Yeah! Let them in!" someone else shouts. The statement rolls through the crowd.

A glass door bursts open and we file through the hallway: doused with sparks, water, steam, and then wind.

When we enter the last chamber, guns are aimed at our heads and strong hands grasp our arms.

CHAPTER 35

With guns jabbing into our sides, we're prodded into a large, round cement room.

Two Sentinels bring a stretcher and Rubaveer gives them Brett. The crowd parts as they carry him away.

The bulging blue-eyed man motions to his people to step back. Then he turns to us. "Remove your armor now."

I find my mom in the crowd and try to make pleading eye contact with her, but she's looking at the man.

Adam takes Jacqueline's hand. "Some of us are naked under here," he says.

"And three of us cannot breathe Earth's air without the armor," I add, my voice unsteady.

"I count two Ancients. Who is the third?" He asks.

"Me," I say.

He gives me a long, icy stare. "You, a *half* human, cannot breathe oxygen?"

"Not this much oxygen." He somehow makes me feel ashamed for what I am.

My Mom, beside him, looks away.

Another woman steps forward, carting two transparent domes that are large enough to go over an Ancient's head. Clear tubes connect both of them to a small round tank labeled, "Carbon Dioxide Additive."

"Ancients —" the man says, but stops when Rubaveer positions herself between him and our group. She looks down at him, her golden armor a menacing reminder of what Ancient technology is capable of. All around the room guns are lifted and fingers hover over triggers.

Rubaveer raises both hands, straightening her fingers beside her head, and brings them down so they are pointing at the man. "My name is Rubaveer," she says.

I sigh with relief as the guns lower.

Rubaveer turns to Topazious and speaks in Emi. Topazious looks at the man and repeats the same gesture. As he does, Rubaveer adds, "This is Topazious. I speak for him because he cannot speak for himself. His ability to translate has been removed."

"I see," the man says. "And you speak English yourself, Ancient? Without a translator?"

"Yes," Rubaveer nods pleasantly.

"Impressive," he says, but doesn't show it.

"Thank you, human. Now that ye know what wee are called, ye do not need to only refer to us as 'Ancients.' What is yer name?"

"Patrick," the man says impatiently. "*Rubaveer* and

Topazious," he over-emphasizes their names. "These helmets will support you until you get your breathing implants in a few minutes." He turns to me. "You —"

"Harper," I correct him.

"Yes. Sure. *Harper.* You will also get breathing implants. I hope they work for you, because they're all we have." He looks to Rubaveer. "Since you seem to be the leader, remove your suit first."

I get worried. Once she removes her suit, she's much more vulnerable.

What if they don't give her the helmet?

She collapses on the floor, heaving for breath.

We reach out to help, but they keep us back with guns.

We're forced to watch as she struggles to breathe.

It's not real, Harper! I snap my fingers to stop the thoughts. They need her to stop the Syndrome.

A man comes up and removes Rubaveer's collar so she can take off her suit. Rubaveer draws the loop-de-loop on her chest. The golden armor crashes to the ground. It doesn't float down gracefully like it did when we removed it from the guards at the Base of Ki. The hallway must have destroyed our Volucris.

Rubaveer stands there in the black bodysuit that was underneath. Her frame looks significantly bonier without the armor. The black frostbite around her eye and at the tip of her finger has started to turn a weird green color.

To my relief, the woman with the breathing helmets gives one to Rubaveer. When she puts it on, Rubaveer looks like she's got a fishbowl on her head. In only a matter of seconds, the slits running down the center of Rubaveer's face start to work harder, visibly opening and closing for breath. The man who removed Rubaveer's collar reaches under the helmet and snaps it back on.

"Now *Topazious*," Patrick says.

Rubaveer draws on Topazious' chest. After his armor crashes to the floor, he's given the other breathing helmet. The frostbite on the side of his head is also turning green.

"Now you three," Patrick says to Jacqueline, Adam, and Tucker. A woman hands her weapon to the soldier next to her and removes their collars.

Adam clears his throat. "As I said, two of us are naked under here."

Without warning, a man throws the three of them a towel. Jacqueline and Adam wrap the towels around their backsides, leaving the front open for Rubaveer's signature – Rubaveer signs their chests. Their armor falls to the ground, as if wetsuit material were falling around their ankles.

They close the towels around their naked bodies. Tucker still has his gray hybrid uniform under his armor, and is holding his towel with confusion.

"Remove that too," Patrick says, pointing to his gray uniform. "Ancient clothes are useless here. There's no Ancient technology to work with it."

A woman comes forward with what looks like a silver blade and runs it down Tucker's back. Tucker removes the top half of his uniform, then the rest under the towel.

Jacqueline, Adam, and Tucker are given a stack of folded clothes.

Patrick nods to the walls that surround us. It's then that I notice the windows that run around the room like spokes around a wheel. Each window looks into a small cell with a cot, sink, and toilet inside.

"You three hybrids pick one. The others will come with me."

Surrounded by Sentinels, Rubaveer, Topazious, and I are led down a tunnel that's large enough to drive a tank through. It looks as though it's been carved straight through a mountain of gray stone. Pipes run along the ceiling and cold lights shine down on a nearly white, polished concrete floor.

We round a bend and warmer light floods a much larger chamber. In this massive space are five glass-walled rooms, each surrounded by a lush arrangement of plants. Tubes of fluorescent lights hang from the high ceiling on wires, which hover just above the plants.

We are locked in the first room and are told to sit on cots that look to be at least fifty years old. Rubaveer runs her hands over a teardrop-shaped object, the size of a human head. "Curious. This is an old Enbrotici processor." Her hand traces to the flat screen attached to it. "What is this?" She gives it a tug.

A guard bangs on the door, shaking his finger, then points to the bed.

As we wait nervously, I peer out of the glass walls, past our room's lowered cement ceiling. Outside the room it looks like we're in a garden.

In the waiting silence, Rubaveer and Topazious' wheezing becomes more apparent under their fishbowl helmets. "Hang in there, guys," I say. "It'll be okay. They can't hurt you, Rubaveer. They need you."

"Is that why ye saved me, Harper? To save thee humans?"

I'm not sure how to answer that, because it's partly true. "One reason. I also really like you. You're my friend." I smile, but I feel like a complete jerk for not telling her earlier.

She's thoughtfully quiet for a moment before she responds, "That's okay. If these humans are nice to me friends and me, I will help them."

Her answer is like a warm ray of sunshine on a cold day.

There's motion and muffled talking at the door. The guard moves over and a very tall figure comes in. She has pastel green skin and no hair ... another Ancient.

It's odd to see her wearing lax, gray human scrubs, and not the perfectly fitted clothes I've grown accustomed to the Ancients wearing.

Rubaveer speaks in Emi.

"No need for that," the Ancient responds in a tinny, low quality computer voice. "We do not need to hide anything, we are all allies here." Her speech seems to be coming from a small speaker hanging from her necklace.

She does the Ancient greeting. "I am Humusi. I will be administering your implants today."

Rubaveer returns the gesture, saying her name in English.

"You speak human very well. I have never met another Ancient who can speak a human language organically. It is so difficult with our anatomy. Where did you learn?"

"Iii taught myself on Procell, before coming to Earth."

"Procell," she says. "Impressive. Who is that? Why hasn't he spoken?"

"That is Topazious."

Topazious makes the greeting gesture, saying his name in

Emi.

"Hello," Humusi says to him in English.

"He had his Scanner removed, so he can not translate right now," Rubaveer says.

"Maybe we can do something about that later. Let's hurry up and get these carbon dioxide converters in. Please lie down on the bed, Rubaveer."

Rubaveer lies back. Her feet dangle over the end of the bed from her height. Humusi brings over a metal tray. On it are little metal beans with a bunch of holes. Out of each bean emerges two claws, like a tiny crab. "These are carbon dioxide converters," Humusi says. She pauses a moment and examines the dark, greenish ring around Rubaveer's eye. She takes Rubaveer's hand and looks at the missing finger tip. "I see you had cold injuries, which are healing now."

Humusi hovers the wand over the metal tray. A carbon dioxide converter jumps up and sticks to it like a magnet.

Rubaveer lifts the giant fishbowl, trying to keep all the tubes attached to it from tangling. Humusi goes along Rubaveer's face, setting a converter into each of the breathing holes that runs down her nose-like ridge.

After doing the same to Topazious, she comes to me.

Humusi removes my collar and Rubaveer signs her signature. Almost as soon as my suit falls to the ground, Humusi pierces a converter into each of my nostrils, opens my mouth and pierces another one into the back of my throat, making me gag.

"Take a deep breath in," she says with one hand on my chest and one hand on my upper back.

My nose and mouth sting from the piercings. I cautiously take a breath.

"Harder, hybrid," she says. "Good. Now out." She pulls away. "The punctures should stop hurting soon."

I touch the outside of my nose. I wonder if these will bug me. The one in the back of my throat is too far away to reach with my tongue.

She takes the collar from the bed and snaps it back around my neck.

"Your Ancient suits need to be taken off. Since there is nothing for them to sense, they will not open to use the restroom, or rinse with the shower, or regulate body temperature, or help with circulation and health. Eventually they will stiffen up and be difficult to remove." She holds up a blade, waiting for me to give the okay to remove my Ancient clothes.

We are returned to the circular room. Jacqueline and Tucker look up from the cots in their cells, now dressed in the same dark gray shirts and pants as us.

We're shuffled into separate cells. A giant iron door, the entrance to the large circular room, bangs shut. The lights are switched off and we are left alone in the near darkness.

"Are you guys alright?" Adam asks.

"Yes. They gave us breathing implants," I say. "An Ancient doctor put them in."

"So there are other Ancients here?" Jacqueline asks.

"It looks that way," I respond.

"I guess that makes sense. We suspected there were

Sentinels among the Ancients at the Base of Ki," Jacqueline says. "And it looks like they have some Ancient technology."

We all go quiet and I plop down on the cot. My emotions swing back and forth between heart-palpitating alertness and utter exhaustion. My pants and shirt are rough against my skin, like wool. It will take some getting used to after the weightlessness of the Ancient clothes.

Have we made a mistake by coming? I curl into a fetal position on the lumpy cot and continuously adjust the pinching collar around my neck. I'm at war with myself. Did Mom let Olivia die? Will she let the Sentinels do horrible things to me? To my friends? I struggle to keep all the worst-case scenarios at bay.

CHAPTER 36

Someone's knocking on the window of my cell. I turn from the wall I've been staring at all night. There stands my mother. Two Sentinels with Ancient guns are at her side.

The door to my cell is open and hints of light come from circles on the prison lobby floor.

I sit up.

"I have three quick questions," she says.

"Okay."

"What were the names of your three closest friends?"

"My three friends ..." I stare at her. Her face is disturbingly impassive. "Maria, Katie, and Jane." Saying their names is like a hammer to the heart. I'm not ready to think about what happened to them.

My mom lifts an eyebrow. "What was your favorite subject in school?"

"I didn't go to school. But in homeschool ... my favorite

subject was science ... " How far away that sounds now. Like it belongs to another lifetime.

"What color was the carpet in the house we lived in?"

"Green."

"She passed," she says to the two gunmen. She glances back at me. "Come this way. I have things to tell you."

She looks straight ahead as we walk, avoiding eye contact, which leaves me to fear the worst. I try to fathom what it will be like if she tells me Olivia's dead.

The tunnel we're passing through gives way to an early morning sky. As we emerge, to my astonishment and confusion, we walk out onto a little town.

As we walk, it starts to make sense. The clouds are made of paint brush strokes, the sky is backlit, and the buildings look like they're from a movie set, except their patina and age is real. The whole thing has the charm of something like a Brooklyn brownstone neighborhood. The buildings are squished together with storefronts and apartments made of brick and timber. They are all adorned with dark wrought-iron window coverings, railings, and lanterns. In between each of the brick front steps are trees — fake or not, I can't tell. On nearly every front door are Christmas wreaths tied with red bows.

"What is this place?" I ask.

"It's the Reno Bunker. It was originally built during World War II when the Sentinels suspected that Hitler was an Ancient."

"They can disguise themselves as humans?"

"They can, very convincingly. We no longer think he was an Ancient, though. That was just paranoia at the time. This whole place sits between hot spring veins to keep it warm and prevent anyone on the outside from using heat detection technology to find us. Impressive, isn't it? The idea is to make the environment mimic real life as much as possible. If you're going to live in an underground bunker for possibly decades at a time, you may as well build it in a way that keeps people from going crazy. The sky-ceiling even gives off UV rays to prevent vitamin D deficiency and make people feel like they're outside."

She points. "Down the street, over there, is a park with a hot spring fountain. That way is the library. That way is the theater and game room. And that way are the government and business buildings." It distinctly seems like she's trying to sell me a place in this community.

"Where is everyone now?" I ask.

"It's early in the morning. People aren't up yet."

"How many people are here?"

"A good amount," she says, slipping back into her cold tone.

We stop at a place with a Starbucks sign, large sliding glass doors, and a porch with outdoor seating.

"Don't get too excited," Mom says. "This isn't a real Starbucks or anything. They just thought it would be funny to steal the sign since the city was in shambles anyway. Coffee isn't what it used to be, but you'll get used to it." She pulls out a key and presses it into the doorknob.

"I don't remember the last time I had coffee," I say.

The two gunmen stay outside, which makes me nervous. I've seen all the awful things humans can do with those guns. I adjust the collar on my neck, taking note of yet another way

I could be killed here. Then I wipe my sweaty palms on my pants.

The coffee shop looks like most coffee shops. Taupe walls are the backdrop for artsy black and white photography, and dark wood tables sit on dark wood floors. White mugs line the shelf behind the counter and tin cans are labeled with things like mocha, eggnog, pumpkin, and caramel.

My mother slips behind the counter. She places two cups under a spout and what looks like pond scum drips in. She moves the cups to the second spout and steam rises from the tip. She opens a cupboard, holds up brown bottles to the light, bends over and adds two drops of brown liquid to each cup. She mixes them with a metal spoon and places them on a table near the front window.

It's been a long time since I've tasted anything but Gewd. I wrap my fingers around the coffee. The cup is warm and welcoming in my hand. There's a pleasant aroma of chocolate and nuts. I take a sip ... and spit it right back out.

Laughter breaks my mother's icy facade. "I told you it's not the same!"

"What is this?!" I wipe at my mouth with my sleeve.

"Think of it like tapioca pudding coffee. That chunky stuff, or Sludge as we say, is an ingenious invention we stole from the Ancients. A nutritious concoction made of algae and vitamins, flavored like the coffee one you just tried."

"There was food made from algae in the Base of Ki too. We nicknamed it Gewd, a mixture of goo and food. It was kind of like a watery Jell-O and a little sweet. I wasn't crazy about that either, but at least it didn't have *this* unique fishy aftertaste."

"Yeah. Well, we don't have the same technology as the current Ancients. This is the best we could do with what's available."

"Are there more Ancients here?" I ask. "Ancients who side with the Sentinels?"

"Yes. It was hard to trust them at first. They started showing up after they saw the destruction of the human race. The Ancients who came to us are the ones who disagreed with it. In the end, we couldn't turn down their knowledge. This war is about the survival of the human race and we are nearly hopeless without them. I really hope your friend can help. We're losing millions a day out there." She points at the ceiling.

"Where's Olivia, Mom?"

She sighs and leans back in her chair, her expression goes sullen. She looks me in the eyes, with an unexpected glimmer of empathy. "Her story actually starts with your father. Both of your stories do." She glances at the people standing guard outside.

"I assume you know that Brett is not your real brother?"

"That's what I was told ... Are you my real mother?"

"I am."

The news is more confusing than I thought it would be. How can someone treat their flesh and blood the way she treated me? Maybe a small part of me was hoping she wasn't my mom. That there's some maternal person out there missing me. Wanting me around. Wanting to tell me I'm the daughter they've been waiting to meet.

We fix on each other for a moment. Then she breaks eye contact, looking down at her cup. "It's tough for me to say this, I've kept it quiet for so long." She runs her hand across her chest and it settles on her heart. "I used to be a different person. I had a great job in New York as a civil engineer. I had parents, two sisters, friends, a life, the works. Everything was going so well ..."

She hesitates, then looks back at me. Her mouth is open for a second before words come out. "Late ... Late one night, many years ago, I finished up a major project at work. My mind was buzzing too much for sleep, so I stepped into this little bar under the office.

"I was finishing off my martini, watching a news report, when the most gorgeous man took the empty stool next to me. He asked what I did for a living. Once I got the guts to answer him, he asked if he could buy me another drink.

"After talking for hours, we discovered that we both loved dancing and technology. He studied biology for some fancy science institution and he was impressed with the methods my firm was using to construct a new skyscraper downtown. After the bar's last call, he made sure I got safely into a cab with his phone number." Her fingers trace the rim of her cup and she smiles a little.

"He was so charming, Harper, I couldn't believe my luck. The courtship was fast and somehow, despite being very careful, I got pregnant. I wasn't going to keep it, our relationship was too new, but he begged me. He insisted that we would make the most beautiful babies and that we would be together forever ... "

For an instant, I can imagine my mom as a pretty twenty-something woman sitting across the table from me, only a few years older than Jacqueline. Was she more carefree back then? When she didn't have children like me holding her down?

"So I kept the pregnancy ... or you," she goes on. "It was awful. I was sick all the time. So much so that I had to give up work projects because I couldn't keep any commitments. But your father took care of me. He made sure I had everything I needed during my pregnancy.

"But ... after I had you ... your father changed." She gulps. "He started disappearing on long business trips all the time. I got suspicious. We fought a lot ... well ... I fought a lot. He was always calm and collected and swore he had no control over his work schedule. Before I knew it, I got pregnant a second time with Olivia. Suddenly his work schedule lightened up and he was home more often again. I thought he had changed for the better ... that things would go back to the way they were before." She gets up and paces back and forth in small circles around the table.

"Our apartment in Manhattan was too small for our growing family, so we did what all New Yorkers swear they'll never do —" She laughs in an ironic way — "and moved to Jersey."

She goes to the window, looking at the street and buildings; then turns back to me and stiffens, brushing the loose hair from her ponytail behind her ear. "That's where strange things started happening. I kept having nightmares about waking up and finding your father running laser beams over my pregnant belly. Those terrible dreams eventually involved a group of people. All of them poking and prodding me, hidden behind these silver helmets." She pulls her shirt away from her body, as if it's too tight. "I told your father about my dreams and he insisted I see a doctor. That it was probably the pregnancy hormones acting up. The medication helped the dreams a little, but as soon as Olivia was born, he began disappearing again."

"I'm sorry," I say, not knowing what else to.

"At the time, I suspected him of cheating."

She bats her hand like it's nothing, but there's an obvious pain in her words. "Suspicion isn't proof. I needed proof to confront him about it. So I left little Olivia and you with my sister. I disguised myself and followed your dad to a diner. I settled into the back of the cafe to see what he would do there. He was wearing this red scarf he always wore, so he was easy to spot. I sat and waited while he read the newspaper. After about a half hour passed, he got up to use the restroom. Then a different man came out and sat in your father's spot with the exact same red scarf. But this man was chubbier and bald."

She starts pacing faster. "For a moment, I thought the worst, imagining that this man had robbed your father and left him for dead in the bathroom. After I did a quick check of the men's bathroom myself, I found it completely empty. When I returned to my seat, I was shocked to find that the man with the red scarf was now sitting with a woman and a baby at the same table." She freezes, placing her hand on the back of a chair, as if to steady herself "I ... felt like I was in some awful, confusing nightmare. I watched this man, who kind of had Lucian's nose, stroke this woman's back like he stroked mine —"

"That's my dad's name?"

She shrugs. "It's the name he told me."

"You told me his name was John."

"I did. It wasn't safe to tell you his real name. I'm sorry."

Across the room, I see parts of my white face reflecting in the chrome of an espresso machine. *Lucian.* Putting a name to the *man* who made me this way is strange and distant, yet at the same time, like I've always known it somehow. Like destiny. I imagine a handsome, well-built man named Lucian walking with my mom down a New York City street, hand-in-hand like a cheesy jewelry commercial.

"Anyway," she continues, "Not sure of what was going on, I hurried home upset. Then came the knock at the door. I remember a very plainly dressed man and woman standing at it, claiming they'd come to help me. I almost slammed the door in their faces, but the woman was holding up photos of a man in a red scarf caring for babies with other women. After I finished going through all those photos, the woman handed me even more containing your father's coworkers, in identical scenarios. I could barely hold the photos, I was shaking so much," she says with a shudder. "The lady explained that she and the man were with an organization they called the Sentinels. An ancient group that monitors Earth for interstellar activity. I thought it was some kind of sick joke."

"I would have too," I say, listening intently.

"She explained that your father was part of a group of very advanced scientists from another solar system. They had the technology to transform into different people and display attractive traits for viable candidates and make offspring with them."

"Wait. What traits?"

"The Sentinels suggested these scientists were looking for

different levels of intellect, skills, and physical capabilities."

"Do you know why they wanted you?" I ask.

She smirks. "Probably intellect, since when I first met your father, he kept asking questions about my civil engineering work. Anyway, as I sat with these people on the couch at our apartment, I was dumbstruck. The woman told me that the Sentinels could help. She said they had saved other women just like me. They promised to give me a new identity, and keep you and Olivia from being found. They had compounds. Lovely little closed communities where you two could grow up safe.

"So I agreed to go. I had to say goodbye to my family and go into hiding with you two. I tried living in a compound for a few weeks, but it was suffocating.

"After pleading, the Sentinels allowed me to return to normal society under the conditions that I maintain absolute secrecy and care for aging Sentinels in a retirement community. I was not allowed to tell you or Olivia anything because they didn't trust children. I could not enter you into normal schools because your potential special abilities could draw unwanted attention. I had to completely abandon my old life and become a different person so I couldn't be traced. I abandoned everything for you two," she says with a tinge of anger.

"The Sentinels moved me to Reno, Nevada. Not too big and not too small of a town. Then they gave me Brett. He was an orphan and highly trained young soldier meant to help watch over you two. You probably remember Patrick coming over and dropping him off." She stops walking, sighs, and lifts her eyes to me. "And I assume you know the rest." She fans herself with her shirt.

I let the thoughts wash over me, reflecting on it all. "Was that why you were so freaked out when the Syndrome popped up in New York?"

She nods. "I thought your father and his friends were trying to kill us, and maybe other women they impregnated. The Sentinels were very suspicious of the RSE Sleeping Syndrome."

Suddenly she starts welling up, mopping tears from her face. The speed at which her demeanor changes makes me feel like a little girl again, curled up on the floor, ribs aching after she's kicked me. She would apologize with tears like this then too.

"I can understand why you thought I was a horrible mother," she sobs. "I didn't mean to hit you and your sister. I would just get so angry that I couldn't control myself. In those moments of rage, I blamed you and Olivia for hijacking my life and shackling me to this destiny that I didn't want. I lost everything because I got pregnant with you two. *Everything.*" She puts the napkin to her eyes. "It's just been so hard. And still, even after all the sacrifice, secrecy, and being so careful ... you and Olivia ..." Her voice cracks as more teardrops fall. She hides her face in her hands.

Her reaction pummels into me like a violent wave. "Where's Olivia now, Mom?"

CHAPTER 37

Mom inhales sharply. "The Ancients have Olivia, just like they had you. She was captured a few weeks after you, when we were hiding in the forest — then I came here. I know it was probably a long shot, but I was hoping that maybe you would find each other and stay together."

More tears run down her cheeks, and she swiftly blots them away. "I'm so sorry I failed to protect you two. I tried. I really did. I gave everything," she sobs.

Something clicks and I get a terrible, terrible sinking sensation. "Wait. Mom. You were in a forest?"

Mom blows her nose in a napkin and then pauses at the question. "Yes?"

"What happened there, when she was taken?"

"Um. The cabin we were staying in caught fire. She got stuck inside." Mom stares off. "The roof caved in and I thought ... she was dead. Then, somehow, magically, she was beside me, telling me to hide. I didn't know how she was still alive. Her face was covered in soot ... and then she ran away so fast that she was a blur, and that's the last I saw of her. Robert, another Sentinel, was with us. He went after her. A few seconds later, I heard him firing his gun into the woods. Then he came back empty handed. He thought he saw one, but he didn't hit anything."

Mom takes a ragged breath. "She was gone after that. Disappeared. We suspected they took her, just like they took you. After all, she disappeared without a trace."

I have trouble speaking. "What did this forest look like, Mom?"

"What?"

"What did the forest look like? Was it a really green, birch tree forest? Were there purple flowers everywhere?"

Her face goes blank. "How do you know that?"

All I can manage to say is, "Aleena."

"What?"

"There was a girl ... Aleena." My voice crackles. "She couldn't remember anything. She said she thought her name sounded something like Aleena. That must have been Olivia ..."

Mom goes ashen.

"Damn it!" I stand up and knock over a chair. "She was there! I was right with her! David said she escaped from a Sentinel camp! He was lying! I didn't ... I didn't ..." I drop to the floor. Hot tears rush down my face.

"You saw Olivia?"

"Yes, but I didn't bring her! I didn't know it was her!" I sob, knocking over a nearby table.

"Was she okay? Did they hurt her?"

"They ... they ... took Aleena — I mean Olivia away ... "

Mom clasps her hands together. "She's alive. Thank God you're both alive." She helps me to my feet, but I haven't got any strength in my legs.

"For all we know Olivia's better off than we are." She helps me back into a chair.

"Harper," she says, giving me a napkin and taking my other hand. "Olivia won't suffer. She won't be stuck in this hole. We'll be the only ones suffering, missing her. After so, so many people have died, I am happy to know that my daughter will live a decent life. Even if she is brainwashed."

"No!" I scream. "You don't understand. Alee—Olivia was taken from the hybrids and put somewhere for 'repair'. Who knows what they're doing with her now! And if she survives that, who knows if she'll be taken back to Cooms! Gone forever!" I heave.

Mom shakes her head. "From what I know, Ancients are more reluctant to hurt their own kind. And hybrids are half their kind."

I think of Rae, floating in suspension in her tank. Maybe that's where Olivia is too. Sleeping, but alive. "But who knows what they really want with the hybrids. They said they want to stop the creation of hybrids because when the Sentinels created us, it advanced the human race too fast." I take a flustered breath. "They're going to wipe out every human anyway. So what's the point in keeping hybrids alive?"

"The Ancients were lying to you, Harper. I told you how you were made."

"So what reason would they have to send an Ancient here to create Olivia and me? What do they want hybrids for? That contradicts everything they said."

"We aren't sure. It seems the Ancients leave some hybrids alone and some hybrids are taken without a trace."

Someone is lying. "The Ancients also said the Sentinels were creating hybrids to build an army against them. Is that true?"

"What were we supposed to do, Harper? We didn't originally create the hybrids, but why not use their skills to defend ourselves? That's all we've ever been doing—defending ourselves."

"Were you preparing me for an army? To fight them?"

"I ... I ... didn't know yet. I wanted to keep you in the dark until you were eighteen at least. See what you'd grow up to do. I told the Sentinels you or your sister weren't showing signs of abilities, so you weren't of any use to them yet."

Yet? But that's not true. In my dream, Mom and Olivia were taking my clone, who they thought was me, to California to help with the fight. "Is there a hybrid army now?"

"Yes. There's a few training at different bunkers throughout the country."

That must be where she was taking human Harper. "Who was the clone then, Mom?"

She stops fidgeting and glances at the gunmen behind her with alarm. "How do you know about that?"

I decide not to tell her about my dreams. Only my Leveling. "The Ancients showed me. Who was she?"

"So the Ancients were spying on us?"

"I don't know. That's why I'm asking you!" I hit my fist on

the table.

"The clone must have been sent from the Ancients. I thought it was you. I waited for you and Brett outside the quarantine zone at our meeting spot after you were supposed to escape. But only you came back, by yourself, without the car."

She picks up her cup and stirs the foul coffee. "I should have known it wasn't you when you — I mean she — hugged me that way. You've never hugged me like that. She said that Brett had been killed by stray gunfire. So I took her on the escape route with us.

"We were traveling to a bunker in California. Olivia started to get suspicious and said the clone didn't know things she should. Then, the clone disappeared after Olivia started asking her questions. A few days later, after we'd found refuge in an old cabin, it got set on fire. And as I just told you, Olivia disappeared after that."

One of the armed men knocks on the door and holds up two fingers. Mom waves to them.

"Two minutes left to talk," Mom says. "They need me for something."

I'm having a hard time sorting it all out. What the Ancients told me. What my Mom just has. Violent human images even add themselves to the mix.

"You're shaking," Mom says. "It's okay, Harper." She reaches out to put her hand on mine.

I pull away. "Don't!"

"It's all going to be okay. I should clarify about the clone. That's why I asked you those questions when I got you out of your cell this morning. To make sure you were you. The other

Harper was quiet. Didn't talk much, which I assumed was because you — I mean she — was sad about Brett and all that she'd been through at the time. I thought she was mad I left her in the quarantine zone." She laughs nervously.

"Is Brett still alive?" I ask.

"Yes. He will recover. I'm so sorry, Harper. I know this is all a lot to take in. I can't imagine what you've been through."

I look at her, searching for the truth. Her eyes respond with pity as they survey my face. I almost feel ashamed for what I am. Ashamed of what I look like and that in a way, I've caused all of this suffering.

Does she even see her daughter anymore? Do I now look more like my Ancient father without his human disguise? I wonder if she's wondering the same thing. I wonder if anything she says is even real. I clench my fist.

The gunman knocks on the door and gestures with one finger.

"Harper, I —"

I hold up my hand. "Are we going to try and save Olivia? To fight back against the Base of Ki?"

"We want to. The Ancients are far more powerful than us right now. If Rubaveer can help us slow the casualties of the Syndrome, it gives us more time to find the great weapon."

This is news. "How long have you been looking for it?" I ask.

"For thousands of years, ever since it was left by the Ancients who visited Earth long ago."

"So it could take much longer. If ever. Olivia could be gone to Cooms by then," I say coldly.

Mom says nothing.

I look out the window at the fake sky, which has gotten lighter since we started talking. People have begun populating the street. Who knows how long my friends and I will be stuck here. "Do you think they'll accept us? Especially since we look different from everyone?"

"Well, there are Ancients here. There are other hybrids here too, though they still look fully human. So I think people will get used to you. Not that you all look bad, just different." She pulls down the sleeve of my shirt, straightening the seam. "We may be able to make you look more like your old self, if that's what you want. Perhaps some Ancients here can help. Your father was a great scientist, though. I'm not sure if his work can be matched."

The gunman knocks on the window. My mother stands. "I must go. A friend of mine has volunteered to escort you to our big Christmas Day brunch. I'll see you there."

CHAPTER 38

The boy from earlier, who is about my age, with black curly hair and tattoos, is waiting for me outside the coffee shop.

"Hi," he says with a grin that's almost too eager and friendly given the circumstances.

"Hi," I respond quietly as a great wave of exhaustion rolls over me. When I step off the coffee shop stoop, I stumble.

The boy catches my arm. "You alright?"

"Yeah just ..."

"Tired A-F?" he says with a more genuine smirk. The gaze of his burgundy eyes brings an unexpected warmth to my cheeks. "Well, I'm here to show you the way to brunch with your friends. Hopefully some food will help. This way."

I follow him down the sidewalk, along all the brownstones with Christmas wreaths and lights hanging from their railings. I can't believe it's the end of December. I think I've been gone since August.

"Must be shocking to come back and see how much the world's changed, huh?"

"Yeah," I respond.

"Aren't you the talkative one? No need to be so gloomy. You made it out! There's a lot to be *thankful* for! You're *alive*!" He says excitedly, doing a dorky dance to go along with it.

I let a small smile slip. He stops and holds out his hand. "I'm Mowgli, by the way."

"Mowgli? Like *The Jungle Book*?"

He laughs. "Yup. Great times for me in primary school with that one. What's your name?"

I'm about to do Ancient greeting, but stop myself. "Harper." I shake his hand.

"Ah, after Harper Lee? So your mum's a book nerd?"

"I don't know, I thought I used to," I say.

Three excited wolves race down the street past us, playfully nipping at each other.

"What's the deal with the wolves?" I try to change the subject.

"Impressive, aren't they? We have a fleet of wild animals trained to go outside because we can't."

I finally notice that Mowgli has a bit of an accent. English, maybe, or Australian.

We pass another cobblestone street and I notice kids' drawings of hand-traced Christmas trees and cut-outs of menorahs hanging in the windows of apartment buildings.

"Sorry to hear about your sister," Mowgli says. "I lost my little brother to the Syndrome before we came here."

"I'm sorry to hear that. How old was he?"

"Twelve."

"Wow. That's awful." So many have been lost. It's another kick in the chest.

"Here we are," he says. I help him push open two large wooden doors on a fancy building with pillars. It looks straight out of photos I've seen of Rome.

A loud humming sound, emanating from hundreds of people fills the air. The space is as big and beautiful as an old concert hall. Hundreds of people bustle below wrought-iron chandeliers, around tables with white linens, set with white china. Holly and candles are the centerpiece of each, accompanied by glistening turkeys, cranberry sauce, yams, salads, and rolls.

"Wow!" Mowgli says, "Our cook's really outdone herself!"

"Yeah," I say. I don't know if I've ever seen food this fancy before.

Mowgli laughs, shaking his finger. "But don't let this delightful *looking* food fool you. It's made of Sludge. Our cook used to make those high-end, ornate cakes, so she's an artist. *Clearly.*" He motions to a turkey.

"Come on, then." He leads me down an aisle between two long tables. We weave between people who are chatting happily with each other. Until they see me — then they stare. Their stares make my stomach churn uncomfortably.

"Don't worry about them," Mowgli says. "They've just never seen someone like you before. I assure you, you're not bad looking. Just unique. Kind of in that high-fashion runway model way. It's a good thing. Who wants to be like everyone else?"

I'm having a hard time focusing on him. "Yeah," I say, wiping my sweaty palms on my pants. I almost prefer the cells to this. *Where are my friends?*

Suddenly Jacqueline's arms are wrapped around me. "Are you okay? Have you been crying?" she whispers into my ear.

The warmth of her concern almost makes me cry again. I squeeze back. I need this hug more than she knows. "No. I have a lot to tell you after this," I whisper back.

She pulls away. "Okay." She takes my arm and leads me to where everyone else is sitting.

Finally I see Adam, Rubaveer, Topazious, and Tucker seated at the end of the table with Brett. Brett is in a wheelchair. His purple face lights up when he sees me. Rubaveer is waving.

"Harper, I'm so happy you're okay," Brett says, "I kept thinking the worst when I was —"

"Shhhh ... We can talk about that later." I give him the lightest embrace I can. *I wish I knew if I could trust you, Brett*, I think as I smell the strong disinfectant permeating off his skin.

I take a spot next to Jacqueline. "Are you guys all right?" I ask.

"Yes we just got done with questioning," Jacqueline says. "Will fill you in on that later, too." Her fingers entwine with Adam's. Next to him is Tucker, then Rubaveer and Topazious. The sight of them seems to lift a thousand pounds off of me.

Adam pulls Jacqueline close and kisses her forehead. She laughs and nuzzles her head into his neck.

Tucker has a knife and fork in each hand, watching the turkey as if it might sneak off. I wonder if he knows about the Sludge yet.

Rubaveer and Topazious are looking around awkwardly at the food and decorations, continuously scratching their collars and clothes. Then Rubaveer points something out to Topazious: Tall blue, yellow, and pink heads bobbing among all the fleshy human tones: more Ancients.

"Gotta check in with my mum," Mowgli says.

"Oh, sorry! I forgot you were standing there. Hey everyone," I say, "This is Mowgli."

They all introduce themselves.

"Great. I'll see you all around. Let me know if you ever need to talk, Harper," Mowgli says.

"Thanks," I say. "I will."

Mowgli waves and disappears into the crowd. I notice more people looking at our group, especially at us hybrids. I scoot in closer to Adam and Jacqueline.

"Oh la la. *'Let me know if you ever need to talk,'*" Adam mocks in a British accent, winking at me. Jacqueline chuckles, adding a nod of approval.

Tucker puts down his silverware and frowns. "That guy looks like a girl with hair like that."

"And what's wrong with having hair like a girl, Tucker?" I ask.

"Yeah," Adam says. "And he's a good-looking guy who's around her age. Seems like a good match to me."

I pull my shirt collar over my chin, to hide a blush.

Tucker huffs, takes his plate, and goes to search for another seat.

"That was all it took?" Adam says. "Wish I thought of that at the Canopy."

My mom comes to the table, taking a seat beside Brett. Olivia's absence barrels into me again. I'll never forgive myself for leaving her behind.

"Harper?" a shaky voice asks.

I turn. *Maria* is standing behind me, her two little siblings in tow. I leap at her and my arms wrap around her instinctively.

"Watch my ribs, Harper," she laughs. "Your hug is powerful." She looks older than when I saw her last, but healthy. And freaking alive!

Patrick starts tapping a fork to a glass at the front of the room, signaling for everyone to quiet down.

"Holy crap! Sit with us!" I say, shoving over chairs and making more room. "I need to know everything! How did you escape the quarantine zone?!"

Patrick clinks the glass again.

"Your mom saved me," Maria says. "After his speech, I'll tell you everything."

Patrick takes the microphone. "Merry Christmas and Happy Holidays!"

The audience mutters it back.

"The holidays are very hard for everyone this year." He pauses. "But last night, on Christmas Eve, we were brought hope. Molly Loomis' daughter was able to find her way back to us." Patrick motions to us sitting at the table. "And she brought with her an Ancient scientist who can cure the Syndrome."

Everyone stands and starts cheering, making the dining hall overwhelmingly loud with clapping and pounding on tables.

Their faces look upon us with so much hope. Maybe it's all been worth it?

"Thank you," Patrick says in a gracious way that sounds completely opposite of how he treated us last night. Everyone quiets and sits back down.

"This will give us more time to find the weapon Glock left for the Sentinels so many years ago."

"Glock left a weapon?!" I say to Mom. "He didn't die?! In the ship fire?"

She gives me a confused look. "No. He faked his death and hid with the humans in the desert with Emmera for many years."

I exchange looks with Adam and Jacqueline.

"— We will fight back and reclaim Earth!" Patrick shouts, followed by chanting.

Patrick doesn't elaborate on Glock past that, and starts to give the rest of his speech, going at length how everyone has been there for each other and we will need each other if we are going to survive. His voice fades into the background of my thoughts.

My eyes land on the spot where Olivia should be. In that moment, I make a promise to myself. I don't know how and I don't know when, but I will get Olivia back.

ACKNOWLEDGMENTS

To Rachael, the very first person to ever brave these pages, and to Josh, the second. You both gave the first draft of this novel thoughtful and meaningful feedback — and continued to engage with The Glow throughout the L-O-N-G process of finishing it.

Lexy and Olivia, thank you for reading the ever-evolving versions of this novel over, over, and over again ... carefully considering every detail and pretending you weren't tired of being my sounding boards.

Thank you, Guido, my husband, who has always encouraged me to have faith in myself. Who understood when I obsessed over this book and used most of my free time to write it. You've helped me lift my dreams from the ground and listened as I talked about this book on our nightly walks: over, over, and over again.

To my dad, who first enchanted me with the whimsy, intricacies, and more profound questions of storytelling. To my grandparents and mom.

For Ruby and Topaz, my initial writing muses, my two amazing dogs, who brought color to my life when I felt I was drowning in gray. Who stayed by my side and loved me purely until they were here no longer. I miss you both dearly. And to Jet, my newest loyal friend, who has big paws to fill but does so in her own adorably dorky way.

To Alia Moore, Geoff Smith, and Kim Stinson-Serrano, who all helped me chip away at this initially massive manuscript and streamline it into what it is today.

Thank you, Victoria Hughs-Williams, my final story editor. You helped me understand the importance of moving the plot along and getting to the heart of the story at a quicker pace. Also, thank you for taking the time to answer all my publishing questions.

And finally, to all the readers and beta readers who's candid feedback — though painful at first — has helped and will continue to help me become a better writer. I hope you enjoy the final version of The Glow that you helped create.

ABOUT THE AUTHOR

Aubrey Hadley has always loved two things in life: words and design. For a while, she put writing to the side (she wasn't sure if she was any good) and moved to the Bay Area to focus on design in Tech. After a while, she finally decided to write her first novel, The Glow. Aubrey still designs professionally, hangs out with her husband and dog, and geeks out on audiobooks, cool shows, and interior design.

Made in the USA
Las Vegas, NV
13 February 2021